Praise for *Albatross*

"[*Albatross*] has a fable-like quality and philosophical depths that Fallis plumbs with deceptive subtlety—you'll come for the story about an athletic whiz kid, and leave contemplating where true happiness really lies, both in Adam's life and your own."

—*Globe and Mail*

"Fallis is on point with his vivid observations. *Albatross* exposes some essential truths, such as the fundamental importance of following your own path." —*Winnipeg Free Press*

"Fallis writes from another time, when Wodehouse and Leacock and Twain roamed the earth. May he never become extinct."

—Linwood Barclay

"It's hard not to get excited about a new Terry Fallis novel, and it is equally hard not to fall in love with Adam Coryell, the big-hearted, sarcastic, fountain-pen-obsessed hero of *Albatross*, a young golf prodigy who just wants to write short stories. In his inimitable style, Fallis has crafted a tender, funny, and compulsively readable novel about what it means to stay true to your dreams, and to yourself. Do yourself a favour and pick up this book—you won't put it down again until the final page has been turned."

—Amy Jones, author of *Pebble & Dove* and *We're All In this Together*

ab

"Booklovers, rejoice and buy this book! In *Albatross*, Terry Fallis has found the antidote for what ails our sorry world. May millions of you benefit!"

—Alan Bradley, *New York Times* bestselling author of *The Sweetness at the Bottom of the Pie*

Praise for *One Brother Shy*

"An ode to one of the most unique emotional bonds a human can experience."

—*Toronto Star*

"[*One Brother Shy*] follows software engineer Alex MacAskill who must face a humiliating incident from his past after his mother dies. It sounds depressing, but, like Fallis' other books, is filled with humour and warmth."

—CBC Books

"A two-for-one flight of invention, full of hilarious one-liners. Terry Fallis has written another fast-paced, incisive, and wry novel that doesn't shy away from the enjoyably genuine and the genuinely human."

—Gary Barwin, author of *Yiddish for Pirates* and *Nothing the Same, Everything Haunted*

"*One Brother Shy* is funny, heartbreaking, and sensitive, just like its reluctant semi-hero, Alex MacAskill. Terry Fallis has worked his magic again in this story of a young man battered by the fates and healed by his own courage and the kindness of an unlikely assortment of people. *One Brother Shy* is life-affirming and an absolute joy to read."

—Susan Juby, author of *Republic of Dirt*

"Mark Twain once observed that the 'secret source of humour is not joy but sorrow.' In *One Brother Shy*, Terry Fallis locates this secret source in a very moving yet often funny story about a young man's search for lost family, lost identity, lost confidence and lost time. The result is a wonderful, powerful tale of pain and redemption."

—Joseph Kertes, author of *The Afterlife of Stars*

A NEW SEASON

Also by Terry Fallis

The Best Laid Plans

The High Road

Up and Down

No Relation

Poles Apart

One Brother Shy

Albatross

Operation Angus

A NEW SEASON

A NOVEL

TERRY FALLIS

McClelland & Stewart

First edition published 2023

McClelland & Stewart and colophon are registered trademarks of
Penguin Random House Canada Limited.

Library and Archives Canada Cataloguing in Publication
Title: A new season / Terry Fallis.
Names: Fallis, Terry, author.
Identifiers: Canadiana 20230141080 | ISBN 9780771094743 (softcover)
Classification: LCC PS8611.A515 N49 2023 | DDC C813/.6—dc23

ISBN: 978-0-7710-9474-3
ebook ISBN: 978-0-7710-9481-1

Book design: Matthew Flute
Cover art: (Eiffel tower) iStock / Getty Images Plus; (snow) Cattallina / iStock / Getty Images Plus; (lamp post) Kora_ra / iStock / Getty Images Plus; (figure) A-Digit / DigitalVision Vectors / Getty Images
Typeset in Electra LH RegularOS by M&S, Toronto
Printed in Canada

McClelland & Stewart,
a division of Penguin Random House Canada Limited,
a Penguin Random House Company
www.penguinrandomhouse.ca

1 2 3 4 5 27 26 25 24 23

Jack Evans (1935–2022)

Chris Paterson (1966–2016)

*For Stefania Szlek Miller, John Di Costanzo, Dan Jenkins,
Kristen, Ben, and Kate Paterson, and all those who live with loss.
And for my brothers in the Withrow Park Ball Hockey League.*

PART 1

TORONTO

CHAPTER 1

"NOW THAT'S USING YOUR FACE, Jack-Mac!" a spectator shouted as the buzzer sounded to end my weekly ball hockey game. To be clear, I actually knew who yelled from the sidelines, but let's just go with "a spectator," shall we? Why encourage him? My teammates gathered around to congratulate me on the winning goal. Yes, it's true. For once, I was the hero. Let me give you the slow-motion replay of my big moment in case you're blissfully unaware. And also because my clutch goal, spectacular though it was, did not make the highlight reel on *SportsCentre* that night.

With the game tied in the final minute of play, I had assumed my position in front of the net to try to screen their goalie. The ball somehow found its way to one of our stronger defencemen back on the blue line. I watched him wind up for one of his terrifying slapshots as I trembled in the firing line. My mission—and I chose to accept it—was to try to deflect the ball to make it even tougher for their goalie to stop. Miraculously, the blade of my stick caught a piece of the orange plastic sphere as it whizzed towards the net at a speed that had me waiting for a sonic boom. It was sort of a good news/bad news/good news scenario. I did deflect the ball—good news—but right into my own face—bad news. That may sound painful, but for years I've worn a full wire cage on my helmet—smart, right?—so the ball bounced harmlessly off my well-protected face and into the net to win the game with about two seconds left on the clock—good news, again.

It used to be that my ball hockey game was a high point of my week, which is saying something for a guy who had just about everything I could have ever desired. My life was nearly perfect. That all changed two years, five months, and fourteen days ago. Despite it all, I still loved and needed my ball hockey and the roughly ninety guys who made up the six teams in our community league. In fact, I think I needed the game and the guys more than ever. You see, for an hour or so every week from April to October, my mind was completely and singularly focused on playing the sport I've loved since I was about six years old. Okay, let me spell it out. It was an escape. An escape for just a brief moment each week, but an escape nonetheless. It was only after the game, and after the post-game "analysis" at our local watering hole, that reality returned and settled over me like falling ash from a volcanic eruption.

I chucked my sticks and aromatic hockey bag onto my front porch, just across the street from the park, and then headed a few blocks north to the Danforth and a sports bar we had kind of adopted, known simply as Rivals.

Speaking of rivals, the two co-captains from the team we'd just played, Bobby Hazlett and Nathan Steiner, great guys, both clapped me on the back and congratulated me on the big win as they waited for a couple pitchers of draught at the bar. Bobby, a corporate lawyer and partner at a big downtown Toronto law firm, was a good friend, but I wouldn't want to mess with him. He was intimidating enough in our games, never mind facing him in a courtroom. Nathan was also a lawyer but about as far away from Bobby's legal world as possible. Nathan worked for the provincial government as a mediator. Such a lovely guy with a wonderful family—three sons, hockey players all. And Nathan could still make things happen in a game, too.

"Jack McMaster, the man of the moment!" Bobby said. "But seriously, that may be the luckiest goal I've ever seen. Hilarious way to win a game, and a heartbreaking way to lose it."

"Hang on, hang on," I replied, feigning indignation. "Lucky? I am affronted! I'm offended! I'm, I don't know, maybe even outraged. I'll have you know that's a set play our team has been practising for months, and that I've been perfecting since I was a kid. So, yes, it was amazing to pull it off in a real game—you know, for the winning goal and all, with, um, next to no time left on the clock, as I recall. And did I mention it was for the victory, you know, against you guys?"

They just laughed and handed me one of the draught pitchers, which I carried to the table at the back that we often used for our post-game celebrations. We don't necessarily sit with our own teams. Everyone in the league knows one another and has played with, and against, each other for years, so we all just pull up chairs.

"I gotta say, that was quite a spectacular finish, Jack," my co-captain, Harris Unger, said when I dropped into the empty seat beside him. "You looked like Cristiano Ronaldo, except he uses his head to score. I like that you changed it up and used your face."

"Well, I guess it could have been worse. The ball could have bounced off my ass and into the net," I replied. "Wait. Now that I think of it, that very thing happened a few years ago. All I can say is it takes great kinesthetic awareness to direct the ball into the net with, um, body parts ill-designed for the task."

"A win is a win, Jack-Mac," Harris said, clinking my glass.

Harris was one of the first guys I'd met when I joined the league all those years ago. He was a savant-like mechanical engineer at a GM automotive research facility in Toronto. He was a smart guy with very good hands, whether he was using them under the hood of his Chevy Blazer or on the ball hockey floor. The researchers at GM would cook up a new design for a more efficient engine, or a lighter, smoother transmission, and Harris would build it. At that point he was heavily involved in the development of electric vehicles, and he loved every minute of it. I was in awe of his gifts. He could build anything, and never met a machine he couldn't diagnose, tear down, and rebuild to be better, stronger, and faster than it was before. Meanwhile, I hadn't even been able to assemble our new gas barbecue, and there were only four pieces to put together using a single screwdriver. So I had called Harris. He came. That's what friends do.

The pregame trash-talking at the park softened into good-natured banter at the bar, and there was even some non-sports-related discussion at times. Still, most of us kept one eye on the several flat-screen TVs prominently arrayed throughout the bar. The Blue Jays were playing the White Sox and, regrettably, had just managed to snatch defeat from the jaws of victory with two boneheaded errors in the ninth. A couple of hours passed quickly when hanging with the boys. It was just such a comfort to be among these guys. Good, close friends I'd known for nearly twenty years. I needed them.

By that time—late summer 2022—very few of us wore masks anymore. No one had really worn them for a few months. As for vaccinations, we'd all had at least five shots, with additional boosters to be administered at regular intervals for the foreseeable future. The pandemic, after several false finishes, finally seemed to be petering out. Life was very nearly back to normal, at least as far as government-mandated restrictions were concerned. I couldn't remember what normal even felt like anymore. Would I ever feel normal again?

Around eleven forty-five, Harris stood up, paid his tab, and looked over at me.

"You coming?"

I nodded and said my goodbyes to the guys. That always took longer than you might think when you threw in some high-fives, several fist bumps, and a hug or two. I also had to re-enact my goal—Bobby threw a rolled-up napkin at my face and I redirected it into a draught pitcher on the table. It only took me seventeen attempts before sinking it. I suffered a few more funny jabs about my unorthodox scoring technique, but as we'd already established, a win is a win.

Harris lived near me, and we walked home through our

neighbourhood. Riverdale is a lovely and diverse Toronto community just east of the Don Valley. Danforth Avenue, an east–west thoroughfare, is the heart of Riverdale, with an eclectic mix of restaurants (many of them Greek), cafés, bars, fashionable boutiques, a microbrewery, a music venue, and a few bookstores—this message brought to you by the Danforth Business Improvement Association. North and south of the Danforth, quiet leafy streets and nice family homes create a very desirable neighbourhood. Withrow Park, vast, green, and treed, sprawls south of the Danforth and is a community hub for dog walkers, yoga practitioners, soccer players, tai chi aficionados, and families, not to mention nearly a hundred aging ball hockey players who use the hockey rink in the centre of the green space for the spring, summer, and fall.

Riverdale is, in my mind, almost a perfect little community in the middle of a thriving, growing metropolis. We moved here when Will was not yet a year old. It's really the only home he's ever known.

Harris and I stopped in front of our house. He looked up at it and shook his head—in a good way, just to be clear.

"I've always loved your home, Jack. It's one of my favourites in the neighbourhood."

"Well, you know who you can thank for that. She found it and was smitten. I confess I fell pretty hard for it, too," I replied. "It's always been a great house for us. I can't imagine living anywhere else."

I looked up and noticed the light on in Will's second-floor bedroom.

"I'm glad to hear that. We wouldn't want you going anywhere."

The three-storey red-brick home was on a corner lot facing the park. It was built in the 1890s, but we'd purchased it just following a significant renovation that resulted in what I've always considered the best of both worlds. It still looked like a home that was more than a century old, but inside it had all the modern conveniences—air conditioning, a fantastic kitchen, big walk-in closets, and a finished basement—while preserving the best of the original home: beautiful wooden staircase and banister, working fireplace and gleaming mantle, big bay windows. And we had our own driveway, a Riverdale rarity.

Harris put his big, calloused hand on my shoulder.

"You're going to be okay, Jack. We're here for you."

"I know, Harris. Thanks. That means a lot."

"Maybe your game-winning goal tonight was a sign of good things to come."

"Kind of you to say, Harris, but just to remind you, the shot ricocheted off my face and into the net. I'm not sure we should read too much into it."

"Yeah, but we won."

He squeezed my shoulder one more time before continuing down the street to his home a few blocks farther south.

Will was already home, so the front door was unlocked. I always felt better knowing he was okay and in the house. Riverdale is a safe neighbourhood, but there's no escaping the fact that Toronto is a big, bustling, cosmopolitan city with many of the attendant problems, including crime, lack of affordable housing, some gang-related violence, too much traffic, smog, and an NHL team that hasn't won the Stanley Cup since 1967. When you're a parent, protecting your kids is an instinct that never leaves you, even when they grow up and enter the ranks of responsible tax-paying citizens. Still, you worry, always.

"Will?" I called as I entered, dragging my hockey stuff with me from the porch.

"Hey, Dad. Upstairs."

After stowing my gear in the basement, I climbed to the second floor. Will's bedroom door was open, and he was working on his computer. I could see he was doing some audio editing or mixing, or both. There were two guitars on stands in the corner, a Guild acoustic and a Fender Telecaster, the cheaper version from Mexico, but still a great axe. A Yamaha keyboard rested on his bed. He pulled off his headphones when I stuck my head in his door.

"How was hockey?" he asked.

"Well, I'm happy to report that we won a very close game, and I scored the winning goal with the clock running out," I said.

"Hey, that's great. Congrats. You're a legend."

"Yes, well, I would have preferred to have scored on a solo rush capped off by a stunning deke, or perhaps a ninja snipe to the top corner, but, you know, a goal is a goal, and a win is a win."

"Don't tell me, the ball bounced off your leg and in," Will said.

"It wasn't that haphazard," I replied. "I actually banked it in off my face."

"Your face?" Will replied. "Now, that takes some skill."

"Yes, well, you know, I'm very good with my face," I said. "But enough about my unique and unheralded hockey skills, what are you working on?"

"It's a song I wrote a few months ago, and I'm just trying to get a passable version recorded so I can try to sort out some harmonies, add a few more instrumental tracks, and work through some different arrangements."

"Have I heard it?"

"I don't think so."

"Can I hear it?"

He paused, thinking about it.

"Sure, why not," he said.

He unplugged his headphones, the sound defaulting to the two monitors that sat on a shelf just above his desk.

It started with a soft and melodic piano intro before an acoustic guitar joined in. It was a ballady love song about meeting a woman in a grocery store and hitting it off. Will really did have a lovely voice, much better than mine. During the verses, the vocal was in his middle register, but it stepped up to his higher range in the chorus. I'd always thought his voice was better in his upper register. The song showcased his vocal strengths. It sounded great, with a catchy hook and what I thought was a nice but unconventional chord progression. The bridge did what bridges are supposed to do—you know, provide a brief musical departure from the verses—before returning to the, by then familiar, chorus. A tight package that told a story with a beginning, a middle, and an end.

"Nice!" I said when it was finished. "Autobiographical?"

"I wish." He sighed. "More like aspirational."

"Can you play it once more?"

"Sure."

This time around, I tried out a few quiet harmonies during the chorus, one above and then one below Will's voice.

"Those work well, Dad," Will said, as he plugged in a microphone secured in its stand and adjusted the pop screen so it was perfectly positioned to do its job.

"Okay, let me layer on a few new tracks this time. You do the lower harmony and I'll take the higher one. That will fill out the chorus nicely."

We recorded two or three takes with our heads close together in front of the single mic. He recorded just the lower harmony, then the higher harmony, and then a version where we sang both harmonies together. I then stood and watched as he moved the harmony tracks into the song. He left the first chorus as one voice only. Then he inserted the lower harmony into the second chorus and both harmonies into the chorus after the bridge, organically building up the song from start to finish.

Twenty minutes later, and well past my typical bedtime, we listened to the new version with the harmonies fully integrated. What a difference they made. The song was really strong. You only had to hear it a couple of times before it stayed with you. That's one sign of a good composition.

"That sounds fantastic," I said. "A great tune, powerful lyrics, good storytelling in the verses, a killer chorus, and a bridge that meshes well with the rest of the song. Not easily done. I love it."

"Thanks. The harmonies make a big difference," Will said. "They really give the chorus some power."

"Let's listen again tomorrow. If it still hits the ear as well then as it does now, I'd say you've got something there."

"Tomorrow morning it is. But right now, I assume you're heading to the shower."

"I was just about to. Why? Is it that bad?"

"As you can see, my window is open," Will said, pointing. "I could smell you when you were still two blocks away."

I laughed, hoping he was exaggerating, and rose to make my way to the bathroom.

"Hey, Dad," Will said. "Are you okay? I mean, are you doing all right?"

He looked concerned. I knew he worried about me just as I worried about him.

"I'm okay, Will. I'm not the same as I was, and we're not the same as we were. How could we be? But I think I'm okay, learning to live in a new reality. But thanks," I replied. "How about you?"

"Better, I think. It's been more than two years. I'm coming around. I hit rough patches now and then. I think it's different for each of us. But I'm better, I think. The old 'time heals all wounds' cliché seems to be doing its thing, slowly."

"Good, son. Good."

I moved to give him a hug. He moved out of range.

"Um, maybe after your shower," he said.

"Right. Sorry."

"Hey, will you be home for dinner tomorrow night?" Will asked.

"Where else would I be on a Wednesday night?"

"Well, you could be out with the boys, or maybe even on a date," Will replied.

"Ahhhh, that's a hard no. Not out with the boys, and definitely not out on a date. I'll be here."

"Good. Then it's settled. I'm cooking us dinner. I want to test out a new recipe I'm thinking of offering at the store."

"Will I like it?" I asked.

"It's called tortilla pie with chicken. A Mexican dish, if the word *tortilla* didn't give it away. Use your imagination. Even your narrow palate shouldn't be offended."

"Thanks! Count me in," I said. "I don't think I can book a mariachi band on such short notice, but maybe I'll pick up some tequila, which just might have the same uplifting effect, anyway."

Will was a good kid. Always had been. Twenty-seven years old. He had a degree from McGill in history and music, and a passion for food and cooking. He'd been holding down two jobs since before the pandemic. He spent most days as a chef, conceiving and cooking prepared foods in the kitchens of Atchison's, a high-end specialty food store on the Danforth. He seemed to enjoy it, and even after cooking for eight hours at the store, he still loved to come home and create in our own kitchen, for which my stomach and I were grateful. Then, on the weekends and some evenings, he worked as a kind of apprentice sound engineer at a recording studio downtown, learning the ropes and refining his already advanced audio editing and mixing skills. He was young and living a full life.

Will used to have an apartment closer to downtown but had moved back home when the pandemic hit in early 2020. He'd been here ever since. I loved having him around. We leaned on one another. We needed one another. I may have needed him more than he needed me. I can admit that. I wasn't sure what I'd do if he weren't back living in the family home with me.

I hadn't stretched after hockey, largely because, well, I hated stretching. I completely understood and accepted the importance of stretching in recovering from a sport as physically intense and demanding as ball hockey on a concrete floor. But apparently my knowledge and acceptance just weren't enough to get me to do it reliably, let alone competently and for the appropriate duration. Making matters worse, I'm about as flexible as cast iron, which I'm sure makes it look like I'm not stretching anyway. But I took a long and very hot shower and then completed about five minutes of my fifteen-minute stretching routine. That was five minutes more than I'd done in a long time. It's just so boring, and more than a little uncomfortable. The shower was to address my post-hockey bodily fragrance issues. The stretching was, however briefly, to ameliorate the pain and stiffness the morning would surely bring. To complement my half-assed stretching regimen, I also popped a couple of extra-strength Advils before going to bed, and I would do the same after waking up.

I may not have mentioned it yet—in fact, I know I haven't—but I am sixty-two. There, I said it. I still don't believe it, but at least I said it. Yes, I'm as shocked as you are. I don't really know how it happened. There I was, in my early forties, minding my own business, living my life. Then I went to bed one night and woke up as a sixty-two-year-old. I can't fathom it. I just don't understand. I refuse to accept "time flies" as an adequate explanation. Not good enough. But I admit, it all happened so fast, though I do have a theory. I'm always good for a theory.

I don't claim to have created this idea. I'm sure I heard or read about it somewhere, but it stuck with me as compelling. If you think about it, from the time we're born to, say, our early twenties, many experiences we have are brand new. Learning to walk. Trying new foods. Going to school. Riding a bike. Making friends. Feeling those first romantic stirrings. Going to high school. Asking someone out.

Being turned down. First time holding hands. First kiss. First time doing more than kissing. Going to university or getting a job. These are all experiences that we have for the first time, usually early in our lives. So they loom large in our memories and take on greater significance. Thinking back, there's just no comparison between how slowly my first twenty years seemed to pass and how lightning-fast my thirties, forties, and fifties zipped by. Why?

Well, in our thirties, forties, and fifties, we tend to be settled into a routine. We go to our jobs, do our work, come home, spend time with our families, eat what we like to eat, cut the lawn, shovel the snow, do the laundry, shop for groceries, fill the car up, do the kids' homework—of course, I mean *help* with their homework—watch *Jeopardy!* at seven thirty and maybe the news later on, and we do all of this day in and day out, week in and week out, month over month, year over year. As an adult, because of the repetitive nature of our daily experiences, they all seem to run together, with few, if any, new experiences to interrupt the treadmill (perhaps a happy treadmill) of the long-established routines that become our lives. Without any variety to break up the benign monotony, the time slips by at what feels like an incredible pace. Sure, perhaps our vacations are opportunities for new experiences, but they aren't long enough and don't happen often enough to change our perception of time. Yes, time flies. It's a cliché because it's true.

So that's my less-than-original theory on aging. It feels like the best explanation I've heard to account for my experience of turning forty and then, in the blink of an eye, waking up at sixty-two.

There's another reason this theory seems to hold water for me. I realized in hindsight that I've been inadvertently testing and proving this hypothesis for years, albeit on a smaller scale, during our annual golf pilgrimage to Virginia. A few buddies from the league and I make a yearly drive down to a lovely golf course in rural Virginia. Here's how it all unfolds, with virtually no deviation over the twenty-five years we've been making the trip. We get up early each morning. Eat the same things for breakfast. Play thirty-six holes of golf, with lunch in between. Then shower, have dinner, and catch a movie, during which most of us fall asleep, even if it's a tense and suspenseful thriller. Then we go back to the less-than-luxurious motel, turn in for the night, and do exactly the same thing the next day, and the next day, and the next day, until a week passes and we drive home. Very rarely does this routine change. And consequently, the days all blend together, and we're back home long before the trip feels like it should be over.

To me, it's the golf-vacation microcosmic controlled study that proves the broader theory. If our days, weeks, and months don't appreciably change, if we repeat the same patterns for a few decades in our adult lives, man, do the years slip by in a blink. And they have. They really have.

But beyond the theory, I simply don't identify as a sixty-two-year-old. When I read about a sixty-two-year-old in the newspaper I don't picture me. My own father seemed sixty-two when he was forty-five and fifty-five. I still feel, in my own completely objective mind, around thirty-five years old. I like the same things now as I did when I was thirty-five. I do the same things. It all feels the same.

Sometimes when I'm driving, I ask myself, as I'm sitting there belted in, hands on the wheel, eyes on the road, does anything feel even the slightest bit different than it did when I was thirty-five and driving down the same road? Is my vision worse? No. Am I just as comfortable? Yes. Does it feel just the same? It does. I know what you're thinking. That's not exactly a double-blind, peer-reviewed, rigorous scientific study in the *New England Journal of Aging and Delusional White Guys*—you know, the very respected *NEJADWG*—but I swear I feel exactly the same. I assumed at sixty-two, I'd feel physically different than I did when I was thirty-five. But I don't. Not often.

Okay, there are two situations when I do feel different, and perhaps actually feel my age. One is when I wake up in the night, often more than once, to pee. Apparently, my prostate no longer feels thirty-five but has fully embraced life at sixty-two. And secondly, the morning after a ball hockey game when, I swear, I wake up occupying someone else's body, someone maybe in their eighties with enough stiffness in the legs to make rigor mortis a viable diagnosis. But usually, the achiness and compromised mobility only last for about . . . well, a full week, just in time to take to the concrete again for our next game. But other than that, I'm still thirty-five years old. So those are the only two instances when I feel sixty-two and not thirty-five. Just those two.

It was late. I crawled into bed and turned out the light, too tired to read. I dreamt about her again, as I did many nights—okay, most nights. It's why I looked forward to going to bed and dreaded it at the same time.

It's often the same scene. I'm watching her speak at a big conference to hundreds of lawyers. She doesn't know I'm there until her eyes catch me at the back of the room, where I stand, chest puffed out, utterly failing to disguise how proud I am of her. Our eyes connect briefly. She smiles at me and, without missing a beat, carries on with her talk about current trends in mergers and acquisitions. There is love and life in that smile. The dream ends before she finishes her talk.

I woke up. It was shortly after four a.m.

Coincidentally, if not conveniently, my prostate was also awake. I took a deep breath and hauled my aging carcass out of our bed and began that long and arduous ten-foot walk to our ensuite bathroom. Despite having played ball hockey on concrete just hours before, I was able to make it almost in an upright position, navigating on sore and stiff legs that seemed more than just unfamiliar. Rather, they felt like poorly maintained rentals about to be retired from active service. I made yet another mental promise to stretch after next week's game. By the time I shuffled back to bed, moaning with every step, I was wide awake. To distract myself from my dream and its star, I returned to a book I've read often, Sylvia Beach's Paris memoir, *Shakespeare and Company*. I think of it as literary comfort food. I soon fell back into a fitful sleep.

I was up, or at least awake, in good time the next morning. To be fair, I'm awake around sixish every morning regardless of what's gone on the night before. I really haven't been able to sleep in since I was about fifty. Okay, yes, you got me. Maybe there are just three situations when I kind of, sort of, feel my age. I mean, I could sleep in just fine when I was thirty-five. But no longer. So, other than my near inability to walk normally the morning after a game, my frequent nocturnal trips to the bathroom, and my internal alarm waking me up at six o'clock every morning, I still feel like I'm thirty-five. Just three.

I got up and took another hot shower, gently kneading my leg muscles and even stretching in a way that was not too taxing. In other words, a keen-eyed observer likely wouldn't know I was stretching even though I was, you know, "stretching." I dried off and stood in front of the full-length mirror in our walk-in closet. I'd pushed myself really hard in the previous night's game. But it was not a pretty sight staring back at me. My legs were still stiff. My knees hurt and even looked a bit swollen to my eye. My ankles were tender. And my hips felt like my ball-and-socket joints had been replaced by the less common block-and-socket joints—I understood why they'd never taken off. Finally, a perfect angry red circle on my stomach glared at me. I'd unintentionally stopped my own centre's slapshot from the slot when I was creating traffic in front of the goalie. I'd seen my teammate wind up for the shot and did my best to curl out of its path. I just wasn't fast enough. Maybe I would have been at thirty-five. However, I was fast enough to collide with the goalpost in my haste to get out of the way. It spun me around to take the gut-shot face-on. It hurt. A lot.

The colour of the bruise was quite impressive: vivid, vibrant, and still changing. It had started out as a classic deep red, but around the edges I could see other colours emerging. I knew the progression. A few days hence a veritable colour wheel of reds, blues, yellows, and purples would blossom from the bruise and keep evolving for weeks. I considered posting shots of the bruise's various colourful incarnations on Instagram but decided against it. I just couldn't be bothered. Hmmm. Now that I think of it, my bruises didn't look like that when I was thirty-five. At sixty-two, they're now much more colourful, visually arresting, almost symphonic in their chromatic complexity. So, just to complete the catalogue, I've now identified four examples of when the reality of my age asserts itself. Just four. Otherwise, I'm still thirty-five.

I limped back to our bedroom and pulled on my work clothes—you know, sweatpants and a T-shirt. I looked at the two walls and eight drawers of our walk-in closet filled with her clothes. *Nope, not today*. I hobbled past Will's closed door towards the staircase. I stopped when I heard faint but familiar sounds escaping from within. I figured I knew what I was hearing—I'd just never heard it coming from Will's room. I almost knocked but thought better of it. Instead, I shuffled downstairs, grunting in discomfort with each step, for the elixir of coffee. Twenty minutes later, Will bounded down the stairs and headed for the front door. I was still staggering around the kitchen, wincing and moaning with each step.

"You sound in pain," Will said as he grabbed his jacket.

"Yes, well, playing ball hockey at such a high level requires some bodily sacrifice that usually manifests itself most profoundly the morning after, and, at my age, maybe three or four mornings thereafter for good measure. So not only do I sound in pain, I actually *am* in pain. But nothing I can't handle as long as I don't have to walk more than ten steps in a stint."

"Good luck climbing up the stairs to your office," he said.

"I'll take rest stops," I replied. "Hey, um, are you okay? I thought I may have heard you, you know, dealing with stuff, when I walked past your door."

Will sighed. We both waited until he'd pulled on his jacket.

"Yeah, it wasn't a great morning. I had a dream about her just before I woke up. I haven't dreamt about her for a while now, and it kind of caught me off guard," he said. "Anyway, I've learned not to resist it. I just let it wash over me. I give in to it, you know?"

"You don't have to explain. That's how I've learned to deal with it, too," I said. "And I don't know about you, but after a few blubbery sobs and some rattling inhalations, when that big lump in my throat shrinks, I feel, I don't know, almost refreshed, rejuvenated, even energized, ready to go. Oh, and calm. I feel calm afterwards."

"I know, right?" Will agreed. "I always feel so much better after a quick release. That's why I stopped fighting it."

"Wise decision. And you know I'm always here if you want to talk things through and compare notes," I offered. "I'm not sure I have any answers, but we might as well feel our way through it together. I mean, we're both on a path here, right? But we're not necessarily going to make the same gains at the same pace. And there'll be relapses and setbacks. There always are. I'm fine for a bit, and then I stumble. Maybe you do, too. So we need to be there for each other, okay?"

Will looked at me, nodded, and gave me at least the nascent phase of a smile.

"I just miss her," he said. "I miss talking to her."

"Yeah, me too. In a big way."

"Hey, on a happier note, don't forget I'm cooking tonight," Will added.

"Trust me, I never forget when I'm off the hook for dinner. Kitchen clean-up is on me."

Will waved and ducked out the door for the walk to the Danforth and Atchison's.

I forced myself to eat some yogurt and granola, then filled a large travel mug with coffee and milk. Will was right. It was a bit of a hike up two flights of stairs to my office on the third floor, so a travel mug seemed the right choice. I somehow did manage to haul myself up to my workspace, with only a half-dozen rest stops along the way to massage my legs and guzzle some coffee. I paused in the large room just outside my office door that we used for family storage. Thirty-plus years of marriage yields lots of stuff—from meaningful mementoes to pure detritus—that all needs to be stored. Every house has a storage room, either in the basement or the attic. For some reason, we chose the attic. Why descend one flight of stairs with tons of stuff when instead, you can climb to the third floor? Brilliant. Without much conviction, I made a mental note to sort through everything in the room—you know, sometime.

I sat down at my laptop in front of the window, the roof lines sloping down on either side of me. I may not have mentioned this yet, but I'm a freelance writer. Have been for nearly thirty years. My wife had the high-flying and high-paying career, so I worked from home and took care of Will in the early years. It felt like he was taking care of me now.

Over the years, I'd built up a strong and loyal client base writing annual reports, speeches, advertising copy, brochures, marketing bumf, and even a few ghostwritten corporate histories privately published as expensive, glossy coffee-table books that graced, well, coffee tables in C-suite lobbies around the country. I liked the flexibility of working from home, in elastic-waistband pants and slippers. The real bonus was saving all the childcare costs in those early years when I stayed home with Will. Now that he's a fully practising adult with only rare relapses, I'm still freelancing from home, and having a few relapses of my own.

I spent an hour or so working on an annual report for a staid insurance company. Scintillating, I know, but even insurance companies need an annual report. In fact, they're required by regulation, and often by legislation. The client called at eleven o'clock, as planned. We exchanged pleasantries before she got down to business.

"Jack, we just really want the report to be powerful, compelling, maybe even gripping. You know, a real page-turner," she opened.

You might think she was kidding about the page-turner part, but she wasn't. Gripping?

"Susan, I like the direction, but this is an insurance company's annual report, with much of its content dictated by regulatory authorities. It is not a novel or a screenplay for a suspense-filled thriller. And, perhaps more to the point, you know how conservative the company tends to be about such things. I remember a few years ago when I tried to make the writing a little more animated, active, and vital—I needed senior management's approval to use a single exclamation mark, while they rejected four others."

"I know, I know. But can you try to add a bit more zip to it? The last draft, well, it just didn't quite seem up to your normal standards. Just saying. So really dig in, you know, and deliver. I know you can. You have every other time."

I sighed, I hoped silently.

"I hear you," I replied. "Will do, and thanks for the feedback."

"Sorry, Jack. Just trying to get us both across the finish line."

We kicked around some ideas for adding more spirit and energy to the prose, but her comment about my last draft not being up to snuff had left me a bit discouraged. We weren't that close, so she probably didn't know what had been weighing me down and making it so hard to turn a hidebound insurance company's annual report into a powerful, compelling, and gripping page-turner.

CHAPTER 2

I HUNG UP THE PHONE, the client's disappointment still rattling in my ears. My eyes tracked around my home office as I tried to stay focused on the task at hand. The family photos on the corner of my desk did not help keep my mind on the client's annual report. Annie's beautiful face smiled out at me. She had that mischievous look on her face that usually preceded some prank or witty line. Annie Barnes. We were married for thirty-one years. Then she died. Two years, five months, and fifteen days ago.

"Annie Barnes," I said aloud, seated alone at my desk. "Annie. Annie Barnes."

Sometimes I said it out loud just to make her memory feel more real, more present. She was a victim of COVID-19, the global pandemic that took so many lives around the world. A cruel fate. Annie was one of the first in Toronto, the first of many—thousands, in fact. She drove herself to the hospital on her way home from the office. She'd been following the news. We all had. She recognized her sudden symptoms, and she knew what they meant. She did not come home. They admitted her right away. Six days later she was gone. Six days. I never saw her again, let alone held her, or kissed her, or felt her head resting on my chest, her hand in mine. Never again.

In those early days, they knew so little about the virus that no one was allowed in to see her. We FaceTimed when she was up to it, but I was never in the room with her. Could never touch her. Hold her hand. Hug her close. She was alone, except for the dozens of other patients and the true heroes—the nurses, doctors, and other frontline workers. And she was declining at breathtaking speed, and I mean breathtaking in its most literal sense. The last time we FaceTimed was the day before she died. She was really struggling to breathe and speak. She knew. She told me she was sorry she was going. I protested but she stopped me. Saying, "No, no, this is happening. I love you, and I know you will be sad. You will mourn. But if you love me, you will not let this be your defining moment. You must come back to life and honour me by living. And take care of Will. We made him. Part of me is in him." I could barely hear her last words to me: airy, breathless, barely a whisper. Fourteen hours later she was gone. Fourteen hours.

While we'd known what was coming and that it wouldn't take long, still, when the doctor called with the news, I couldn't respond. That familiar lump in my throat seemed to block any sound. I had nothing. Will took the phone and thanked the doctor for letting us know and asked those practical, benign questions around disposition of the body and funeral arrangements, all while I collapsed into my grief. It seemed impossible, though that reaction was almost universal among those who had known her. Annie was so strong, so together, so confident, and so good at everything she tackled. People like Annie didn't just die. They conquered everything thrown in their path. They rose above that which would have defeated others. They were resilience personified. That is, until COVID. Two years, five months, and fifteen days ago.

I married well above my station. Annie is . . . Annie was smart, strong, and completely committed to us as a family, for the long haul. She made partner at Borden Mackenzie, one of Toronto's top law firms, in record time, establishing a reputation as a tough, creative, and savvy mergers and acquisitions specialist. When the complexities of a transaction stumped everyone else, on both sides of a deal, Annie would somehow find her way to a solution. With a string of ever larger, and more prestigious and lucrative, transactions—initially as an associate, and then as a partner leading the deals—she had socked away loads of retirement savings that had just continued to grow.

The massive deals she led and the time they required meant that I was the constant on the home front. Working out of our house allowed me to take care of Will in the early years while still adding to the family income, mainly writing speeches. Though my income was about a quarter of what Annie drew, we saved a bundle on childcare, and paid off the mortgage, too. In short, when Annie passed away, the combination of her life insurance payout, our healthy retirement fund, and our lack of debt meant that I'd never need to work another day in my life. I say again, I married well above my station. But I kept right on freelancing anyway. I didn't know what else to do. I needed the familiar to help me navigate the daunting—a world without Annie.

I have a theory about grief—yes, another of my theories. This is how I try to figure out why life works the way it does. I don't claim these theories are necessarily true. They just feel right at the time I concoct them. I do try to keep an open mind and amend my little postulates from time to time to reflect new knowledge and life experience.

It seems to me that when a loved one dies, we have a finite amount of grief to endure, whether the passing was sudden and shocking or prolonged and predictable. This idea first occurred to me when I lost my younger brother to a car accident when he was backpacking around Europe, the summer he turned nineteen. Like all nineteen-year-olds, he was invincible, and excited about life. On the cusp of so many important experiences. Gone in an instant, when a driver fell asleep at the wheel on a hot, humid, and hazy afternoon and struck my brother down as he hitchhiked along a country road outside of Brindisi, Italy. He'd been headed for the ferry to take him to Corfu. I remembered the rugged beauty of Corfu when I'd thumbed my way across Europe in my early twenties, but my brother never made it there. He'd been denied all those little experiences and adventures that I'd enjoyed on that Greek island. That stuck with me for a long time.

So when a death is unexpected, the grief rushes in hard and fast. It's a shock, and the pain and surprise submerge you all at once. If, on the other hand, a loved one is diagnosed with, say, some form of terminal cancer, death is often not imminent even if it's certain. Death takes its sweet time in some cases. So that finite allocation of grief is spread out over a longer period. In fact, if the outcome is inevitable, it's almost impossible not to start grieving long before the loved one actually passes. You might argue that grief management may be easier in this more prolonged scenario. Perhaps, but that can be a long and painful haul.

So I don't really know which grief scenario is worse, the sudden and intense conflagration or the slow, debilitating burn. (Is neither an option?) Okay, so maybe it's not much of a theory after all. But when Annie died, it happened so fast, the pain of it all hit me like a runaway train. No warning. No ability to help. No time to be thoughtful and rational. Just the inescapable fact that someone I loved more than anyone else in the world was somehow, inexplicably, undeniably, irrevocably . . . gone. In the months that followed, Annie's death hollowed me out and filled me up with a grief that literally made me feel heavier, physically. As if concrete were now part of my bodily constitution, hardened and heavy. Walking was taxing and tiring. So was the very act of getting out of bed. Moving from room to room seemed to take more effort. When I started playing ball hockey again, I was no longer the same player. I couldn't do the things and make the moves I used to be able to pull off. I'm not suggesting I was a great player before Annie died. I wasn't. But I was definitely better before than after. Grief is hard—physically hard. And don't get me started on my erratic and frustrating sleeping patterns.

Having said all of this, I had started to feel more like myself in the past few months. I think watching Will slowly emerge from the shadow of his mother's passing helped in my recovery. I just felt better and was actually able to enjoy myself at least a little—not like before, but certainly more than I could right after Annie died. Friday night at the Dora, having a few beers with the guys. Hanging out in the park. Playing my ball hockey games. Being around my friends. All were starting to feel almost enjoyable. Again, not like before. But not like just after either. Baby steps.

One thing was certain. Having lost Annie, I needed to hold on to Will, physically and emotionally. I worried about him, perhaps unnecessarily. Maybe I was really just worrying about me, through him. But he was my one tangible living link to Annie. I was not looking forward to the day he moved back out on his own. I still needed him and perhaps he still needed me.

In the corner of my office was a cardboard box with the words "Magic Tree House" scrawled on it in my nearly illegible hand. We'd been trying for nearly a decade to clear out stuff in the house that Will had outgrown. But in the last two years, five months, and fifteen days, I just hadn't been able to load that box into the car and drive it over to the Goodwill drop-off station. The box was filled with every available book from the Magic Tree House series that Will had devoured as an early reader. The books featured two young kids, Jack and Annie (of course), who were able to travel to faraway places and times through their, yes, magic tree house. When he was still very young, Will actually thought the books were about his mother and father, and I confess I did little to disabuse him of the notion. I lifted the cardboard flap, reached in, pulled out one of the books at random, and sat back down at my desk. The book in my hand was called *Dinosaurs Before Dark*. It had been one of Will's favourites. Mine, too. Before he was old enough to handle them on his own, I would read the stories to him. I flipped through the book

I'd read to Will dozens, perhaps hundreds, of times. The story, the words, the dialogue, the illustrations all rushed back to me in a flash. I read the entire book, sometimes reciting sections from memory, while remembering the physical feeling of little Will sitting in my lap, spellbound at the exploits of Jack and Annie.

I gave in to the memories for a while but then returned the book to the box and kickstarted myself back into the scintillating insurance company annual report that still lacked the ever-elusive scintillating part.

Shortly after five o'clock, I heard Will arrive home from work. Soon after, he was clattering around the kitchen creating his promised tortilla pie. I would have loved him whether he could cook or not. But man, it's great having a talented chef living under your roof. I was grateful every day, usually around dinnertime.

I abandoned my annual report—just temporarily—and headed downstairs. When I entered the kitchen, Will was spooning refried beans between layers of soft tortillas in what I believe is called a springform pan. He had already stuffed in cooked chicken along with several other ingredients, all of which looked and smelled fantastic.

Will looked up, saw me, and did what he did every time he came home from work. He hugged me. Always a favourite part of my day. I hugged back and held it for a little longer than usual.

"Hey, Dad," he said, brow furrowed. "Are you okay? Tough day?"

"I'm okay, Will. Just trying to make a hidebound insurance company sound hip, young, and interesting in that exciting and captivating communications vehicle traditionally known as the annual report."

"Wow. Now, that sounds like mission impossible."

"Yes, it is, but that's why they pay me the modest bucks—you know, to do the impossible," I replied. "Beer?"

"Oh yeah. Thanks."

I handed him a beer from the fridge and I opened one, too.

By this stage, the kitchen was smelling amazing. Half an hour later or so, Will flipped on the broiler to brown the shredded cheese he'd loaded on top of the pie. When it came out of the oven, it was perfect. I nearly passed out from anticipation. Will served it as he might an apple pie, carving out sizeable wedges for us both. It was delicious.

"Holy shite, this may be the best thing I've ever eaten," I said, chowing down on seconds, or it could have been thirds by that time. "So good."

"And the leftovers should get us through the week," Will said with a nod to the hefty portion of tortilla pie still nestled in the springform pan.

"I wouldn't count on too many leftovers," I said. "The night is young and I'm still hungry."

"You make a cook's heart swell, Dad."

"Will, you do know how much I appreciate all you do around here, particularly in the kitchen, right?"

"I know, Dad, I know, and it's fine," he said. "I'm not paying any rent and I work full-time. So cooking dinner hardly makes us even. Besides, it's one of my favourite things to do. It calms me down after a stressful day at work."

"Excellent points, well made," I agreed. "Then by all means, keep those meals coming."

He'd brought home from work two small glass jars filled with chocolate mousse for dessert, and now he set them on the table with a couple of small spoons.

"Ahhh, not chocolate mousse again?" I asked, as I inhaled my little jarful.

Will laughed.

"Um, Will, son, are you going to eat yours?"

He pushed his jar over to my side of the table.

"It's all yours, Dad. I ate a couple servings when I made it this afternoon. You can only take so much chocolate mousse before the richness defeats you."

"Actually, that's not been my experience, though I should perhaps undertake more testing."

Will laughed at what he called my dad jokes. Some might have been offended by the term, but I'd always embraced it with pride.

"So, Dad, any new songs lately?" Will asked.

"Not really." I sighed. "I haven't picked up my guitar in quite a while."

Will paused and looked down at the table for a few seconds before looking back up at me.

"You know, Dad, eventually you're going to have to start doing those things again that once made you happy. They might just make you happy again, or at least happier." He paused again before continuing. "So why not write a new song? Hey, did you ever finish that song you started about the ball hockey league?"

I'd begun working on the song not long after Annie died, but it had stalled, and I just hadn't been able to get back to it since.

"I only wrote the first two verses and the chorus," I replied. "I'll get back to it sometime."

"Dad, I really liked the chord progression you came up with, and the words in the chorus were great," Will nudged. "How did the chorus go again? Something about not being able to score, and sore knees? Solid lyrics."

I smiled, remembering the words. I liked them, too.

"If I remember correctly, the chorus went like this," I said, and then proceeded to sing in my serviceable but hardly memorable voice.

My knees are sore
And my hands won't score
My head is pounding in pain
The will is strong
But the legs are gone
Every week it's the same.

Then Will joined me on the final line, which came back to him at just the right moment.

It's so much more than the game.

"Right, right. That's it. Love it," Will said. "I guess when you're over sixty, you stop writing love songs and start writing ball hockey songs."

As soon as the words left his lips, he seemed to realize what he'd said.

"Shit, Dad, shit. I didn't mean that. I wasn't thinking," he said, his hand pressed against his forehead. "I'm such an idiot."

"Will, Will, please, relax, it's fine," I said, and meant it. "I wasn't writing it because I couldn't write love songs anymore after losing your mother. I started to write it out of gratitude for what the league has given me all these years. In a way, I think of it as a love song, just an unconventional one."

An awkward silence reigned for a few seconds, so I filled it.

"You know, I was forty-three when I joined the league. I mean, how often at that somewhat advanced age do you get involved with something that bestows on you a whole new circle of great, close friends? It's rare, and it really tells you something about this community," I said. I worried about the silence, so I just kept prattling on.

"Did I ever tell you about my first game in the league?"

Will smiled.

"Many times, Dad, but tell me again. I like the story."

"Okay, so I'm sitting on the bench in my very first game in the league—2003, I believe—and I ask the guy sitting next to me—I don't even remember who it was—'So, who's the oldest guy in the league?' I see him scan the other team's bench and then the floor before he points and says, 'Do you see that guy with the red helmet in the corner? That's Irwin Holst and he just turned fifty-two.'"

I paused for dramatic effect before barrelling on.

"'What? There's a guy playing in the league who's fifty-two? That's incredible. Fifty-two!'"

"Right!" Will said, still looking engaged even though I'd told this tale quite a few times over the years. "And now you're sixty-two and still playing in the league. Good on you, Dad. Good on you."

"And I've got a few years left in me, I figure."

A knock at the door interrupted our conversation, or perhaps spared Will from more old stories.

"You get that, Dad, and I'll clean up the kitchen," Will suggested.

I lifted myself off the kitchen chair and shuffled to the front door, my body still protesting the previous night's game. I found four of my closest hockey buddies—Harris, Nathan, Bobby, and Ted "The Apple" Appleton—standing on our porch with pizzas, beer, and what appeared to be trepidation on their faces.

"Oh, hi, guys. Did I forget to put something in my calendar?"

"Ummm, no, not really—you see, we just thought we'd, um, stop by and maybe watch the Jays game with you," Harris said, as they hustled past me and plunked down on the couch and easy chairs in the family room. Bobby handed me a beer and a slice.

"Thanks, Bobby," I said, taking the beer only. "But I literally just finished eating a few minutes ago."

"Such a nice place you got here, Jack," Ted said.

"You've been inside our house before, Apple. You were here last week."

"I know, but I'd just forgotten how nice it is inside. I mean, this couch is really comfy," he said, plumping a throw pillow before sliding it behind him—and no, I don't know why they're called throw pillows.

Something was going on. They just sat there and looked up at me as if they were about to kick off a Tupperware party, or maybe a captains' meeting. Then they all turned to Harris and kind of nodded. Ever subtle, Bobby actually motioned with his hand as if to say, *Okay, let's get on with it.* On cue, Harris stood up and cleared his throat.

"Well, Jack, you see, it's like this. We came over because, well, we're still worried about you," Harris started. "You've been through a lot, a real shit storm you certainly didn't deserve. Anyway, we just want to help you. You can lean on us."

I didn't know what to say and for once in my life, instead of saying something stupid, I just said nothing. Harris seemed to understand that he still had the floor, so he started up again.

"I mean, it's great that through it all, you've still played ball hockey."

"Yeah, but we've noticed a marked decline in your play," interjected Bobby. "Ahhhh, I mean, I hope you're not injured. Is your Achilles acting up again?"

"Jesus, Bobby, we agreed not to mention his play," Ted said. "Stick to the script."

"There's a script?" I asked. Ted and Bobby actually nodded.

"Guys, please," piped in Nathan. "Not to get too metaphysical about this, but you don't need to be physically injured for your game to suffer. Playing with a broken heart could affect your play, too. Give the guy a break. It takes time."

"Hang on. Let me just add a point in my own defence," I started. "You seem to have forgotten that I'm sixty-two—holy shit, it's even hard to say that out loud. Think about it—I figure my skills have been on a slow and steady decline since I turned fifty, just like all of yours have. So don't blame Annie for the slide in my play. I'm sure it hasn't helped, but did I mention that I'm now sixty-two and I'm still playing? It's not like skating, you know. There's no gliding in ball hockey. It's all cardio, all the time."

I made a mental note to add "declining ball hockey skills" as the fifth, and I hoped final, example of how life at sixty-two is different from life at thirty-five. It was quite clear to me that I was no longer the ball hockey player I was at forty-five, let alone twenty-five. But I think that should complete the inventory. Just five. That's it. Five.

"Whoa, Jack. We're getting off track here, thanks to Bobby's big yap. Of course, you're right. We're all getting older, but this is not about how we're aging or about the state of your game right now," Harris said, glaring at Bobby. "Um, look, Jack, you're one of us. You're our friend. We've been through a lot together over the years, and not just in front of the net. This little intervention . . ."

"Intervention?" I interrupted. "It's more like a home invasion."

Harris knew I was joking so he just ignored me and carried on.

"This little intervention is just to remind you that we are here for you. And we don't care if your play is a little off—at least until the playoffs roll around. I'm kidding! We're just worried about you, and we want to help."

Despite their less-than-refined approach, I was touched. They were serious and they meant well. Even shoot-from-the-lip Bobby.

"Guys, that's very thoughtful of you, and I'm touched, I really am, but I'm feeling better. I'm getting there. I'm sure my game will be back up to par soon. But I've never gone through anything like this before, so I'm still a rookie at this kind of thing. There is no instruction manual. I'm sort of feeling my way through it and doing my best to keep an eye out for Will."

"But there must be something we can do to help," Nathan said. "How about we set up a schedule and bring you meals, so you don't have to worry about that?"

"Boys, remember, I live with my own personal chef," I said, pointing to Will in the kitchen. "It takes him half as long to make meals that are twice as good as the Shake 'n Bake chicken and tuna casseroles you guys could pull together. Not that I wouldn't really appreciate it, but there's just no need. How about you just hand over the money you'd spend on those meals and that could defray Will's higher-end food costs?"

Four guys reached for their wallets.

"Guys, stop! That was a joke. You're supposed to laugh."

"Well, shit, man, it's not always easy to tell when you're being funny," Bobby said. "Before, you were always funny. Now I really have to think about it to know for sure."

"Look, I am grateful for all of you, and even for this little intervention, as you call it. But we're going to be okay. Time will do its thing. I'm not back yet, but I'm headed in the right direction. Just being around you guys helps. Playing in the league helps. Sharing a beer after the games helps. This, tonight, helps. But in the end, I'm going to have to navigate the tough stuff pretty much on my own. But seriously, I love you for caring and coming over. I'm lucky to have you and I'm sure I'd be really messed up if you weren't around. So, from the bottom of my broken heart, thank you."

"Well, just try to pick up your game a bit, will you?" Bobby said.

Everyone laughed.

Their kind message delivered and received, we settled down to eat some pizza and watch baseball. Nathan was on his feet, his head tilted almost horizontal, scanning the bookshelves in the family room.

"So, what's with all the books on Paris?" he asked.

"Oh, well, you see, I haven't talked too much about this with you guys, but I have a thing for Paris in the 1920s. It's one of my, um, interests. You know the players, Hemingway, Fitzgerald, Stein, Pound, Picasso, Salvador Dalí . . ."

"Who did they play for?" Ted asked.

I ignored this, but persevered. "You know, that was a time of cultural revolution, with new ways of writing, new ways of painting, new ways of seeing the world after the horrors of the Great War. These artists were known as the Lost Generation. For some reason, I've always been fascinated by this city and this time period, though I'm not really sure why."

"When was the last time you were in Paris?" Harris asked.

"That's the strange part of the story," I replied. "I've never been."

"What? You have shelves full of books about it, but you've never been?" Bobby asked. "It's only a seven-hour flight. I've been three times and knew nothing about these guys or who they played for."

"Twice Annie and I booked trips to Paris, but, you know, shit happened to scupper our plans both times. We never made it, and I just haven't felt like going through with it on my own."

"You should go, man. You know, a reset, a fresh start. A new beginning. You should definitely go," said Nathan.

"But not until after the season ends, unless your play continues to suck. In that case, you can go anytime."

"Thanks, Bobby, that really means a lot to me."

More laughter.

"Hey, the game's starting," Ted said, checking his watch. "Who's got the remote?"

And that was it. Intervention concluded as the Blue Jays game commenced. Paris would have to wait. Still, I felt blessed. Truly blessed.

The Jays lost, but I found just spending time with the guys watching sports on TV was, if not therapeutic, at least calming and comforting. After the game, the guys lined up to hug me and whisper encouragement and support in my ear before they left. We were a group that hugged, on the ball hockey floor and off. Truly blessed.

Will had disappeared upstairs after he'd finished in the kitchen. But he appeared at our bedroom door as I crawled into bed.

"Dad, you should really go to Paris."

"Oh, you heard that idea, did you?"

"It's inspired," Will said. "I should have thought of it before now."

"So tell me, Will, did you know about this little intervention?"

"Well, um, it's possible that I may have known something about them coming over for a visit," he said.

"And by cooking me dinner you made sure I was here for them."

"So they could be here for you."

"Touché. Thanks, son."

"I really think you should consider going to Paris. There are literally zero obstacles stopping you. And if you went at the end of the ball hockey season, I'd come over for Christmas."

"But then you'd be alone here," I said. "I worry enough about you when we're living in the same house. Being an ocean away would be, well, hard."

"Dad, do not use me to justify sitting around here when the city and history you're passionate about are out there just waiting for you. I'm fine. I have a job. I have two jobs. And, as I think you've noticed, I am able to cook my own meals and take care of my twenty-seven-year-old self. So no, I kept you away from Paris once before—it's not on me this time. This is on you, Dad. Paris is right there. It would take you ten minutes to book a flight and an Airbnb, and you could be there later this week. Come on. I mean it. It's important. Will you at least think about it?"

"Well, after your spirited defence of the idea, I feel honour-bound to give it serious thought. And I will."

"That's all I ask," Will said.

"Hey, Will, thanks again for the tortilla pie. Even though it was part of a conspiracy to foment an impromptu therapy session in our own family room, that dinner made it all worthwhile."

"You're welcome, Dad," he said. "You can take me out to dinner in Paris over Christmas."

I lay awake for a long time that night, and not just mulling over the boys' intervention. Even though its execution may have fallen short of their expectations, there was nothing more genuine and heartfelt than their desire to support a friend they were worried about, perhaps justly. But my mind kept coming back to Paris and Will's insistence that I think about it.

I cannot really explain why I'm so fascinated by the Paris of the 1920s and what it represents in our cultural history. It's just one of my things. And I seem to have many. It's likely one of the consequences of having been blessed with more than my fair share of curiosity back when, you know, allocations of curiosity were being handed out. Have I mentioned that I have a theory about curiosity? Well, I do. I've come to realize that curiosity is one of life's great gifts to me. At least, that's how I think of it. Perhaps curiosity is a zero-sum game across the world's population. Some people have little curiosity so I can have loads. Anyway, whatever the explanation, I have derived such joy and fulfillment over the years from following where my curiosity has taken me. Paris of the 1920s is one of those places. It grabbed me one day when I read a magazine piece about the Lost Generation and the revolutionary changes unfolding at that time in many cultural corridors, particularly literature. I was fascinated, which Annie suggested was code for obsessed.

I wonder if part of my interest, keen interest—okay, obsession—may have been connected to the fact that I had never been to Paris. It was arguably easier for the city to remain almost unattainably idyllic and mythical in my mind when my idea of Paris had never had to compete with the real thing. The bubble might well burst as soon as I breached the Boulevard Périphérique and set foot in Paris proper. But I hoped not.

Annie and I had made two valiant attempts to visit Paris and in particular the Left Bank, where my interest really lay. Our first trip was called off a week before our flight due to a veterinary emergency. For the ten days Annie and I were supposed to be in Paris, we ended up waiting hand and foot (perhaps paw?) on our now long-gone beloved labradoodle, Miller, as he recovered from urgent abdominal surgery. Our rescheduled trip was canned when Will broke his leg in a ball hockey game, and we had to wait on him hand and foot until he recovered. Miller was a slightly more demanding patient than Will. But still, Paris was set aside. Ironically, we'd christened our pup Miller after Hemingway's middle name.

Having our trip to Paris twice thwarted had done little to quell my interest in the City of Light. The upshot was, I now had shelves of books about this pivotal period in Paris when writers, artists, and other creative types from around the world gathered on the Left Bank. Many were American (Hemingway, Fitzgerald, Gertrude Stein, Ezra Pound), and some British (Ford Madox Ford, for instance). But a few Canadians were there, too, Morley Callaghan and John Glassco among them. Oh, to travel back in time and be a fly on the wall in the Paris cafés and salons of the 1920s. After Will's impassioned plea, not to mention my pals' earlier appeal, perhaps it was time to put Paris back on my radar. Maybe Will was on to something.

CHAPTER 3

NATHAN'S BRIEF, even terse, text message arrived just as I was waking up on Saturday morning.

> Jason is gone. Happened late last night. Private cremation.
> Public memorial service at Holy Name, Wednesday at 2 p.m.
> Captains' meeting today at Rivals at noon.

We had known it was inevitable and so had Jason. You'd think that having plenty of warning—knowing that this outcome was inevitable—would somehow make it easier to handle. That wasn't my experience that morning. So much for my vaunted theory that amortizing grief over a longer period might be easier. I cried in bed for a bit and thought about Annie. After a while, I couldn't tell whether my blubbering was for Jason or Annie.

Jason Clayburn, one of our long-time ball hockey captains and another all-round great guy, had been on a slow—and then, towards the end, an all-too-rapid—decline since he had been diagnosed with colon cancer less than a year before. It was hard to witness a vital, energetic, if a tad paunchy, friend waste away until he was nearly unrecognizable. But through it all he inspired with a clear-eyed acceptance and a positive attitude. I can only describe his last six months as noble. I hope that were I ever in the same position, I might adopt a similar philosophical approach. But I have my doubts.

I well remember how shocked we all were at the captains' meeting when he told us his diagnosis and prognosis. When he first broke the news, he said, "Boys, I'm afraid this is not one of the good cancers." We were reeling, but Jason was so composed and still filled with good humour. He somehow put it all in perspective for us.

"Come on, guys. There are ninety of us in the league. At least one of us, probably more, is statistically guaranteed to face a life-threatening illness. I just drew the short straw this time. Don't get me wrong. I'm not happy this is the lottery I won, but given the size of the league, someone's number was going to come up. It just happened to be mine. I'm surprised it hasn't happened sooner."

I will never fathom his equanimity, his bravery, that day—not to mention in the months that followed—while the news devastated the rest of us. As we processed Jason's words, I remembered when, years earlier, at the end of a long night of music and drinking at the Dora, he'd told us how he felt about the league.

"Other than my wife and daughter, you guys, my ball hockey brothers, mean more to me than anyone else."

I also remembered my response.

"You should maybe get out more, J-man."

Everyone had laughed at my line, but we all understood Jason's point. We felt the same way but were still learning how to express it. Friendship among guys is governed by all sorts of asinine, time-honoured behavioural rules and expectations. Don't express your emotions and don't even think about shedding a tear, let alone full-on crying. Don't you dare reflect any kind of vulnerability. Do not under any circumstances tell your male friends how much they mean to you. Absolutely no physical demonstrations of affection (i.e., no touching), except for the sports loophole that permits a hug, a helmet tap, or even a slap on the ass in celebration of success (e.g., a goal scored, a save made, a game won).

I know those sound a bit extreme, but they're certainly recognizable to boys and men almost everywhere. My friends and I in the league, all older now, were learning to shed these unwritten rules, seeing them for what they were, outdated and often damaging reflections of stereotypical masculinity. Or, put in the simplest of terms, those rules were just plain stupid. Ubiquitous, but stupid.

Okay, soapbox back in the closet. Rant over.

A few of the guys were already at Rivals when I arrived. Everyone looked terrible—but this time it was due to the sad reason we were gathered and not the typical Saturday after-effects of the Friday night before. A few minutes later, all of the captains were present and accounted for, except of course for Jason Clayburn.

"Guys, thanks for coming," Nathan said. "Look, I know it's a very sad day, but we knew this was going to happen. We just didn't exactly know when. The end was quick, and for that we should be thankful."

We all nodded but said nothing to interrupt Nathan.

"So I've spoken to Cindy, and she's either okay or in complete denial. I can't really tell. Frankly, I may be in that camp as well."

Lots of nodding heads around the table before Nathan continued.

"But it's going to be a tough few weeks for Cindy and their daughter . . . um . . ."

"Zoe," I said.

"Right, Zoe. So I think we need to step up our support plan. Can we just go around the table for updates in each area?"

We all nodded.

"Okay, let's start with meals. Bobby?"

He scanned his notes before reporting.

"The Clayburn freezer is completely full right now, and I have another freezer at my house full of meals ready to take over when there's room in theirs. Will McMaster has been a big help upping our game. The meals are top-notch."

Ted patted my hand.

"I'd say we're covered at least for the next two weeks, but we'll need to rev up our efforts again after that to keep them well stocked," Bobby continued. "Just a reminder, Cindy and Zoe don't really like seafood, but anything with chicken, pork, or beef is great. Italian and Asian dishes also score well. So I'll pass around another sign-up sheet to take us into October. And Jack-Mac, they particularly liked those chicken casseroley thingies that Will made, so maybe he could whip up a few more."

"Done," I replied, thinking of ways to make it up to Will, though he never seemed to mind using his superpower for good.

"Cindy is so grateful," Bobby concluded. "So let's keep it going for a while longer."

"Thanks, Bobby." Nathan stepped back in. "Okay, staying with Jack, where are we with the obit?"

"You may recall that I wrote it with Cindy a few months ago and Jason approved it then," I started. "Before coming here, I added the date of his passing in the first sentence, and Cindy added the memorial service arrangements at the end. It's already been submitted to the *Star* and the *Globe and Mail*, as we planned. It'll run Monday, Tuesday, and Wednesday."

My voice cracked on the word *passing* but I held it together. Nathan put his hand on my shoulder and squeezed. I used to be so much better at controlling my emotions when I was younger. Now I can lose it watching two cats hugging on YouTube.

"Great, Mac, thanks," said Nathan. "Okay, I can update you all on Zoe's tuition. As you know, our goal was to raise enough dough to cover her final year, starting just about now. We passed that goal a month ago and I transferred the money over to a very thankful Jason and Cindy. Donations are still coming in and this morning's sad news will likely trigger even more. So we're in good shape. I'll shut the fundraising down when the donations stop. Whatever Zoe doesn't need for tuition and books, they can maybe spend on a mother-daughter trip somewhere. They'll need it."

Heads nodded all around the table.

"Bobby, back to you for the memorial service stuff," Nathan said.

"Right. The service will be Wednesday at two p.m. at Holy Name.

Just to confirm, Nathan will be speaking on behalf of the league. Stein-man, you're a braver man than I. Thanks for doing this."

Nathan looked briefly at the ceiling in what might have been fear, then just nodded before looking at Ted Appleton.

"Finally, Apple, remind us, where are we on the trophy?"

"Sure thing," started Ted. "I talked the idea over with Cindy some weeks ago and she felt strongly that we should tell Jason—that he'd want to know. So I visited him last week and told him about our plan. He was weak but just so thrilled and happy, so I'm glad we let him know. It was kind of special, you know? I wish more of us were there when he heard the news. Anyway, I'm getting the new plate engraved now and I'll be picking it up next week. To cut to the end, it means that the championship team this year will be lifting the Clayburn Cup." His voice cracked, too, and almost gave way. He paused, gathered himself before speaking again. "Man, he was beaming when I told him. We did a good thing here, boys."

"Okay, gents, one final, unrelated item since all of us captains are here," Nathan said. "You already know that Mike Westlake lost his shit in the late game last week and bodychecked Lucas Grant into the boards. Lucas is fine and will play this week but has a bit of a hip pointer. You've all seen the email traffic, and it seemed a consensus was emerging on how to proceed. Jack, can you draft the letter to be sent to Mike confirming the automatic one-game suspension Brian handed out at the time?"

"Will do," I replied.

"Mike already apologized to Lucas, right after the game, and they're all good. It was an intense game. I think we all agree that

Mike is a good guy who just lost it for a minute. I think one game is enough. He's filled with remorse, and it probably won't happen again."

Nathan looked around the table.

"Does anyone have a different view?"

All of us shook our heads.

"All right then, confirmed by consensus. That's it, guys. Thanks for coming. Let's be there for each other and for Cindy and Zoe. This is a tough time."

Harris, my co-captain, hadn't said much the entire meeting and looked almost stricken. He's an emotional guy at the best of times and wears his feelings on his sleeve—and, when his sleeve is insufficient, sometimes across his chest—for all to see. He'd been one of Jason's closest friends. After the meeting, I approached him.

"Are you, okay, Harris?" I put my hand on his shoulder, just as he had for me earlier in the week. He looked up at me with eyes that seemed angry and shook his head.

"I am definitely not okay. With so many dicks walking the earth, it makes no sense that Jason gets called. Where's the justice in that? It makes no sense."

"I hear you, but we both know there's really no answer to that age-old question. It seems unfair, I know, but we just got to keep putting one foot in front of the other. Time heals . . ."

"Don't give me the 'time heals' line, please," he said, raising his hand. "Just don't."

"Sure, Harris," I said, and squeezed his shoulder. "I'm here," I said before stepping away. "I'll see you at the game. I'll look after the lines if you'd like. Just come and play."

"Thanks," he said, as I moved towards the door. "Hey, Jack-Mac. Sorry."

I just smiled and waved him off.

"No worries, Harris."

We spoke to Brian and the other referee just before our slate of games on Tuesday night. Then, before each of the three games, one of the captains on the floor talked about Jason and what he'd meant to the league and announced that from then on, we'd be playing for the Clayburn Cup. The players tapped their sticks on the concrete—you might call it the ball hockey players' version of the twenty-one-gun salute. Then we had a moment of silence. It was short, sombre, and moving. Then it was game on, just as Jason would have wanted.

The game was just a few minutes old when it became clear that my co-captain, Harris, was playing unusually aggressively. He looked angry and played that way. He was digging in the corners as if his life depended on it. In one battle with Tony Rossi, Harris kicked his aggression up a notch.

"Watch your stick, Harris," warned Brian, our head referee. "Your stick!"

Too late. While swinging for the bouncing ball, Harris's stick hit Tony on the thigh, hard. Tony's a good guy. He's a great guy, but when you get slashed in the leg, even nice guys sometimes react. He shoved Harris, who then shoved back with such intensity and apparent hostility that Tony wound up on his ass in the corner. I was just a few feet away as this was happening and, on instinct, I rushed in to smother Harris, who was getting ready to drop the gloves.

"No, no, no, Harris, don't do this," I started, as I wrapped him up with my arms and moved him away from Tony. "Just breathe. You don't need this, and the team doesn't need this. Let's just cool off."

Brian approached, and he did not look happy.

"Okay, Harris, I don't know what's going on with you tonight, but you were the clear aggressor there. You're off the floor for the rest of the game, and an automatic one-game misconduct comes with it. You're gone."

I still had my hands on Harris's upper arms. He said nothing but shook me off, grabbed his bag and second stick from the bench, and headed for the gate.

Not that it matters, but we went on to lose the game. Harris's outburst and ejection were the talk of the evening at the park, but he didn't stick around to join in. I watched my email after I got home and was rewarded around midnight.

> Fellow Captains,
>
> I'm sorry. I messed up in a big way tonight. I understand that as a captain, I have to do more than just promote the competitive but recreational tone of the league. I also have to model the kind of behaviour we expect from everyone. I didn't do that tonight. I regret it and I'm sorry.
>
> I thought playing would make it easier to deal with Jason's death, but it just reminded me even more of him. It just makes me so angry that he's gone. I know that's childish but it's how I feel. I've already called Tony to apologize. I know I have an

automatic one-game suspension, but I'm going to sit out for a couple games after that until I feel more like myself. Sorry, I know there's no place in our league for that kind of play and it's never been part of my game. So I'm pulling myself out for a bit, till I get a handle on it. Thanks for your patience and apologies, again.

Harris

Good. Well-crafted and clearly heartfelt. Then my doorbell rang. It was nearly twelve thirty. Will was already in bed. I opened the front door and found Harris standing there.

"It couldn't wait," he started. "I've been a complete asshole. I don't even know who I am right now. And for me to complain to you, of all people, about good people being taken from us too soon, well, I just wasn't thinking. I'm so sorry."

"Bring it in, Harris," I said, and gave him a hug right there on the front porch.

I patted his back in the collegial way guys do, and then released my grip. That's normally the cue for the "huggee" to do the same. But Harris hung on and wasn't letting go. I could feel his shoulders shaking as he snuffled into my shoulder. I steered him—more like slow-danced him—into the house without him letting go. I'm sure it looked a bit odd to any late-night observers on the street. I guided him to the family room and lowered him onto the couch as *SportsCentre* aired on the TV, the sound down low.

"What the hell is happening to me?" he asked as I handed him a cold beer.

"Seriously, you don't know?" I asked. He looked at me, bewildered. "You really haven't put it together?"

He just looked up at me from the couch.

"Harris, look, your very close friend, who has only ever been a positive force for good on this earth, just died from a bastard form of cancer that strikes at random. Anger is natural, expected, totally understandable," I began, not really knowing where I was going. "Grief is hard, man. I've learned a thing or two about it in the last couple years. It's hard and it hits us all differently. Some days it lays me low, and I just don't feel like getting out of bed. Will makes me get up. Without him, I'm not sure I would some days. I get up for him and I get up for Annie."

He was nodding slowly, which I took to be a good sign.

"Hey, let's walk over to the service together tomorrow," I suggested. "I'll knock on your door at, what, one forty?" He nodded again.

Harris was divorced with a daughter living in Barcelona, so he had no one here to lean on. He was all by himself. I pictured what it would be like for me to deal with Annie's passing without Will around.

I stopped talking then and we did what some guys do when we're trying to deal with heavy stuff. We watched sports on TV. For many of us, it's our last line of defence in avoiding reality, or conflict, or pain. At one in the morning, that meant watching Australian rules football, followed by snooker from England. Coming up next on The Sports Network was a rerun of last year's U.S. national spelling bee. So we shut it down around two thirty and Harris walked home.

I woke up earlier than usual and didn't feel like being in the house just then, with so many sad thoughts of Annie and Jason commingling. So I pulled on jeans and a sweater, grabbed a book, and went across the street into the park to read for a bit. I found a bench under a big tree. The sun was only just peeking above the eastern horizon, but it was warm enough that at least the dew had evaporated. I was reading *Paris Was Yesterday*, a collection of columns by Janet Flanner, the long-time *New Yorker* correspondent based in, you guessed it, Paris in the 1920s. Her "Letter from Paris" in each issue of the *New Yorker* quickly became required reading and captured, almost in real time, what was going on around her in one of the cultural hotspots of the world. Her writing made me feel like I was right there, right then, standing just behind her as she rubbed shoulders with some of the great writers, artists, and outsized personalities of that pivotal period and place.

I looked up as a beautiful young woman approached the bench, smiling at me. Nothing makes a guy who's sensitive about his age feel better than to have a young and stunningly attractive woman smile at him. (Yes, we are often that shallow. Or should I say human?) She'd clearly been out for a run. I wondered how I looked and glanced at what I was wearing. Nothing special but it all fit well, was clean, and didn't smell. She sat down at the other end of the bench, still smiling. In my empty head echoed the refrain *maybe I still got it* as I held in my stomach as long as I could.

Then, still smiling, she turned to me and said, "I think you play hockey with my dad, Steve McMann? I'm Natalie."

Shite. Don't misunderstand me. I wasn't seeking the attention let alone affections of a gorgeous young woman. Not at all. But it at least soothes the ego of this sixty-two-year-old (who identifies as thirty-five) to know that women don't find me repellent.

"Right, Steve. Right. Great guy. Played with him for years. Solid player, too. But don't tell him I said that. I wouldn't want it to go to his head. You know, it could affect his play."

She laughed.

"My dad says you're a good player, too, but that you maybe pass a little too much."

"Good to know," I replied. "Good to know."

"Anyway, sorry about Mr. Clayburn, and um, so sorry about your wife."

"Thanks. That's good of you."

Then she resumed her run and I, my reading. So I guess that would be number six in my growing list of things that make me feel my age. A young and attractive woman smiles at me and then says she thinks I'm a friend of her dad's. Yep, okay, that's definitely number six. But just six things. And probably no more. Six.

I kept an eye on my watch and an hour later walked back home to change. The brief reading respite in our beautiful park had made me feel much better. I ate some breakfast and spent a few hours punching up that insurance annual report. Then it was time.

I called on Harris and we walked up to Holy Name on Gough Avenue, just off the Danforth. We arrived at the church at about ten minutes to two.

"Give me a sec," Harris said when he noticed Tony Rossi, already seated a few rows up. Harris leaned over, put a hand on Tony's shoulder, and spoke to him. Tony smiled and I read his lips. "Don't worry about it." Tony offered his hand and Harris took it, looking relieved. Case closed. Troubled waters calmed.

The service was powerful and heart-wrenching. Where his emotions were concerned, Harris had always been an open book, and I perused most of the pages that afternoon as he sat next to me at the memorial service for one of his best and oldest friends. Jason's wife, Cindy, spoke quietly and bravely, saying she could not have made it through the last nine months without the guys in the league and all we'd done. She was strong, but when she broke down a few times towards the end, Harris started to lose it beside me. Tears leaked from his eyes, spotting his grey suit pants. I could hear him breathing heavily as he fought it. I didn't really know how to help. I patted his thigh as he quietly wept, but it felt more like a gesture I'd use if he'd just scored a goal. We weren't at the park playing ball hockey. I decided Harris needed more right then. So, while it felt a little weird, I put my arm around his shoulder and left it there for a few minutes just so he knew I was there for him. I'm quite sure I've never had that much sustained physical contact with one of my guy friends before, but then again, nor had I ever had to comfort someone at his best friend's memorial service. After the first few minutes with my arm draped over his shoulder, my hand squeezing it periodically, it didn't feel strange at all.

Nathan held it together and spoke very well about Jason and what he'd meant to his ball hockey "brothers." I looked around at my fellow co-captains and so many other friends who played in the league. Most were composed, but few seemed unaffected. Most hands clutched Kleenex and virtually all eyes were streaming. I was thankful that Jason had already been cremated. The pall-bearers would likely have been largely drawn from among the co-captains, and looking around the church, we weren't in a state for the safe shouldering and transport of a heavy casket.

When the service ended, Harris turned towards me, embraced me, and whispered in my ear, "Thank you, brother. I couldn't have made it through without you."

I walked home after eating far too many of the little squares and crustless sandwiches without which no memorial service is complete. Many of us in the league gathered that evening on the Danforth at the warm and welcoming Dora Keogh, to support one another, toast our fallen friend, and even critique his play. Some might have thought it unseemly, but Jason would have loved it and laughed. Perhaps he did.

A couple of nights later, Will cooked dinner again. He got a healthy discount at Atchison's and had brought home a couple of outrageously expensive strip loin steaks. He had smashed potatoes in the oven while barbecuing the steaks out on our back deck. Even though it was technically the fall, it was sweltering outside, so we ate in the air-conditioned comfort of our kitchen. The steaks were beautifully cooked and so tender that no teeth were required to ingest and enjoy them.

"Wow, such good steaks," I said after powering through mine. "Thanks, Will."

"Tough to mess up steaks when they're so perfectly aged and marbled."

"I don't know much about steaks, but those were about the tenderest I've ever eaten."

Will pushed his plate away, took a deep breath, placed his hand on my arm, and looked me in the eye. Something told me he wasn't about to describe what he had in mind for dessert.

"So, Dad, um, I wanted to talk to you," he started. "It's kind of important."

"Of course, son. I'm here for you. Whatever you need, and that's not just the amazing steak talking."

He smiled.

"Dad, this is less about me and more about you," he said.

I wasn't expecting that, but despite my curiosity I held my tongue. I waited.

"Dad, I think you're still struggling. You're not the same as you were before," he said, still resting his hand on my arm.

"Will, the love of my life, the only woman I've ever truly loved, died, and I couldn't even be with her at the end. We had no time to prepare. One day we had breakfast together. The next, she was in the hospital. The next day, she was on oxygen and declining fast. Then she was gone," I said. "Of course I'm not the same as I was. I never will be. That's what grief is. That's what grief does."

"Dad, I know. I know. No one should have to go through what you went through."

"What *we* went through," I corrected. "What we're still going through."

"Right, I know. But eventually, you'll need to emerge from this fog, because nothing will change if you don't," he said, his voice becoming more animated. "Dad, Mom is gone. She's not coming back. She would not be happy with you if she knew you rarely leave the house except to walk the hundred metres to the ball hockey rink, or up to the Danforth for groceries. Dad, I think it's time to restart living your life instead of just existing with Mom's death."

While I was a little caught off guard, I was engaged enough to recognize a powerful sentence when I heard one. It's the curse of the writer. His hand still rested on my arm. I smiled and put my hand over his.

"That's not bad, Will. Did you come up with that last line?"

"Funny you should ask. I did not. Mom did," he replied. "They're not my words, they're hers."

"What do you mean?"

He looked up at the ceiling.

"Dad, I was really hoping it wouldn't come to this, but I think Mom would agree the time is right. So listen, when Mom knew she was dying and when she knew there was no stopping the virus, she was thinking about you. She was so concerned about how her death would affect you that she FaceTimed me the day before she died."

"I know. She told me on our last call," I said. "I'm glad you could speak with her at the end. That was important for you—well, for both of us, in helping us accept what was happening."

"But there was more to my call with her," Will said, looking at me. "She looked miserable, weak, and sad, and was breathing rapidly behind her oxygen mask. Beyond saying goodbye, she had one more item on her agenda. First, she said that you, Dad, will need to find someone else to, um, be with."

He paused to let that sink in, but I was still processing it when he spoke again.

"As you can imagine, I was shocked and asked her, 'You mean another woman?' And Mom said, 'Yes, Will, to the best of my knowledge after thirty years of marriage, I'm quite sure your father is straight.'"

Despite reeling from what I was hearing, I smiled at her line. Even close to the end, her humour sparked. Still, I was stunned at what she'd said to Will.

"Dad, Mom then basically told me that if, after a reasonable time, you weren't back up on your feet, living again and participating in the world again, I was to play this video for you that she'd recorded just before, you know, the end. Then she texted me the download link."

I clearly was not adept at masking my emotions.

"Um, are you all right?" Will asked. "I know it's a shock, but . . ."

"Hang on," I said. "You mean you've had a video message for me from your mother that you've been sitting on for two and a half years without telling me or showing me?"

"Don't do this, Dad," Will said. "It's been a burden for me to have it, but I promised Mom that I'd, as she put it, 'only break the glass in case of emergency.' I was honouring her final wishes. It was painful keeping it from you, but I'm not going to apologize for fulfilling Mom's final directive. And Dad, you said it. It's been two and a half years. That's a long time."

After I made it past my instinct and could think more rationally about it, I felt terrible about my comment.

"Right. Of course, you're right. I'm sorry, son. And I'm sorry you've had to carry that load all this time." I leaned over and gave him a hug before continuing. "But it seems you—and she, in a way—have decided I'm not doing well, so you're now breaking the glass?"

"Reluctantly," he replied. He pulled out his mobile phone. "It's quite short. She's very weak," Will said as he handed it to me. "Do you want me to leave while you watch it?"

I thought about it for a few beats.

"No, son, we're sharing this struggle. Plus, I'll need you here in case I have a stroke or some other medical emergency, which, given how I'm feeling, seems a distinct possibility."

I took Will's phone from his hand. Annie's gaunt and stricken face was immobilized on the screen, waiting for me to press play. Will stood up and came around behind my chair. He rested his hands on my shoulders. The closeness, the contact, felt good. I paused for a few seconds and took some deep breaths.

"You don't have to watch it right now," Will said.

"Yes, I do," I replied. "I really do."

I hit play.

And there she was, looking as I'd last seen her, propped up in her hospital bed, oxygen mask on, the privacy curtain behind her not really living up to its name. She spoke very quietly, not only because she was so weak but so she'd not disturb the other three patients in her room. Considerate, literally to the end.

"Jack, love. You're watching this, so you must still be hurting. I'm sorry. I know it's hard. I'd be a mess too if our places were reversed. But you must stop looking back and dwelling on my, you know, my death. So weird to say that. You have Will. We made him. He needs you and you need him. Look, love, you made me better for thirty-five years. But you are not good alone. I understand you. It took a while, but I do. I love you. But I know in my heart that you cannot be your best self and live your best life or honour the rest of those clichés if you are alone. It's the truth. You're allowed to be happy. I want you to be happy. So please, and I hate to be dramatic, but my . . . my, um, dying wish is that you will now restart living your life instead of just existing with my death. Go to Paris like we planned. Go for me. Find someone. Be good to someone. Be good *for* someone, as you were good to, and for, me for so long. I mean it, love. Do not let my death define your life."

She collapsed back against her pillow and closed her eyes, exhausted from the effort. She'd struggled to get out the words, but only because she had trouble breathing, not because she doubted what she was saying. She was sure of herself right to the end. I could tell. I knew her well. She opened her eyes for just a second, long enough to look directly into her phone, and nod her head once. Then the clip ended.

Will squeezed my shoulders and then sat down across from me again.

"Dad, I'm sorry I held on to this, but I was doing what I thought was right. I thought you were getting better, but then you stalled."

"I like to think of it as plateauing," I said. "And there's no call for you to apologize, son. I'm so sorry you had to bear this burden for so long. But I'd have done the same thing were I in your shoes."

"So, Dad, I've got one word for you. Paris."

CHAPTER 4

IT TOOK ME A FEW DAYS—actually, more like a week—to recover from seeing Annie talking directly to me on Will's phone, nearly two and a half years after she'd gone. Eventually I realized I needed to process what she'd said and how I'd respond. It was so like her to be worrying about me and my future when she was just hours from passing. I certainly wasn't interested in finding another partner. I could barely get my head around the notion that I no longer had Annie, let alone actively pursue her successor. But after hearing Annie's heartfelt words—and beginning to see at least some vestige of truth in them—I felt an obligation to give serious thought to what she'd said about starting to live again. Since she'd died, my world had played out in monochromatic tones of grey. Maybe I needed to start letting some colour back in, or if necessary, forcing some colour back in. Paris had colour and checked several more boxes, too. Paris seemed like it could be a step in the right direction, a step forward in my recovery. I could find an Airbnb on the Left Bank and carry on my freelancing from there while immersing myself in the history of the city. I didn't mind the idea of being on my own. I've always been comfortable in my own company. I'd miss Will and the guys, but thought it was manageable.

As shocked as I had been to see Annie's video, I began to see that in a way, it had released me from the paralysis my grief had inflicted. Something had shifted. Perhaps a threshold crossed on the grieving trail. I had a long way to go. I knew that. But Annie had helped me at least understand that it was time to navigate my way out of the dark place in which I seemed to have resided since she died. Two and a half years later, her voice, uttering what were surely among her last words, shook me from my grief-stricken lassitude. She knew me so well, knew just what buttons to push, what cards to play. Her thinking was sound, and her gambit from beyond the grave, effective.

I feared if I didn't act quickly on my change in thinking, lethargy would once again overtake me. So I acted. I made a plan, of sorts. I first looked for a place to stay. I figured the beginning of November, a week or so after the ball hockey season ended, would be a sensible departure date. While Paris seems always awash in tourists, November is considered low season. If I wanted as authentic a Paris experience as possible—whatever that means—November struck me as the right time to arrive. And I'd aim to return to Toronto towards the end of March, so I was home in time for the draft of the new teams and the start of a new season in early April.

Could I really go away to Paris for five months? Maybe it would be more prudent to go for a few weeks and see how I was doing before committing to such a long stay. No—it was Annie's voice in my head. *It's Paris. Lots to see and do. The lives of the Lost Generation to trace, their haunts to visit. Come on!* Five months would slip away in a flash. Will had already said he'd come for Christmas so we could be together. I could find no logical arguments against the full-blown, all-in, damn-the-torpedoes, five-month adventure in the City of Light. I did come across several illogical arguments, but I ignored them, which I think would have pleased Annie.

I spent a Friday morning online searching for a place to stay on the Left Bank, in either the fifth or sixth arrondissement. I was impressed with the number of options available, including some apartments for longer-term rentals. It's easy to pay an arm and a leg—sometimes topped up with a few lesser-valued appendages—for quite lavish and spacious apartments on short-term contracts. But if you dig deeply enough, there are also many smaller, clean, charming, well-appointed, and centrally located flats available at reasonable rates. I found one I really liked located deep in the heart of Saint-Germain-des-Prés. It was not enormous, but it was clean, with warm wooden ceiling beams, a modern kitchen, and an amazing bathroom. The location was perfect for learning all about the writers and artists who had congregated in that neighbourhood almost exactly a century before. The five months would run me about sixteen thousand dollars. I thought that was a pretty good deal. I hesitated, but only for a few minutes, before booking the apartment. I worried I might feel freaked out after committing to the five-month rental, but I didn't. I actually experienced a sensation that approached peace and contentment—that is, when I was finally able to identify those unfamiliar feelings.

Lest I falter, I felt the need to keep up my momentum, so I immediately booked my flights. This was happening. This was really happening. When my resolve finally overpowered my trepidation, it only took me a morning to find, book, and pay for a very cool apartment in the heart of the Latin Quarter, and the flights to wing me there and back again. And I felt fine. No trembling, or cold feet, or second thoughts—at least not yet, anyway. That gave me a month or so to get my act together for, you know, flying to Paris. I figured Annie, looking down on it all, would be pleased. I realized I felt different. Annie's video and Will's encouragement had pushed me across a new threshold.

That afternoon, I was sitting in my third-floor office, but I was not writing. I was bored with the speech I was working on for a tech CEO and a little preoccupied with my impending trip to Paris. So I picked up my guitar from its stand just in front of my bookshelves. It felt good to hold the old familiar friend after neglecting it for too long. It was still in pretty good tune, but I made a few minor adjustments and it sounded crisp, clean, and clear. I played what I'd already written of that new song about the ball hockey league. I know what you're thinking. Who writes a song about ball hockey? Well, since you asked, I guess I do. But it's not a song about ball hockey as much as it's a song about friendship and what it's like to live in the midst of a strong and supportive community. Frankly, if the music is good and the lyrics tell a story, I think you can write a song about nearly anything, and over the years, I have.

Most of my songs have only ever been heard by close family or unsuspecting patrons of the Dora Keogh on certain Friday nights when the house band, led by a ball hockey friend, talks me up onto the stage. While I've been playing guitar, writing songs, and singing for more than forty-five years, and even played in a band in university, I was never labouring under any delusions that I might one day break into, let alone make it big in, the music business. No, I don't think so. I'm smart enough to know that I don't sing and play well enough to make it. It was always just something that I've really enjoyed as a creative outlet.

There are many ways to write a song. Some songwriters start with just the lyrics and perhaps the vibe of the song before the music emerges to meet the words. Others can only write lyrics or only write music, but not both. I tend to need a good chord progression to kickstart my musical creativity. Usually, I won't even develop a melody until I have a nice-sounding chord progression, either strummed or fingerpicked. The melody follows, sometimes easily, sometimes not. Then I map out the structure of the verses, still without having any lyrics. After that, I'll develop the bridge, always a tricky part of songwriting. The challenge is to make the bridge different enough from the verses to signal a true break in the proceedings, while still fitting well musically so in the end the song hangs together as a whole. When I think I've got the chords to accompany the melody, the verses, the bridge, and some kind of ending, I play it through on my guitar, often with dummy lyrics or just humming, until the song becomes kind of entrenched in my musical memory. Then it's time to lay down the lyrics.

A good song has a catchy tune and solid lyrics. These two

elements seldom come together in the same song, but you can usually tell when they do. I've written a few dozen songs, but only a handful would I consider to be worthy of sharing with anyone.

I wrote down the lyrics for the first two verses that I already had in my mind, then I worked on the words for the bridge. The bridge doesn't just signify a shift in the music and sometimes the feel of the song, but it often signals a brief lyrical departure as well, where you step outside, or above, the story being told in the verses. I knew what feeling I wanted the bridge to evoke, so the words came easily for a change. It's always nice when the right words also happen to fit the rhyming scheme. Serendipity.

I spent another half hour working through a closing verse and how to end the song. Of course, the ending is the last thing the listener hears, so you don't want to half-ass it. It's an important part of the composition. I had a hazy idea for overlapping voices at the end, but I'd need Will to try that part out. So after a good ninety minutes of focus—which seemed like fifteen minutes—I finished the song and typed out the lyrics. The fruits of my labour:

More Than the Game (Jack McMaster, © 2022)

Beyond the trees and the falling leaves
In the dark of night
Aging teams still live their dreams
Underneath the lights

When the game begins, I go breaking in
I'm almost in the clear

I fire a shot that the goalie stops
His teammates stand and cheer

Although it's rare when tempers flare
Still, everyone plays hard
And in the end, we're all still friends
As we head up to the bar

(Chorus)
Well, my knees are sore
And my hands won't score
My head is pounding in pain
The will is strong
But the legs are gone
Every week it's the same
It's so much more than the game
Oh, much more than the game

When your game is done, whether lost or won
You hate to leave the park
So you stay to the end and heckle your friends
Whenever they miss the mark

But we all know when the whistle blows
And it's time to pack it in
That it won't be long till the week is gone
And the game is on again

(Bridge)
When the season finally ends
What rewards have we reaped?
Look around and count your friends
That's the score we keep

(Chorus)
Well, my knees are sore
And my hands won't score
My head is pounding in pain
The will is strong
But the legs are gone
Every week it's the same

(Repeat chorus)

It's so much more than the game
Much more than the game
We'll still play
We'll still play

I played the song through four or five times in an effort to lock it in my mind. I determined it was in the right key and so didn't need any capo adjustments to raise the pitch a couple of semitones. I liked it where it was. The descending chord progression was kind of catchy, I decided, and the lyrics, though not those of your typical love song, held heartfelt meaning for me, and I hoped perhaps for others who played in the league. At my age and stage—I still can't believe I'm sixty-two—a heartfelt song is also a kind of love song.

Speaking of sixty-two, I thought of something else that actually makes me feel my age. I think we're up to six now, so this would make seven. My hair. Until I was about forty, my hair was thick, wavy, and just starting to grey. But it soon became clear that I'd inherited my grandfather's thinning hair. On top, there is an ever-growing bald patch. There's no debate anymore. I took a selfie of the top of my head, and it's definitely a bald spot. But in my every-day life, I can't see it. Everyone else I meet, provided they pass behind me, is well aware of my thinning hair, but from the front, my customary vantage point when looking in a mirror, it still looks like I have a full head of hair. My forehead may be a little higher than it once was, but from the front, I still wouldn't know I look like Friar Tuck when photographed from a drone. Because I don't see it every day, I can easily forget about my bald spot. Call it denial if you like, but it can pass completely out of my mind for long stretches of time. But the other day, I was at an automatic bank machine grabbing some cash. It was one of those with the security monitor up in the corner near the ceiling. When I glanced up at it, somebody with a glowing bald spot lit up the screen. I was the only one in the small glass room housing the ATM. What the hell . . . oh yes, I remember now. I'm losing my hair. Have been for years. Okay, there you have it. We're now up to seven instances when I do feel my age. Just seven.

After I sang the new song through one last time, I heard the front door open and Will come in after spending his day cooking. After he took a shower, he climbed the stairs to my office.

"Hey, Dad, I'm home."

"I'm glad it wasn't a stranger I heard in the shower," I said. "How was your day?"

"It involved, in part, creating and assembling thirty-six trays of lasagna, thirty-six trays of shepherd's pie, and seventy-two single-serve jars of lemon mousse. But it all went well."

"Now you're just making me hungry."

"Good, because we're having a lasagna that didn't quite make the grade. I tipped it over by accident and could not get it to look right, even in a new pan."

"I don't care what it looks like. I'm happy to ensure no lasagna is left behind."

"Hey, glad to see you strumming. Are you working on that song?"

"I think it's finished, as of about fifteen minutes ago."

"Let's hear it," he said.

"It's still a little rough, but . . ."

"Come on, Dad, let's hear it."

"Okay, but be kind," I replied, before breaking into the intro of descending chords.

Will listened intently, nodding his head. When I hit the chorus for the second time, he put a harmony over top of my voice that fit really nicely.

He also seemed to like the bridge. I could tell because just before I moved back into the last chorus he said, "Love that bridge!" while vigorously pointing at me. I'm a quick study.

When I reached the closing lines where I wanted overlapping voices, I handed him the lyrics and told him to restart the first verse underneath my voice singing the final phrases, *We'll still play. We'll still play.* He picked up what I meant immediately and sang his part perfectly. He has a better voice than I ever will.

"Ooohhh, that worked great at the end," Will said. "I love the song, Dad, and the bridge you've written is killer. We really need a bass line to anchor those guitar chords walking down."

"That makes sense," I said. "Can you add that in sometime?"

"Sure. I have access to a Fender P bass at the studio, or if it's not available, I could just add it with keyboards."

"Great, Will. Thanks. The song is growing on me," I said. "Although I haven't played it often enough yet to grow sick of it, but ask me tomorrow."

"I'd better get that messed-up lasagna in the oven," said Will as he turned to head downstairs.

"Hey, Will," I said. He turned back to me. "Um, I wanted to let you know that, believe it or not, I'm now booked for Paris from November to the end of March, so I'll be back home for the start of the spring season."

Will clapped his hands and punched the air.

"Dad, that's fantastic! Good for you. That's what you needed to do. Congratulations. We can FaceTime as often as you like, or at least until you've established a closely knit group of friends in Paris, and I'm rendered redundant."

"Well, I'm not sure I'll have my Parisian posse up and running anytime soon, given my high school French," I said. "So you're safe for at least a while."

"You'll be great, Dad, even with your accent."

"What's wrong with my accent?"

"Well, it's not so bad. But it does kind of sound like you're just pronouncing French words with a dull, flat, and monotonal English accent. No real tonal character. No panache. No vocal flourishes."

"Well, that's very encouraging to hear. Thanks very much. I know you had the good fortune of enlightened parents who put you in French immersion, but that wasn't available when I went to school. And I don't want to start sounding like some Pepé Le Pew impersonator," I complained.

"Actually, Dad, just to clarify, Pepé Le Pew speaks in English, with a French accent. But he's speaking in English."

Hmmm, true, but I ignored him and kept talking.

"You do know that ever since, oh, I don't know, I was eighteen months old, my first language has been dull, flat, and monotonal English."

"Dad, don't take my comment the wrong way," he pleaded. "Your grasp of French vocabulary, grammar, and verbs is actually not bad, but maybe I can help you work on your pronunciation and intonation—you know, rolling your *r*'s a little, and punching certain syllables, working on that guttural sound in your throat."

"*Bon*," was all I said in reply.

"That's just what I mean, Dad. *Bon* should sound more like *bong* when you kind of cut off the *g* at the end. It shouldn't sound like the German city."

"Bon, bon, bon, bon," I said. "Bon."

"Better! See, that didn't take long," Will said. "Tomorrow, we'll try *bonjour*."

"Funny, guy," I said. "But you'll come to Paris for Christmas, right?"

"Of course I'll be there. We've never been separated at Christmas and we're not going to start this year," he said. "I'll book flights."

"Just give me your dates and then I'll book the flights. It's on me."

"Deal. Thanks, Dad," Will said. "Oh, by the way, can you send me that recording you made of 'Until the New Year'?"

"Sure. Why?"

"Um, I just like it," he replied. "If you can send me the full GarageBand file, I may just dial back the guitar a little bit. I think it overpowers your voice in some of the quieter sections. But I think it's one of your best, and I want to be able to listen to it."

"Sure, Will."

"Until the New Year" is a song I wrote for Annie shortly after we started seeing each other, when we were both students at the University of Toronto. It was the first and only Christmas love song I ever wrote. After we had been virtually inseparable for the fall term, Annie had headed back home to Vancouver to spend Christmas with her family. It was written quickly, in the emotional throes of her absence. I missed her. The lyric at the end of the second verse, *as coloured lights frame my thoughts of you*, occurred to me as I wrote the song playing my guitar on my bed in my residence room on campus. I had hung up a small—and a little tacky—string of Christmas lights around the periphery of my window. As I worked on the song, I could see my reflection in the glass bordered by the twinkling, coloured lights. Sometimes lyrics come from what's right in front of you.

Now, more than forty years later, I still really liked the song, which isn't how I feel about many of my tunes. I figured out a fingerpicking pattern and a chord progression unlike any in my other songs. Then, to hit the sweet spot in my voice (and "sweet spot" is very much a relative term), I used my capo to bump it up two or sometimes even three frets, so it better fit my vocal range. In our early years together, I used to sing it to Annie every Christmas Eve. It was a song about longing, waiting, and separation. My first thought was to call it "Annie's Song," for obvious reasons. But for equally obvious reasons, the estate of the late great John Denver might have had an issue with that title, so instead I lifted the title from a line in the chorus to reinforce the idea that I was desperately awaiting her return.

When Will headed downstairs I put the capo on the second fret and quietly sang "Until the New Year." I made it two-thirds of the way through before I had to stop. Though I'd tried before, I still couldn't quite make it through the whole song. But it sounded good to my unbiased ears, even if some of the lyrics were a little cheesy. But I was twenty-one years old and in love when I wrote it.

Until the New Year (Jack McMaster, © 1981)

The leaves were falling then
Now snowflakes ride the wind
And Christmas carols fill the air
As people bustle everywhere I go

Laughing children smile at me
As they sit upon his knee
And winter clouds surround the moon
As coloured lights frame my thoughts of you

I know it can't be . . .

(Chorus)
But I wish that we could spend this time together
Celebrating everything that comes along
My heart will be with you until the new year brings you back
And then we'll play it day by day, 'cause time is ours

On the street school kids sing
As skinny Santas' sleigh bells ring
And visions of you danced in my head
On Christmas Eve

(Bridge)
Some people say that I'm tied down again
But they don't know who we are
I can't tell you what you've done for me
I fly higher than before

(Chorus)
But I wish that we could spend this time together
Celebrating everything that comes along
My heart will be with you until the new year brings you back
And then we'll play it day by day, 'cause time is ours

Now you're at home
A million miles to phone
But you know where my feelings are
All my love at Christmas time for you
All my love at Christmas time for you

—

Perhaps because I was booked for Paris, I was in a better mood for our game that night. Who really knows if it improved my play? But I did score a goal and set up another. A rare performance of late. I have a theory about ball hockey—of course I do. Ball hockey is a time machine.

I realized during a game recently that, for me, ball hockey has become a weekly return to my past. I know and accept that the morning after hockey feels far different at sixty-two years old than it did at fifteen, or twenty-five, or even forty-five. But the feeling during the game itself is another matter. I've played hockey for nearly my entire life. In the moment, in the heat of the game, in the flush of an intense play, it's nearly impossible to think about anything else except the game—the pass you're about to make or take, the opposing player you're chasing, the goalie you're trying to beat, the slapshot you're about to block (sometimes with your gut yielding a Technicolor bruise with incredible staying power). You can't possibly play your best if even a portion of your brain is committed to other thoughts. 'Twas ever thus. It's the same feeling I had playing hockey when I was nine years old, and it never changes.

For about an hour each week, it takes me back to a time in my life when all I worried about was what Mom was making for dinner that night, whether I was in trouble for anything, and whether we'd win our game. Sure, at sixty-two, you make a pretty quick return to reality when the final buzzer sounds, but for that one hour each week, I'm on a therapeutic time-travelling vacation. I feel renewed, restored, content. Perhaps even happy. And so does every other guy out there on the floor. It clears my head so I'm better able to confront all those other issues being a grown-up throws in your path. Yes, ball hockey is a time machine.

Harris bought me a beer at Rivals after the game.

"Well, if I'd known all I had to do was score a goal to score a beer, I'd have worked much harder on my offensive skills," I said.

"I think you're already offensive enough," he commented with a smirk.

"Hey, Harris, thanks partly to your intervention a while back, and to some other encouragement I recently had from Will, and, um, someone else, I've booked that trip to Paris I've wanted to take for so long."

"That's friggin' awesome, J-Mac," he said, clapping me on the shoulder. "You need this, man. I'm thrilled for you. Spill with the details."

"I'm leaving in early November, and I won't be back until late March. And yes, fear not, I will be home for the April draft."

"Priorities, Mac. Priorities!" he joked. "So where are you staying?"

"I booked a nice and cozy little Left Bank apartment in the very part of Paris that I've been reading about for years. So I'll be right in the thick of it. I'm excited about it, and I haven't really been excited about anything for a long time."

"I'm so happy for you, and I'm happy for me and the rest of next year's team, too," he said. "This could also be the cure for what ails your game. Maybe it will lift your performance to its previously lofty heights. A win-win!"

News spread fast through the bar and by the time I left about an hour later, nearly fifty guys had stepped up to shake my hand and congratulate me on the Paris adventure. I also had far too many drinks delivered to my table. I didn't want to offend anyone, so in the true spirit of league camaraderie, I downed them all. I was feeling no pain when Harris and Nathan walked me home—carried me would be more like it—and left me in Will's capable hands. I don't remember Will helping me up the stairs to our bedroom, my bedroom, but I woke up there in the morning, along with a headache that felt like an anaesthetic-free lobotomy.

It's hard to imagine this happening two and a half years after she died, but when I first opened my eyes in the dark of the very early morning, groggy, likely still drunk, the hangover not even out of the starting blocks yet, I reached for Annie. I did, and not for the first time. On instinct alone, I moved my hand over to her side of the bed in search of the comfortable contours of the sleeping form that I knew so well after so long. Catching myself, realizing my mistake, was a stiletto piercing my heart, again. This happened more frequently than I would have expected so long after she died. I was not in full command of my faculties when reaching for her. I was half-asleep, or perhaps fully under. My subconscious clearly hadn't yet come to grips with Annie's passing. And did I mention my conscious self was also still struggling to adjust to this unwelcome and still unfamiliar absence in my life?

But I was getting better at recovering from these little shocks. And by the time I could lift myself out of bed and lumber to the bathroom without too much damage to my surroundings, I felt more myself. Then, to counter the melancholia that comes with briefly thinking your loving wife is lying next to you when she's not, I remembered I was going to Paris. That helped. I still felt good about my plans. I'd be alone, but I'd be in Paris. A reasonable trade-off.

I started packing two weeks before I was scheduled to leave. I packed several times to try to get a clear sense of what I was taking with me. It's not easy to figure out what to bring when you're headed to a city you've never visited but only ever dreamed about. I had an ever-evolving packing list as I added and subtracted different items in the run-up to departure day. In the end, there were several things that I considered to be absolutely essential cargo. Some of these were on the list for practical reasons, like my passport, and my laptop so I could keep serving my clients and they could keep paying me. Other items were more personal, and their relative importance to me helped them make the cut. Possessions on the list included my guitar—despite not playing much since Annie died, I never considered not taking it with me—some family photos, a good pair of walking shoes, a few of my older Paris books—with many of my others preloaded on my iPad to save weight and space—and a few prescription refills for the statin I'd started taking a year or so back.

Hmmmm . . . that reminds me. Okay, the eighth thing that makes me feel sixty-two is the cholesterol-lowering wonder drug I'm on, like most men in their sixties. And, no, I absolutely do not feel any freer to indulge in favourite foods that were verboten in my pre-statin days. Absolutely not. That would be irresponsible and silly. Right? So we're now up to eight. But just these eight things. Otherwise, I'm thirty-five.

—

Despite my growing anticipation, departure day arrived faster than I'd expected. My Air Canada flight was on a Sunday evening. I piled all my luggage on the front porch and prepared the car for loading, one of my specialties. I opened the back of Annie's BMW 330i wagon—largely because it was the only car we owned—and began to exercise my well-developed packing gene. It's really the only superpower I have. Ever-helpful Will knew enough not to involve himself in packing the back of the car. When I'd finished, I was able to close the hatchback door, but only just.

At the appointed hour, which was about four hours before my flight, Will slid into the driver's seat and I got in beside him. Airports were still flummoxed in the pandemic's aftermath, and delays checking in and passing through security were common and long.

"Okay, just before we go, I want to review the list I left on the kitchen table for you," I began.

"You mean, I can't forget to water the plants, take out the garbage Wednesday mornings, shovel our driveway and sidewalk and Mrs. Kiniski's next door when it snows, switch from Cool to Heat on the thermostat when winter arrives, rake and bag the leaves for pickup, and check for messages that no one ever leaves on our phone anymore?" Will replied.

"I see you've already reviewed the list. Well played, son."

"Dad, I was going to do all those things anyway, even without your list," Will said. "I'm twenty-seven, so I've been an adult for several months now. I've got it all covered. No need to worry. Plus, you can harangue me via FaceTime at your leisure. I don't want you sitting in

Paris thinking about everything that could go wrong here in Toronto. That makes no sense. Enjoy yourself. Indulge yourself. Maybe even meet someone who sparks a new song. Trust that I have everything well in hand here, and start planning for my arrival in December."

"Got it, Will," I replied. "I just don't want to forget anything. And I doubt I'll be meeting anyone song-worthy."

Will started to pull out of the driveway. He looked in the rear-view mirror and stopped the car. Then he backed up again.

"Um, Dad, were you planning to take that suitcase that's still on the front porch?"

"Shit."

We made it to Pearson International Airport with plenty of time to spare. Will grabbed a baggage cart and I loaded it up with my guitar, my computer backpack, and two suitcases, including the one I'd nearly forgotten on the front porch.

"Thanks for driving me," I said to Will as I hugged him. "Be good and be smart while I'm gone."

"Always, Dad. I've got it covered."

I hung on to him for longer than seemed customary for a familial bon voyage hug.

"Uh, Dad, I'm in a no parking zone, and I should be getting home," he said. "I have about sixty friends coming over tonight for a little party."

I laughed and released him.

"I love ya, Will."

"I love you, too, Dad. Now go and, I don't know, kickstart the next part of your life. I know you can do it. And give my regards to Hemingway and Fitzgerald."

"And Callaghan," I added. "The Canadians are always left out."

I waited till he drove away before I muscled my overburdened baggage cart into the Departures area. I still felt anxious but excited about Paris. I still missed Annie.

PART 2

PARIS

CHAPTER 5

IT WAS AN UNEVENTFUL FLIGHT. I mean, no oxygen masks dropped from the ceiling panels above our heads. No one threw up on the passenger in front of them. And no one complained that the pretzel packets were too large. Although, I wasn't sitting in my assigned seat. A family of three—mother, father, and the child who appeared to be their six-year-old son—were seated in my row, but not together. I was in my preferred spot, the booked-early window seat, while the mother and son were next to me. The father was across the aisle, not just in the middle section but in a middle seat in the middle section. Not sure if the father planned it that way, but I always think families would rather be seated all together. I much preferred the window, but the little boy next to me was bouncing on his seat like an Olympic trampolinist. Those around me assumed my offer was driven by kindness and thoughtfulness, and perhaps some of it was. But there was also a healthy dose of self-interest at play. I spoke to the mother, suggesting I switch seats with the father as part of what you might call a family reunification program. She was thrilled and so was the little boy. I'm not certain about the expression on the father's face as we passed in the aisle, but I don't think it was gratitude. He seemed worried he'd now be on trampoline-spotting duty for the duration of the flight.

I found myself seated dead centre of the plane, about as far away as I could be from an aisle, let alone a window or an exit. The older woman next to me renewed our acquaintance—I'd helped hoist her carry-on bag into the overhead compartment when she'd boarded—and kept up a congenial stream of conversation for an hour or so, until she eventually fell asleep, leaving me wide awake with another five hours to go. The little boy whose father was now in my seat may well have been on a caffeine diet as he pinballed from mother to father, oscillating from loud laughter to even louder temper tantrums. The father was grimacing and rubbing his forehead as if shooting a Tylenol commercial. But his eyes shot open when the boy literally seized the opening and shoved a finger up his nose—to be clear, the father's nose. The desperate man looked down at the floor as if deciding whether his son might be stowed under the seat in front of him. I decided I was happier next to a loquacious but lovely senior.

I really tried to sleep. Honestly, I did. I wanted to arrive in Paris for my first time well rested and refreshed. Alas, no. But I tried. As I'd boarded and walked through the plane to my seat, I had pined for the spacious seats with ample leg room up in business class. I had had the opportunity to book a seat in that section, or even upgrade at the gate just before departure, but just couldn't bring myself to pay what seemed like such an enormous cost. About halfway across the Atlantic, I would gladly have paid twice the premium for a fully reclining throne up front, where I'm quite sure I could have caught some serious Zs. At six foot two, I ultimately decided that comfort in steerage was a lost cause. I could manage to pretzel my body into a specific position that was actually comfortable, but only for about seventeen seconds. Then I'd have to shift again.

I closed my eyes, and my mind immediately went to Annie. It was not surprising. When my thoughts were even momentarily unoccupied, Annie was my brain's go-to default destination. It made sense. We'd planned this Paris trip together twice, before both attempts were thwarted, as you will recall, by unforeseen family emergencies. Yes, our labradoodle's unexpected surgery was considered a family emergency. And now I was going to Paris on my own, a pale imitation of what the trip would have been with her. Yet I was going, in a way, for her.

I still missed her terribly, but the shock of her death had eased, as had the early intensity of the grief. Now it was more a persistent dull ache, an emptiness, a loss in the colour of everyday life, the melancholy knowledge that I'd never make her laugh again. In retrospect, I decided that was how I'd managed to be with, and stay with, Annie. I made her laugh. It wasn't a Sherlock Holmes–level deduction. Annie often straight-up told me—and plenty of others, too. I knew she was out of my league in so many ways. But my ability to make her burst out laughing, or make coffee shoot out her nose, or make her rock gently while clutching her stomach in paroxysms of mirth, apparently compensated for what I always considered—though she never did—a host of other shortcomings. These included my somewhat average looks, a dated, out-of-fashion wardrobe, the buckets of money I didn't have, and an aversion to seafood, her favourite. I like to think there were other reasons we clicked. More common ground. Like our simpatico political views, a passion for books, and a shared love for the community centred around the park near our home. But Annie always led with the laughing. Who was I to argue?

With my eyes still closed, yet no closer to sleep, I thought about Annie's haunting exhortation to "find someone else" so I could move on and live my life to what she saw as my full potential. An extraordinary gesture on her part given how very sick she was. Yet, I was still grieving. I couldn't imagine a future when I wasn't mourning her sudden loss. At the same time, I felt as if I could function in daily life a little more easily and willingly than I could before. It no longer took a Herculean effort to step outside the house to do the grocery shopping or play my hockey game. I was managing somehow. Sure, I did feel a little better, as if I could at least see my normal self somewhere in the distance. But the idea that I might ever find someone else—let alone seek someone else—was a bridge too far.

Will's support, even just his presence, was a significant factor in my modest improvement, though I doubted he appreciated the important role he was playing in my slow return to everyday life. And now, going to Paris would be, I hoped, a new and welcome distraction to keep me from backsliding, wallowing. Paris just might help me move forward. There was so much to see and do in Paris, I figured at the very least it would keep my mind off what a brutal couple of years it had been. I confess, I did worry about the nights, the long stretches of time for thinking and remembering. But Paris gave me a real sense of excitement and anticipation, something I hadn't experienced in a long time.

When the drinks cart finally made its way to my section of the plane, I bought two beers, their medicative benefits outweighing the eventual trip to the cramped washroom they would prompt later in the flight. I drank the beers down quickly in order to make a final, last-ditch attempt at sleeping. I needed to think about something other than Annie, as difficult as that was. So I turned my mind to the ball hockey league, which was seldom far from my thoughts.

Countless times over the years, I've tried to figure out exactly why the league has come to mean so much to me. It runs much deeper than the fact that I've played and loved hockey for nearly my entire life. That certainly helps, but I think it's more about the values that we try hard to entrench and sustain in the league. It's hard to spell them out without sounding like a children's after-school TV special. But it is purely recreational ball hockey, without the win-at-all-costs mentality that pervades other, more competitive leagues. We have certified, experienced referees to call the games with a zero-tolerance approach to rough play and unsportsmanlike conduct. Beyond the refs, we co-captains often impose additional sanctions against players who consistently contravene the standards of conduct we've tried to establish and enforce. This can include suspensions for a game, a few games, or even sometimes for an entire season. This has a way of encouraging players with a more aggressive, violent style to find a different league. After more than twenty years, every player, veterans and the few rookies alike, understands what we have and how to keep it. We have a code of conduct that every player must read at the beginning of each season. The code is more than words on a page. It captures the ethos we've tried to create.

We change up the teams every season so that over time, everyone gets to play with everyone else. Our friends are in the league, not just on our own teams. This means any simmering rivalries from the previous season are long forgotten as the newly formed teams come together. Of the ninety or so guys in the league, there are only a couple whom I've not yet had as teammates. I've already inflicted my "ball hockey is a time machine" theory on you, but I also consider the game to be the great leveller. We have players in the league from all walks of life. Lawyers, writers, financial services guys, restaurant workers, city employees, CBC staff, journalists, musicians, doctors, engineers. Blue collar, white collar, well off, and just getting by—we cover the socioeconomic waterfront. But here's the key point. When the game starts, nobody thinks about checking a lawyer, taking a shot on a retail worker, or passing to the banker. Those differences among us are as irrelevant as they are unseen when everyone is wearing a team jersey and holding a hockey stick. We're all just hockey players locked in a game we loved long before any of us became lawyers or city workers or anything else. The great leveller. The great equalizer. Anyway, for these and other reasons, the players the league has attracted and kept are solid guys who have a stake in protecting and promoting the kind of league we've created. Beyond my family, I can't think of much else that has given me more satisfaction in my life. Here endeth the sermon.

—

I still hadn't slept, and there remained two hours before touchdown at Charles de Gaulle. I'd been sleeping better at home after trying two nightly capsules of a THC and CBD oil blend. With cannabis legal in Canada, I confess I still hadn't smoked any legal weed, but I was sleeping better. I didn't want to risk being kicked out of France for attempting to import cannabis products for the purposes of trafficking, so I had left my oil capsules at home.

I gave up on sleep, slipped my AirPods into my ears—which is where I find they work best—and started watching the Woody Allen movie *Midnight in Paris*. I'd seen it a dozen times or more and loved it. Naturally, I promptly fell asleep while the opening credits were still running—a trick worth remembering for future transatlantic crossings. I woke up as we touched down in Paris. It was a bit of a rough landing, so when I say I woke up as we touched down, it doesn't quite capture the speed, intensity, and terror with which I regained consciousness. The older woman next to me put her hand on my arm after I flinched awake.

"It's all right, dear, we've landed. We're here."

Charles de Gaulle Airport was busy, though I suspect it always is. There was a long line at customs. I've never had a bad experience entering a foreign country, other than being strip-searched by two Moroccan border guards who had confused the small Tupperware container of peanut butter in my backpack with something more illicit and less nutritious. But on the heels of the pandemic and virtually no international travel in the last three years, I was a little nervous as I inched my way towards the front of the line. I masked up for the procedure, as did many of my fellow passengers. We Canadians are a cautious and responsible lot.

"Bonjour," I said as I pushed my passport across the counter to the young woman in her customs uniform.

Expressionless, which seems to be standard operating procedure for customs officials around the globe, she flipped through my passport and asked a few standard questions, including length of stay. I realized she was speaking accented English, so I abandoned French and stuck with my native tongue. I tend to babble when I'm nervous.

"This is a trip my wife and I have been planning for years," I blurted. "I'm really excited."

"Is your wife with you?" she asked, looking behind me.

"Um, no, I'm travelling alone," I said. "She died of COVID two and a half years ago."

The customs woman's head snapped up to look in my eyes. Hers were glistening.

"I'm very, very sorry. That is very sad," she said. "My mother also died from the COVID, seven months ago. It is unfortunate that your wife is no longer with you."

"Thank you, and I'm sorry about your mother," I replied. "My wife's last wish was that I make this trip. So here I am."

I didn't bother explaining that Annie also wanted me to find someone with whom to make a new life. I knew she had said it out of love, but it was still hard to fathom. I couldn't quite wrap my mind around the idea.

The officer stamped my passport as I concentrated on not tearing up any more than I already had. I took my passport back and saw that she had offered me her hand as if introducing herself. On instinct I shook it. She held on a touch longer than one might expect.

"I hope you find what you're looking for in Paris. It has always been a city of new startings. I mean, new beginnings. My English is not so fine."

"Thank you very much. You've made me feel very welcome. Merci. Merci beaucoup."

She smiled in a quiet, sympathetic way, then waved the next person up to the counter and restored her standard stone-faced countenance. I nodded and wheeled my carry-on bag ahead of me, following the signs with suitcases on them to the baggage carousel.

I'd felt anxious and a little depressed at times on the flight. But I was struck by how much better I felt after my brief encounter with the young, uniformed woman who seemed more kindred spirit than customs official. At the carousel, my suitcases arrived right on schedule—you know, the last two bags to appear after a forty-five-minute vigil. But by that stage, I'd already assumed they'd been lost. Needless to say, I was so thrilled when they appeared on the conveyor belt that I completely forgot about the long wait. Then I hustled over to yet another counter, this one beneath a sign that said *Les services spéciaux*. I handed over my baggage tag in return for my guitar in its hard case. I opened it up to make sure my six-string was actually inside. It was, and there was no damage, at least not that I could discern at first glance. I hoped the neck would not spontaneously detach from the body of the guitar as soon as I made it to my apartment.

I had everything I was supposed to have, which I thought was an achievement worthy of at least some modest celebration.

I managed to find an empty luggage cart sitting forlornly off to the side of the corridor and loaded it up. I pushed all my earthly possessions, at least for the next five months, out the main doors of the terminal and into the lineup for a taxi. With so much luggage, taking the train was a non-starter.

"Merci. Rue de Seine, juste à côté de la rue de Buci, s'il vous plaît," I said to the driver in my best French after he loaded my bags into the trunk.

"No problem, monsieur," he replied. "Traffic is good this morning."

I was pleased that I understood him so well before I realized he'd also spoken in English, just like the customs official. I'm sure he was trying to be helpful, but the Paris experience was supposed to include dusting off my high school French, taking it out for a spin, and trying to make it work. So it was a bit of a letdown that my first French phrase instantly betrayed me as an anglophone.

There wasn't a lot to see for the first twenty minutes or so of the drive into Paris. But when we crossed the Boulevard Périphérique at the north end of the city, the world outside the taxi's window started to look and feel like Paris proper. I was excited, though I projected a calm and cool demeanour, as if driving through downtown Paris was an everyday thing for me. That lasted until I suddenly realized we were crossing the Seine at Île de la Cité. I recognized the landmark church instantly.

"Notre-Dame!" I blurted, pointing, as if my startled driver had never seen it either.

When he regained control of the car, I saw him chuckle in the rear-view mirror.

"Yes, monsieur. Notre-Dame."

The cathedral was still closed after the terrible fire of 2019. I could see the scaffolding that had been set up as part of the reconstruction, but the two iconic towers at the front stood tall. We crossed over the bridge and into the Latin Quarter. We were almost there.

"The address on Rue de Seine, monsieur?"

I made a point of giving him the street address in French.

The Latin Quarter was just as I'd imagined it. Of course, the dozens of Left Bank walking tours I'd watched on YouTube had helped give me an accurate sense of the place, but still, it was nice to have my mental impression confirmed on the ground. The streets looked as if they'd been laid out at random, almost never meeting one another at right angles. Cafés, restaurants, galleries, and boutiques dominated the streetscapes, with what I assumed were apartments on the floors above.

As agreed, I had texted the owner of my rental apartment en route from the airport, and she was waiting for me at the big arched wooden doors that opened into a courtyard within the building. She was in a rush, so she led me up a staircase to the third floor, opened the unit, handed me the keys, and said, "Au revoir, monsieur."

It was a relief to be alone in the space I'd be occupying for the coming five months. There was no need for a more elaborate tour. It wasn't big. The photos in the Airbnb ad must have been taken with a very, very wide-angle lens. The front door opened directly into the bright but snug living room. A couch faced the front window overlooking the courtyard, with a matching chair off to the side. A glass-and-wood coffee table featured a glass bowl in which rested wooden spheres of various sizes. Two large books about Paris sat next to the decorative bowl. Yes, judging by their size and positioning, you could call them coffee-table books, so at least they were in the right spot.

Behind the sitting room was a galley kitchen that included a small oven and fridge, a double sink, a reasonable amount of counter space, and glass-doored cabinets with all the dishes and glasses I'd ever need. I noted there were four juice glasses and six wine glasses, perhaps reflecting the drinking preferences of Parisians. There was also a microwave, a toaster, a blender, a block of nice knives, and, in the cupboards below the counter, pots, pans, cutting boards, and a fiery red Le Creuset baking dish (I lived with a chef so I recognized the brand). Simply put, the kitchen was well equipped to support my solid though limited culinary repertoire. A small table for two pressed up against the back of the couch gave me a place to eat and write.

A modest bathroom opened off the kitchen. There was a shower but no bathtub, which suited me fine given that the last bath I took was in the early 1980s. Finally, the bedroom was small but quite adequate for one person. The queen-sized bed was beautifully made up with a white comforter and four large pillows, and the bedroom window opened onto Rue de Seine. Oddly, the closet was as large as the bathroom, and its built-in drawers and double-decker hanging bars easily accommodated my clothes. There was even room to store my suitcases. My guitar slid nicely under the bed. Hardwood floors gleamed throughout, while ancient wooden beams held up the ceiling, not to mention the floor above. All in all, I was very happy with my little apartment and its location. Not bad for booking online.

It took me about half an hour to stash all I'd brought with me and make the place my own. That entailed hanging a Toronto Maple Leafs cap on one of the hooks on the back of the door. I was starting to feel the effects of my new time zone, a long flight, and a short sleep. But it was only noon in Paris. I figured I should push myself to stay awake and try to make it at least till early evening before succumbing and inaugurating the bed. So I took a quick shower and pulled on a pair of jeans, a T-shirt, and a sweater. I sat down on the couch to tie my shoes. Then I looked at the empty spot next to me and pictured Annie sitting there. I'm not religious, or even spiritual. I don't have hard and fast views on life after death. But for a flash, I thought I felt something. I can't explain it. It was just a feeling, a very fleeting feeling. It was not so much her presence I sensed, but more like her approval, her blessing, or perhaps her happiness that I was in Paris, if only on my own. After all, she had wanted me to come to this special city. It was her idea. Then the sensation passed, if it had been there at all. I like to think she was pleased.

To forestall an afternoon wallowing in memories of Annie, I forced myself to get up and get out to explore my new neighbourhood in the City of Light. Sure, I was tired, but the idea of strolling the streets of the Latin Quarter, in the footsteps of the Lost Generation artists and writers from a century ago, more than compensated. This was why I'd come, or at least it was one of the reasons. I slipped on my jacket and headed out the door.

Walking in Paris is so different from walking in Toronto, or in any other modern city. In Canada we've grown accustomed to a history that is calibrated in decades. In Europe, and in Paris in particular, history sprawls out before you in centuries. Exploring the meandering streets of Saint-Germain-des-Prés, it was clear I wasn't in Kansas anymore—not that I've ever been to Kansas, but you know what I mean.

Save for the major thoroughfares like Boulevard Saint-Germain or Boulevard du Montparnasse, the streets are narrow, as are the sidewalks, where there are any at all. The buildings are neither tall nor set back from the streets as they tend to be in North America. But they are crammed together, cheek by jowl, so that walking the side streets of Paris feels a bit like navigating winding canyons, with apartment blocks rising above the cafés and shops encroaching on either side.

I wandered around, trying to orient myself to my new neighbourhood. I headed south on Rue de Seine. When I hit Rue de Buci, I noticed a place on the corner called Café Paul. I realized I was hungry. I steeled myself and rehearsed my order in my mind before going inside. I approached the counter and the young man standing behind it.

"Um, un café au lait et un pain au chocolat, s'il vous plaît," I said in my best French accent.

"To take away or eat here, monsieur?" he replied without so much as an instant's hesitation.

Damn. It was annoying to have them switch immediately to English. Was my accent that bad?

"Ici, s'il vous plaît," I persisted.

I paid with the Apple Pay app on my iPhone and sat outside in one of the classic Paris café seats facing the street. It was cool—it was November after all—but heat lamps mounted below the awning made it not just tolerable but comfortable. And wow, the café au lait was amazing, surpassed only by the chocolate croissant. I've had lots of both at different cafés in Toronto, but none compared to what I was enjoying now. I wondered if the thrill of being in Paris was somehow affecting my taste buds, but I rejected that notion almost as soon as it occurred to me. This was Paris, where they knew their way around coffee and croissants. They were brewing and baking both long before the city of Toronto even existed.

Restored and a little more awake, I continued my walk along Rue de Buci and then the street it turns into, Rue Saint-André des Arts. I followed it down towards Place Saint-Michel, marvelling at how many tiny food stands there were, with an impressive range of international offerings. The neighbourhood seemed crowded for a Monday afternoon, but I suppose the narrowness of the streets could have just made it feel more congested.

About a half hour after my visit to Café Paul, jet lag descended like an offshore fog. I'd never felt fatigue like that come on so quickly. I turned around and started back to my apartment, glad that I'd remembered the way home. There was a small grocery store—or should I say *épicerie*—on my way back. I stopped in and picked up enough provisions to keep me nourished for a few days. I was home by two thirty and ready for a nap—or more likely a coma from which I might not awaken. So much for making it to early evening. I loaded up the fridge and cupboards, drew the bedroom curtains, and crawled into bed.

When I woke up, it was nearly six thirty in the evening and I didn't know where I was—well, only for a few seconds. Then I remembered what bed, and what city, I was in. I grabbed another quick shower and felt quite well rested thereafter. Rested but ravenous. I walked back up the street to a restaurant I'd seen earlier on Rue de Buci called L'Atlas and grabbed a seat outside. The temperature had dropped with the sun, but those heat lamps did their job, and it was lovely watching the crowds streaming by.

"Oui, monsieur," the server said as she delivered a basket of bread and what would turn out to be the best butter I'd ever tasted.

"Risotto à la truffe, s'il vous plaît."

"Excellent," she replied. "Would you like something to drink?"

"Is my French really bad?" I asked.

"Well, I would not call it bad," she backpedalled. "The words were fine. Perfect. But I could tell it is not your birth language. I was just trying to help you feel more comfortable."

I paused to work through a line in my head and tried it out.

"Oui, je comprends. Mais, pouvons-nous essayer en français? Pour moi?"

"Bien sûr, monsieur," she said. "Qu'est-ce que vous voulez boire, monsieur?"

"Un verre de vin rouge, s'il vous plaît."

"Quel vin, monsieur?"

Uh-oh. Stay calm. Think.

"Um, peut-être le vin rouge de la maison?"

"Parfait, monsieur."

"Merci, madame, ou mademoiselle?"

"Mademoiselle," she replied. "De rien, monsieur."

She smiled as she turned and headed for the kitchen. I felt as if I'd made some kind of Anglo-tourist breakthrough.

The server and I kept up our rudimentary conversation in French right through the tarte Tatin I ordered for dessert. She kindly spoke slowly and carefully enunciated her words. Dinner cost me about forty-five euros. *Ouch.* I decided not to stress about the higher cost of living in Paris. What could I do? I was living in Paris. Don't think about it. Just pay. So I did.

I thanked the server and left her a sizeable tip, or as we say in French, *pourboire*. Then I continued exploring my neighbourhood. At night, there was a completely different vibe out on the streets. It didn't seem possible, but there were even more Parisians out and about. The cafés were packed with young and old alike, huddled under the heat lamps and enjoying the street scene. I kept walking, keeping track as best I could of where I was. I walked a long section of Boulevard Saint-Germain and saw Les Deux Magots, Café de Flore, and Brasserie Lipp, three iconic establishments that Hemingway had frequented. I made a decision not to visit any of them that night—I wanted to prepare myself before walking into those key Lost Generation haunts I'd read so much about. But at least I now knew where they were. Instead, I just walked aimlessly for a few hours to begin to settle into Paris.

I already noted that ball hockey is a time machine. But in a completely different way, Paris is also a time machine. The city's very layout, its architecture, its history all seem to resist change and progress. Paris has hobbled most attempts at modernization. I'm grateful for that, though perhaps not all would agree. After spending a few hours strolling the city streets, I could understand why dragging Paris into the twenty-first century was so difficult.

It's nearly impossible to build a large restaurant or a big box store in the Latin Quarter. You simply can't find a single property large enough. Instead, you'd have to negotiate with the owners of six or seven contiguous properties to give you the space you'd need. And of course, finding six or seven individual owners who all were willing to sell at the same moment would likely never happen. This keeps Paris from changing. It hasn't physically evolved or modernized in the way many newer cities have. As I say, Paris is a time machine. Large portions of the city, particularly on the Left Bank, have changed very little in a century or more. Most of the popular cafés from the 1920s are still operating just as they were in Hemingway's day, including the three I passed that evening and most of those on Boulevard du Montparnasse, like Café de la Rotonde, Le Select, La Closerie des Lilas, La Coupole, and many more. If I took off my glasses, the Latin Quarter through my blurred vision would appear much as it did a hundred years ago. Only the cars parked outside the cafés and the customers' fashions inside would betray the year. Even the parks look just about the same, including Le Jardin du Luxembourg, though at that point I'd not yet visited it.

I supposed the same phenomenon could be seen in other European cities and towns that had not been not devastated by war—Madrid, Prague, Venice, and Florence, among others—though I hadn't travelled enough to be sure. But it only took me one day to realize that Paris was a time machine. Perhaps I was born out of my time. When we finally perfect time travel, hopefully before I'm dead, I'd live in Paris in the 1920s. That's what I'd do. Until then, living in Paris in the 2020s will have to do.

My day caught up with me around eleven thirty, and I returned to my apartment and fell into a deep and dreamless sleep until eight thirty the next morning. I did not wake up once in the night. In Paris, even my prostate took a vacation. Now, that's how you manage jet lag.

CHAPTER 6

THIS TIME, I knew where I was when I woke up. I'm not suggesting I deserve any special credit for this. I know that most people know where they are after a good night's sleep. But still, it was a relief. I just lay there for a while basking in the knowledge that I was no longer in Toronto, across the street from Withrow Park. No, I was in Paris, on the Left Bank, and I felt different. As if I'd turned a page. I wasn't sure which page, or even what book, but something had shifted. I was excited about exploring a city I'd only ever read about. After a horrendous few years, I sensed my head was above water for the first time in a long while. I savoured the realization without completely letting go of the grief that had pushed me under in the first place. But it was a start, and I held on to it.

I bounded out of bed—well, more accurately, I rolled out of bed with great care, my legs feeling the effects of my walking the day before. It wasn't quite the physical incapacity I often felt the morning after a ball hockey game, but my legs made it clear I'd walked for several hours on very little sleep. I stretched a little bit and then took a long, hot shower. The bedroom was so small that I was able to open the curtains while sitting on the bed. How convenient. I sat there and watched the streetscape below me. I pictured Hemingway or Fitzgerald or Morley Callaghan, or all three, walking up Rue de Seine, perhaps on their way to Les Deux Magots for breakfast. It continued to hit me that the scene from my window would not have looked much different in the 1920s than it did that morning.

On the surface, the Parisians walking through my field of view seemed utterly unaffected by Paris. Many looked world-weary, presumably wrestling with the range of everyday issues that weigh us all down—money, jobs, relationships, health, children, aging parents, and yes, even the death of a loved one. These are universal challenges whether you live in Paris, Munich, Beirut, Seoul, Nairobi, or Toronto. I guess when you've lived in Paris for years, the thrill, the history, and the wonder of the city fade after a while. Still, I couldn't imagine not being awed on a daily basis, living there amidst all that had unfolded in Paris over the centuries of its considerable cultural influence. But perhaps that would change after I'd been living there for a few months. Perhaps I was destined to become blasé about it all, too. I hoped not.

It was eight thirty when I pulled on my clothes, ready to head out for my first full day in Paris. I had no big plans other than exploring the Left Bank. Just before I left, I texted Will to let him know that I had arrived safely, and all was well. Obviously, he was sound asleep at the time, so I didn't want to call him. I'd do that later in the afternoon when he was home from work.

A few minutes later, I joined the crowds of Parisians walking south along Rue de Seine. Most were going to work and looked it. I was going to explore and indulge my curiosity about a special city and a special contingent of artists who had changed the world a century before. My first stop? Café Paul. I braced myself for another exchange in my second language—in case it's not clear, I don't have a third or fourth language. I stood in line and slowly made my way up to the counter. Most of the staff were younger, likely putting themselves through school—perhaps at the Sorbonne, also in the Latin Quarter. But when I reached the counter, I looked up to see the warm, open, and smiling face of an older woman—at least, older than the other counter staff. I put her in her mid-fifties, though I'd never been particularly adept at estimating ages and had learned the hard way to keep my yap shut on the subject. Greenish eyes, and curly—or at least wavy—short brown hair that was just long enough to frame her quite lovely face. Not that I know much about women's hair, but hers struck me as a low-maintenance style that looked great on her. Wash and go with a shake of her head. And no, I don't know why that occurred to me. Lean—despite working in a café-bakery—and tall, she just gave off a happy and pleasant aura. The name tag on her black Café Paul T-shirt said *Calla*.

"Um, un café au lait et un pain au chocolat, s'il vous plaît," I said in a manner that could generously be described as slow and deliberate.

"Plaisir, monsieur," she replied. "Café à emporter ou pour rester ici?"

She spoke slowly and used hand motions to make her words clearer. I could tell by the few key French words I recognized that she was asking whether I wanted my coffee for *here or to go*.

"Uhhh, ici, s'il vous plaît."

She beamed at me and nodded. I beamed right back, pleased that I'd been able to respond to what had admittedly been a rather simple question. I silently gave thanks to all my French teachers over the years, who, based on my classroom performance, would surely have rejoiced to see just how far I'd come.

After exchanging more smiles with Calla, I paid and took my little tray to a free table alongside a large window offering an unobstructed view onto Rue de Buci. I could easily have devoured two or three pains au chocolat, but I controlled myself and only ordered one. My powers of restraint weren't particularly well developed, so I'd see how long that lasted. My mind drifted to Annie as I lamented yet again that we were never able to experience this beautiful city together. I realized I'd never be able to say, "We'll always have Paris."

Café Paul was packed, but only with people lining up to grab coffee and croissants *à emporter*, as they say in France. So, few tables were occupied beyond mine. After deciding to take my time and savour my pain au chocolat, I simply inhaled it. I was utterly defenceless. The flavour was something I'd never quite experienced before. As penance, I sipped my café au lait as slowly as its amazing aroma—and caffeine rush—permitted. To ensure this wonderful coffee did not become the very centre of my existence, I pulled out a book to read while also taking in the daily Parisian parade just outside the window.

I was rereading for the umpteenth time *Memoirs of Montparnasse*, John Glassco's entertaining recollections of his time in Paris during—yes, you already know—the 1920s. A Canadian and sometime poet, Glassco seemed more interested in partying than poetry when he arrived in Paris at the tender age of eighteen. But his memoir captures the feelings and attitudes of artists—many of them expats—in Paris as the world emerged from the shadow of the Great War. To the greatest extent possible, I wanted to immerse myself in the Paris of that period. My location in the Latin Quarter helped with the Paris part, and the books I was reading sent me back in time a century to the days of the Lost Generation.

I figured I shouldn't take up space in the café after I'd finally finished my coffee, so I made my way through the takeout crowd—now much thinner—to the door. The older woman who'd served me smiled and waved. That was nice. I waved back. Just outside the door, an elderly woman sat on a piece of cardboard on the sidewalk. She looked at me with a mournful eye. I stopped.

"Un café, madame?" I asked.

"Oui, monsieur. Merci, monsieur."

"Et un croissant aussi, peut-être?" I asked.

"Oh, merci. Merci, monsieur," she replied, nodding with some vigour.

"Un instant," I said, again quite pleased at my ability to carry on a conversation—yes, I know, calling it a conversation might be a modest exaggeration.

I stepped back into Café Paul, waited my turn, and found myself once again standing directly in front of the older woman server.

"C'est un plaisir de vous revoir, monsieur," she said, casting her happy countenance upon me once more. I wasn't exactly sure what she'd said, but I deduced it was a reference to seeing me again so soon.

"Ahhh, yes, oui, bonjour encore, madame."

"*Rebonjour*, monsieur. Pas *bonjour encore*. Et *mademoiselle*, pas *madame*." She smiled, almost in a shy way, as she gently corrected me.

"Ahh, excusez," I said. "Rebonjour, mademoiselle. Um, merci pour la clarification. C'est vrai?"

"Parfait, monsieur."

The other counter staff, not to mention the lineup behind me, were urging us with their eyes and hands to conclude our little French tutorial so I could place my order and make my much-anticipated second exit.

"Ahh, yes. Un café et un croissant, s'il vous plaît."

"Bien sûr, monsieur."

After I'd paid, I realized I didn't know if the old woman wanted cream or sugar. So while the older woman named Calla poured the coffee, I popped back outside and received a perfunctory "non, merci" on both counts. When I stepped back in, Calla looked past me at the woman seated outside and then back to me. She put her hand on her heart when she spoke.

"Ohhh, monsieur, vous êtes très gentil," she said as she slipped a second croissant into the bag and handed it to me.

Then I pointed at her and said, "Non, mademoiselle, vous êtes très gentille. Merci."

She waved and I felt her eyes still on me as I slipped out the door and handed the coffee and croissants to the old woman. I stole a glance back and as I'd thought, Calla was watching me, with her hand still over her heart and a look of pure, unadulterated sympathy etched in her face. I didn't think Calla would make a good poker player. It seemed clear what she was feeling at all times. I liked that. I was still hungry and had briefly considered snagging for myself the second croissant Calla had added to the bag. But I figured the older woman could use it more than I.

I checked the time and realized I needed to hustle to get where I needed to be on time. I was due outside the Cardinal Lemoine Métro station at ten thirty. Guided by the Maps function on my iPhone, I walked for about a dozen blocks along Boulevard Saint-Germain before cutting right along Rue Monge for a few more blocks, until I hit Rue du Cardinal Lemoine and the designated Métro station. I saw a few people who had gathered in a clump on the corner. I figured I was in the right spot. I hovered nearby until I was sure. At ten thirty sharp, a middle-aged man with a backpack stepped out of the group and turned to face the others.

"Good morning, all. I'm Chris from Paris Tours, and this is our Hemingway's Paris walk."

Most of the assembled group were from England and the U.S., rounded out by a Swedish couple and an older man from Vancouver. Our first stop was just a short walk up the street. We were headed for 74 Rue du Cardinal Lemoine, the site of Ernest and Hadley Hemingway's first apartment in Paris. They'd arrived in December of 1921, staying briefly in the Hôtel d'Angleterre on Rue Jacob before landing their first flat in January of 1922. I'd made the virtual pilgrimage to their apartment several times on guided walks livestreamed on Facebook and YouTube. But of course, I'd never done it using my own feet, as it were.

I should come clean about Hemingway. Given how many books I've read and documentaries I've watched about Ernest Hemingway, you might think that I'm an unabashed fanboy. In fact, I like neither him nor his writing. He was a selfish and self-centred bastard of the first order who also happened to revolutionize literature at a time when the winds of change were sweeping through Western society and culture. He married four times, treated his wives, friends, supporters, and everyone else badly, incessantly embellished his own exploits—okay, he was an inveterate liar—failed as a parent, and then descended into mental illness, taking his own life when he was sixty-one but looked eighty-one. He lived hard and looked it at the end. As for his writing, he undoubtedly changed the literary landscape with his spare, barren, simple, declarative prose at a time when that was bold and new. But I just don't like his writing. I hail from the "why use six words when twelve will do" school of writing. English is a rich, diverse, and bountiful language, and I like to splash around in it and explore its outer reaches. My approach to writing and my preferences when reading are about as far from Hemingway as one can get. Yet I can't ignore his impact on literature and the formative role Paris played in his life. In fact, I find it fascinating, compelling, and endlessly interesting. Certainly, those close to me would eagerly testify—likely in rather strenuous terms—to just how "interested" (read: obsessed) I am with Paris of the twenties, even though they may not find it quite as gripping a subject.

"All right, gather round, if you will," Chris said in front of the nondescript building. "So, on the third floor, the newlywed

Hemingways rented a two-room flat that had no hot water, and a shared bathroom down the hall. Apparently, they slept on a mattress on the floor and by all accounts had never been happier."

It was surreal to have read so much about this address, seen so many photos of it from multiple angles, and watched countless YouTube videos of the building from inside and out, and now, finally, to be standing right in front of it, in the flesh. On instinct, I pressed the palms of both my hands against the dirty white outside wall, as if performing a Vulcan mind meld on Hemingway's apartment building. I know that's silly. The Vulcan mind meld only works on other living beings, not buildings. Still, I thought I felt something passing into me through my now-dirty hands.

To be honest, and it certainly wasn't the fault of our very capable tour guide, I learned nothing on the tour that I hadn't already assimilated through fifteen years of reading a mountain of books on Hemingway, 1920s Paris, and the Lost Generation. But it was wonderful to be there, standing on the same front steps where Hemingway once stood. Reading works well for amassing a store of knowledge, facts, and anecdotes. But being there is something else again. Something that filled an empty space inside me that I hadn't quite realized was there.

We then walked the short distance to 39 Rue Descartes, where Hemingway rented a room with a fireplace on the top floor to write in during the day. The plaque on the outside wall erroneously said Hemingway had lived in the building. Not true. It was just a workspace. Tour guide Chris clarified this for the group, though I already knew.

Over the next hour or so, we visited more of Hemingway's haunts, including Les Deux Magots and Café de Flore, where he often wrote; Église Saint-Germain-des-Prés, just across Rue Bonaparte; and the strip of cafés and bars on Boulevard du Montparnasse. We even paid homage to Woody Allen's *Midnight in Paris* by visiting the stone steps where the Owen Wilson character sits before travelling back in time to hang out with Fitzgerald and Hemingway. The time passed without my notice. I can't describe the feelings and even emotions I had traipsing around in Hemingway's footsteps. I was a little unprepared for how it all made me feel. It helped that every stop of the tour looked essentially the same as it had in 1922. This made it so much easier to imagine myself in that world all those years ago. I loved every step of the tour, though my lower back was protesting after all the walking.

Okay, okay, yes, a stiff lower back after walking may well be another tangible sign that I am in fact sixty-two years old. I grant you that. I think that brings us up to eight. But only eight. That's not many, you know.

After the tour, I thanked Chris for a thrilling morning and made my way back towards my neck of the woods. Yes, having been in Paris for a couple days by then, I had already demarcated, and claimed, "my neck of the woods." I was famished by that stage, so on my way back, I grabbed a classic Parisian sandwich from a street vendor. It was a long, thin baguette with butter and ham, known *en français* as a *jambon-beurre*. Just ham and butter on a baguette. Could there be a simpler sandwich? Yet it was an extraordinary and unexpected gastronomic experience. It's difficult to describe exactly what made it so good. It was perhaps some combination of the taste of all three ingredients, the texture of the bread, and the complementary creaminess of the butter. Okay, I guess that wasn't so hard to describe. It was so good that when I finished it, despite my aching lower back, I turned around, walked back, and bought a second.

I made it back to my apartment just in time. I sat down on the couch and pulled out my iPhone. Will's image flickered onto the screen of my FaceTime app.

"Hey, Dad."

"Hi, Will. You look good," I started. "Just checking in, as promised."

"Good to see you, Dad. Paris hasn't completely changed you," he said. "You still look like Dad to me."

"Give it time. In a few more weeks I might be rocking a beret and a pencil-thin moustache. You never know."

"So is it everything you thought it would be?"

"A bit early to tell. It was only yesterday that you dropped me off at the airport," I replied. "But in the short time I've been here, Paris has lived up to all my expectations. It's amazing to be here and to see in person what I've only ever read about or seen in photos and videos."

"But do you feel any different?" he asked.

"I do. I do feel different. I'm alone but I'm not lonely, if that makes any sense," I said. "I miss your mother. We were supposed to be here together, so there's an added poignance to being here."

"Sorry about breaking my leg, and I'm sorry Miller needed surgery," Will said. "But you're there now, which I have to think is better than not being there."

"It surely is, son," I replied. "And I've told you before never to hold any guilt about breaking your leg. That wasn't your fault. The other kid was suspended, if you'll recall. It was a dirty check and he sat out the rest of the playoffs. So no need to apologize. When you have kids, you'll understand."

"I know, Dad, but I still feel bad about Mom and you missing that trip. If I'd scored on the play or set up the winning goal before he took me down, that would have at least given me something positive to hold on to."

"Well, how about me driving you and your crutches to school every day for two months? That was some good father-son bonding time. I seem to recall we laughed a lot."

"Dad, I remember *you* laughing a lot, but you were the one telling me the jokes and, well, let's just say that not all of them measured up to the strict definition of humour. But it was fun hanging out and not having to hobble to school each day."

"Wow, tough crowd," I said. "So, how's everything at home? No fires? No water in the basement? The roof is still where it was when I left?"

"Everything is fine, Dad. Not a lot has happened in the thirty-six hours since you left. Even the dishwasher is still working."

Will was sitting on the living room couch.

"Good. So, how's work? Any news?"

"Busy at the store today, but I was in the downstairs kitchen prepping desserts for the week. Lots of chocolate bread pudding."

"What about your other gig?" I asked. "Were you in the studio last night?"

"Yep, I was," he replied. "I was helping an up-and-coming band lay down some tracks for a few originals. They're making a demo. It was good, I think. Some days you feel like you're on and some days not so much. But I'm learning a lot, including when and how to trust my own musical instincts and judgment. So yeah, I think it went well."

"That's great, son. You're lucky to be working in fields that you love. Not everyone does. In fact, relatively few do. So stick to it. You'll get there."

Movement on the screen behind Will caught my attention. A young woman was stirring something on the stove. Short black hair and a black T-shirt. She may have been of South Asian descent, but on FaceTime, the kitchen is a long way from the living room.

"Hey, Will, I don't want to startle you, but someone's in the kitchen."

"Thanks, Dad. I know," he said, laughing. "That's Ariel. We work at the store together. We're test-driving a few new recipes."

"Ariel, as in *The Little Mermaid*?" I whispered.

"Yes, Dad, but she gets that every day, so let's not go there, okay?"

"Of course. I get it," I said.

He lifted the phone up so I could see her more easily.

"Ariel Banerjee, say hello to Dad," Will said.

She looked up and offered a radiant smile and waved.

"Hello, Dad!" she called. "I heard the *Little Mermaid* reference. You're not going to break into 'Under the Sea,' are you?"

She was laughing now.

"Oops, sorry about that, Ariel. I thought I whispered that part," I said, chastened. "Very nice to meet you. And you're in luck, I don't know enough of the lyrics to attempt 'Under the Sea.'"

"I'm just messing with you, Mr. McMaster."

"Ariel, please, call me Jack."

"Like in the Jack Reacher movies?" she asked.

"Touché, Ariel, touché," I said. "And yes, exactly like the Jack Reacher movies. Thank you for asking. I'm often mistaken for Tom Cruise."

She just laughed, nodded, and waved before turning back to the stove.

All right, all right. When my son's friend calls me "Mr. McMaster," I feel every one of my sixty-two years. I think that brings us up to nine things that make me feel my age. Just nine. Still single digits. That might be it.

Will and I talked for a few more minutes before signing off. I wondered if Ariel and Will had anything more cooking than what was on the stove. Though I only had spoken to her for a few seconds, she seemed nice, happy, funny, and very confident. I liked that and figured Will would, too. Good for Will.

The next few days passed by in a blur. I'd start each day at Café Paul for café au lait, pain au chocolat, and a warm exchange with Counter Calla, who remained the only Parisian to continue speaking to me in French when I started in French. We'd wave to one another when I left. I'd deliver a coffee and croissant to the old woman sitting on the corner and then I'd start my exploring. I didn't want to become isolated on the Left Bank and miss other important sites in Paris. So I spent Thursday and Friday of my first week across the Seine on the Right Bank. I toured the Jardin des Tuileries, a beautiful public garden just across from the landmark spire of Place de la Concorde. I don't mind gardens, but it didn't take long before its relentless beauty washed over me and I became somewhat immune to the horticultural magnificence of it all. So I then walked up the Champs-Élysées all the way to the Arc de Triomphe, one of the more recognizable Paris tourist hotspots. There were swish boutiques and movie theatres along the Champs-Élysées, and some very bad drivers navigating the gigantic roundabout that encircles the Arc de Triomphe. I spent an entire afternoon walking through the Louvre. Yes, I saw the *Mona Lisa*. It's rather small. And by the end of the day, I didn't want to see another painting for quite some time. It was all a bit much, but still amazing to see such famous and classic masterpieces. Another day, I enjoyed the Musée d'Orsay, including several van Goghs.

I did not climb the Eiffel Tower, though I stood below it and gaped for a few minutes. I spent a couple of hours walking along the big shopping street Rue Saint-Honoré. Chock full of expensive stores, Rue Saint-Honoré is your street if you're looking for an Hermès scarf or a Gucci handbag (if that's what they're called). I also stepped into the famed Ritz Hotel on Place Vendôme and paid an exorbitant amount for a drink in the Hemingway Bar, allegedly liberated from the Nazis by the famous writer in 1944.

Of course, I walked along the Seine and crossed over the famous bridges, including the Pont Neuf. I must have walked a few dozen miles in my early days in Paris. But I always felt more comfortable, more at home, more content when my feet hit the Left Bank again. I visited more sites in the Latin Quarter, including Brasserie Lipp on Boulevard Saint-Germain, where Ernest and Hadley Hemingway often dined, several churches, and the Sorbonne. I stood in front of 27 Rue de Fleurus, just west of the Luxembourg Gardens, where Gertrude Stein and her partner Alice B. Toklas convened their regular salon, a gathering place for writers, artists, entertainers, and celebrities in the 1920s. I checked out the former location of Sylvia Beach's English bookstore, Shakespeare and Company, on Rue de l'Odéon. She was the legend who single-handedly published James Joyce's groundbreaking novel, *Ulysses*, when no mainstream publisher would touch it. Another morning, purely by chance, I stumbled upon the site of the Hôtel d'Alsace, where Oscar Wilde died, no doubt with a witticism still on his lips. I visited the Musée de Cluny, better known as the National Museum of the Middle Ages. Yes, there's an entire museum in Paris devoted strictly to the Middle Ages, and it was fascinating. Well, it was fascinating for the first half hour, and then my eyes may have glazed over a bit, but that was my issue, not the museum's.

I was usually in bed and sound asleep by nine thirty. Sometimes I dreamt, and sometimes I didn't. When I did, Annie was always in the cast, usually in the leading role. Sometimes I felt better after waking up, but often . . . not so much. So I'd get up early and start walking the streets. Despite my daily intake of pain au chocolat, I'd lost six pounds in my first six days wandering around Paris. I FaceTimed with Will every couple of days just to make sure all was well on the home front. It also did my heart good to talk to him. I missed him. I missed Annie.

On the seventh day in Paris, a Sunday, I did not rest. I decided to return to some of the places I'd already visited on the Hemingway walking tour, but this time on my own, without the gaggle of tourists in tow. I started by walking along Boulevard du Montparnasse and cut down Rue Delambre to number 10, where the Dingo Bar originally stood. This was where Hemingway is said to have been introduced to F. Scott Fitzgerald. Suffice it to say, when they met, alcohol was involved. Lots of it. It's a restaurant now, but I still wanted to see it. Then I had a coffee a few doors down at Le Dôme, followed by an espresso and croissant at La Coupole. Finally, even though I was no longer hungry and was very much caffeinated, I ordered lunch at La Rotonde, just across the street from Le Dôme. I ordered—what else—French onion soup, and it was stellar. The interiors of the three cafés have not changed dramatically from the days of Callaghan, Hemingway, Glassco, and Fitzgerald. So it was easy to sit at my table and feel what it was like to be there a century before.

By that time, it was early afternoon, and I felt the need to walk off my morning indulgences. I made my way back to Rue Descartes to take another look at Hemingway's rented writing space, or rather the building that housed it. I'm not sure why I went back, but I did. I didn't stay long. I mean, how long can you stand in front of a building as people flow around you, giving you annoyed looks? Well, in my case, about twelve minutes. Afterwards, I strolled along Rue Descartes, just enjoying the cool temperatures and clear skies. I was picking my way through the Latin Quarter back towards Boulevard Saint-Germain when I heard a sound that stopped me in my tracks. Surely not. I rotated on the spot in an attempt to pinpoint its location. I confirmed the right direction and continued walking along Rue Descartes, guided by my ears.

The sound was getting louder, and I was getting closer. I assumed, as I neared the source, it would morph into something more appropriate and native to Paris. But it didn't. I knew that sound. The familiar yet out-of-context music to my ears was coming from a gated school. I was in the right place but still couldn't see what I was hearing. I followed the property onto a side street and found the driveway that, according to the sign, led around the corner and into the parking lot. I edged around the bend, and there it was, in all its glory. A full-blown ball hockey game was playing out before my eyes in a school parking lot on the Left Bank of Paris. To say it seemed incongruous would be an understatement. There were real nets, inhabited by goalies in full equipment. Judging by their matching shirts, there were four runners on one team but only three on the other team. All were clearly younger than I, and likely younger than the thirty-five-year-old I felt like inside, except of course in those nine instances I've enumerated. As far as I could tell, two were women, and they were good. Really good. The players were even using the regulation hard orange plastic ball. It was so strange to see the distinctive rooftops of the Left Bank as the backdrop for a ball hockey game.

I sat down on a parking curb and watched. It didn't take long for me to realize that the players were bantering with one another in a language that I understood quite well. These were almost certainly Canadians, playing a Canadian game in a foreign city.

Just as English-speaking expat American, British, and Canadian writers flocked to Paris a hundred years ago to reshape the literary landscape, so too did these ball hockey–playing Canucks come to Paris to, well, um, play ball hockey.

I knew that no ball hockey players worth their salt wanted to play with unbalanced teams. I was surprised they weren't playing three on three and letting the fourth runner sub in when a teammate tired, just to keep the teams on the floor even. But they had opted to play four on three. Perhaps this was my opening. In a break in the play as one goalie adjusted his pads, I stood up and walked over to the players.

"Hi. I was just walking by and was happily surprised to come across a game of ball hockey," I said. "Do you want another runner to even out the teams?"

CHAPTER 7

I COULDN'T HELP BUT NOTICE a look of skepticism crossing at least one of their faces—or perhaps it was all seven of their faces, and the skepticism was really incredulity. I mentioned earlier that they were all younger than I. (That was not surprising. At sixty-two, most people were younger than I.) Just to clarify, none of these players looked older than thirty. So, yeah, I was old enough to be their father.

"I've played in a league back in Toronto for the last twenty years and, well, I'm not as old as I may look."

"Good for you, man," one of the young guns said. "I think it's great that you're still playing ball hockey in your fifties."

"Ahhhh, right. Fifties, yes, well, thanks. Cool, cool, cool," I said. "So, um, if you have an extra stick, I can fill in, at least for today, and try not to embarrass myself."

They looked at one another, shrugged, nodded, and I was in. Knowing what a drag it was to play with uneven teams, I figured they'd have let me play even if I'd been a plastic orange pylon—you know, to match the plastic orange hockey ball. I prayed to the gods of geriatric ball hockey that my play would surpass that of a pylon, but the jury was still out.

Someone handed me a stick, and I shed my jacket. I stretched a bit in the hopes that when the game restarted, I'd be able to impersonate someone in their fifties. The stick they loaned me was a little short for me, but better too short than too long. It had a nice curve in the blade and at least it was warped the right way for me.

I learned in their brief introductions that most of the players were finance types working in the Paris offices of international banks and consulting firms. One of the guys and both women were American while the rest were Canadian. They played a pickup game every Sunday afternoon and then hung out in a nearby café afterwards.

The game resumed with me playing defence, at least until I found my feet, let alone the ball. My fellow players had more energy than I, but I'd played ball hockey for a good thirty years longer than they had, so I could compensate for my age-reduced speed, mobility, skill, and endurance with hockey IQ and smart playmaking. I let the ball do the work, making long, crisp passes rather than sprinting from one end of the parking lot to the other, the way my new friends did. Not that I could have sprinted from one end of the lot to the other, at least not more than once—and I'd likely be the only one who knew I was sprinting.

I was nervous at the start, but quickly grew more comfortable and accepted after setting my mates up for two or three great goals. I also still had a relatively accurate snapshot that served me well as I potted three or four goals of my own. The pace of the game was faster than I was used to, but on the other hand, the parking lot was smaller than the regulation hockey rink we played on at home. So my dubious physical conditioning was not taxed as much on the smaller surface, particularly when playing defence. The only thing tougher than keeping up with my fellow players without collapsing from some kind of fatigue-induced seizure was keeping up with them without *looking* like I was about to collapse from some kind of fatigue-induced seizure. I managed. I paced myself. I breathed deeply. I was happy. I had fun. I had missed playing more than I appreciated. And these were nice folks. Young, brash, even a little cocky, but still nice.

Having been down by three goals when I'd entered the fray, our team came back to eke out a win by one goal. I won't dwell on the fact that I scored the winning goal. That would be unseemly—true, but unseemly. So, without dwelling on it, I did score the winning goal. (To me, "dwelling on it" means mentioning it at least three times. I'll not cite my game-winning goal again. But I must say it was a nice solo effort that involved a slick deke and a laser-guided shot to the top corner, short side. But I'm not dwelling.)

The other players worked hard and played hard, but they also had fun. They weren't so into the game that the fate of the world turned on the outcome. I seemed to have overcome their initial wariness and proved my proficiency at the game despite having been born thirty years before they were. As far as I could tell, they were good people, but were still from a different world than mine.

So I was pleased when, at the post-game gathering at the café-bar around the corner, they told me I was welcome to be a regular and join them every Sunday afternoon. I handed over my email address for the group list and told them I'd be there. I was in. That felt good. Ball hockey in Paris. Who knew that was a thing?

The sun was setting as I slowly dragged my creaky carcass back to my little Left Bank neighbourhood. In an act of sheer brilliance, or at least modest forethought, I had not sat down at the café-bar for the hour we'd spent there after the game. I may not have been able to stand up if I had. I could feel my leg muscles protesting and filing injunctions against any more physical activity for the foreseeable future. But I plodded on, almost there. On a whim, I popped back into Café Paul on my way home. I can't exactly tell you why, or on what whim I was acting. I'm not withholding information; I'm just not clear in my own mind. But while I was there, I did pick up a baguette to accompany the frozen lasagna I planned to heat for dinner. Oh, and I noticed that Calla wasn't there. Her shift must have already ended.

After slowly and gingerly scaling the flights of stairs to my apartment—quiet groans under my breath—I took a long, hot shower, focusing the spray on my aching legs. Then I even completed about two-thirds of my stretching regimen, in an attempt to protect my ability to walk the next morning. While the frozen lasagna was in the oven, I opened my laptop and ordered two Sher-Wood T90 composite sticks with my preferred curve, a pair of ball hockey gloves, and some black hockey tape. A few minutes later, I thought of Annie and headed back to Amazon to order a mouthguard and protective eyewear. Annie always insisted I be well protected. I was too old to have my teeth knocked out. Ten minutes later, I made my third visit to Amazon, this time to order a jock strap. Even at sixty-two, this should have been my first purchase. No one wants a slapshot in the, um, family jewels, with a plastic orange hockey ball that in the moment—not to mention in the crotch—feels slightly harder than granite.

The lasagna wasn't half bad—more like one-third bad—but the baguette was the best part of dinner, although the half a bottle of red wine I downed was also in the running. I fell asleep easily that night, and I dreamed. Annie. I dreamed of Annie, again. This happened sometimes, though perhaps not as often as it had in the early months following her passing. Beyond the recurring dream where I'm watching from the back of the conference hall as Annie speaks to a few hundred delegates, my nocturnal hallucinations tended to be snapshots of our everyday life together, before COVID. So they weren't freighted with the emotional pain of her death and its numbing aftermath. We were just interacting normally, happily, as two people who loved one another would. When immersed in them, I didn't know I was dreaming. I was fully invested in the illusions. I had no idea she was gone. It was only when I woke up that the cruel truth hit home again . . . like a sledgehammer.

Those days after dreaming of Annie were tough. Sometimes I forced myself to get up and get out into Paris, if only for the distraction. It sometimes worked, but not terribly well. Other times, I just stayed in bed and indulged in a bit of recreational wallowing, submerging myself in her loss. Having tried both approaches, I can say that neither was particularly effective. I loved her. She was gone. It was going to hurt. I was going to be miserable. There was no escape. In a way, I didn't want to escape. Yes, remembering her so intensely after dreaming of her was painful, but sometimes it was preferable to the numbing catatonia that occasionally enveloped me. It's not rocket science. Grief is hard. I knew that. Sometimes feeling loss is better than feeling nothing.

Paris was helping, albeit slowly. I still missed Annie terribly, every day, sometimes every minute. But since embedding on the Left Bank, I'd noticed that the monochromatic greys had given way to some emerging hues—muted, but definitely real colours.

I noticed it about two and a half weeks after arriving in Paris. It was a Wednesday morning following a dreamless night. It wasn't an epiphany or a bolt from the blue. No, it was an almost unconscious nascent sense that I felt at home in that little apartment, in that arrondissement, on the Left Bank, and in Paris. It just kind of snuck up on me. I felt comfortable, even content. I had a routine of sorts. Into Café Paul in the morning to start my day, exchanging witty, urbane, charming banter with Calla in my broken French. The language barrier admittedly challenged my ability to be witty, urbane, and charming, limiting me to what amounted to the vocabulary of a Parisian preschooler. But I persevered. Then I'd continue my explorations of the city. Sometimes, I'd even venture across the river to the other side, like when I visited the Musée des Arts et Métiers, a fascinating museum with a great collection of early aircraft, including the famous monoplane designed, built, and flown by Louis Blériot. You likely know this already, but he was the first to fly across the English Channel, from Calais to

Dover, in 1909. And I was right there in the same room with his famous plane. I thought that was amazing.

But I'd always come back to the Left Bank, and when I did, I'd instantly feel more comfortable, more at home, more relaxed. I'd usually cook dinner for myself, unless I was just not feeling like it, and then I'd slip out to a café or restaurant in the area, of which there were dozens, perhaps hundreds, within walking distance. I probably cooked about seventy-five per cent of the time. So that meant some grocery shopping now and then, but I was getting better at that, too. I tended to use the self-checkout stations to forestall the cashiers' immediate switch to English when they saw me coming. I knew they meant well, but I always found it a little irritating.

Some days I'd need to deliver a writing assignment to a client, but I wasn't working my network for more projects. I only wrote when a client request came in over the transom. In short, I did not seek the work, but delivered when it was requested.

I'd speak to Will several times each week. I always enjoyed our FaceTime calls. I was discreet and tried not to pry, but through seemingly innocent questions posed in the guise of everyday conversation, I learned that his collaboration with Ariel ran deeper than test-driving meals. I could tell from his face and voice when he spoke of her. Will was clearly smitten. Sometimes Ariel would join our calls, and soon I too was smitten. Wrong word. I just mean I really liked her as a match for Will. My initial assessment of her was more than borne out by further conversations. She was funny, thoughtful, smart, and clearly comfortable in her own skin. Once, she let her hand rest on Will's shoulder while standing behind him, almost unconsciously. It looked so casual and natural yet signalled an affection for him that did my heart good.

Anyway—still on my routine, here—I'd be in bed in reasonably good time, reading my way through the Paris books I'd brought with me before falling asleep, sometimes to dream, but often not. It was a loose daily schedule that seemed to work and gave me something to follow as I settled into this city and life after Annie. Oh, yes, and there was my weekly little piece of home, ball hockey Sunday afternoons in a school parking lot on Rue Descartes.

One day, after breakfast at Café Paul and a delightful exchange with Calla, I walked over to the Luxembourg Gardens. There's an apocryphal story about Hemingway being so poor in the early Paris years that he'd capture pigeons in the Luxembourg Gardens to bring home to Hadley for dinner. This likely never happened. In reality, Hadley's family allowance enabled the young couple to live quite comfortably in what was then a very inexpensive city. My how times have changed, judging by what I was paying for my humble little apartment.

In the centre of the gardens is a sprawling, shallow stone pool and fountain where children can manoeuvre radio-controlled toy sailboats. Before leaving my apartment, I'd watched colourized video footage of children in the late 1890s sailing boats in the same pond. Nothing had changed—well, back then, the boats were controlled only by long sticks, not the radio transmitters used today. I sat on a bench in the park and read my book for an hour or so, just as Parisians had been doing since the gardens first opened more than four hundred years ago. I was rereading, yet again, Morley Callaghan's *That Summer in Paris,* his memoir about the months in 1929 when he and his wife, Loretto, lived in the City of Light. I enjoyed it each time I read it and always discovered new insights with each pass through it.

The walk to and through the gardens had spurred my hunger. It was around eleven thirty by then—close enough for lunch, in my mind—so I walked back to Café Paul. I took my place in the lineup. Fortune or fate or some other force acted in my favour, for when it was my turn, there was Calla facing me behind the counter.

"Bonjour, Calla," I said, greeting her with a smile.

"Ah, encore, monsieur," she replied.

I assumed she meant I'd been in for breakfast not all that long ago.

"Vous connaissez mon nom," she continued.

I sheepishly pointed to her name tag.

"Ah oui, bien sûr," she replied. "Comment vous appelez-vous?"

I was pretty sure she'd just asked me what my name was, as opposed to those other basic questions we all learned in French class. You know, like what time is it? What's today's date? What are you wearing? What is your dog's name? Did you eat the chocolate cake?

"Jack," I said.

"Jacques," she corrected.

"Ah oui, Jacques."

"Bonjour, Jacques."

"Bonjour, Calla."

I'll spare you my halting attempt at ordering, but I somehow managed to secure a ham and cheese croissant, a lemon tart, and yet another café au lait. I thanked Calla and sat down at my usual spot by the window. I pulled my book back out from my backpack and continued reading while I munched. Man, the ham and cheese croissant was unbelievable. Such flavour. For a time, I was lost in a gastronomic reverie.

"I can't believe you're reading that book," a woman's voice said in perfect English with a lovely English accent.

I looked up to see a beaming Calla, no longer wearing her Café Paul T-shirt but instead a black sweater, jeans, and a dark brown leather jacket. Clearly her morning shift had ended. It took me a minute to process that she might not be the native Parisian I'd assumed she was. She just waited, smiling as always, as I tried to catch up.

"You speak English. You are English," I said. "I had no idea."

"I'm a Brit through and through, but I live here because it seems that Paris is where I'm supposed to be."

"Your French is beautiful—at least it sounds beautiful to me," I said. "And I really appreciate that you don't immediately switch to English when you hear my appalling accent."

"Nonsense. Your French is perfectly understandable and acceptable," she replied. "I respect your efforts to speak in a language that is not your own, and I just don't want to discourage you by switching to English."

"Um, merci, mademoiselle."

"De rien, monsieur," she said. "This may sound forward, but would you mind if I joined you and your wonderful book?"

I only then remembered her opening comment. I looked at the book in my hand.

"Of course not. Please. Sit."

I stood up and pulled out her chair as my mother had taught me when I was very young.

"Do you know Callaghan's work?" I asked.

She just nodded and sat down.

"Are you a Callaghan fan, too?" she asked.

"Yes, but not just Callaghan. My interest is fueled by a broader fascination I have with Paris in the 1920s. You know, the Lost Generation, and the seismic impact they had on the literary and artistic landscape. All that stuff intrigues me."

Her eyes widened.

"Wow. I can't believe you just said that, and with such eloquence, too. It seems we're both seized by that era," she replied, shaking her head and smiling all the while. "Wait a minute, is this a set-up? Are you stalking me?"

"Um, ahhh, no, not at all. I live nearby, and I just like this café and, you know, Paris in the 1920s . . ."

"Relax, I'm just kidding around," she said, beaming at me. "But I was serious when I said we share an interest in the Lost Generation. Starting in 1920 my grandmother owned an apartment not far from here that she passed on to me. She lived among the Lost Generation—they were her friends—and it changed her life."

"No way!" I said. "You're kidding! That's amazing. That is, um, wonderful! Very cool."

"Wait, there's more," she said, reaching into her purse for her wallet. "Morley Callaghan was a favourite of my grandmother's. She knew him and his wife, Loretto, when they lived here in 1929. I promise you that what I'm about to tell you is the absolute truth.

My full name is Callaghan Hughes, named for Morley Callaghan, courtesy of my grandmother."

With a flourish, she flashed her passport to back up her claim. It read *Elizabeth Callaghan Hughes*.

"I'll leave where the Elizabeth comes from for later. I don't want to overwhelm you," she said.

"Holy shhh . . ."

"It's okay, you can say *shit*. I'm familiar with the word and am not offended in the least. I've even been known to hurl the term around myself, along with other more colourful profanities. Such a rich language we have."

"Why, thank you," I replied. "Holy shit! I can hardly believe I'm sitting with someone whose grandmother befriended the Callaghans here in Paris a century ago. Such a wonderful connection to that era. What's more, here I am, on the Left Bank, talking to you, a woman named Callaghan in honour of that friendship. I'm overwhelmed. This is a lot to take in."

I made a mental note always to call her Callaghan, in tribute to a fellow Canadian writer.

"Even here in Paris, I've not met many people who still care about those halcyon days," she replied.

"And you know the word *halcyon*! Where did you come from?"

She smiled and picked up my book to hold, almost to caress.

"I still can't believe you're reading this book. It's one of the lesser-known memoirs of that time."

"Yes, but it's written by a fellow Canadian, one of our most famous writers," I said. "So, like many Canadian success stories,

Callaghan and his memoir both deserve more recognition and profile than either has earned thus far."

"So you're Canadian," Callaghan said. "I should have known."

"Really? Why?"

"You just don't seem like a brash, jingoistic, self-absorbed American. We get a lot of them in here."

"I'm many things, but I like to think that brash, jingoistic, and self-absorbed aren't among them," I said. "Plus, as far as I know, Canada is still part of the Commonwealth family, so we're practically related."

"An important bulwark against the creeping cultural hegemony of the U.S. of A."

"Right. The last line of defence!" I said, my clenched fist in the air. She laughed. "First *halcyon*, and now *hegemony*. If this were a job interview, I'd already have made you an offer."

"And I didn't even know you were hiring."

We both laughed.

"Okay, I'm dying to hear more about your grandmother," I said. "I mean, if you don't mind. She sounds very cool."

Sitting and talking with Callaghan just felt so comfortable, natural, easy.

"My grandmother defined cool, in so many different ways," she began. "I'll give you the abbreviated version or we could be here all day."

"I've got nowhere to go," I said, a little surprised at my own comment.

"My grandmother was Constance Stanley, a name that just seems to fit the 1920s, doesn't it? She was born in 1902 into a wealthy but stifling family. She was expected to marry the son and heir of another rich English dynastic family, but she wasn't very good at doing what was expected of her. She was what you might call a problem child who seemed not to recognize any form of parental authority. She had her own ideas, interests, and plans—plans that involved Paris. She made such a nuisance of herself at home that her parents finally succumbed to her incessant requests to spend her eighteenth summer in Paris. Her father figured it would be a calm and pleasant season on the home front if Constance was across the channel in Paris. Rather than pay for a hotel, they did what most rich Brits did at the time, when real estate was so cheap in Paris—they bought her an apartment on the older, more affordable Left Bank. It's where I live now, more than a hundred years later."

"How extraordinary. Man, those were the days," I said, shaking my head. "They bought an apartment on the Left Bank for their daughter and bought themselves some familial peace at the same time. A win-win, as they say."

"I like a man who can use *familial* correctly in a sentence," she replied. "So, my grandmother arrived in Paris in the late spring of 1920, just for the summer, and didn't return home to England for a decade. She basically refused to leave Paris, and I don't think her parents minded very much."

"How did she live here at such a young age?" I asked. "Did she work?"

"Nope, her parents funded the whole thing, though she didn't really live that extravagantly. She was an aspiring poet, but she knew in her heart that she wasn't good enough to make it a career.

So she focused on meeting the right people and insinuating herself into the community of Lost Generation expat writers and artists that made that period so fecund and fertile."

"'Fecund and fertile.' That's so much more impressive than using *familial* properly, not to mention the alliterative bonus."

She threw her head back and laughed freely, loudly, without inhibition. Others in the café glanced her way, but I didn't care, and Callaghan certainly didn't.

"But how did she get back to Paris after returning to England?" I asked.

"Even when she did finally come home, in the fall of 1930, she still kept her Left Bank apartment. She knew she'd make it back to Paris one day. She eventually agreed to marry Sir Edward Best, the scion of a local wealthy family. It wasn't exactly a love match, but it did yield one daughter—my mother. Then Sir Edward died at quite a young age and my grandmother inherited all of his worldly goods. Without a financial care in the world, Constance took it in stride and raised her daughter on her own. But as soon as my mother married, Constance reverted to her maiden name, pulled up stakes again at fifty-something, and fled back to Paris, where she lived out her days in the city she loved."

"Wow," I said. "What an incredible story."

"Well, she was an incredible woman," she said, looking wistful. "I really loved her. Despite what her strained relations with her parents might suggest, she was kind and empathetic, and always helpful to those around her. She was certainly very good to me. She was more than my grandmother. I thought of her as a kindred spirit."

She paused and looked out the window with a faraway look in her eyes.

"Anyway, I've prattled on too long already. I'll tell you the whole story sometime. We have not yet scratched the surface."

"Okay, we can leave your grandmother, but only for the time being. But what about you?"

"Short version now, longer version later," she said.

"Agreed."

"I grew up in the same stifling, wealthy family but thankfully seemed to inherit my grandmother's rebelliousness. I left home right after finishing a graduate degree in fine arts. I'm an artist, a painter. My apartment doubles as my studio. I've lived in Asia, Australia, and also for a time in Mexico City, but have always come back to Paris. It's my true home, my centre. I've spent most of my adult life right here. Even as a teenager, I'd spend my summers here with my grandmother. When she died in 1989 at eighty-seven years old, she left me her apartment. She'd told me for years that she was going to, but I never knew if she was serious. Turns out she was. I've been here ever since."

"What about your parents and siblings?"

"Only child," she said, pointing to herself. "And both my parents, with whom I never really connected, are now gone. All right, enough about me. Who are you? I just know your name is Jack."

"Jack McMaster. I'm a freelance writer from Toronto and am realizing a long-held dream by spending five months living in Paris, a city I've never visited before despite being a little obsessed with it."

"Hence the Callaghan memoir."

"Right. I have a son, Will, who is twenty-seven years old, a chef, and an emerging recording engineer. He lives at home with me."

Callaghan was looking quizzically at me, waiting for me to complete the story of our family.

"Oh, right," I said, looking down at the table, suddenly feeling the weight of the last two and a half years. "Yes, um, as for his mother, well, that's a sad story . . . um, perhaps for another time," I said, trying to swallow the lump that had suddenly germinated in my throat.

"Of course. I'm sorry, Jack," she said, briefly touching my wrist. "Changing the subject, how old are you now?"

That question caught me a little off guard, though I knew the answer. I paused and pushed the lump down, trying to regain my balance.

"I know I may not look it—please tell me I don't look it—but I'm sixty-two."

She didn't bat an eyelash.

"You misunderstood my question, Jack, though I can see how you easily could," she started. "I'm not interested in how many years you've been walking this earth. I want to know how old you are."

I still didn't understand, and my look must have made that clear.

"Do you feel sixty-two years old?" she asked.

"Absolutely not."

"Do you self-identify as a sixty-two-year-old?"

"Definitely not."

"Can you believe you're sixty-two?"

"I cannot."

"Right, then. Tell me how old you are in your head."

"Oh, like when I'm not thinking too hard about it, how old do I think I am? How old do I feel?"

"Yes, exactly."

"Thirty-five."

She gasped and brought both hands up to her mouth.

"Me too!" she whispered. "The very same. Thirty-five."

"Um, how many years have you been walking this earth? Not that it matters much, given that you're really thirty-five."

"Fifty-six."

"No way!" I said, shaking my head. "You look much closer to your own perceived age than to your actual years."

"Well, you don't look sixty-two, but who really cares? Who we are and what we do are what's important, not how old we are."

"Nice. I like that," I said. "Um, I was just about to walk over to Shakespeare and Company. I haven't visited there yet. Would you like to go with me?"

I don't know what came over me. That was about as bold as I'd ever been.

"I love that bookstore, and would love to go sometime," she started. "But I volunteer Wednesday afternoons at an immigrant support centre off Saint-Germain, and I should probably get moving."

"Oh? What do you do there?"

"There's French language instruction all afternoon, so I keep the students' children occupied until their classes are over."

"So, how do you keep them occupied?" I asked. "Poker? Karaoke? Square dancing?"

"Ha! No, but I'll add those to my list," she said, laughing. "I teach art classes."

"Right, you're a painter."

"Yes, I am," she replied. Then her eyes widened. "Hey, we're always looking for models. Would you consider coming and sitting in a chair, or standing against a wall, maybe gazing into the distance, for an hour some Wednesday afternoon?"

"Uh, do I have to be naked?" I asked, thinking of my modest but still-there pandemic paunch.

(Damn, and there's number ten leaping up into my lap at the worst possible time! Like most aging men, I've discovered that my metabolism seems to slow down with each passing birthday. I suspect others have discovered this, too. I used to be able to eat anything I wanted without gaining any weight. Then I turned forty and my body said "all right, the free ride is over," or something to that effect. In my forties I gained ten pounds. In my fifties I gained another five—or maybe it was ten. I seem to carry the extra weight in two places—my neck, and my belly. Tough to hide extra weight when you wear it on your neck and your gut. So when I see myself in photos now, my double-chin-in-training and my well-established abdominal roll make me feel like I'm no longer thirty-five, and more like sixty-two. So there you have it. Only ten things make me feel my age. Ten isn't a big number, right? I mean, it's not like it's eleven or twelve.)

"Naked?" she replied. "Jack, these are adolescents and teenagers, I'm not sure they're ready for that yet."

"That's just fine by me. I'm not sure I'm ready for it either," I said. Then I heard myself saying, "I think I could pose for a while some Wednesday afternoon. I just need to shoehorn it into my very busy schedule. Somewhere between my lunchtime pain au chocolat and my twilight pain au chocolat."

"Oh, that's fantastic!" she gushed, clapping her hands. "Thanks so much. So maybe next Wednesday afternoon, then?"

I nodded.

"Oh, that's brilliant. That is great news. The kids are getting tired of drawing the janitor," she said. "And then we can consider the naked modelling idea after we see how you do next week."

She stood to leave.

"Well, Jack McMaster, that was a lovely little interlude in my day. Will I see you here tomorrow?"

"Yes. This is my spot."

"Great. Until then."

I realized after she left that she'd made me laugh several times in the preceding half hour or so. She was kind of wacky, in the best possible way. My body actually felt different—energized somehow—after the laughter. I hadn't had much cause for laughter lately. I'd nearly forgotten what it felt like, until an English café worker named Callaghan reminded me.

I watched her leave. I liked how she walked. She stopped and spoke to the old woman seated on the cardboard outside the door and gave her some money. After she'd crossed the street and started walking up towards Boulevard Saint-Germain, she turned to look back at me. I smiled and waved. She stopped, then jumped up and down like a little kid, laughing and waving back at me. She then returned to her adult persona and carried on her way. She was different.

Something else changed that day. From that moment forward, all the Café Paul counter staff stuck to French when taking my orders. A Callaghan kindness, I was sure.

—

On the very edge of the Left Bank, Shakespeare and Company faced the Seine just across from Notre-Dame. It's the most famous English-language bookstore in Paris, and the successor to the original bookshop started by Sylvia Beach back in 1919. I'd read books about S&C, including *Time Was Soft There*, and also Beach's own memoir. But of course, I'd never been. It only took me about ten minutes to walk from Café Paul to the bookstore. It was a magical place. Unlike any other bookstore I know of, this one takes in young literary vagabonds and gives them a roof over their heads in return for working in the store. Aspiring writers have come from around the world for a stint at Shakespeare and Company. The store is a bit rundown, overstuffed with books, downright chaotic in places, and almost always crowded. I loved it.

I explored every nook and cranny of the store. In almost every corner there were rolled-up mattresses and bedding that would be unrolled and made up after closing time for the kids who worked there. The new books were out at the front, with the older, used books filling the back of the store and the second floor. As I turned to climb the stairs, I noticed a quotation in large letters painted on the wall. It read *Be not inhospitable to strangers, lest they be angels in disguise*.

A wonderful sentiment and a good rule to live by. The quotation's provenance is a bit hazy. Some attribute it to Yeats, but the international consensus seems to be that it's from the Bible—the book of Hebrews, I'm told. Regardless, it's a lovely expression.

I didn't buy any books during that visit but knew I'd be back often. No need to rush. Just take it in and savour it.

CHAPTER 8

CAREFREE AND KIND. Those were the two words that came most often to my mind when I thought of Elizabeth Callaghan Hughes. And I thought of her often. I didn't mean to. It just happened. In the week since Callaghan had first sat down at my table, we'd repeated the rendezvous daily, as soon as her morning shift ended. By our third get-together, it felt like we'd been friends for years, not days. She just had such an easy, open, and warm way about her. My mother would have described her as a "free spirit." Nothing seemed to get her down. She was always upbeat and optimistic. Often before joining me, she'd bring a croissant or a baguette to the old woman—Callaghan told me her name was Clementina, a Romani name meaning "merciful"—who was a fixture on the sidewalk outside the café.

Wednesday afternoon, following our daily conversation, while sharing a ham and cheese baguette, we set off for the immigrant support centre, just off Boulevard Saint-Germain. It was a sunny but cool day. Perfect for an afternoon stroll. We gabbed to one another all the way, touching on a range of topics, from how evolution could ever come up with the bizarre praying mantis to the interesting relationship between Gertrude Stein and Alice B. Toklas. We could pretty well talk about anything. It was an exercise of learning and laughing, but heavy on the laughing. She seemed to have a boundless range of interests. I liked that. I liked that a lot.

The centre was in an old building on a side street. Imagine that—an old building in Paris. But this one was a little tired, a little rundown. After all, it was a community-service hub for newly arrived immigrants. It was not the executive suites of the Banque Nationale de Paris.

Callaghan and I stood in the foyer as students, mainly mothers and their children, entered before splitting off. The parents turned left into the language classroom on one side of the foyer, while their kids turned right into the art room on the other side. When all were present and accounted for, Callaghan took my hand and led me into the art room. She wasn't being romantic or overly familiar but rather just practical. She wanted me to accompany her into the room, so she innocently grabbed my hand and led the way. It was not a calculated move. Having said that, the warmth and softness of her hand felt—well, it felt really nice. Human touch. I'd missed it. I hadn't held hands with anyone since, well, since Annie. I trailed Callaghan into the room, my hand in hers. She guided me to a chair at the back and then moved up to the front of the room. Most of the dozen or so kids, ranging in age from about fourteen to nineteen, spoke better English than French, but were fluent in neither. Callaghan skillfully used both languages to ensure they understood her but also improved their French.

The kids then set up their easels and fixed large sheets of paper to them using big metal bull clips. The easels were arranged in a circle, in the middle of which sat a table with a chair resting on top. Callaghan indicated they were ready for me. As I walked towards the table in the centre, the kids clapped, I assumed because I was not the janitor. Again, Callaghan took my hand, this time to help me up onto the table. Again, I registered her hand touching mine before I settled into the chair. She crossed my legs and had me bring my hands together in my lap. She asked me in a whisper not to move if at all possible. In a blend of French and English, she introduced me as a Canadian friend on my first visit to Paris. They were all looking at me intently. I broke the "don't move" rule briefly to wave and smile—kind of an ice-breaker—before returning to my statue stillness.

Callaghan then led the group in a brief demonstration of technique, her charcoal flying across her paper as she showed them the proper way to sketch various parts of the human body—in this case, my human body. The kids started sketching, with Callaghan wandering among them offering one-on-one advice and encouragement. I was able to follow most of what she was saying, particularly when she spoke in English. At one point, as she demonstrated to one young woman the technique for capturing the subtle shading on the wrist as it flows into the arm, she stepped over to me. She lifted my arm and showed the group how supple the connections were between hand and wrist, and wrist and arm. I was wearing a short-sleeved shirt, so my bare arm was at her disposal.

During this, she ran her fingers up and down my arm, deep into her instruction, and held my wrist as if it were an inanimate object. But it wasn't inanimate at all. In fact, it felt quite animate to me, thank you very much. Human flesh and bone. My human flesh and bone. As when she had held my hand earlier, it was not lost on me that her very innocent, even educational, human touch felt good on my skin. I was reminded again how important human touch is to our species, or at least to me.

One young woman, likely around eighteen years old, engaged Callaghan in a discussion in broken French and English. In the course of their conversation, the young art student gestured my way and said two words that I recognized. I heard her say "sans vêtements." You know my French has a long way to go, but I knew what "sans vêtements" meant. I snapped my head around to lock eyes with Callaghan, but she put her hand on the young woman's arm and said, "C'est dommage, mademoiselle. Mais il est impossible et totalement inapproprié. Jack n'est pas un mannequin professionnel."

I was relieved to learn that my clothes would be staying on, given that I'm not a professional mannequin and all.

I survived my debut performance as an artist's model. Callaghan said I'd done an amazing job, and who am I to question her judgment on the matter? I can now add sitting very, very still to the list of things I apparently do well. It was nice watching from my frozen position how she interacted with the kids. She was just as comfortable dealing with them as she was with her customers at Café Paul, or with me. I decided that to be that at ease with such a broad cross-section of people meant that she was at peace with who she was and what she believed.

When the French classes were over next door, the parents gathered their sons and daughters from the art room. The kids took their charcoal sketches of me with them. Only a few of them looked remotely like me. When they'd gone, Callaghan hugged me and thanked me for giving up an hour or so of my time. The hug felt nice.

The next day, we broke our routine of sitting and talking at Café Paul after her shift. Instead, she took me to Les Deux Magots, just a five-minute stroll away on Saint-Germain. I was excited to be there. Most of the Lost Generation writers at one point or another had frequented this famous café. Hemingway in particular liked to write there. His favourite table is marked by his photo hanging on the wall behind it. We lucked out and arrived just as someone was vacating the Hemingway table in the corner. Just sitting there was a thrill.

At Callaghan's suggestion, we ordered what the English translation of the menu described as "a selection of matured cheeses from our regions." My cheese tastes tend to be limited to medium cheddar with an occasional foray into the exotic realm of Gouda. So it was a revelation to me not only that I agreed to this menu item, but that I loved every different cheese on the plate—none of which was cheddar or Gouda. One expands their horizons when in Paris, or perhaps when one is with Callaghan Hughes.

"You promised to tell me where the Elizabeth in your name comes from," I reminded her as we devoured the cheese.

"Yes, I did, didn't I?" she replied. "Well, this may sound a tad far-fetched, but I assure you it's the gospel truth and is even recorded in my grandmother's diaries. My parents were hopeless at coming up with name options for me, so they sought her advice.

When she suggested Callaghan she did not connect it with Morley and Loretto, knowing that my parents really had no interest in Paris of the 1920s, let alone literature. So she claimed it was an old family name that would have some meaning if it were given to me. As for the Elizabeth, my grandmother said she proposed it because it seemed to flow nicely alongside Callaghan Hughes."

"But I assume there's more to it," I suggested.

"Indeed," she replied. "Hadley Richardson—her maiden name—and my grandmother were good friends. Because of her loyalty through those tumultuous early Paris years, my grandmother despised Hemingway for cheating on Hadley and then divorcing her. Elizabeth was Hadley's first name, and it's no coincidence that I now carry it as mine."

"So, thanks to your grandmother's subtle subterfuge with your parents, you are named after Hadley Richardson and Morley Callaghan. I can't tell you how amazing I think that is. Extraordinary."

"Well, few would believe it, but I do have the documentary evidence should it ever be called into question."

"You have your grandmother's diary?" I asked.

"Diaries, plural. I have many volumes."

"Do you think that maybe, at some point, I might be able to see them or even read them?"

"Well, let's just see how it goes, shall we?" she replied with what I interpreted as a mischievous smile. "So, when we met, you said you felt like you were thirty-five years old. What has kept you feeling like you're thirty-five?"

It wasn't the first time I'd thought about that, but to at least give the impression that I wasn't about to trot out a practised, carefully contrived response, I looked up to the ceiling—you know, wracking my brain, giving her question serious consideration. Then I lowered my eyes to hers.

"Curiosity," was all I said.

Her eyes widened in surprise, her mouth agape.

"Was that the wrong answer?" I asked, a little concerned with her reaction.

She maintained her startled look but slowly shook her head.

"I've asked so many people that question in the last ten years or so, and none has given me the answer I've been looking for. Until today."

"I don't know what to say."

"You are the first to share my belief in the boundless power of curiosity," she said, with some gravitas.

She then rolled up her sleeve and turned her arm to show me a small tattoo in lovely cursive script. It read *The cure for boredom is curiosity. There is no cure for curiosity. Dorothy Parker.*

"My grandmother loved Dorothy Parker and would recite that all-too-true line over and over like a mantra."

"I've never heard that quotation, but I love it," I said. "It's a much classier and clearer representation of curiosity than a tattoo of a dead cat."

It took her a beat or two, but then she laughed.

"Very nice," she said, nodding her head. "Clever boy."

We spent the next hour tackling the deep, unanswerable questions that I've considered often, without ever drawing any conclusions. Is curiosity cultivated or innate? Why does it feel so invigorating when we get turned on to something new? Why had curiosity played such a role in *our* lives when it had no real impact on so many others?

When we seemed to have exhausted the topic, Callaghan put her hand on my wrist.

"I like you," she said. "So, what else keeps you thirty-five?"

"Well, I still play ball hockey at least once a week, in a community league back in Toronto. That always makes me feel young," I said. "In fact, my carefully constructed and continually tested theory is that ball hockey is a time machine, at least for me. When I'm playing, I can't concentrate on anything other than the immediacy of the moment. I am utterly focused. And to me, playing today feels just like it did when I was ten or fifteen, or twenty-five or forty-five. The game stays the same and when I'm playing, I feel just as I did playing decades ago. Perhaps it's not really a theory, but I have given it a lot of thought."

"Oooooh, I love the concept of a familiar activity being a time machine. That works perfectly," she said. "I guess it could be anything we've done our whole lives. Say, singing, or baking cookies, or reading favourite books, or playing hockey. Whatever. They all transport us back in time. Brilliant!"

On the spur of the moment, Callaghan and I decided to make the short walk over to the Church of Saint-Sulpice, just a few blocks southwest of where Rue de Seine meets Boulevard Saint-Germain. Of Catholic denomination, the original Saint-Sulpice was built back in the thirteenth century. But the current version was built in the 1600s and is now the second-largest church in Paris.

I could sense Callaghan watching me as we entered through the heavy but quite ordinary wooden doors. Her scrutiny was rewarded, as I nearly gasped when we stepped inside. The interior space was enormous, with giant stone columns supporting the high vaulted ceiling. We sat down quietly in two of the hundreds of wooden chairs provided to accommodate the congregation and stared at the stone beauty surrounding us. It was breathtaking.

"What an incredible space," I said.

"I thought you'd like it."

"I'm pretty sure this is the church where Hemingway came in desperation when he was plagued with a bout of impotence shortly after marrying Pauline Pfeiffer. He prayed here for divine intervention, and it seems his prayers were answered. When he returned home, Pauline was waiting and, according to Hemingway, 'we made love like we invented it.'"

Callaghan burst out laughing but quickly restrained herself. Several other visitors glared our way.

"What an absolute prat he was," she said, stopping short and looking at me, I assume in case I was offended.

"Don't worry. I couldn't agree with you more, if I understand what a prat is," I replied. "He was a revolutionary writer who lived in a fascinating time, but that doesn't mean he wasn't a grade-A jerk."

Callaghan looked relieved.

"Hmmm. I just realized I told you a story about Hemingway and Pauline's sex life," I said. "Apologies. That was a little offside and probably not something I should have raised."

"Ha! You're hysterical, Jack McMaster," she said. "Fear not. I find discussing Hemingway's sex life to be far more interesting than his novels."

We wandered aimlessly through the streets surrounding Saint-Sulpice until late in the afternoon, when it was time for Callaghan to leave for a meeting with a gallery owner.

We stood at the entrance to the Mabillon Métro station back on Saint-Germain.

"Hey, while I'm thinking of it, I have to attend an art exhibition opening tomorrow evening at a gallery near the Sorbonne," she said. "Would you like to meet me there and maybe we could grab a bite to eat afterwards?"

I found myself answering before even thinking about it.

"Hey, thanks. I'd like that. It's time I learned something about art, anyway. Maybe you can help with that."

"Great!" she replied with a full-wattage smile. "I promised to be there a bit early, but you can arrive any time after seven."

She gave me the address, hugged me, and hustled down the stairs to the Métro. I walked back to my place and called Will to check in. All was well on the home front. Ariel was with him, again. I liked that. She looked very much at home bustling around the kitchen behind Will on my FaceTime screen. The more I saw and spoke with Ariel, the more I liked her. Will deserved the happiness she seemed to be bringing him.

I arrived at the gallery shortly after seven. It looked like a small but elegant storefront operation—until I was inside. Then I saw that it opened up towards the back and was actually quite large. There were lots of fashionably—or fancifully—dressed beautiful people taking in the art, sipping on champagne, and nibbling on exotic hors d'oeuvres that did not look like any identifiable food I'd ever seen. It didn't take me long to realize that this wasn't just any art show Callaghan had invited me to. It was *her* art show. My first hint was the eye-catching, larger-than-life photo of her hanging on the wall just inside the door. Her name ran across the bottom in a large, flowing, almost swirling font that screamed class and sophistication. We're not talking Comic Sans here. The words *Paysages urbains* were emblazoned across the top. If I'd already seen the paintings, I could have translated the show's title by inference. But I hadn't yet checked out the art, so Google Translate told me the show was called *Cityscapes*.

There were about forty beautifully framed paintings on the walls, and they were all Callaghan's. She was the only artist showcased in the exhibition. Each painting featured the distinctive, but certainly not showy, signature of Callaghan Hughes in the bottom right-hand corner. I think the best way to describe my reaction at the time is thunderstruck. Yes, I was thunderstruck.

The paintings themselves were of a certain realist style—a term I just made up meaning the opposite of abstract. If you were squinting at them from afar, they might seem at first blush to be photographs. They were stunning and featured street scenes from four very different cities—Paris, Singapore, Melbourne, and Marrakesh. Despite my fascination with the Lost Generation, I was not drawn to the art of the era. The works of Picasso, Matisse, Dalí, Man Ray, and others who had made visual art in Paris a century before just did not appeal to me. But, man, I really liked Callaghan's paintings and was nearly knocked off my feet by her obvious talent. Even an artistic philistine like me could see it.

I quickly scanned the gallery space for Callaghan but didn't see her. Well, that's not quite true. I saw her but just didn't recognize her. I'd only ever known her in a Café Paul T-shirt or post-shift casual attire, so my eyes passed right over the tall, elegant, and arresting woman in the blue form-fitting dress and matching blue high heels. My ignorance of women's fashion prevents a more informed description. She'd already struck me as a lovely and beautiful woman when I'd first encountered her at Café Paul. But that evening, at her own art exhibition, she was lovely and beautiful on an entirely different scale.

She saw me look right through her, so she waved, beamed, and headed right over to me. When she smiled, I finally recognized her.

"You made it," she said, giving me a hug and then keeping her arm hooked through mine.

"I'm just trying to process both what I'm seeing on the walls and what's now on my arm," I said.

"Sorry, I just didn't want to make a big deal out of this," she explained. "I suppose I could have been a little more forthcoming with the details of the show."

"Well, it is a big deal," I said. "And you look, um, amazing. Not that you don't always . . . well, you know what I mean."

"Ha! Very smooth, Jack," she replied, laughing. "I get it. You've really only seen Café Callaghan. Tonight is one of the rare occasions when Couture Callaghan emerges from her chrysalis. But it's not exactly my thing. Just playing the part for the show."

"And your art," I gushed. "I love it. I'm not just saying that. I think it's stunning."

She said nothing but squeezed my arm and pressed her head against my shoulder.

Likely because Callaghan had British roots and perhaps a following in her home country, the cards describing the paintings were in both French and English. And when the gallery owner—a Brit—clinked her glass and called the room to order, she spoke in both languages. (I'll just stick to the English.) She motioned for Callaghan to come closer to the front and she did, leaving my side, but seemed reluctant. I'm pretty sure it had more to do with having to speak to the crowd—a terrifying prospect for many—rather than the pain and misery of standing further away from me. The gallery owner spoke.

"Welcome, ladies and gentlemen, to Smithson Gallery and the new Callaghan Hughes exhibition, *Cityscapes*. I'm Dorothea Smithson," she began. "We've all been eagerly anticipating this new collection, and I know you share my view that it is simply wonderful and extraordinary and reflects a maturing artist at the top of her game. Her technique is exquisite and her commitment to detail and colour and perspective and composition has been pushed into an even higher echelon than in her previous work. Having shown her for many years now, I have so enjoyed watching Callaghan beginning to take her rightful place among leading contemporary artists. And not only is she a gifted and supremely talented artist, but many of you will know that she is also just such a delight in every other way."

I glanced at Callaghan then and watched her look down and blush, leaving the "aw, shucks" implied. It was clear to all that this was not false modesty. This was a humble person obviously uncomfortable in the spotlight yet looking like a star.

"The four cities Callaghan has captured in these pieces are all very different. You can see her technical ability to capture diverse places and cultures in a way that invites you right into the scenes themselves. Now, to descend into the commercial for just a moment, all of these paintings are for sale this evening—in fact, many have sold already. So please speak to anyone on the gallery staff or me—we're all sporting pink name tags so we're easily found—and we can process the transactions. The turnout tonight tells me that the value of these paintings is on the rise even as we stand here admiring them. Let me now introduce Callaghan Hughes to say a few words before we let you return to the real reason you're here, to view and perhaps acquire new paintings from my friend, the fine artist Callaghan Hughes."

Callaghan shook off her discomfort and moved up to stand next to Dorothea Smithson.

"My, I'm a little overwhelmed by all of you here and by Dorothea's very kind words. I want to thank you all for coming to see my work. I've lived in each of the four cities represented in these paintings and have done my best to capture not only the diversity and contradictions inherent in these special places but also the mood they engender and how it actually feels to be there, in the moment. I'm excited and grateful to share my work with you, and I want to thank my friend Dorothea and Smithson Gallery for always being so supportive of my artistic journey. Thank you all again for coming."

We all applauded as Callaghan turned to embrace Dorothea. Then a squadron of servers fanned out across the space to peddle more high-end appetizers and champagne. Callaghan was swept up in a crowd of well-wishers, on which I did not want to intrude. So I took my time and stood in front of each painting, marvelling at what I was seeing. Each city's works were incredible, but my heart was lost to the Paris paintings. Knowing how Callaghan felt about the city, I was not surprised to see that twelve of her fifteen Paris paintings were scenes from the Latin Quarter. I liked them all but was utterly possessed by a smaller streetscape scene captured from what I was sure was an elevated position on Rue de Buci. I could see Café Paul and, further down, L'Atlas restaurant, along with the other cafés that gave the street such a warm and welcoming vibe. In my mind, it was a quintessential Left Bank scene. Worried I'd missed my chance, I buttonholed a gallery staffer with a pink name tag and discovered it was still available. I bought the painting on the spot. It was not inexpensive, but I really did love it and the bonus of knowing the artist made it an easy call.

In hindsight, I honestly wasn't trying to ingratiate myself with Callaghan. I felt no obligation to purchase one of her paintings. At least, I didn't think so. I just loved that Rue de Buci scene. My sense of Paris was perfectly captured in that one eighteen-by-twenty-four-inch frame. Okay, fine. I admit it. I also found myself drawn to Callaghan. I liked her in a way I couldn't yet quite define. I just knew that when we were together, I thought about her. And when we weren't together, I thought about her. It was a feeling that was unfamiliar to me, or at least one that I'd long forgotten.

As the event wound down, Callaghan was occupied thanking everyone and hugging many as the crowd thinned and eventually dispersed into the Paris evening. After she'd escorted the last visitor to the door, she turned, closed her eyes, and took a long, deep breath. When she opened her eyes again, she was looking at me, still standing in front of the very first painting I'd ever bought. She came over to me and once again looped her arm inside mine as she looked at her, or rather my, painting.

"This is one of my favourites," she said. "I just love that view."

"Where were you when you painted it?" I asked. "It's not a street-level perspective."

"Well, I painted it in my studio, but the photos I worked from were shot from a fifth-floor window of Hôtel de Buci. The concierge there, Sanjay, is lovely, and he let me photograph the scene from one of the rooms."

"It's amazing," I said. "I'm so blown away by all of your paintings, but this one is special."

"Well, the good news is, the show was a success. Everything sold, and Dorothea says that doesn't happen very often."

"Callaghan, that's fantastic, congratulations!" I said, hugging her. "Wait a sec. So what's the bad news?"

"It's not bad news. It's just, the tough part of this work is that I labour over these paintings, and then someone buys them, and I never see them again. It's hard. I get attached to them."

"Well, you can come and look at this one anytime you like," I said.

Her eyes widened.

"You bought this one?"

"I did," I said. "I had to. It's perfect. It's my quintessential image of Paris."

She threw her arms around me and kissed my cheek. I didn't know what to do so I just hugged back.

"You are a saint," she said. "This was the one I was really worried about losing. I almost pulled it from the show, but Dorothea talked me out of it. Now it's safe with you. I couldn't be happier."

"I'll take good care of it, and visiting hours are quite flexible," I said.

"Don't go anywhere," she said. "Just stay right here."

She broke away to speak with Dorothea. At one point she pointed to me and to the painting. Shortly thereafter a gallery worker came over and took the painting away. I'd been told I could pick it up the next day, but a few minutes later, the same gallery worker returned with the painting wrapped up securely and handed it to me. Then I watched as Callaghan embraced Dorothea again before walking over to where I stood.

"Okay, let's go," she said, grabbing my free hand—the one that wasn't holding a brand-new Callaghan Hughes painting. "I have to get out of these medieval misogynous torture devices."

Back on the street, Callaghan immediately stopped and put one hand on my shoulder for balance while she removed her high heels. Then she pulled a pair of flat sandals from her purse and onto her feet.

"Much better," she said as we started walking again. "You're not busy right now, are you?"

"I'm in your hands, or rather, hand," I said, looking at my hand in hers.

She laughed and swung our arms up and down, together.

"I just want to get out of this dress and have a glass of wine," she said. "My studio is not far from here. What do you say? Fancy a glass of wine?"

"Lead on, as long as I can bring my new painting with me."

We crossed back over to the north side of Boulevard Saint-Germain and walked a little ways along Rue de l'Ancienne-Comédie. We stopped in front of an old wood-and-glass door as she dug for her keys. It was a lovely building, a classic five-storey Paris apartment block with a small café on the ground floor. We entered and squeezed into the tiny elevator. When it opened on the top floor, there was only one door beckoning from across the corridor.

"Your studio occupies the entire floor?" I asked.

She smiled at me a bit sheepishly.

"My grandmother knew a good real estate investment when she saw one."

Callaghan opened the door and waved me in. Wow. The large, open space featured a lounge area, a dining area, and a fully equipped modern kitchen. A small powder room—if that's what you call those small sink-and-toilet-only bathrooms—was just to the left of the front door. The floors looked to be the original light-coloured hardwood. Above us, the high ceilings were supported by original wood beams, spaced at regular intervals. Large windows, flanked by billowy, sheer white curtains, faced onto the street. A low glass table sat beneath the window with a framed photograph of an older woman sitting in an easy chair, a painting hanging on the wall behind her.

"Is this your grandmother?"

"None other," Callaghan replied. "That photo was taken in this very room."

Bookcases were built into the far corner of the lounge area. The furniture looked super-comfortable. The couch and its overstuffed cushions were calling my name.

"It's wonderful. What a place to live."

"I've been very happy here, ever since I first came to spend a summer with my grandmother when I was just a teenager," she said. "Let me show you the rest that you can't see from here."

She once again took my hand—she seemed to like holding my hand, and it felt natural—and led me through the lounge area to an arched French door of glass and wood. Beyond it there was a spacious bedroom, a large ensuite bathroom with all the modern conveniences, and a generous walk-in closet. It was all beautiful. Finally, off the other side of the lounge area was a smaller door that opened into a large room that was obviously her studio. I made that call after seeing several easels, a long workbench, and stacks of canvasses leaning against the far wall, some unfinished and plenty not yet started. Here, large windows opened onto the interior courtyard. The light was wonderful. Everything was wonderful.

"Your apartment is spectacular," I said, and meant it.

"Thanks. I sometimes forget how lucky I am to be able to live and work in this space," she admitted.

"It's a lovely space in which to be marooned with your paints and palette."

"Okay, how about that Bordeaux I've been saving for a special occasion?"

"How nice of you to consider my visit a special occasion."

"Well, yes, there is that, but I may have been thinking also of the art show," she replied.

"Forgive my twisted sense of humour," I said. "Believe me, I know we're celebrating your great artistic triumph tonight, but I do think we should include my recent acquisition of a Callaghan Hughes original in our festivities."

"Well, that goes without saying."

By this time, she'd poured two glasses of Bordeaux and led me over to that very inviting couch. I sank into the cushions, far deeper than I'd expected. Very comfortable. She sat down next to me and curled her feet up under her. It was not lost on me that her knees were nudging my thigh.

"You look very, very happy," I commented.

"I'm positively joyful," she replied. "I never in my wildest dreams thought we'd sell every piece. But it happened. I'm still recovering."

"That reminds me," I said as I leapt up and grabbed my new painting from its spot leaning against the wall next to the door. "I have to see this again."

I opened the rather extensive wrapping and set the painting on the easy chair opposite the couch so we both could see it. Then I resumed my place on the couch, restoring the contact between her knees and my leg.

"I really love that. I'm excited to have it."

"I'm so glad it's yours. It makes me happy," she said. Then she turned to look me squarely in the eyes. "But I'm still trying to get a handle on you. Still trying to figure you out."

She was smiling almost dreamily as she said it, but there was a serious ring to her tone that had me a little worried I'd done something wrong.

"I mean, you're smart, kind, curious—as we've discussed—young at heart, and you're funny, which in my experience is all too rare."

"So far, so good," I said, with not a little trepidation.

"But below the picture-perfect veneer, beneath the surface, I sense melancholy. It shows itself from time to time. A sadness. An emptiness. An uneasy reserve at times. It's almost as if your humour is a shield, so others don't notice what's roiling underneath. The sadness feels newish, fresh, even a bit raw, like you're not yet yourself again."

She put her hand on my arm as she spoke.

"If I'm right, I'm so sorry that you are hurting. Because, as I've said before, I like you. Plus, you just bought one of my paintings, so I kind of feel compelled to be nice to you."

Without that last line, I may well have burst into tears. She'd read me like a book. Her funny line at the end gave me the emotional outlet I needed. I laughed instead of the less desirable alternative. I nodded my head for a few more beats to gather myself. Then I put my hand on top of hers and turned a bit so I could look at her.

"You are very perceptive," I started. "And I haven't even started to be funny yet. I used to be the funniest guy in the room, but I haven't been that person for a couple of years now."

She stayed silent and waited.

"Annie, my wife of thirty years—Annie Barnes was her name—died in April 2020, one of Toronto's earliest COVID deaths."

Callaghan recoiled and drew both hands to her mouth.

"I couldn't even be with her in the hospital. I couldn't hold her hand or touch her face. The hospital was not far from our home, but it might as well have been on a different planet. She was alone in a crowded hospital, and . . ."

I stopped talking, knowing that my voice, not to mention the rest of my composure, was about to break. Callaghan, ever kind, knew where I was and filled the air.

"Oh, no, no, Jack, I'm so sorry. No wonder you're not fully yourself after that tragedy. How could you be? You don't have to explain anything. I'm sorry if I was prying. I'm just trying to know you—to know who you really are."

"No, it's okay. I'm glad we're having this conversation. It feels right," I said. "Annie understood me so well that she even told me in a video from her hospital bed, just hours before she died . . . well, she told me not to stop living because she was gone. Not to be defined by her passing. She understood me better than I did myself."

Callaghan had tears brimming in her eyes. That just about made me lose it again, but I held on. She moved her hand from my arm and placed it on my hand, not in an aggressive *fear not, I'm here now to save you* way, but just gently and quietly. I sat for a minute or so saying nothing, collecting myself, feeling the warmth of her hand. I took my time before resuming. Callaghan let me.

"I've had a lot of help from my son, Will. He's strong and we're close. It was he who encouraged this trip as part of helping me, you know, somehow come back from Annie. I've also been given so much love and support from the guys I play ball hockey with. I know that may sound weird, but it's much more than a ball hockey league. We've been together for years now. It's a community of good friends who really care about one another and look out for one another. I'm not sure I'd have made it through without them."

Callaghan squeezed my hand but didn't let go.

"Annie sounds like an extraordinary person who loved you very much. When and if you're ever ready and comfortable, I'd love to hear more about her. Jack, my heart breaks for you," she said.

"Thank you. You would have liked her, and she would have liked you."

"And I'm impressed with your hockey buddies. They sound like a special group," she said. "It's good to know that guys can come together like that and be there for each other."

"They have lifted me up so often in the last two and a half years. I really am lucky to have them."

"Okay, well, that's a good start," she said. "Thank you for telling me, a relative stranger."

"You're not a stranger," I said. "Not anymore."

"I've had some pain in my life, too, but I don't think it's on the same scale as you've endured," she said.

"Pain is pain," I said. "Maybe you'll tell me about it sometime."

"Maybe I will."

I said good night about an hour later, after rewrapping my new acquisition to keep it safe on my walk back home. Standing at her front door, Callaghan held me for a long time. Then she kissed me once on the cheek.

"Are you okay, Jack?" she asked. "Do you want me to walk with you?"

"I'm much better now," I replied. "You're a great artist and a pretty good listener, too. I'm just fine to walk home. Thank you, though."

Then she kissed me a second time, on the other cheek, while her hand cradled the back of my head. I tend to remember details like that. Always have.

CHAPTER 9

CALLAGHAN INSISTED.

"Are you sure?" I asked. "It's just a bunch of sweaty and smelly expat guys and a couple of women—of course, they don't sweat, they glow—playing ball hockey in a parking lot. It's not exactly a compelling spectator sport if you're new to the game."

"I am new to the game, and that's precisely the reason I want to watch," she said. "Curiosity."

I couldn't argue with that and didn't really want to. I'd just told her about my weekly game on Rue Descartes. I couldn't tell whether she was curious about the sport in an academic sort of way or looking to learn more about something that was a big part of my life. I guess it could have been a combination of the two, but regardless, she was set on coming. Obviously, I had to bring my A-game that day and keep up appearances.

My Amazon orders had arrived the previous week and I'd spent the requisite inordinate amount of time taping my stick, so it was just as I liked it. There is a science to stick-taping that I've always taken seriously, even though there's little empirical or even anecdotal evidence to suggest my game has benefited from the ritual. (Having been taping my stick in a certain, very particular way for more than thirty years, I concede that *ritual* is an appropriate term.) So I was all set for the game. And apparently, so was Callaghan.

Perhaps it was her innate curiosity, but Callaghan had this childlike sense of wonder that I found very endearing. She seemed constantly amazed by what she saw in the world around her and it showed in her charming, unfiltered reactions. And even with all the negative, malevolent, destructive forces at play in the world, she still sustained this optimistic, glass-is-half-full perspective that was rare for someone in her mid-fifties. And only a few days following her triumphant, sellout art exhibition, she still had the mental bandwidth to get excited about watching a ball hockey game in a Latin Quarter parking lot.

I confess I was a little nervous playing with Callaghan watching from the bleachers, or rather a parking curb. It brought back memories of being in high school, when my girlfriend at the time would come to watch my house league games—to clarify, those games were on ice, and the relationship didn't last. I liked my new sticks and they performed well for me. In the warm-up I blistered several snapshots and a few slapshots that actually hit the net where I was aiming. I did no happy dance to celebrate my shooting prowess but just maintained my cool, I-meant-to-do-that demeanour.

The very same complement of players showed up again that

week. I introduced Callaghan to them all—I was pleased that I'd remembered which names were attached to which faces. She was her usual charming and witty self. We threw our sticks in the middle and one of the guys divided them up to create the teams. Then it was game on. I held my own in the early going, setting up my teammate Julie for a couple of goals, and potting two myself. But we gave up three goals in the process. So it was a close game. Callaghan clapped, hooted, and hollered when our team scored, shouting encouragement to our players by name. Such a Callaghan thing to do. My teammates loved it.

At about the halfway point in the game, I heard what sounded like a muffled cellphone ringtone—that's because it actually was a muffled cellphone ringtone. Our goalie had mistakenly left his phone in his pants pocket before pulling on his equipment. This made answering his phone challenging to say the least. Finally, he dispensed with discretion and decorum and thrust his hand down the front of his hockey pants. He rooted around for a while and finally extracted his cellphone. By then it had stopped ringing, which our goalie found quite irritating. He was standing there glaring at his phone when it started to ring again. He answered and turned away to deal with the call. After he hung up, he walked over to his enormous hockey bag—goalies carry a lot of equipment—and started pulling off his pads.

"Sorry, guys, my son fell and cut his forehead," our goalie explained. "It needs a stitch or two, so I have to bail and get him to the hospital."

"Can your wife get him there and then you can meet them at the hospital after the game?" asked one of the other players.

Our goalie just looked at the guy and shook his head.

"You're not married, are you?" he asked. "This is a shared responsibility, and a ball hockey game does not take precedence over my lacerated seven-year-old. Sorry, but I gotta go."

"Right, of course," the other guy backpedalled. "I guess we're done. Can't play with one goalie."

"I'll play," Callaghan said, raising her hand. "Leave your equipment and I'll play."

"I don't know," one of the other players said.

"It's just standing in the net and letting the ball hit you, right?" Callaghan said.

"Well, there's a little more to it than that," the goalie said. "Otherwise, goalies wouldn't always be such extraordinary athletes."

Then the other goalie chimed in.

"Just leave your stuff and I'll drop it off at your place later."

By this stage, our goalie had almost fully shed his stuff.

"I'm good with that," he said. "Thanks. It'll save me some time getting to the hospital."

With that, he dashed to his car and peeled out of the parking lot.

"So, how about it?" Callaghan said. "I'm up for trying."

"Are you sure?" I asked. "It's not as easy as it looks. And you might be overcome by the smell itself."

"Well, surely I'll be better than no goalie," she argued.

"Fair point," I replied. "Okay, let's give her a shot."

Everyone nodded in agreement.

She was already pulling on the equipment. I helped her, because there's a certain order to be observed in donning a goaltender's kit. You can't put your hockey pants on if you've already strapped on the pads. I learned that the hard way as a kid. Our goalie's equipment was not just smelly but sweaty, too. I don't mind my own perspiration and aroma when playing, but I draw the line at immersing myself in someone else's stench and sweat. Apparently, Callaghan had somewhat lower standards.

"Everything's so big," she giggled as she struggled to put on the equipment. "Do I have to wear this, too?"

She held up our goalie's jock strap.

"Um, I would if I were you," I said. "That ball packs a punch."

She dutifully pulled it on.

Ten minutes later she was fully kitted out, though she was swimming in the equipment. I'd tightened everything I could, but she still seemed to disappear in the jersey and chest protector and shoulder pads. She laughed with glee when she slipped on the mask, and I adjusted the straps so she could actually see out of it.

"Mmmmmmm, this smells just wonderful," she said, still laughing.

"Yes, we call it *essence de hockey bag*," I said as I led her over to the net.

"Okay, this is your net. Your job is to protect it," I explained. "Just stand in a slight crouch, with your stick on the ground and your catching hand raised, and focus on facing the shooter directly, head-on. If the shooter passes to another player, shift to face the new shooter. Half the work of playing in goal is positioning yourself in the net so you're as big as possible. It's all about not giving them much net to shoot at."

"Got it," she said, nodding her head. "Face them head-on, make myself big. That's a plan."

The game started up again. My teammates and I did our best to keep the ball out of our own zone to minimize the shots Callaghan would face. But inevitably, the play shifted to our end of the parking lot. She did remarkably well. You could tell by the way she moved in the net that she was well coordinated, even athletic. She played without fear. The shots fired on her came in hot and hard, but she faced them without once flinching. It's possible she never saw the shots, but there was no flinching. She managed to put her body, or her hands, or her stick, or occasionally her face, in between the ball and the net. Every time a shot hit her and bounced harmlessly away, she'd shriek with delight, even when the shot ricocheted off her mask. After a while, she even started to trash-talk the other team, in a pleasant, amiable way.

Of course, she did let in several—okay, maybe a dozen—easy goals. But she also made some spectacular saves, whether fluky or not—and admittedly, most of her saves involved at least a bit of luck. But she was true to her word. She was much better than no goalie, and she clearly earned the respect and camaraderie of the other players. She was quite excited by the end, and hugged her teammates and the opposing players, too. She gave a memorable performance and it made me like her even more. As we walked back to her apartment, she asked thoughtful questions about the game and her play and offered her own informed observations about the experience. She was sweaty and smelled like most humans would after playing ball hockey for an hour in someone else's stinky equipment, but she didn't care. She just seemed exhilarated by it all.

—

"I'm going to head home and grab a shower," I said when we reached her door. "I'm either smelling you or me, but either way, a shower seems like a good idea."

"But you're coming back, right?" she asked. "The best pizza in Paris is being delivered at seven o'clock, and you don't want to miss that."

"Count on it," I replied. "I'll be back to celebrate your startling and memorable debut in net."

"Hey, did we win the game?" she asked.

"Let's just say you were a big winner and not worry about the score."

"Probably wise. See you in a bit," she said, squeezing my hand. "I don't really think a hug is a good idea right now."

"Well, not the way you smell," I replied, shaking my head.

"You're not smelling me, you're smelling our first goalie and his rancid pads," she said. "I always smell lovely."

"Fair point, but the moratorium on hugging still stands, at least until I get back to your place."

She just laughed.

I hustled home as fast as my post–ball hockey body could carry me. And that wasn't very fast. My legs were stiffening up, and my feet were sore. I knew why. When you're growing tired late in the game, you tend to slap your feet down on the pavement when you're running rather than purposefully placing them. So later on, your feet hurt. In this case, my feet hurt.

Watching the clock, I lingered in a very hot shower for as long as I could. But I didn't want to be late returning to Callaghan's. By the time I'd returned, my body felt a little more like my own—the next day, however, would be another story.

We sat on her couch again, drinking wine as we waited for the pizza, jazz from the 1920s playing in the background. It was nice. Callaghan was leaning against me, and it felt right. Annie was never far away—would never be far away—but that didn't seem to conflict, in my heart or my head, with what might or might not be happening with Callaghan. Annie had seen to that.

I refilled our glasses and sat back down. Callaghan again leaned against me.

"You know, I would never rush you into anything, given what you've gone through—what you're going through," she said, almost in a whisper. "You are in full command of this situation. I will just note that if or when you feel like we might have something here, something between us, you already know that I like you. I felt it in my gut when I first laid eyes on you. And if I'm reading the signals correctly—and as a Pollyanna, I don't always—I think you like me. But you clearly had something very special with Annie, if I can say her name. It seems that you and she were meant for each other, were made for each other. I never want to compete with that. I never could compete with that. Annie is irreplaceable. But maybe, just maybe, there's room somehow, sometime, for something more. It's in your hands. I'm in your hands, but I won't push, and I won't pressure. You're vulnerable. I'm vulnerable. Let's just do what feels right, when it feels right."

When she started talking about Annie, I very nearly lost it again. That had been happening a lot. I no longer had much control over my emotions. I'd noticed this long before Annie's brief illness. It was another manifestation of aging. Yes, okay, I see it now. There's another. That would be number eleven in my growing list of things that actually do make me feel my age. At thirty-five, I could go to funerals or watch tragic, heartbreaking movies or read sad, sad novels and never feel at risk of crying. Not so much now. At sixty-two, my tear ducts now operate on a hair trigger, and you never know what might set off the waterworks. So, eleven. Just eleven. It's not like there are forty-seven. Just eleven.

Callaghan was still leaning on me but had fallen silent. I waited until I knew I could speak without my voice quavering. In the meantime, I reached my arm around her and pulled her in a little closer. Still felt right.

"I honestly don't know how this happened. It almost feels fated. I mean, I saw you on my first full day in Paris. What are the odds?" I started. "And what's happened in the weeks since has been, well, it's been amazing to me. You are amazing to me. I don't know much right now. I'm still sorting out what's happened already, what's happening right now, and what might happen in the coming weeks and months. But I do know one thing with crystal clarity. Before we met, the notion of a new relationship seemed utterly unthinkable. That has changed in the month since we met."

"Wooohooo! So you're saying there's a chance!" she said, pulling back to look at me.

I laughed and nodded my confirmation. Then, with Hollywood timing, the entrance buzzer sounded, signalling that the best pizza in Paris had arrived to rescue us from a heavy moment.

I soon understood why Callaghan considered this the city's best pizza. It really was good. Soft, cheesy, and filled with flavour. I learned that night for the first time that I loved caramelized onions on pizza. I ate far more than I should have but rationalized it with the knowledge that I still had to walk home.

When Callaghan got up to refill our wine glasses, I headed over to the built-in bookshelves. Normally books were my first stop when visiting someone's home, but I still hadn't checked out Callaghan's. Most of the shelves held art history books, which I guess made sense in an artist's studio. I also saw several shelves of books about Paris in the 1920s, many of which I also owned, including a dog-eared paperback copy of her namesake's *That Summer in Paris*. Along the top shelf was a collection of about two dozen leather-bound volumes. They looked old. Turned out there was a logical explanation for that.

Callaghan returned with our refilled glasses and sat back down on the couch. I pointed to the upper shelf.

"Can I ask what those leather notebooks are?"

"Ahhh, you have struck upon what is of greatest value in this room," she started. "Those, Jack, are my grandmother's diaries from June 1920, when she'd just arrived in Paris at the age of eighteen, through to November 1930, when she returned to her family home in London—though the diaries are silent on what prompted her return to England."

"Extraordinary," I said. "Have you read them?"

"Every word, and more than once," she said. "It's a who's who of expat Paris, recounting one adventure after another, with my grandmother in the middle of it all."

"She sounds . . . incredible. I wish I could have met her somehow."

"She was a true original. A feisty feminist long, long before the movement entered the mainstream. Her family tolerated and financed her decade in Paris, I believe because having her at home making everyone else miserable was not an appealing prospect. So in Paris, in the 1920s, she lived the artistic life of the amateur poet and salon aficionado. How I wish I could have seen and done what she saw and did."

I figured the time was right.

"I know we haven't known each other for long," I began. "But I would dearly love to read those diaries if you don't think the invasion of your grandmother's privacy would be too much. I've read so much about Paris a century ago, but mostly from historians. Of course, we've all read A *Moveable Feast*, but Hemingway wrote that thirty years after his initial stay in Paris, and we now know that his version of the truth may have only a passing affiliation with what really happened. So to read a first-hand account from one who was right there in the midst of it all would make me a fly on the wall. It's the next best thing to being there. I would love that."

"Jack, of course you can read them," she said, as if surprised that I'd thought she might say no. She sprang from the couch and stood on her tiptoes to retrieve the first volume. "I have an early start in the morning, so I'm going to bed, but please, plunk yourself down on the couch and read to your heart's content." She kissed me on the cheek and disappeared into her bedroom.

"Good night. And thanks for this, um, this privilege," I said, holding the leather-bound notebook.

I followed her instructions and immediately sat back down on the couch, sipped my wine, and read the first volume. Simply put, it was amazing. There were snippets of her poetry but more than that, there were vignettes vividly describing wonderful scenes, including some with familiar figures. The young woman of means, Constance Stanley, had a gift for language and writing, and turned an honest and often entertaining eye to the people and events around her. And she was blessed with more than her fair share of chutzpah. Later in the volume, in the spring of 1921, she saw the famous American poet Ezra Pound walking along Rue Jacob. She described it this way:

> *I recognized Mr. Pound and his red hair immediately, even from across the street. How fortuitous! I decided in that moment I was not going to let this poet out of my sight. Seize the day and seize the poet! He stopped a little further down Rue Jacob and entered a large and beautiful sandstone (I think) home of no fewer than six floors. I was close behind him, and with the front door open, I could hear music and the unmistakable sounds of clinking glasses and gay dancing. I am quite familiar with the sounds of celebration. It was a raucous party that sounded near its zenith. After Mr. Pound disappeared into the house, I hastened up the steps and, giving the impression of one who belonged, I simply pushed open the door and entered. I daresay my heart was beating a storm.*
>
> *Without unduly blowing my own whistle, I looked like I belonged at that party. As good fortune would have it, I was wearing my favourite slim, drop-waist, lavender dress topped by my new cloche hat, the kind that's all the rage in*

the cafés and dance halls of Paris. I swiftly snared a drink from a tray on a foyer side table. I have no idea what it was, but it did tickle my nose. I gulped it down to steel my nerves and snagged another. Then I introduced myself to Ezra Pound, who'd been watching me since I'd crashed the party. I stuck close to him until the celebration wound down many hours later. I learned I'd invaded the home of the American heiress Natalie Barney, who was hosting this so-called salon, though to me it very much resembled a grand party.

Endearing myself to Mr. Pound was my mission, and I set myself on it, and on him, with vigour. By the end of the evening, I'd wrested a commitment from Mr. Pound to review some of my poems. I am well aware that as a young and not unattractive woman of some means, doors occasionally open for me, though far fewer than were I a man. When they don't, I fling them open myself, as I did tonight. But I'll not apologize for employing my wiles and guile to make for myself an artistic life in this most artistic city.

Wow. How could you not love Callaghan's grandmother from that one passage alone? I was wide awake and wanted to read more, but it was getting late. Callaghan had gone to bed at least an hour and a half earlier. I'd been so excited about digging into her grandmother's diaries, I hadn't thought through my exit strategy. Should I wake her up to say good night? Should I pop my head into her bedroom? Should I just turn out the lights and leave? Many questions, few answers. I carefully put the leather notebook back on the bookshelf. Then, on a whim, I pulled a later volume off the shelf and opened it at a random spot. My eyes fell upon the entry for a day late in January 1926. Strange. I didn't know what I was looking at. I stared at the neatly boxed line of gibberish for a long while. It didn't look like any foreign language I knew.

WO pnuvre: Fvk cnprf rnfg bs Cynpr qr yn Pbapbeqr. Gbc. Yrsg raq-obneq.

What was this? What did it mean? Was Constance experimenting with magic mushrooms at the time? Was she so inebriated in that moment that she'd lost her ability to form real words? No, I didn't think so. The indecipherable notation was neatly written and carefully boxed. That made it seem deliberate. It could be a code of some kind, but to what end? While the text was utterly impenetrable to me, still there was something about the look of the line that somehow felt, well, almost familiar. I couldn't explain the feeling. I wrestled with the conundrum for another quarter of an hour before giving up. It was late and I was tired.

I returned the leather volume to its place on the bookshelf and turned out the lights. It felt weird to leave without letting Callaghan know, so I tiptoed to her open door and leaned into her bedroom. She was lying on her side on the far side of the bed, facing the window, her bare shoulders emerging from the sheet and coverlet. Through the window, a streetlight illuminated her face, serene and beautiful. It was the face of one at ease with herself. It was only then that my eyes strayed to the unoccupied side of the bed. She had turned down the sheet and the pale blue coverlet. I was quite sure it had not been that way before she'd said good night.

I stood there in her doorway for a few minutes as I spun through the stay-or-go options so fast they were just a blur in my mind. Then a movement caught my eye. Still seemingly asleep facing the window, Calla slid her right hand to the spot where the covers were turned down and patted the mattress. Then I heard her voice, again just above a whisper, her eyes still closed.

"We don't have to do anything. Sometimes it's nice to hold hands with someone you really like, just for the comfort and the warmth."

That's when I started to cry. Shit. Outstanding timing. I didn't mean to. I didn't plan to. I didn't want to. I just did.

"Oh no, Jack, I'm sorry. I've botched it up. I said I wouldn't push you and this probably looks to you like pushing. Oh, bollocks." She sighed. "Hmmm . . . it kind of looks like pushing to me, too. I'm sorry. I don't want to be that person. I just want you to feel safe with me. But it's too soon, I know. I'm sorry. I'll shut my bleeding cakehole now. So sorry."

I got my little breakdown under control, then, in the dim light, pulled off my clothes—not all of them, I left my boxers on—and crawled in beside her. It just felt right. Different, unexpected, even strange, but right.

"Please, Callaghan, you've done nothing wrong. I cry at the drop of a hat these days. I cried when I scored a goal back home, before I flew over here. I cried at the last nature documentary I watched. I have no idea why, but I did," I explained. "I do want to be here, with you. I'm just working through a lot of different emotions and feelings I've never experienced before, let alone all at the same time. I'm trying to sort through them, navigate them, manage them, somehow. And you're actually helping me with that, whether you realize it or not."

In response, she just turned towards me and searched for my hand with hers. Her hand was so warm. I tried to focus my mind on the strange line of indecipherable text I'd just read in Constance Stanley's diary. Instead, I fell asleep almost immediately, Callaghan's hand in mine.

When I next opened my eyes, light was streaming through the white sheer curtains and falling in patches across the floor, across the bed, and, oh yes, across Callaghan lying beside me. Right. I remembered. I was nearly naked in Callaghan's bed. I could tell that she was completely naked, as she was pressed up against my back—I believe the term is spooning, if that's not too much information. In the morning light, I examined my mind, my thinking, my heart, my feelings, my gut, and every other internal resource I could tap for any indication that I'd made a colossal mistake, but none leapt out at me. I thought of Annie. I missed Annie, and in the same emotional spasm, I realized I really liked Callaghan, too.

Her arm was draped over my hip, her hand resting on the side of my thigh. Nothing had happened in the night. I would have remembered that. She'd made no exploratory moves and I'd stayed still, apparently deep in sleep. But now, in the morning, it was not lost on me that after so long, the physical human contact felt so good. I found it almost moving.

"Coffee?" she whispered.

Her voice had a way of calming my thoughts.

Not quite yet awake, I made a barely audible guttural sound in my throat that even I could scarcely decipher. She apparently knew right away that my monosyllabic uttering meant "yes."

"Be right back," she said.

She slid out of bed humming a cheerful tune and blithely walked to the kitchen, naked. I soon heard the sounds of drawers opening, spoons rattling, and cups being pulled from cupboards.

"Big noise," she warned from the other end of the apartment.

Then I heard the always grating and grinding sound of coffee beans being pulverized into powder. I knew she'd be back soon because the milk frother on her machine was doing its thing and that's usually the last step. I then heard her padding across the floor, and in she came bearing two cups and just as naked as when she'd left a few minutes earlier.

"Oh, sorry," I said, closing my eyes and then covering them with my left hand to reinforce my commitment to gentlemanly decorum.

"What? You know, ninety-one per cent of doctors surveyed say that drinking hot coffee with your eyes closed is hazardous to your health," she said, as the penny dropped. "Oh, I'm so sorry. I get it now. I'm making you feel uncomfortable. I'm an idiot. I should have told you earlier. I swear I'm not being provocative or promiscuous. This is not an entrapment stratagem. I'm barely conscious of it anymore. It's just that ever since I spent a summer in Sweden when I was twenty-six, I have completely shed the nudity hang-ups that seem so prevalent in England and North America. So you can open your eyes and take your coffee. I just feel more comfortable like this."

So I did. I mean, I didn't want to spill my coffee.

"I can put something on if you like."

"No, I think I can handle it, though I may still have some North American nudity hang-ups of my own to work through."

She casually sat on the edge of the bed beside me, and we drank our coffees and smiled at one another.

"This way, all my imperfections are on full display. I am an open book," she said.

I hadn't detected any imperfections at all, though I was doing my best to look her in the eyes.

"Did you know that when Churchill was visiting the White House during the war, Roosevelt accidentally walked in on him while he was in the bathtub?" she said. "As the story goes, Churchill apparently said, coolly and calmly, 'You see, Mr. President, I conceal nothing from you.'"

I laughed and so did she.

"Good line from a true master of the witty riposte," I said.

After a while, her unconscious manner and utter lack of inhibition made it all feel quite natural. It really did seem to be just part of who she was.

"Okay, I'll work on my North American nudity issues," I said. "But I doubt I'll be ready any time soon to model in the buff at your art class."

"I don't think that was ever in the cards, anyway. But you do have a great body, lean and sinewy."

"Ha! Kind of you to say, but not as lean as it used to be. COVID bequeathed what I call my pandemic paunch."

"You look good to me. I assume it's the ball hockey that keeps you in shape."

"Yes, and the DNA lottery win that came with several generations of taller, skinny forebears. Though after forty, those benefits seemed to diminish, even disappear."

"Well, I can see why you self-identify as a thirty-five-year-old."

"Right back at you," I said, still trying to keep my eyes focused on hers.

An easel with a canvas was set up in the bedroom, facing away from me. It had not been there when I'd slipped into the bed. Uh-oh, I thought.

"You didn't, um . . ." I said, pointing to the easel.

"I may have," she replied. "I woke up in the night and was struck by how the streetlight through the window fell across you."

"May I?" I asked, pointing again to the canvas.

She nodded and stood up from the bed and turned the easel, so the canvas faced me.

"Wow, that is incredible," I said, and meant it.

Rendered in charcoal, there I was, lying on my side, fast asleep, my head on the pillow, my arm crooked and resting on the mattress a few inches in front of my face. A slash of light illuminated my forehead, ear, eye, and part of my mouth and chin, with the rest of me in the shadows. It looked just like me. It occurred to me again just what a talented artist she was.

"It's so beautiful," I said. "Despite the model."

"Well, you know, I have to work with what I have on hand." She slipped back into the bed.

"Fair point."

From that night on, we alternated between staying at my little apartment and staying at Callaghan's studio. To be fair, we both agreed that the studio was much nicer, so more often than not, we stayed there.

"Son, it's Dad calling."

"Dad, we're on FaceTime. I can see you and I recognize you as my father."

"Right, sorry. Force of habit," I said. "How's everything?"

"It's great, Dad. Weather hasn't been awesome, but it is December in Toronto, so it's par for the course."

"Work is still going well?"

"I'm having fun and still learning a ton at Atchison's. You've been missing some solid meals here at home."

"So, how's it going with your friend Ariel?"

"Still going strong. And, yeah, I was going to mention, she's been staying over now and then. Hope that's okay."

"Son, you do not need my permission to have her stay over. I'm really happy for you. She seems like a great person. Good on you, Will."

"Thanks, Dad. Yeah, she's very cool. I'm happy."

"Listen, Will, while we're on the subject, um, I've been meaning to mention something to you," I began. "Um, I wasn't expecting this to happen, I wasn't looking for this to happen, I wasn't trying to make it happen, but it seems I've met someone. Someone I like more each time I'm with her."

"*Yes!*" he shouted. "That's just fantastic, Dad! I'm thrilled for you."

"Well, that's a relief. I was worried about telling you."

"Come on, Dad, you should not have been worried," Will said.

"I'm happy for you, and, you know, Mom would be pleased, too. She probably is."

"Thanks, Will. That means a lot."

"Okay, I need details. What's she like?"

"Well, she's a real free spirit. She's an artist, a painter, who is very different from your mother and very different from anyone I've ever, um, been with. We discovered we both share an interest in Paris and the Lost Generation. Her name is Callaghan Hughes."

"Cool handle," Will said.

"Very cool. In fact, it gets cooler," I replied. "She's actually named after Morley Callaghan."

"You're kidding."

"Nope, her grandmother lived here in Paris in the twenties and was good friends with Callaghan and his wife."

"Well, she sounds like a great match. How old is she?"

"Twenty-two."

"*What?* Really? You're kidding!"

"Of course I'm kidding. But I must say, your shocked reaction hurts a little," I joked, and Will laughed. "She's fifty-six but lives like she's thirty-five, and could probably pass for forty-five."

"So, do I get to meet her when I'm in Paris?"

"Of course, unless it all goes off the rails in the next few weeks, but I see no storm clouds on the horizon. I want you to spend time with her. I have no idea where this is going, if anywhere. I'm just going with it, day by day. But your view of her is important to me. I think you'll like her. And I know she'll like you."

"Dad, this is such good news. You deserve it. Does she know about Mom and me?"

"Yep, I came clean early and she's still around. So I take that as a positive sign."

"Great, Dad. Just awesome. Can't wait to meet her. I'm serious. Good for you."

That was just the reaction I was hoping for.

After finishing up my call with Will, I again turned my mind to cracking that coded diary entry that I'd found on my first night at Callaghan's. It felt like the answer was orbiting just out of my reach, but I also had a strong sense that I was close and would eventually figure it out. I'd just have to be patient and the answer would strike me. Or perhaps I had it all wrong and the garbled text would elude me forever. I really had no idea. Just a feeling that felt almost like faith.

CHAPTER 10

CALLAGHAN INSISTED, again. Last time it had been about watching me play ball hockey. This time it was about her desire to hear me play my guitar and sing some of my own songs. She'd asked me repeatedly after spying my guitar in the corner of my apartment. Though I'd talked about music and its important role in my life, she'd not yet heard me play. I was quite sure missing out on Jack McMaster's greatest hits had not compromised her life to date in any major way, yet still she insisted. I understood. As soon as I had learned that Callaghan was an artist, even before I'd discovered she was in fact a talented and accomplished artist with considerable commercial potential, I was very keen to see her work. Curiosity alone was reason enough, but when you discover that you care about someone, the need to figure out just who they are, where they come from, and what has shaped them is even greater.

Yet when you care about someone, the need to perform well for them increases—whether it be with a hockey stick or a guitar—and, in lockstep, so too does the anxiety.

So, with trepidation that bordered on panic, I slid my guitar—a lovely, slim, and compact Yamaha APX-5A acoustic-electric—into its hard case and walked it over to Callaghan's "flat," as she called it, true to her British roots. I also packed some courage for what would follow. Why? Well, to be honest, I don't care much about what people I don't know might think of my music and my voice. I'm not a seasoned performer. Unless you happened to be wandering through my bedroom or bathroom at just the right moment, you likely wouldn't know there was any music in my life at all. Believe me, I'm comfortable enough in my own skin and objective enough in my own self-assessment to know that neither my voice nor my guitar-playing is up to a professional standard. I've known that for years, even decades.

Yes, I've always had a realistic view of the role music plays in my life. It's a satisfying and enjoyable hobby that I would never attempt to take beyond the recreational realm. I was not labouring under any delusions about my musical prospects. Yet I just knew that when playing for Callaghan, I'd be feeling nervous, and worrying about what she might think if I fell short of her expectations. That told me something about my feelings for her.

When I got to her apartment, I cracked open the courage I'd brought. It was a lovely bottle of Beaujolais. I poured us each a glass, though mine was a much heftier serving. I drank it down fast.

"Won't that affect your playing?" she asked as I refilled my glass.

"Likely, and probably my singing, too, but not as much as my inherent anxiety at the prospect of playing for you. So I've opted for the lesser of two evils, which in this case is three glasses of wine administered over a very short time period."

"Why are you nervous? You're not playing at the Stade de France in front of eighty thousand fans. You're just playing for me," Callaghan said.

"Exactly. For me, it's not the number of people I'm playing for—it's more about the particular person for whom I'm playing. Without getting too confessional here, the more I care about someone, the more nervous I am to play for them," I explained. "The question that orbits in my head is, how will you feel about me after I butcher a few songs?"

She laughed, thinking I was joking, then realizing I wasn't.

"Chill, Jack. Relax. Any interest I have in you is not so shallow that it'll be affected by how well you sing or play guitar. Surely you don't think that."

I drained the second glass of wine.

"Well, when you put it that way, it does sound a little juvenile, or superficial," I admitted. "But yes, I do think that. I like what we have here. So I want you to remember I'm not trying to break into the music business as a solo artist. That's not the goal. I just like playing guitar, writing songs, and singing them in the privacy of my own company. It makes me nervous to have an audience, even an audience of one, and particularly when *you* are that audience of one."

"Well, I'm honoured you'd boldly confront your performance anxiety for me," she quipped. "But regardless, I'll still be here, even if you can't carry a tune in a plastic beach bucket."

"Okay, that calls for more wine. If only I had a plastic beach bucket."

She laughed again. She had this way of throwing her head back in amused abandon when she laughed. Utterly unfiltered, unselfconscious, uninhibited. Natural.

I proceeded to pour and then down my third glass. I could feel the alcohol relaxing me, calming me, filling me up with illusory resolve—you know, that aforementioned courage. Time to get started before my jangled nerves pierced my wafer-thin willingness to perform.

"So, what would you like to hear? A little James Taylor? Maybe some Eagles? Or even a Cat Stevens tune? Though you might be a bit young to know him."

"Hmmm. If you really want to play some covers and force me to compare your performance to James Taylor's or the Eagles', that's fine. Your call. But I'd much rather hear some of your own songs, because you undoubtedly perform them better than anyone else on the planet."

"Smart thinking. I see what you're doing there, pumping me up and all," I replied. "Very smooth. And, having just chugged three glasses of wine, I'm very nearly inclined to agree."

"Then it's settled," she said, patting my knee.

I played her three originals, three of my favourites. Two were songs I strummed on my guitar. They were more up-tempo. One was about an earlier relationship I'd had while in university, and the other was that more recent song I'd written about our ball hockey league, "More Than the Game." The third song was quieter and called for fingerpicking rather than strumming.

It was a more generic love song, written without anyone specific in mind. I just liked the chord progression and figured a love song fit the sound.

I was learning that Callaghan had an emotional side to her. I figured this out when I looked at her in the middle of "More Than the Game"—I'd been avoiding eye contact with her while I was singing lest I lose my place, my voice, my nerve, my mind, or all four simultaneously. There were tears streaming down her cheeks during the bridge, where I try to convey the idea that the weekly ball hockey game is not the most important part of playing in the league. Yes, she was crying—or at least tearing up—in a song written about a community ball hockey league for aging men. Thereafter, I made a point not to look at her again until I was finished. I was glad I'd avoided lifting my eyes to hers during the love songs.

"Sorry, Jack. I'm a mess," she said when I'd let the last chord ring. "First, you tell me you're purely a recreational, sing-in-the-shower kind of guy, then you hit me with three really melodic, meaningful, and memorable songs, played beautifully and sung beautifully. I feel like I've been set up."

I said nothing. I had no idea how to respond. So I just looked at her, which I was finding was a nice way to occupy my time. When she'd finished wiping her eyes, she motioned for me to put my guitar down. I excel at following instructions, so I gently lowered my six-string to the floor. Then she wrapped me up in her arms, squeezing me so hard I had to hold my breath for a short span.

"You are a very special man with very special gifts," she whispered in my ear.

"Well, if I'd known it was going to go that well, I would have played for you weeks ago, and perhaps limited my wine intake to two glasses."

She laughed and squeezed harder.

I did not play the first love song I'd ever written for Annie, "Until the New Year." In my humble, perhaps twisted view, it may be my best and is certainly my most meaningful song. But I wasn't ready to play it for Callaghan. I just couldn't. But as it turned out, someone else could.

A few nights later, we were both sound asleep in the wee hours when my phone rang, waking us both and perhaps even a few of Callaghan's neighbours for good measure. My hands seemed to be still asleep as they fumbled around the nightstand before gaining a tenuous grip on my phone. Despite feeling a little groggy, I was able to decipher the letters on my screen as the word *Will*.

"Will? Are you okay?"

"Sure, Dad, everything's fine," he replied. "Oh, oh, right, so sorry. It's the middle of the night for you, isn't it? Shit, sorry, Dad. I didn't think that one through."

"It's fine, as long as you're okay."

"Dad, I'm fine, but I have to talk to you about something kind of important."

That's the kind of opening that sets the wheels in one's mind a-spinning.

"Okay, and now—you know, three forty-five a.m.—is the best time?"

"So sorry, but yes, it's kind of urgent, and now that you're already awake . . ."

"Okay, son, shoot."

"Great, Dad. Okay, I've just texted you a download link for a song. I'm asking you to listen to it, without freaking out, and then I promise I'll explain everything, okay?"

Those wheels in my head were now spinning so fast they were smoking.

"Okaaaay, but you're kind of freaking me out a bit here."

"Dad, in my last sentence just a few seconds ago, I specifically asked you to listen *without* freaking out."

"Right. Okay, okay. I'll be back to you after I listen. Stand by."

I slipped my AirPods in and clicked on the link Will had texted me. An acoustic guitar intro started, one that sounded familiar yet at the same time completely new to me. Then the unmistakable voice of Jim Cuddy, Canadian country-rock singer-songwriter and ball hockey legend, started singing . . . my song? Yes . . . he was singing my song. In fact, it was "Until the New Year," the very song I'd written for Annie more than forty years ago.

Just to help with context, Will and I actually knew Jim. Despite being Canadian rock royalty, he'd lived in our neighbourhood and played in the ball hockey league for years. Wonderful guy, great musician, gifted singer, and no slouch with a hockey stick.

I don't think I was breathing as I listened. The song was fully and beautifully arranged for Jim's band, with bass, drums, two guitars, violin, and the perfect addition of sleigh bells in a few choice spots—after all, it was a Christmas song. There were new harmonies I'd never contemplated in the chorus, and a stirring violin solo. It sounded amazing. Jim's soaring voice in particular elevated the song to an entirely new plane. But I had no understanding of what had led to this.

"Will, what exactly is this, and how did it happen?" I asked after the final strains of the song died away.

"Dad, it's okay, just take a few breaths and let me explain," he started.

If we'd been in the same room, he would have been placing his hands on my shoulders to calm me down while he spoke.

"Remember when I asked you to send me the GarageBand file for your song, back in the fall before you left for Paris?"

"Yeah, I remember."

"Well, it may be that I, um, was not quite as forthcoming as I could have been. You see, I wanted to surprise you by remixing the whole song, adding some strings, bass, sleigh bells, and some harmonies. It was going to be part of your Christmas present," he explained. "So, I had almost finished all of that and was in the studio four days ago doing the final mix. I was listening to it back through the monitors when Jim Cuddy walked by the open door of the studio."

"Why was the door open?" I asked, trying to control my breathing.

"Dad, the studio is in an old house and the windowless studio I was working in is an overheated sweatbox. I was just trying to get some air into the control room," he replied. "Anyway, Jim stopped in the hallway to listen and fell in love with the song. He stepped in and asked about it and was shocked when I gave him the song's history. He said to me, 'You mean Jack wrote that song in 1981 for

Annie? It's a great song. Stands up over the years, the way all great songs do. It works because he was obviously truly in love.'"

"Wait a minute! Jim said that about my song?"

"He did, Dad. He did," Will replied. "Dad, think about it. You've played that song hundreds of times over the decades. You have no idea what it feels like to hear it for the very first time. Jim heard it for the first time and . . . well, um, Dad, he wants to release it. He's been looking for a Christmas single and has been coming up empty."

"What! You're kidding!" I said. "But it's already recorded? How did that happen?"

I realized in that moment that Callaghan, wide awake, had placed her hand on my arm and was watching me with elevated eyebrows.

"Dad, that was my idea, or my fault, depending on how you look at it. Jim asked me what he could do to persuade you to let him release the song. And I told him recording the song and letting you hear his take on it would be a start. So that's what he did. No one other than the band and I have heard it. I helped mix it. But it's completely up to you whether it's ever released."

My head was hurting from processing what I was hearing.

"Will, I just don't know. It's kind of a private, intimate love song for your mother. It's personal. Releasing it for the world to hear seems like a violation of some kind, a betrayal of your mother and our privacy."

I then remembered that I was lying next to Callaghan. I looked at her and smiled and whispered so only she could hear: "Everything is okay. It's all good."

"Dad, hear me out. Don't write it off just yet," Will started. "Mom loved you. She loved that song. She loved Jim and his voice. And she was proud of you as a songwriter, even if few others knew. I really think she'd want this to happen . . . for you."

I said nothing. I was mulling. I wasn't good at talking and mulling at the same time.

"Dad, one more thing."

"Yeah, I'm here, Will."

"You once told me that writing a song that made it to the airwaves had been on your bucket list since you were seventeen years old, when you wrote your first song on your first guitar," he said. "Dad, that was forty-five years ago. Isn't it time?"

"Man, you are good, son."

"So you're not pissed at me for this?" he asked.

"No, son, I don't think I am. At least not yet," I said. "I kind of see where you're coming from and how all this played out. I'm just trying to come to grips with it. It's a lot to take in. It's a shock."

"Yeah, but doesn't that track sound awesome?"

"It does, son. Wow, it really does."

After the call ended a few minutes later, I had to explain the whole thing to Callaghan, who was wide awake and nearly paralytic in her curiosity. I came clean. I had no choice, and I actually wanted to. I explained everything, including the story of the song, when and why it was written and for whom, and how Jim's stellar recording had come about. I worried a bit about how she'd react, that she might feel like she was somehow competing with Annie, or at least with her memory. But she just seemed excited and happy about it all.

"Jack, this is such good news and I'm thrilled for you. I don't want to intrude, but do you think I could hear the song?" she asked quietly. "I'm dying to, and I'm pretty sure this is not one of the originals you've already played for me. But I'd understand if you'd rather I didn't hear it."

I was both anxious about playing her such a personal song and excited for her to hear one of my own compositions recorded so beautifully by a true professional, a bona fide star, and his very tight band. I nodded, cued up the song, gently pressed my AirPods into her ears, and hit play.

I'd already learned that Callaghan was an open book. She wasn't very good at masking her emotions. In the dim glow cast by the streetlight outside her apartment window, I watched her cycle through a range of facial expressions as the song played. I could just faintly hear the track spilling from the AirPods, so I could connect her reactions to the lyrics.

When the acoustic guitar launched into the introduction, her eyes widened, and her mouth formed an *o* before morphing into a smile. That's how good and clean the intro sounded. Then, another expression of joy when Jim's voice cut in with the first verse. By the second verse, her mouth was closed, her bottom lip slightly protruding. On the lyric *and coloured lights frame my thoughts of you*, her bottom lip trembled. In the chorus that immediately followed, tears formed. They were my tears, but I did notice that Callaghan's eyes also glistened as she watched me and listened to my song.

When the recording finished, she turned to me.

"Again, please."

I hit play again for her.

When the song finished playing for the second time, she put her arms around me and whispered in my ear.

"That is a masterpiece. It's what a love song is supposed to be and do," she said. "You were so very lucky to love someone who inspired such heartfelt creativity and beauty and . . . longing."

That was one of the nicest things anyone had ever said to me.

We talked for a while about the decision I had to make—whether or not to let Jim release the song, my song, Annie's song.

"I know it's hard, but what would Annie think?"

I tried to sift through my feelings and how I truly thought Annie would react.

"Well, she loved Jim's voice and loved the song," I said. "I'm guessing she'd be pretty chuffed to hear it on the radio or at a concert."

"Right. Well, shouldn't that factor into your thinking?"

"Yes, I guess it should," I agreed.

"Jack, did you ever play her song for friends and family in Annie's presence?"

"Now that you mention it, several times over the years, and always at her request," I said, nodding.

"Clearly, she loved that song and was proud of its creator," she said. "All right, then, so what's holding you back?"

"I don't know."

"Let's listen to it again and pretend we're hearing it on the radio," she suggested, taking one AirPod from her left ear and inserting it gently in mine. "But when you're listening, think of it as a tribute to Annie, an homage to her, because that's really what it is. A testament to your love. Okay?"

I nodded as she held my hand.

We eventually fell back asleep. I woke up as Callaghan was dressing for her Café Paul shift. She sat on the bed to tie her shoes as I looked around her spectacular apartment.

"You don't really need to work at the café, do you?" I asked.

"If you mean, do I really need the money, then no, I guess I don't," she replied. "My great-grandparents bought this place outright before my grandmother even moved in a hundred years ago. My needs are not extravagant, and my art covers them, now. But being cooped up here all day, every day, with only easels, canvasses, paints, and brushes to keep me company is not my idea of a full life. I like people around me. I need people around me. I have lots of, I don't know what to call it . . . social energy that I need to bleed off before I can be my best as an artist."

"Right, I see. So you volunteer at the centre and pull morning shifts at Café Paul to make yourself a better artist," I suggested.

"Yes, and a better person, too, I hope."

"You are quite something."

"Yes, but I've never written a hit song that's going to be on the radio," she said as she kissed my cheek and headed out the door.

"Neither have I," I replied. "Not yet anyway."

A couple hours later, I was back at my apartment, working on a speech for a client, the CEO of a consumer packaged goods company who'd been invited to speak at a fancy Canadian Club luncheon in Montreal. It's hard to go all visionary, eloquent, dramatic, and insightful when outlining your company's first-quarter plans for growth in the adult diaper market, but that was my task. I'd managed to craft about ten minutes of the speech that I thought might hold together. It referenced the aging population and what that generation had sacrificed to help create a prosperous and stable economy. I confess I was struggling with how to close the circle I'd started and bring the audience back to incontinence products and the dignity we owe our seniors. It may well have been a bridge too far. What made it even harder was that my mind was elsewhere.

In the early afternoon, my phone rang.

"Hey Jack, are they letting you play any ball hockey in Paris?" asked Jim Cuddy, a voice I'd recognize almost anywhere, anytime, even when he wasn't singing.

"Good to hear from you, and yes, I've actually got a pickup game every Sunday afternoon in a school parking lot with a group of Canadians. You know, I'm playing right wing on the Left Bank."

He laughed.

"So, I haven't seen you for a while. How are you holding up?" he asked. "I know it's been really hard. I can't imagine."

"Thanks. Yeah, it's been tough, but I'm feeling better. Coming to Paris—Annie's idea—has been the change I needed. It feels like I'm becoming myself again, slowly."

"I'm glad," Jim said. "And all these years I've known you, I had no idea you were a songwriter. Will set me straight on that score, and I gotta tell you, 'Until the New Year' really is a beautiful, heartfelt, ballady love song, and it's right up my street. I think it's great. I wish I'd written it."

Wow. He'd written so many classic songs that most Canadians

could sing by heart at their local karaoke bar or when stuck in traffic. So hearing him tell me he wished he had written my song made me feel a little faint.

"Well, you made it sound so much better than any recording I've ever made of it," I replied. "Your version is fantastic. I love what you've done with it."

"Yeah, but making a great song sound great is easy. Making a mediocre song sound great is impossible," Jim replied. "Look, I spoke to Will, and I know he's spoken to you. I also know the history of the song and what it means to you and what it meant to Annie. I get that it was your love song to her when you were just starting out. And the song we'd like to release will still be your love song for Annie, but many more people will hear it and be touched by it. But it's completely up to you. If you have any reservations, we won't do it. It's your call."

"Jim, I'm honoured and not a little surprised you're interested in doing this. I guess I'm shocked, but I've talked it over with Will and, um, at least one other good friend, and you officially have my blessing. It helps that you knew Annie, and I know she'd be all over this idea if she were, you know, here."

"That is great news, Jack. Thank you. It's a special song, a true song, and it needs to be heard. And it will always be a song that you wrote and that honours Annie."

"Thanks, Jim. I mean it. Thank you," I said. "So how do we go about this? I'm in uncharted waters here."

"Well, if you're up for this, a lawyer will email you a document to sign giving you full writing credit for the song and all the royalties that come with that. Now, don't expect to be able to buy a

Lamborghini, but if the song connects with people the way I think it will, there'll be something in it for you. And remember, because it's a seasonal song, it should come back every year. The gift that keeps on giving."

And it was done. True to Jim's word, the paperwork arrived in my inbox a few hours later. I perused it quickly to make sure it reflected what Jim had said in our call. To the best of my rudimentary knowledge of legalese, it did, but just to be sure, I passed it by fellow ball hockey captain and corporate lawyer Bobby Hazlett. I swore him to secrecy, and he kindly confirmed that all was on the up and up in the legal documents. *Standard boilerplate. Good to go*, was his response.

I signed it and emailed it back to the lawyer. A stroke of the pen and I was the "songwriter of record" on a soon-to-be-released Jim Cuddy seasonal single. I'm sure I looked the same afterwards, but inside I confess I felt different. The more I thought of Annie that day, the more comfortable I became with the decision. Had she been alive, I thought, she'd have been thrilled to be driving to her office on a December morning, turn on her radio, and hear "Until the New Year" and Jim's voice filling up the car. Yep, she would have loved that.

Callaghan was teaching at the immigrant centre that afternoon. She was working with the kids on still-life sketching—you know, bowls of fruit, stacks of books, a wine bottle casting a shadow. So my static human form wasn't required. I hadn't finished my speech, but I knew my work on it was done for the day. Sometimes you have to leave a project and just let it sit for a bit before returning to it with fresh eyes.

I shut down my laptop and reached for my guitar. I hadn't played that much since arriving in Paris, but I increasingly felt the urge. I avoided playing Annie's song, as I still had Jim's version in my head and wanted to keep it there for a bit longer. In fact, I didn't play any of the covers or original songs on my playlist. Rather, I started playing around with a few different chord progressions. I did this almost unconsciously, but I later recognized it as the first faltering steps along a well-trodden creative path that sometimes—sometimes—yielded a new song. But it was early days, without yet a clear topic, let alone any semblance of lyrics. I was just fiddling with chords, fingerpicking patterns, possible melodies, and even potential bridges. It felt good to be cradling my guitar, lost in what sometimes seemed like random experimentation as I searched for chords I'd never played in quite that order before. That's how new songs are born. Two hours slipped by in what felt like minutes.

I let the creative wave carry me until I could sense my energy starting to fade. I'd learned to stop of my own accord while—as Hemingway might say—I still had something in the tank to draw upon when next my musical muse visited. So I made a quick recording on my phone and then put my guitar down.

Eventually, I headed back to Callaghan's apartment and spent some more time reading her grandmother's diaries. I was enthralled. They were such vivid and animated recollections. Her descriptions and judgments of the art and the music, and above all the people, were captivating. She recounted a visit she'd made one Saturday evening to a salon in the home Gertrude Stein shared with her lover and partner, Alice B. Toklas.

Mr. Pound kindly took me to visit Miss Gertrude Stein in her home over on Rue de Fleurus, which was filled with interesting and often strange art crowded haphazardly on the walls with little discernible logic or order. Hadley had warned me that arriving in the company of Mr. Pound, and without any particular evidence that I was an artist or poet myself, established or emerging, Miss Toklas would likely draw me into her orbit, while Miss Stein would probably not speak with me. And truly that is just as it unfolded. Miss Stein was just as I'd expected, having spoken to many who knew her. She was solidly built and quite low to the ground, which I offer merely as observation, not insult. Her hair was closely cropped and to me she resembled the statue of Caesar I'd seen recently in the Jardin des Tuileries. Perhaps she would not be offended—and for all I know, might even be pleased—to be likened to Caesar.

Another poet and friend to Mr. Pound, Mr. T.S. Eliot, was there, too. Pound and Eliot engaged Miss Stein in an esoteric discussion of modern verse on which I tried to eavesdrop, but Miss Toklas kept me thoroughly occupied in banal conversation as she knit in the chair beside me.

In preparation for my visit, I'd borrowed some writings of Miss Stein from Mr. Pound. I found them utterly impenetrable, and I suspended my inquiry awash in a palpable sense of literary inadequacy. Miss Stein created such strange and repetitive word patterns that they defied comprehension, at least in my primitive brain.

So I chatted amiably with Miss Toklas while keeping one eye, and as much of my ears as possible, on Miss Stein and the two poets. On the other side of the room, a little out of the fray, a small, stocky man, his hair flat to his head, sat quietly, keeping his eyes fixed on the walls of paintings. Mr. Pound told me on the way home it was the artist Pablo Picasso. I had seen his works and liked them as much as I liked Miss Stein's writing. Put more clearly, I warmed to neither.

I admit to some irritation at not being able—or perhaps the more appropriate word ought to be "permitted"—to speak with Miss Stein on any topic more meaningful than the weather. And yet I was content to be in the same room with her, and the other two poets, whom I admire so very much.

I lowered the leather notebook to let what I'd just read settle in my mind. There was such immediacy to Constance's entries, as if she'd recorded them just after returning home from her latest encounter. They felt that fresh. And this one short entry brought together in the same room Eliot, Pound, and Picasso, not to mention Stein and Toklas. After reading the account, I felt like I'd been there, too.

I really considered the handwritten diaries of Constance Stanley to be an exciting discovery in the field. And if I could just decipher that one cryptic, unfathomable, inexplicable line of text, nested neatly in its box on the page, I had a hunch it might reveal the diaries to be even more significant. I'd spent a lot of time wracking my brain trying to figure out the answer. I didn't think I was any closer to solving the mystery, yet still I felt I'd get there eventually.

Cracked code or not, I thought the diaries ought to be published. I believed they represented a new and important addition to the scholarship around Paris in the 1920s and the Lost Generation. But what did I know, except that these diaries were fascinating and arresting? Perhaps historians would feel the same way. I thought we needed to find out. But that would require Callaghan's blessing and a careful and thoughtful approach.

During my quiet but mesmerizing afternoon of reading, every once in a while I would suddenly remember that a song I'd written in 1981 would be released very soon by none other than Jim Cuddy. That seemed almost as surreal as being one of only two people alive who had read the diaries of a fearless upper-crust socialite with artistic aspirations in 1920s Paris. If Annie couldn't be here with me—and I knew she couldn't, I accepted she couldn't—I hoped she was enjoying all of this, wherever she was. But missing her still felt like my primary preoccupation, even when communing with Constance Stanley's diaries in Callaghan's apartment.

CHAPTER 11

CALLAGHAN AND I WERE WAITING. She was holding my hand. I'd have been happy to come by myself, but Callaghan wouldn't hear of it and had switched shifts with a friend at Café Paul to join me. When a fresh crop of people started filing through the sliding glass doors, Callaghan let go of my hand and sidled a half-step away from me. I looked at her.

"I don't want to overwhelm him when he hasn't even met me yet," she said, still smiling.

I leaned over and kissed her forehead. It seemed the most natural of acts.

"I've known him for quite a while now—his entire life, in fact—and he's going to think you're great," I said. "He and I generally feel the same way about things."

I turned my eyes back to the flow of visitors pouring into the atrium and immediately found Will looking at me and waving. I was surprised to find my eyes tearing up, but I think I was the only one who noticed. I closed the distance to Will as he crossed the floor towards us. He was beaming. He'd always looked more like Annie than like me. He let go of his wheelie suitcase and hugged me. I hung on for longer than was reasonable and squeezed my eyes shut in a vain attempt to stifle the waterworks. What was happening to me?

"It's okay, Dad," he said. "I'm safe and I'm here."

"Sorry, son. This kind of thing has been happening a lot lately," I explained. "I think it has something to do with your mother."

"Really? You think?" Will mocked. "Dad, grief is hard. It takes time. But I also seem to remember that you cried at my grade three Christmas concert when I sang my solo. Maybe this isn't that different, except I'm not singing. At least not yet."

I laughed, and that really helped at that particular moment.

"That's just the kind of line your mother would have used. And you have a lot of her in you," I said. "I sometimes see her when I see you."

I released him and wiped my eyes with my sleeve. I looked over his shoulder and saw Callaghan looking down and studiously giving Will and me the space to reconnect after a couple of months apart.

"You look good, Dad," Will said. "Have you lost weight?"

"Even here in the land of croissants and pain au chocolat, I have dropped a few pounds purely courtesy of all the walking and Sunday ball hockey," I replied.

I put my hands on his shoulders and gently turned him in Callaghan's direction. She took a few tentative steps towards us, a shy smile playing on her face.

"Son, Will, this is Callaghan Hughes," I said, moving one hand to her shoulder.

She stepped towards him and embraced him—a very Callaghan thing to do. Will looked a little startled, but only for a microsecond, before he hugged her and smiled.

"So lovely to meet you, Will," Callaghan said as she pulled back a bit. "After what your father has told me, I feel as if we have already met."

Will laughed.

"And some of what Dad told you might even be true," he said. "It's great to meet you, too. I think I know why my dad looks so happy. Thank you for that, and I mean it."

Now it was Callaghan's turn to tear up. She hugged him again.

"Very kind of you to say," she said. "Knowing what you've both been through, it means a great deal to me. And I should say, it's no coincidence that I'm very happy, too."

She looked at me when she said it.

"And what's not to love about an English accent?" Will replied.

"Well, sir, you are in luck," she said. "I've been perfecting mine for quite a few years."

Ten minutes later we were all in a cab for the drive into Paris. It took me back to when I'd arrived and made the same trip nearly two months earlier. I realized I felt so much better on my second taxi run into Paris than I had on my first. I knew who was responsible for that.

Will had never been to Paris and was craning his neck in every possible direction so as not to miss anything.

"Don't expect much from the drive in," I said. "The outskirts of Paris look like the outskirts of most cities. You'll know when we're in Paris proper."

Will knew exactly what I meant about fifteen minutes later as we entered the city. We dropped Callaghan off at Café Paul for her rescheduled afternoon shift and then the taxi continued on to my apartment.

"It looked a little bigger on FaceTime, but this is a great set-up, Dad," Will said after carrying his bag up the stairs and into the apartment.

"I'm afraid you're on the couch," I said. "But I've fallen asleep on it several times already, so I figure you'll be okay."

Will was holding his iPhone and looking around the apartment.

"Did you bring your Bluetooth speaker, Dad?"

I pointed to the cylindrical Bose speaker on the kitchen counter. Will turned it on and paired his phone with it.

"So, here's the final track that Jim released this morning to streaming services and radio stations," Will said as he hit play and turned up the volume.

Christmas music had already saturated the airwaves by that stage, but there was still time for "Until the New Year" to make its presence felt on the charts.

I sat down on the couch and closed my eyes to concentrate on the song, my song. It sounded even better than I'd remembered.

"Is this a new mix?" I asked.

"Yep. The earlier version you heard was just a rough take from the floor, with the whole band playing at the same time," Will explained. "This final version was recorded in multiple tracks and takes and then assembled in the final mix."

"Wow," I said when the song was over. "Let's hear it again."

We actually played the track a couple more times. I was hearing something that didn't quite fit.

"This makes no sense, but am I hearing my voice in the harmonies?" I asked. "Am I somehow in this mix?"

"Good ear, Dad," Will replied, smiling. "Yes, you're there, and that new high harmony is my voice. So we're both on the official recording—you know, for posterity's sake."

"Holy shit! But how did you make that happen?"

"It was Jim's idea," Will said. "I still had all the vocal tracks from your original recording. And because Jim had arranged the song in the same key and tempo, we just punched in your harmony track underneath Jim's lead vocal. I had to tweak your timing a bit, but it now sounds like you were right there with us. And then I recorded the new high harmony off the floor."

"It all blends so nicely," I said. "It's so tight."

"Well, that's good, because tight was just what we were going for. And Jim is really happy with it. He wanted us to be on the final track," Will said. "You wrote the song. You should be on the recording."

"Nice that I was actually singing in tune and on key," I said. "That's not always the case, as you know."

"You're way too hard on yourself, Dad. You may not have the best voice in the world, but it's completely serviceable and works just great for backup vocals."

"Good, because completely serviceable was just what I was going for," I replied. "In fact, I may name my first solo album *Completely Serviceable*."

We both laughed. It felt so good to be yukking it up with my son. I hadn't realized how much I'd missed him until he was with me in Paris. But I have to say, the final mix sounded amazing. I already liked the song, even when the only recording I had of it was all me. In fact, I'd liked that song ever since I'd written it in the early eighties. But I loved it now. While listening to Jim singing it, I occasionally had trouble remembering that I had actually written it. For forty-one years, I'd only ever heard my voice pushing out those lyrics.

"Hey, Dad, is this Callaghan's painting?" Will asked, pointing to the piece hanging above the couch. It was the one I'd bought at her exhibition. I nodded.

"I love it," he said. "It looks so real, almost like a photograph."

"That scene is just down the street from here. I'll show you on the way to dinner."

"Wow, she is good."

Will and I went out to walk around my neighbourhood for a while and then grabbed a bite at L'Atlas before his jet lag took a hold of him. We waved at Callaghan as we passed Café Paul. She was working until nine, but we had a plan for the next day. Rather than doing the afternoon nap thing, as I had when I'd arrived, Will was pretty well dead to the world by the time we made it back to the apartment. As my mother used to say, he'd been burning the candle at both ends in the run-up to the flight. He was ready to crash. He took a shower while I made up the couch. And by "made up the couch" I mean I laid a sheet and blanket on top of the cushions, along with one of the pillows from my bed. I tried to make it look like a freshly made bed and not a random pile of bedding but may have fallen short on that score.

Will emerged from the bathroom in sweatpants, drying his hair. He collapsed on the couch, seeming a little more awake than before his shower. I sat across from him in the matching easy chair.

"So, Will, how's it going with Ariel?"

"All is well, Dad," he replied. "She is very cool and we're really getting along well. She's funny, and that counts for a lot."

"I can tell you that a good sense of humour can carry you a great distance," I said. "Your mother claims . . . your mother claimed that's why she married me."

"So not your matinée idol looks or ripped upper body?"

"Well, yes, that was part of it, too. How long have you and Ariel been, um, together?"

"It started before you left for Paris but has been more serious in the last month," Will said.

"Well, I'm happy for you," I said. "If you can find someone with whom you can be yourself while still sorting out how to be better, and on top of that, she can make you laugh, too, you're in a good place."

"Well, I've grown up watching how well that formula works."

I changed the subject before my emotions overtook me yet again.

"So about tomorrow," I started. "I'm afraid that because I'm such an outstanding time management specialist, I have to work tomorrow morning finishing a luncheon speech for a client who runs a company that manufactures adult diapers. So this is not one of those assignments that writes itself, unless it's a *Saturday Night Live* sketch."

"Sounds like a great gig, Dad," Will replied. "I'll just stop myself from articulating all the funny lines that are coursing through my brain right now."

"Thank you, I'm grateful," I said. "But if you're okay with this, Callaghan has the morning off and wants to show you around the Right Bank. You know, the Champs-Elysées, Place de la Concorde, the Arc de Triomphe, Place de la Madeleine, the Opéra National de Paris, maybe even the Louvre. I want to show you around the Left Bank, but we can do that tomorrow afternoon, when I'm finished this brilliant speech that will captivate a luncheon crowd with anecdotes from the world of incontinence products."

"Sounds good to me, Dad," he said. "I can already tell that Callaghan and I will get along just fine. I'll try to sustain the good impression you've somehow managed to make on her. But I don't know if I can make it through the whole morning without the truth slipping out sometime."

I laughed.

"Well, do your best, and I'll avoid telling any stories that position you in a less than glowing light. And there are many, as you know."

"Deal," Will replied. "Seriously, Dad, it was one thing to hear on a FaceTime call that you'd met someone. And I was fine with that, and happy for you. But it was another to then be standing there with the two of you right in front of me. On the plane, I kind of wondered, maybe even worried, about how that would feel—you know, in my gut—to see the two of you together."

"And?" I asked, leaning forward in my chair.

"And, fear not. It felt good, really good. No negative vibes at all. I think she's great, and I trust your judgment."

"I've been worried, too, so thanks for being so open-minded and responding so well. I'm breathing again."

"Dad, you're living again. This is what Mom was talking about," Will said. "I could see it as soon as I laid eyes on you. And ever since you met her, I could tell on our calls that something had shifted. It's all good, Dad. I'm happy for you. I'm happy for Callaghan. And I'm pretty sure Mom is, too. I just know it. I can feel it."

"Me, too," I replied around the lump in my throat. "Me, too."

Will put his head down on the pillow and was asleep within minutes.

Callaghan picked Will up the next morning. Will was awake, dressed, and in full command of his faculties when she arrived. I was somewhat unaccustomed to sleeping in an apartment that was not also occupied by Callaghan, so it was nice to see her when she came through the door. On instinct, I reached for her, but she put her hand on my chest and just gave it a little pat.

"Please, you two," Will said, ever aware. "Go ahead. Don't worry about me. I'm fine. I really am."

Callaghan nodded and smiled before kissing me. Then she gave Will a hug. They left together shortly thereafter and headed for the Métro so I could finally finish my adult diaper luncheon speech. I mean, who wouldn't want to write a speech about incontinence? I spent the next three and a half hours contorting my words, and occasionally myself, to meet the requirements of my assignment. You know, writing a powerful and compelling luncheon speech that also burnished the image of the company and their leadership in the adult diaper category, all without compromising the luncheon guests' appetites. Sure, no problem.

I ended up with a twenty-five-minute address that may have been a little lighter on the diapers and a little heavier on the debt we owe to our seniors, and the societal benefits of ensuring they are more independent and engaged citizens. Incontinence products for seniors actually do help restore some physical freedom, allowing them to go out more and connect with the world. But it was still tough to make it all work in a luncheon speech.

Writing speeches for oneself is hard enough, not that I've delivered many of my own. But writing them for a client whom you might not know well is particularly challenging. I never agree to write a speech unless I can meet and spend some time with the person for whom I'm writing. You might think that's a no-brainer, but you'd be surprised how often a director of communications calls looking for me to write a speech for their CEO without giving me any face time with him or her. If the CEO is new, sometimes the comms director hasn't yet had any time with him or her, either. But I always insist on getting in front of the CEO so I can at least get a preliminary sense of their speech patterns and rhythms. Long or short sentences? Monotone or inflected? Large vocabulary or small? Fast talker or slow and steady? Sense of humour or not so much?

Sometimes when meeting with a CEO for the first time, I ask a lot of questions and draw out the conversation, not so much to learn the answers but rather to have an opportunity to assess how they speak. I'll also scour the Internet for video clips of speeches or media interviews they may have given. I remember one speechwriting assignment where my most valuable resource in preparing to write the address was a shaky video of the remarks the CEO had given at her own wedding. It was recorded by a family member and posted on YouTube. Despite the cinematography, which was clearly inspired by *The Blair Witch Project*, the audio was solid. It really helped reveal how she spoke and allowed me to craft a speech that actually sounded like her.

Fortunately, I knew this diaper CEO quite well, and that enabled me to write for her voice. The speech sounded like she had written it for herself. And that was my goal. But that morning, I was also stewing about how Callaghan and Will were getting along on their tour of the Right Bank. I hoped that after spending some concentrated time with her, Will was still on board the Callaghan Express, and that no reservations had crept in.

I wrapped up the speech and emailed it to my client. I felt my load lighten as I hit send. Then I reached for my guitar again, as I had several times in the last few days. I no longer needed the initial phone recording I'd made of the various chord progressions and melodies I was trying to bring together in a new song. I'd played it enough by that stage that it had officially earned the designation "song in progress." Still no lyrics. They wouldn't come for a while.

Twenty minutes later, Will sauntered through the door.

"Where's Callaghan?" I asked.

"She said to give you a hug, but she's gone over to the immigrant support centre for the afternoon."

"Right, I forgot it's Wednesday. It's her regular volunteer gig," I said, remembering my days of the week. "So, um, how was the tour?"

"Fantastic. What a city!" he said. "It's like stepping back in time, other than the nutbar drivers."

"So you enjoyed hanging with Callaghan?"

"Dad, relax," he replied. "I gotta say, you sure can pick 'em."

"In a good way?" I asked with some trepidation.

"Of course in a good way," he replied. "I think she's wonderful. I figured you'd know that already."

"I do. I do, I just didn't want to make assumptions about my own judgment. You know, drinking my own Kool-Aid, as it were. So you like her?"

"She's great, Dad. So different from Mom, but just as amazing, in different ways," Will said. "It's strange that you're—not sure what the right word is—*involved* with a woman who is so unlike Mom."

"Yeah, it somehow makes this all a little easier that I didn't gravitate towards a replica of your mother," I said. "I don't know why."

"Dad, I know it might feel like it sometimes, but you are not betraying Mom or her memory. In fact, you're honouring her and her last wish."

"Thanks, Will. I'm not sure how you came to be so wise, but I suspect you get it from your mother," I said. "But it means a lot that you're supporting whatever it is that Callaghan and I have going. And I still don't even know what it is. I just know that she makes me laugh, I seem to make her laugh, and we think alike in so many ways. I never expected it to happen, let alone so soon after arriving. And I wasn't even looking. I wasn't trying. I was minding my own business and it just happened. It's like it was fated."

"I say just be thankful. You're very fortunate," he said. "I like her easygoing manner. There's no pretense. No putting on airs. I'm not sure I've ever met anyone who seems so comfortable in her daily life," Will said. "And she's just so nice and so easy to talk to."

"Exactly! Okay, so you see it too, then. I'm not grossly misreading the situation."

"Dad, you done good, and I'm thrilled for you. I kind of worried when I first watched Mom's video that I'd be—I don't know—uncomfortable about you hooking up with someone else. That I'd feel a loyalty to Mom. That I'd accept Mom's message as noble and generous in principle but have trouble dealing with the reality of you being with someone else when it happened. But here I am having spent the morning with Callaghan, and I have none of those reservations. I just really like her and feel happy for you."

"Well, this is all going better than I could have dreamed," I said.

"Let's just hope she's not a really, really gifted serial killer," said Will.

"Thanks for planting that thought, son. I'll be on the lookout for any telltale signs," I said. "Okay, I've got us booked onto the Hemingway walking tour in an hour. It's a good way to explore the Left Bank. I did the tour shortly after I arrived and it's well worth it."

"Great. After that, I have some Christmas shopping to do. But I'll catch up with you and Callaghan for dinner."

And so the days passed. If this were a movie, you'd now be seeing a montage of various scenes of us enjoying Paris, accompanied by some catchy music. Will and I spent most of our time together, joined by Callaghan as often as her schedule permitted. She wanted to be sure I was having quality father-son time with Will.

We toured the city, ate at restaurants, visited the Louvre, climbed the Eiffel Tower, and walked the Champs-Élysées from Place de la Concorde all the way to the Arc de Triomphe. Yes, we lived the tourist's cliché and hit all the spots visitors are encouraged to see. And speaking of movies, one afternoon we even watched a Hollywood blockbuster on the Champs-Élysées, after which we sat in a sidewalk café and watched Paris flow by in front of us. To this day, I can't remember what movie we watched.

We had decided as a group that we should endeavour to visit as many Lost Generation cafés as we could bear. It was just a few days before Christmas and while there was no snow, it was chilly, and it certainly wasn't tourist high season. Okay, I guess the Christmas market stalls conveniently arrayed along the Champs-Élysées were kind of touristy. But it was nice that the streets weren't quite so packed. I'd already been to all our targeted Latin Quarter cafés, but of course Will hadn't, and Callaghan had only visited a few of them.

We were concentrating on the cafés along Boulevard du Montparnasse and found ourselves one afternoon in Le Dôme Café, a spot that Hemingway and Fitzgerald and so many others frequented in the twenties. Like most of the cafés of that era, it hadn't changed much in the intervening years. We had a table right against the window overlooking Montparnasse. Will checked his phone and snapped to attention.

"Bad news?" I asked.

Will's mouth was agape as his fingers worked his phone, sometimes scrolling, other times typing.

"Wow," was all he said.

"What? You can't leave us sitting here in suspense," I said.

"Sorry. Okay, get this. 'Until the New Year' was released last week, just before I arrived. Well, it entered the Canadian top one hundred singles chart at number twenty-three, which I guess is extraordinary for its first week."

"Wait," I said, shaking my head, perhaps to clear it. "The song I wrote more than forty years ago has debuted in the top twenty-five?"

"Woooooooohooooooo!" Callaghan stood up, bouncing on her feet and cheering until the waiter shushed her.

"Okay, Dad, I'm going to text you the 'listen live' link for Q107," Will said. "Callaghan, I'm sending you the one for CHUM-FM, and I'll monitor CHFI. These are the Toronto stations most likely to be playing the song. If it was number twenty-three last week, it could well be much higher today, so we shouldn't have to wait long to hear it. And that is the iconic moment in any songwriter's life, when they first hear their song on the radio."

By then we all had our phones out, our earbuds in, and our assigned stations streaming. We sat nursing our coffees and listening intently. Nobody moved, except to politely wave away the waiter a few times. But after twenty minutes of listening to other people's songs, I ordered another round of cafés au lait. Exactly twenty-seven minutes after we'd started listening to the three radio stations, Callaghan's eyes bugged out. She wrenched the wired buds from her ears, then pulled the wire lead from her phone. She cranked up the volume, sat the phone in her now-empty coffee cup to amplify the sound, and put the makeshift speaker in the middle of the table.

And there it was, my guitar intro, played by the much better guitarist in Jim's band. It was still hard to believe. I was sitting in a

Paris café listening to a song I'd written forty-one years ago as it aired live on a Toronto radio station. We all leaned in closer to Callaghan's phone as Jim's awesome voice launched into the verse. It was as surreal as I'd expected. Jim and his band made the song sound so much better than when I'd cobbled together a recording on my own. I guess that's why Jim is a big star and I'm a freelance writer. But when the chorus came, hearing both Will's voice and my own on the harmonies was quite an emotional experience. Callaghan clutched my hand and squeezed so tightly for so long that gangrene was a legitimate fear. To distract me from the crushing pressure on my hand, Will gripped my shoulder and wasn't letting go, either. Okay, it was exciting and, after such a difficult and emotionally draining two and a half years, a welcome change.

What a moment. As Will had reminded me, hearing one of my songs on the radio had been a goal since I was seventeen years old. Achieving it so many years later was not something for which I was adequately prepared. It was a lot to take in. Of course, I'd been hearing from all my ball hockey buddies, who knew the story behind "Until the New Year." In fact, most of them had heard me play the song at dinner parties when the wine was flowing. Now, every time one of them heard the song on the radio, I'd receive a text. I considered upgrading my cellphone plan to make sure I didn't exceed my texting limits.

To decompress after our Montparnasse café tour, which also included La Coupole and La Rotonde—meaning we were all heavily caffeinated—I took Will to play in my weekly ball hockey game over at the school on Rue Descartes. Of course, I said nothing about the success of "Until the New Year," but evidently Will felt comfortable enough with his new teammates to tell them all about it. Everyone was very nice about it all. Man, it was a day.

We spent most of Christmas Eve at Callaghan's flat—I was learning to use her favoured word for her apartment/studio. There was a whole lot of wrapping going on while we each, in turn, averted our eyes. The entire time, we were streaming Toronto radio stations. We never got tired—at least I never got tired—of hearing my song on the radio.

My cellphone rang in the early evening. It was Jim Cuddy.

"Merry Christmas, Jim," I said when I answered.

"It certainly is," Jim replied. "In fact, that's why I'm calling. My manager just let me know that 'Until the New Year' heads into Christmas at number two on the charts. I wanted you to be first to know."

"Incredible!" I replied. "I can't believe it. We've been streaming different Toronto radio stations here for the last few days, and it's been an out-of-body experience hearing your voice so often."

"You mean hearing my voice singing your really, really great song," Jim said. "And remember, being number two at Christmas is like being number one. No song will ever knock Mariah Carey and 'All I Want for Christmas Is You' out of the top spot. And there's a big drop to the number three spot, so I figure we'll be at number two for a while. So this is just about as good as it gets. Congratulations. You've got a hit on your hands."

"*We*, Jim. *We've* got a hit on our hands," I said. "And given that this is the first time I've ever had, as you say, a hit on my hands, is there anything I should be doing? I feel a little helpless in Paris while our song climbs the charts in Canada."

"There's really nothing for you to do but enjoy the ride, and maybe say 'yes' when reporters call. The story behind the song is powerful and poignant," Jim said. "Anyway, give my best to Will and whoever else you're celebrating with, and we'll see you when you're back in the spring. Thanks again, man. Your song is crushing it here."

I didn't tell Will and Callaghan the news right away. They were deep in conversation as they helped one another with their wrapping. They laughed and gently needled each other as if they were siblings. It suddenly dawned on me as I looked from Will's smiling face to Callaghan's, while Q107 played my song yet again on the wireless speaker, that I was happy—genuinely happy—for the first time in a long while. I realized it was possible to love Annie, to miss Annie, and still be happy. I hadn't thought that I'd ever get there. But I had made it. And I could detect no caveats around my happiness. No twinges of guilt. Annie had made sure of that.

"Hey, was that the rock star Jim Cuddy you were talking to?" Will asked.

"Yep," I replied. "Nice of him to call."

"So, do you have any news to report?" Callaghan asked.

"Well, I'm not sure it warrants the 'news' designation, but he called to say that the song is now number two on the Canadian charts, and it looks like it could be up there for a while based on the long drop to the song in third place."

I don't think I've ever seen eyes and mouths open wider than on Callaghan and Will at the moment. They were on me in an instant, wrapping me up and eventually pulling me down to the floor, hooting and hollering so loudly I feared the gendarmes might soon be knocking on our door. Now I knew how Tom Brady felt when he was sacked for a ten-yard loss. When I pulled myself back up to a standing position, they both hugged me, and the three of us bounced up and down as a unit while Callaghan and Will chanted, "Number two! Number two! Number two!"

We were too tired from all the excitement to cook, so we ordered in pasta. By ten thirty or so, I could barely keep my eyes open.

"Will, I think we should head back before my pasta coma hits," I said.

"Nope. I don't think so," Will replied. "You should stay here. Your couch is really not comfortable, so it would be helpful if you could spend the night here with Callaghan, so I can sleep in your bed. Think of it as an early Christmas present for my back."

I looked at him to make sure I was reading him correctly. His face told me I was.

"Can you make it back okay on your own?" I asked.

"I've made the trip several times already. I'll be home and horizontal inside of seven minutes."

I gave him my key, hugged him, and sent him on his way.

After he left, Callaghan sat down next to me on the couch, leaned against me—she seemed to like leaning against me and I quite liked it, too—and rested her head on my shoulder.

"I'm sorry about Will's back," she said. "He seems a little young to have back issues, doesn't he?"

I put my arm around her.

"Callaghan, he doesn't have any back issues," I said. "He just likes you very much, and what you do for me."

She nodded, smiled, and closed her eyes.

"What a nice boy you and Annie raised."

Will arrived the next morning around nine thirty with croissants and pain au chocolat for Christmas breakfast. Callaghan made omelets and defrosted fresh peaches she'd put in the freezer in the summer. I don't know how French chickens differ from Canadian chickens, but the eggs in Paris have so much more flavour, and the yellow of the yolk is deeper and richer. The omelets were wonderful. And because Will was there, Callaghan was fully dressed when she cooked. It might also have been because frying bacon *sans vêtements* is ill-advised.

It was almost noon before we started exchanging gifts. Even though it was still early morning in Toronto, I'd already started receiving Christmas texts from the ball hockey boys back home. They continued for most of the day. The text from Harris was more than "Merry Christmas." He asked if he could come to visit for a week in late February. Of course, I agreed.

For the just over thirty years of our marriage, I'd only ever spent Christmas morning with Annie, and of course with Will too when he arrived on the scene. The last two Christmases, after Annie died, it had just been the two of us, punctuated by visits from friends in the neighbourhood who were looking out for us. Sitting in Callaghan's beautiful flat, I realized it felt like I was supposed to be spending this time with her, though it had all come about so quickly. I also knew I was still in love with Annie. I always would be. But I could also feel myself falling for Callaghan. It reminded me of that passage in A *Moveable Feast* where Hemingway claimed to be legitimately in love with two women at the same time—his first wife, Hadley, and the woman who would become his second wife, Pauline Pfeiffer. Of course, there were some key differences in our situations that made them a far cry from parallel. Most notably, Annie had died, and with her last breaths had urged me to find someone else to love. In Hemingway's case, he'd carried on an adulterous affair with Pauline right under Hadley's naïve nose. Oh, yes, and Hemingway was a self-centred jerk, while I like to think I most definitely am not.

I handed Callaghan my present and watched as she tore open the wrapping as if she were five and not fifty-six. I loved that streak in her. She held up the signed first edition of Morley Callaghan's *That Summer in Paris*. I'd found it online at an antiquarian book site, and it had arrived just in time. She immediately burst into tears and threw her arms around me.

"Well, I've never given a woman a gift and triggered a reaction like that," Will said. "Well played, Dad."

Then Callaghan handed me her gift. It felt like a framed piece of art. I unwrapped it and it turned out to be a framed piece of art. As I've said before, I'm a quick study. I turned it over and realized she'd finished and framed the sketch she'd made of me as I slept that first night in her flat. Will was blown away by it. Finished and framed, I thought it was stunning. And it looked just like me, only better.

"I love it," I said as I hugged her—there was a whole lot of hugging going on that morning. "It's perfect. Thank you."

"Hang on, there's one more," she said, and I thought I noticed her wink at Will, though I wasn't sure.

She handed me another gift. Deploying my sixth sense for gifts, I divined that it was another piece of framed art, though slightly smaller.

"Okay, this may seem a little weird, but it's truly from my heart," she said, clearly nervous about my reaction.

I opened it and was shocked to be looking at a beautiful painting of Will and Annie together. I recognized the scene. I glanced at Will and he gave me a knowing shrug. He must have sent Callaghan a copy of the photo that we had in a frame on our mantle. It was a great shot of the two of them, both looking as much like themselves as in any photo I'd ever seen of them. And they looked every bit themselves in Callaghan's perfect painting. It took my breath away. I managed not to burst into tears, but it required a Herculean effort.

"I'm at a complete and utter loss for words," I said, still gazing at the painting. "I cannot think of a more meaningful gift." I buried my face in Callaghan's neck and worked on holding myself together.

She knew it had made an impact. She rubbed my back.

"It's a wonderful painting," Will said. "It really captures us both, and that's saying something when you've never met Mom. You two would have liked one another. Okay, with those dramatics out of the way, here's my gift to you both. Merry Christmas."

Through the hastily applied wrapping paper, it felt to me like yet another framed piece of art. I handed it to Callaghan to unwrap. It turned out to be two framed copies of the same candid black-and-white photograph of Callaghan and me. It was a shot of us looking at one another on a street corner not far from her flat, with a café slightly blurred in the background. Only she and I were in focus. It was a fantastic photo that seemed to capture the best of the two of us. There was something in the way we were looking at one other that I found touching.

"Oh my gosh," Callaghan said. "I'm not sure my heart can take much more of this. I love this. We both look amazing, don't you think?"

"There's one for each of you, so when Dad's back in Toronto, you'll both be looking at the same photo," Will said.

Then Callaghan did burst into tears and buried her head in my chest. I rubbed her back as she'd rubbed mine. I was a little taken aback by her reaction, but I just figured it was because Christmas could be an emotional time of year. She recovered quickly and embraced Will.

"I absolutely love it, Will," she said. "I don't think I've ever been given a more thoughtful and meaningful gift."

She looked at me, and I elevated my eyebrows and nodded towards the Morley Callaghan first edition resting on the coffee table. She looked stricken for just a second.

"Right! Except of course for the lovely book Jack gave me earlier," she said as we both laughed. "Definitely the two most thoughtful and meaningful gifts I've ever received."

"I was kidding, you know," I said.

"Yes, I know, Jack," she replied. "But I do love both gifts equally."

"It's a stunning shot, Will," I said. "And just when I thought this day couldn't get any better. Thank you, son."

The rest of the day and evening was a blur. Will and I cooked the turkey and made the gravy, while Callaghan handled the potatoes, turnips, and peas. It helps to have a chef as a son. We all ate far too much that night, and the three of us actually fell asleep on Callaghan's couch.

Three days later, I walked Will to the security gate at Charles de Gaulle.

"Dad, thanks for everything. The last two weeks have been awesome. I feel like I'm seeing you in your natural habitat. You seem really at home here, and I know Callaghan has made that happen," Will said. "So I'm just telling you, please do not screw this up!"

We hugged, and then he was through the door where the security screening awaited. I watched until I could no longer see him. Then I left for Callaghan's.

CHAPTER 12

IN TODAY'S VERNACULAR, Callaghan was "creating content" for a few art shows she had scheduled for later in the spring. In other words, she was painting in her studio. With Christmas behind us, she felt she needed to buckle down and start producing. Her recent sellout exhibition had boosted demand but depleted her inventory, so she was feeling the pressure to paint. She had some pieces already finished in the studio but needed many more to feature in the spring shows. So I stayed out of the way and continued reading Constance Stanley's diaries. I lost track of time when I read them, and the hours slipped by almost unnoticed.

By that stage, I was up to 1926. Callaghan's grandmother wrote so well, with such vivid detail. The scenes she described, sometimes with dialogue, were so richly observed, I felt like I was not just a fly on the wall but rather a full participant. They transported me to the Paris of a hundred years before. Not unlike ball hockey, and Paris itself, Constance Stanley's diaries were a time machine. I knew I had to pursue the idea that had occurred to me when I'd first started reading them. I knew my idea had legs. I just had to figure out how to raise it in a way that yielded the right outcome. It wasn't rocket science. In fact, it seemed obvious. But I wasn't sure how Callaghan would react.

A short time later, she passed through the living room on her way to the kitchen to make coffee. That afternoon, she was flagging and needed a boost to keep her brush doing what it was supposed to do on the canvas.

"You know, I've read so many books about Paris, some of them first-hand accounts. Sylvia Beach's story about her bookshop Shakespeare and Company, which I loved, and fellow Canadian John Glassco's wonderful memoir. Even Janet Flanner's *New Yorker* columns have that personal feel to them," I said. "But your grandmother's diaries are the most candid, interesting, and detailed that I've ever read. So, um, I was wondering, have you considered having them edited and published? I really think a fresh, new voice from that era would add to the scholarship of the period. I have to think you'd be able to find a publisher, even if it's an academic publisher. You know, I could help you pull them together. It would mean going through the diaries very carefully and deciding if you're comfortable having it all out there in the public eye, or if you may wish to redact certain sections or names."

"Whoa, whoa," she said. "Publish my grandmother's diaries?"

"Well, is it such a crazy idea?" I asked. "I know there's an audience for them. We're part of that audience, right?"

"It's just that they've always been my private kingdom. My personal portal to my grandmother's life," she said. "I don't know how I'd feel if they were no longer in my exclusive domain, my little historical sanctuary. Do you understand what I mean?"

"Of course, I understand," I replied. "It would be a big change. On the other hand, your grandmother would finally receive the recognition she deserves for capturing that time so vividly, so personally, and so well. I mean, there's no denying she's a fine writer."

"Hmmmm, I don't know."

"People would know her name and her story," I said. "I know it might be difficult to, you know, share her with the wider world. But there may be an argument that her work deserves a larger audience beyond just you, and now me. It sheds new light on a special city in a special time. It may be bigger than the two of us."

I felt myself wince when I said this, worried that I'd pushed her too far, too fast. But she was deep in thought, staring out the window at much the same view her grandmother would have seen in the 1920s. I left her in silence for a while as her wheels turned. Then she promptly walked into her bedroom without a word. Uh-oh. I'd blown it. I felt sick.

"I'm sorry I mentioned it," I pleaded from where I sat on the couch. "It was not my place. I apologize for . . ."

"Hang on. Just give me a second. I have something to show you," she called from her bedroom.

I clammed up. I could hear the distinct sound of rummaging. I have a history of rummaging myself, so I knew what I was hearing.

"Found it!" she said, and emerged from her bedroom.

She was carrying what looked like a very thick and very old photo album. She sat down next to me on the couch and placed it on the coffee table in front of us. It turned out to be a very thick and very old photo album. On the label glued to the front cover I read *Paris 1920–30*. I held my tongue, still not certain if my somewhat impetuous suggestion required a shift into damage control. My stomach felt funny, and not in a good way.

"Don't you think if we found a publisher for the diaries, they'd want some photos to go along with her words?" she asked.

"Wait, you have photos from that time?" I asked, pointing to the album. "These are her photos?"

"I may have forgotten to mention that she was pretty good with her Brownie, and she had it with her most of the time," she said.

"Oh my gosh, holy shit, oh my gosh . . ." I whispered to no one in particular.

"Okay, Jack, breathe. Just breathe."

She put her hand on my arm as I tried to control what felt like cardiac arrhythmia. Over the years of my interest (obsession?) in the Lost Generation, I'd seen almost every publicly available photograph of the writers and artists of that period, including those in the Hemingway Collection at the Kennedy Presidential Library. And now I hoped I was about to look at a whole new set of photos from that time. I took Callaghan's advice, and a minute to breathe. Just breathe.

"Okay, before we open the album—and let me be clear that I really hope we're going to open the album—who else has seen these?" I asked.

"As far as I know, only my eyes have seen these photos in the last thirty years or so," Callaghan said. "I suspect my grandmother may have shown them to others in her circle over the course of her life, but no one has seen them since I found the album when I moved in here after she died."

"Okay, understood," I said. "Hang on." I stood up and shook out my shoulders and arms before sitting back down. "Okay. I think I'm ready." She laughed.

Then she opened the album and we started turning the pages, very, very slowly. The pages were of heavy black paper, with those little finicky paper corners glued in to hold the photos in place. It must have been quite the labour-intensive ordeal to mount all those photos. But I gave thanks that Callaghan's grandmother had been so dedicated to capturing her life. There were also notations in white pencil beneath most of the photographs, identifying who was in the shots and where the pictures were taken. Very helpful when I came upon someone I didn't recognize—and there were many.

I knew immediately that I was looking through a treasure trove of historically significant photographs. They were all there, sometimes by themselves, and often in small groups. Fitzgerald and his wife Zelda, Hemingway, Stein, Ford Madox Ford, John Dos Passos, Hadley Richardson, Pauline Pfeiffer and her sister Jinny, Picasso, Ezra Pound, Morley and Loretto Callaghan, John Glassco, Robert McAlmon, Harold Loeb, Gerald and Sara Murphy, Man Ray, Kiki de Montparnasse, and so many more. While unfortunate, it made sense that Constance Stanley herself was only in a handful of the shots. Clearly, she was behind the camera for the lion's share of them.

"I can't believe what I've just seen," I muttered after we'd turned the last page of the album. "These are, well, they're priceless, and will be of tremendous academic interest. They're . . . my gosh, they're wonderful."

Because only Callaghan had access to them and she didn't open the album all that often, the quality and clarity of the shots were striking. I noticed my hands were trembling as I turned the pages—such was the anticipation of what awaited on the following page. Callaghan also noticed and seemed almost moved by my uninhibited reaction. I decided to seize the moment.

"So does this mean that you're at least considering the idea of finding a publisher?" I asked. "I think these incredible photos make it almost a sure thing we could find one."

"I'm still working through the idea—getting used to it," she replied. "It's scary to contemplate, but it does seem a little selfish—or maybe very, very selfish—to withhold her writing and photos from others who would really love to see them and study them. It feels like we'd be serving the public good by at least exploring the opportunity. I don't know why it never occurred to me before."

"And remember, you'd always have the originals right here, just for your eyes," I said.

"And maybe your eyes, too," she replied. "Let's wait until you've finished reading the diaries before we take any steps on the publishing front. I'd want your view on how we approach the whole thing. Plus, I may need some time to get comfortable with the idea of no longer having her all to myself."

"Deal."

With that, Callaghan returned to her easel and I to her

grandmother's diaries. I was reading her entries from early in 1926 when I came upon several references to "WO." In one entry it simply said, *Time with* WO. And on January 14, 1926, Constance wrote, *Stole a long weekend with* WO *in Berlin*. I couldn't figure out who WO was after mentally scrolling through all the people I could think of from that era. I came up empty. That could simply mean it was a lesser-known or unknown person. Callaghan didn't know, either. I looked through the photo album again, but there were no notations beneath the images to help in solving the mystery.

Two pages later, I once again read that strange January 1926 entry I'd stumbled upon the first night I'd sat up and read the diaries. There was that scrambled line, neatly boxed at the top of the entry:

WO *pnuvre: Fvk cnprf rnfg bs Cynpr qr yn Pbapbeqr. Gbc. Yrsg raq-obneq.*

As I had many times since first finding that line, I thought about what it could represent. But I still felt no closer to figuring it out. When I'd mentioned it to Callaghan the morning after I'd first seen it, she had said she'd always thought it was a code of some kind. Hmmm. Still, something about the nonsensical arrangement of letters and words seemed familiar to me, but I couldn't put my finger on it. I just kept staring, and sometimes glaring, at it, feeling deep down that figuring it out was important. But I got nowhere. I had nothing. After wrestling with it for an hour or so, I gave up, yet again, and went to bed.

—

Two nights later, it happened. I don't know if it came to me in a dream, but I do know that when I woke up in the middle of the night—clear-eyed and energized—I thought I might have cracked the code. Surely it couldn't be that simple. I slipped out of bed and pulled the diary back down from the shelf. I didn't want to turn on the big floor lamp in the living room for fear of waking up Callaghan. So instead, I lit the big candle on the coffee table, then grabbed a pencil and scratch pad from the kitchen counter. By candlelight, I created two rows of letters:

A	B	C	D	E	F	G	H	I	J	K	L	M
N	O	P	Q	R	S	T	U	V	W	X	Y	Z

When I was a kid, I loved the Hardy Boys books and wanted to be a private eye. For my birthday one year, my parents gave me a book about simple codes so I could send secret messages to a few close friends similarly intrigued by ciphers. And this little table was probably the simplest code of them all. You just transpose each letter in your message with the corresponding letter below or above it in the table. So when coded, *apple* would become *nccyr*. Thanks to my adolescent interest in ciphers—and this simple one in particular—the very look of the boxed gibberish in the diary entry had somehow rung a bell, jogged a distant memory—you know, perhaps triggered a long-forgotten synapse.

I quickly translated the coded message and was shocked to find that the most rudimentary of codes actually worked. (Okay, so it's no surprise that Constance Stanley was not recruited to work at Bletchley Park in the early 1940s.) When translated, the coded line read:

JB cahier: Six paces east of Place de la Concorde. Top. Left end-board.

I gave a little whoop, or perhaps it was a big and boisterous whoop. I was excited. Callaghan emerged from the bedroom with the blue coverlet wrapped around her.

"Jack, are you okay? What's going on?" she asked. "It's the middle of the night."

She sat down beside me on the couch, still half-asleep.

"Usually, you're naked. Was it something I said?"

"All is well. It's just a little chilly out here," she replied, yawning and drawing the coverlet more tightly around her. "So what's all the excitement?"

"I had an epiphany in my sleep and awoke with the solution to the coded message in the diary."

"You figured it out?" she said, sitting bolt upright. "You know what it says?"

I pointed to the scratch pad where I'd transcribed the line.

JB cahier: Six paces east of Place de la Concorde. Top. Left end-board.

She stared at it, moving her lips as she read it through more than once.

"Are you sure that's it?" she asked. "It doesn't make much sense, does it?"

"I'm pretty sure I've got it right. The simple code key I used yields complete and understandable words. We now have to figure out exactly what they mean."

"Well, *JB cahier* probably just means a notebook about JB—whoever JB was—but the rest of the instructions still don't really work if you've ever been to Place de la Concorde," she said.

I pictured the big public square in my mind—except it was round—and I realized she was right. Six paces east would be in the middle of the chaotic, frenetic traffic circle, which made the words that followed even more cryptic: *Top. Left end-board*. What could that mean? Even though I was convinced I'd broken the code, I just couldn't understand the message it revealed.

"And why the secrecy? Why the code?" she asked.

"I think the reason will be clear when we figure out what the message means."

So the coded WO now meant JB, but I still couldn't think of any prominent members of the Lost Generation fraternity with those initials. I supposed it need not be someone prominent. But it was fun to contemplate, given the secretive measures Constance had taken to protect JB's identity.

We kicked around some other ideas for a while, but eventually the fact that it was, by then, three forty-five in the morning caught up to us. We went to bed feeling as if we'd taken two steps forward and one step back. Frustrating. One mystery had yielded another.

—

I couldn't wait. I went the next morning at first light—or at least at the first light I saw after opening my eyes. I was not optimistic but didn't feel we could rule it out until I'd at least gone there to confirm my suspicions. I left Callaghan in bed and walked towards the Seine. Visiting Place de la Concorde in the middle of the morning rush hour for the purposes of pacing off a treasure hunt location seems like a bad idea in hindsight. Actually, it was a bad idea at the time, too. I was certain it was a fool's errand, but I had to make sure. I crossed over the Pont Neuf, incidentally the oldest bridge over the Seine in all of Paris, dating back to 1578. Then I headed west on the Right Bank to Place de la Concorde. Even from a few hundred metres away, I could see that my mission was futile. But I was there, and I wanted to be certain.

An easy way to kill yourself is to be a pedestrian anywhere near Place de la Concorde anytime near rush hour. So it was not the best plan I'd ever come up with. I was just impatient to solve this mystery, and that included eliminating scenarios that already seemed impossible. I took my life in my hands wading through the chaos of traffic circling the large roundabout that was Place de la Concorde. With no lines on the road, it was just a massive vehicular free-for-all with a pedestrian—me—in the middle. I stopped breathing several times as I picked my way to the very centre of the largest public square in Paris and stood next to the seventy-five-foot-high obelisk that towered above it all.

Cars whizzed all around me, and not always in the same direction. Through observation, I learned that once every six or seven minutes, the traffic slowed and almost petered out as part of its natural flow cycle. This gave me approximately forty-five seconds to count off my six paces and see if there was anything of interest on the road to explain the clear yet still unfathomable instructions: *Top. Left end-board.* I knew the answer long before I stepped out into the road, counting off my six paces east of the obelisk. There was absolutely nothing on the road at the designated spot, beyond a discarded COVID mask and an oil stain in the shape of Phyllis Diller's distinctive profile. I nearly stayed there too long coming up with the comedienne's name. When I'd finished closely examining my surroundings, I looked up into the front grill of a speeding Renault. The car's horn sounded as I leapt the final four paces back to the safety of the obelisk.

All right, I had duly confirmed that I had not cracked the puzzle, even though I still felt confident I'd cracked the code. I returned to find Callaghan still in bed. I made her coffee and rejoined her. She stirred, the aroma of the coffee on her nightstand working its magic.

"Well, the Place de la Concorde was a bust," I said when she opened her eyes. "As we suspected, there's nothing there that seems to relate in any way to the coded instructions."

"Just as I feared."

"Now what?" I asked.

"We start again and keep thinking," she said, squeezing my hand. "Something will present itself. I can feel it."

A week later, Harris Unger arrived after visiting his daughter in Barcelona. He had booked his return flight out of Charles de Gaulle so he could stay with me for a few days on his way home.

I confess, I was really excited to see him. I missed my hockey brothers. I was loving my time in Paris, and what—and who—it had brought me. But FaceTiming with my friends back home was a pale substitute for being with them, playing hockey with them, joking around with them, drinking with them, commiserating with them, supporting them, and just growing older with them. Maybe that sounds odd to others, but not to me. It was a special bond that had been forged in the heat of competition but had morphed into something much deeper—a true community of friends.

I decided to walk from my apartment to the Gare du Nord to meet Harris, whose train was due at noon. It was not a short walk, about three and a half kilometres. But walking in Paris is arguably the best way to see the city, provided you survive the all-too-many crazy drivers. I again walked across the Seine over the Pont Neuf, but this time I continued north along Rue du Pont Neuf. With a few jogs and turns here and there and the occasional near-death traffic experience, I made it to the Gare du Nord in about forty-five minutes. Each time I strayed from the Latin Quarter and ventured onto the Right Bank, I was reminded that I much preferred the vibe on the Left Bank. There's nothing wrong with the Right Bank. There is some outstanding architecture there, and lots of touristy things to see. It's just that my introduction to Paris had been through the literature of its expat writers from a century ago. So I gravitated towards the Left Bank in general and the Latin Quarter in particular. And nothing in my four months of living in Paris had changed that prejudice—or perhaps inclination is a better word.

I was on the platform when the train pulled in. It was crowded. As you can imagine, Paris remains an important and popular transportation hub, particularly for train travellers. I kept a weather eye out for Harris and finally saw him step down from the train's second car. We were like two little kids greeting one another after both being away for the summer. We hugged and bounced up and down on the platform, earning a few glares from the sea of passengers parting to flow around us. We were simply thrilled to be with one another again after four months separated by the Atlantic Ocean.

"Holy shit, I can't believe I'm here," Harris said as I shouldered one of his bags. "And again, I say holy shit, I can't believe your song was playing on every radio station in the country when I left. Congrats, J-Mac. It's just friggin' incredible."

"Thanks, man," I said. "It's been an amazing ride so far. You can blame or thank Will for it all, depending on whether you like the song."

"Jim nailed it, but the song is solid, too," said Harris. "He's not saving a bad song with his stellar voice. It's already a great song, and it's making Jim's voice sound even better. And that's saying something."

"Does everybody know about it at home?" I asked. "I haven't told anybody."

"Everyone knows in the neighbourhood," replied Harris. "The old 'local boy makes good' story travels fast. Plus, it's been in the Toronto papers. Beautiful song, man. Just beautiful. I just see Annie whenever I hear it."

"Me, too, Harris. Me too."

We grabbed a taxi back to the Left Bank and yacked all the way to my apartment.

"So how are you doing? I mean, how are you really doing?" Harris asked. "I'll need a full report to give the guys when I get back."

"I'm feeling good. Much better than when I arrived," I started. "The change of scenery has done me a boatload of good. I still miss Annie every day, but I'm having new experiences in a new city and that seems to be helping. Plus, I'm still playing ball hockey once a week, so I'll be in shape for the start of the new season."

"If anyone could sniff out a game in Paris, you could," Harris said. "So that means you are coming home before the season starts?"

"Fear not, Harris, I wouldn't miss the first game. In fact, I'll be back in time for the draft. You don't think I'm going to let you draft our team all on your own, do you? Who knows who we'd be left with?"

"Great. Then we can share the blame for the team's performance," he said. "Now tell me about this Callaghan woman."

"What? How do you know about her?"

"It's all good," he replied. "I bumped into Will on the Danforth when he got back after Christmas, and I insisted on seeing his photos from his visit. Anyway, there she was."

"I met her not long after I arrived, just by fluke," I explained. "She's quite a successful artist—a painter—but she also works in the café where I usually start my day."

"I'm really happy for you, man, and Will was over the moon about it all, which must mean something," Harris said. "I just want to make sure you're okay and that you're not rushing back in too fast."

"I know, Harris, and I appreciate your concern, but believe me, I had no plans to meet somebody. But it happened and we seem to have hit it off, so we're taking it slowly, seeing where it goes."

"Will says she's wonderful, but in ways that are completely different from Annie. That made me feel good, that you weren't just grasping at something or someone who was as close as possible to Annie."

"No worries there. Annie was one of a kind," I said. "This feels completely different, probably because Callaghan is completely different. She's one of a kind, too."

I paused for a moment and then carried on.

"And you may not know, but Annie actually wanted this to happen and urged me to make it happen," I continued. "She knew me very well, Harris. It was she who told me I needed to find somebody, that I was at my best when I was with someone. That's the kind of person I was married to for thirty-plus years."

"Wow, that's some heavy shit right there, man."

"Tell me about it. I'm still processing it all," I said. "Anyway, you'll meet Callaghan soon. I'm pretty sure you'll like her. Everyone else seems to. In fact, now that I think of it, you're going to meet her this afternoon. We're playing ball hockey and she'll be there."

Harris and I had lunch at a café right near my apartment. I had vegetable risotto, a favourite of mine.

"So enough about me, how are you holding up?" I asked.

"Much better, brother," Harris replied. "When Jason died, I admit I went into a bit of a tailspin. I know you remember, because you were there and helped me out. I never really said thank you for that, but you were so supportive through all that, and I appreciate it."

"Hey, I'm still on my own grief journey, so I can relate. I'm glad you're feeling better."

"Oh, it still hurts. It hurts a lot. The injustice of it all. Endlessly asking, why him?" he said. "But then I realized that bad shit happens to people all the time, every day. And I know that guys like Jason, like you and like me, we don't get special treatment. We don't get a free pass on the bad stuff. We suffer along with everyone else. So time has put that into perspective for me and I'm a lot less angry about it all. Plus, I just spent time with my daughter and that helped a lot, too."

"Good man, Harris. I'm impressed. That sounds like a surprisingly mature and thoughtful approach for you." He laughed. I laughed, too.

Harris and I were a little late for the game. We'd already been assigned to a team and jumped in to warm up our goalie with a few shots. Then our players gathered on the side to sort out our lines.

"Harris, meet Callaghan Hughes," I said.

Harris looked confused. Then our goalie pulled off her mask and immediately gave Harris a hug.

"Great to meet another Canadian ball hockey player. I hope you're a stronger back-checker than Jack," she said. "You really do not want me to be your last line of defence."

Harris laughed. He told me afterwards that her opening line charmed him and made him feel like they'd known each other for years. That's what Callaghan does. That's who she is.

"Did I use the term *back-checker* correctly, Jack?" she asked. "I'm still learning the lexicon."

"Well, yes, except for the part when you denigrated my back-checking abilities, of which I am justly proud," I replied, feigning indignation.

"You're still my favourite back-checker. I'm just trying to motivate you to, you know, step it up today, when I'm your goalie." She smiled sweetly.

"I will do everything humanly possible to protect my goalie today."

She then leaned in and kissed me. Harris just smiled.

Our regular goalie was at a mandatory-attendance, command-performance family lunch, so Callaghan had suited up again and assumed her place in goal. She did her best to square up in the net and directly face the shooter. But most of the saves she made were more because the ball just happened to hit her rather than due to her athletic prowess and kinesthetic awareness. When you stand in the right place and in the right position, you can't avoid making saves. That was Callaghan's secret. She was still giggling wildly whenever she made a willful save or the ball happened to hit her.

Even using my extra stick, Harris had a solid game, potting three or four goals and setting me up for a few, too. He was a skilled and generous playmaker.

After the game, Harris and I returned to my apartment and took much-needed showers. Callaghan arrived shortly thereafter, having showered at her flat.

"Tell me more about the league," she said to Harris. "Jack speaks so highly, almost reverentially, about it."

Harris talked about it as a community and explained how closely knit the guys were. Bad apples seemed to find their way out of the league, he said, and the good ones stayed.

"It's a little hard to explain, because I don't know of another league in the city that is quite like ours. Sure, the hockey and the workout are important. So is the competition. But the relationships, the camaraderie, the feeling of belonging to a community that looks out for one another, those are more important," he said. "It's more than the game. Hey, that reminds me, have you heard Jack's song about the league?"

"I love it," Callaghan replied, looking my way. "Jack played it for me a while back. Heartfelt. Even moving."

"Well, I haven't heard it yet," Harris said.

"Can't a guy have secrets anymore?" I complained.

"Not if I'm the only one who hasn't heard it," he said. "I'm your co-captain!"

"Jack, Will has already heard it. I've now heard it. Isn't it time you played it for your co-captain?" Callaghan said.

I played up my reluctance and made a few excuses, but Callaghan gave me this look that dissolved my hesitation in a few heartbeats. I picked up my guitar and played. Now, sometimes when you play a song for an audience, small or large—and for me it was almost always small—your nerves get the better of you. Your voice quavers a little, and your fingers on the frets just don't co-operate as they do when you're playing by yourself. That didn't happen this time. Perhaps it was my comfort with Callaghan and Harris. I don't know. But my song and voice sounded good for a change, at least I thought so. No guitar missteps. No egregious vocal anomalies. It was that rare albino moose of a performance when my weaknesses as a guitarist and singer did not seem to impair the listener's ability to understand and appreciate my song.

Normally I avoid looking at my audience. I didn't look at Harris. After all, I wasn't falling for him. But watching Callaghan watching me seemed to boost my confidence. She looked entranced as I sang. Either that, or the song was such a sonic assault on her senses that she slipped into catatonia. Turned out it was the former. I could tell she was listening carefully to the lyrics from start to finish to get the story, as she had the first time I'd played it for her. In the bridge, she actually put her hand on her heart and gave me such a heartfelt look I nearly faltered. Her reaction came during this lyric:

And when the season finally ends
What rewards have we reaped?
Look around and count your friends
That's the score we keep.

And she'd already heard it once before.

"I never thought a song about ball hockey could hold such meaning," she said after I struck the last chord and let it ring. "I pick up more meaning in the lyrics each time I hear them."

She came up behind the couch where I'd sat to play the song and wrapped her arms around me. Then she kissed the top of my head, no doubt in the middle of my ever-growing bald spot.

"Sweet tune, Jack-Mac," Harris said, shaking his head. "It's a different kind of love song, but it's still a love song."

"Yes!" Callaghan said. "You're right, Harris. It is definitely a love song, and beautiful in every way."

Two days later I escorted Harris out to Charles de Gaulle to catch his flight. Having him with me in Paris for a few days had seemed to quell the separation anxiety I'd been feeling being away from my ball hockey brothers for so long. It had really helped. I had the taxi wait while I said goodbye.

"Okay, so don't forget to review the player rankings when they're ready," I reminded him. "I'll be home before the end of March, so we'll get together then for a beer and figure out our draft strategy and picks."

"Sounds like a plan. Draught beer and draft strategy at the same table," Harris replied. "Hey, I'm glad you're doing so well. I even think your game is back up, almost to where it used to be a couple years ago. You looked good out there in that parking lot."

"Thanks. I feel better. Even though I'm in a strange city and hanging out with a woman who is different from anyone I've ever met, I seem to be feeling more myself than I have in a long time."

"I'm happy for you, man. I really am. You deserve it. And Callaghan is great. Love her."

We hugged, and Harris headed into the airport while I slid back into the taxi for the drive back into the City of Light.

Callaghan had been her wonderful self when Harris was visiting, so I wasn't surprised that he really liked her and was happy for us. But after Harris left, I began to see subtle changes in her behaviour, in how she acted when we were together. There was no blowout, no argument, not even a furrowed brow. At times it just felt like there was some distance between us that wasn't there before. Almost a kind of periodic ambivalence on her part when I was around. It worried me, but at other times, she seemed just as she always had. So, as a recognized expert in avoiding difficult topics, I just let it ride, hoping all was well.

Then, a couple weeks after Harris left, Callaghan and I were doing what we often did in the evenings. We were sitting together on her couch, leaning on one another, and reading. It all felt just so comfortable and right—until, you know, it didn't.

I again detected a certain subtle coolness in Callaghan, as if she was annoyed with me for some reason. It wasn't overt, and perhaps I was misreading her signals. But I'd been tracking it for a while by that time. One moment she was her normal, ebullient self, and the next she was staring at me with eyes that I can only describe as frigid. Then it would pass. Or would it? Perhaps she just suppressed it. Regardless, I was worried enough to overcome my traditional fear of potentially difficult conversations.

"Um, is everything okay with you?" I asked. "With us? I've just been getting a vibe now and then that feels, I don't know, different. Maybe I'm imagining it. Are we okay?"

She looked at me with furrowed brows. Great. Furrowed brows did not seem like a good sign.

"Why wouldn't we be?" she asked, in a way that struck me as cagey.

"No real reason. It's just that you've seemed, I don't know, a little quiet these last few weeks. A little subdued. A little tentative."

She sat up, looked out the window, and then suddenly buried her face in her hands and rocked a bit. She wasn't crying, but clearly something had been brewing and I'd inadvertently lit the fuse. I just waited for her. In a minute or so, she composed herself and turned back to me.

"All right, Jack," she said. "Okay, let's get it out into the open. Let me tell you a story that may shed some light on what you perceptively have noticed in my demeanour. You see, ten years ago, for some unknown reason, I was seeing an American investment banker—Cooper Croft was his Hollywood-sounding name—who worked here in Paris. He didn't behave like your typical high-flying Wall Street finance guy, though that's exactly what he was. We were together for three years and we had a good thing going. Or so I thought."

"Uh-oh," I said. "What happened?"

"Well, out of the blue, he got a promotion to the Hong Kong office and within a few days he just left, and whatever we had together went with him. I never even spoke to him again. He just disappeared. He wouldn't return my emails, my texts, my calls, my letters, and he still hasn't. In modern parlance, he ghosted me. He followed the money to Hong Kong and whatever we had just ended."

"Oh, Callaghan, I'm so sorry," I said. "Not all guys are like that. I'm not like that."

"After that, I didn't go out with anyone until, well, until I brazenly accosted you at Café Paul and sat down at your table," she said. "I cannot go through that again. I thought I knew him, but I clearly didn't."

"So as we get closer to my return flight to Toronto, you've started to put your shields up, thinking that I might be about to pull a Cooper and disappear without a trace."

"You know, once bitten, et cetera, et cetera," she said.

"Callaghan, I'm really sorry Cooper was such an idiot and an asshole, but I'm not Cooper," I said, leaning towards her, perhaps to signal that I was serious. "My home is in Toronto. My son is in Toronto. Much of the life I know is in Toronto. So I do have to go back, but I'm praying—and up to a few moments ago, I've been assuming—that what we have will continue, even though for at least a little while we won't be in the same city. I *will* return your texts and emails and calls, and I'm hoping you'll respond to mine. And I will come back to Paris, or to wherever else you might be, just as soon as I possibly can, perhaps even sooner."

"You make it all sound so simple and straightforward," she said. "Even words like *airport* and *flight* and *long-distance relationship* are triggers for me. I can't even talk about it right now, let alone figure out a solution. I know it was ten years ago, but it still hurts. I can't do that again."

"I'm not doing what Cooper did!" I said, a little more emphatically than I'd intended. "I want us to continue. What we have is worth the effort to keep it going, even when there's an ocean temporarily between us."

"I just can't talk about this right now. I'm not ready to talk about it. I don't want to talk about it. Not yet," she said. "Can we park it for now?"

"Of course, as long as you know, I'm not a finance guy like Cooper with the cool name. What he did to you was despicable. I'm not even capable of that."

We sat there for a time, Callaghan staring at the floor, while I fixed my gaze out the window. Finally, after what seemed like an awfully long time, Callaghan changed the subject. Bless her. Mind you, we were simply re-enacting a conversation we'd already had a week or so before. It was safe territory, so we travelled through it again.

"I really liked Harris," she said. "If all your ball hockey mates are as nice and funny, I'm not surprised you feel so strongly about the league."

I clung to her comment like a lifeline.

"Well, the guys are all different but seem to share the same values, if that doesn't sound too cheesy."

"No whiff of cheese anywhere. In fact, it's nice," she replied, still sounding sad, but making an effort. "You, Jack, are very lucky."

I had barely heard her last comment, because my eyes had fallen on the framed photo of Callaghan's grandmother that rested on a little metal stand on the table below the window. My eyes had passed over it countless times before, but in that instant, I was seeing it for the first time. I stared at it until it all became clear. I tried to stay calm and reserved in the face of the revelation, but instead, I suddenly leapt to my feet, clearly startling Callaghan. She jumped. Well, I mean her surprise seemed to lift her off the couch all on its own.

"Whoa, what the . . ." she said, settling back into the cushions.

"So sorry! But look!" I snatched the framed photo and held it out to her. "Look!"

She didn't get it. She hadn't seen it. Not yet.

"Yes, Jack, it's my grandmother. I recognize her. I've actually seen that photo a number of times before."

"No, no. You're missing it. Just like I missed it. Look at the painting in the shot, hanging on the wall behind her."

She squinted a bit before I watched her eyes widen to what seemed like the size of side plates.

"Bloody hell and curse my crumpets! Why did I not see it till now? It's been right in front of us the whole time. That's it! It must be!" she shouted, and jumped up and down on the couch.

"'Curse my crumpets'?"

CHAPTER 13

IN THE PHOTO, Callaghan's grandmother reclined in her chair in the very sitting room where we were then standing. Behind her, above and to the right of her chair, hung a painting on the wall. You may already have figured out what it featured to cause such a furor, but not all of you may be so quick. So to put everyone in the know—or perhaps more appropriately, in the picture—the painting hanging behind Constance Stanley featured, yes, you've got it now, none other than Place de la Concorde.

"So in the photo, exactly where was her chair positioned in this room?" I asked.

"Right about here," Callaghan said, moving over to stand in front of the sitting room wall.

There was a different piece of art hanging on the wall in about the same place. It was one of Callaghan's works.

"Okay, so let's solve this mystery right here and right now," I said, before reciting the first part of the coded message Callaghan's grandmother had left and that I'd committed to memory weeks earlier. *JB cahier: Six paces east of Place de la Concorde.*

I stood in front of where I estimated the Place de la Concorde painting once hung on the wall, and then I confirmed that east was towards the window to my left. I took six grandmother-sized paces in that direction. I was left standing in front of the near end of the built-in bookshelves that held, among other things, the diaries of Constance Stanley. My heart was beating as if I'd just finished an extended ball hockey shift. Thankfully, I smelled better than I do after a ball hockey game and wasn't sweating like a bush-pig in the seventh circle of hell.

"Okay. 'Top. Left end-board,'" I said, calling out the rest of the coded message.

I stood on a chair I had snagged from the kitchen to reach the top shelf. My heart was still pounding, and my stomach was tight. Callaghan steepled her hands in front of her mouth and bounced up and down on the balls of her feet. I pulled down a few of her grandmother's leather-bound notebooks and felt all around the left end-board, but nothing seemed amiss. Then I happened to push against the deepest part of the end-board and it gave way, apparently swinging on a pin in the middle, to reveal a secret compartment of sorts. You only expect to find secret compartments in movies and novels. But we found the real deal.

Callaghan, who'd been watching what I'd been doing very closely, gasped when the end-board swung in. Without shoving my hand into the compartment, I stepped down off the chair.

"What are you doing?" Callaghan asked in a tone lightly tinged with impatience. "You found it!"

I shook my head.

"You should be the one who discovers what's inside, not I."

She smiled and nodded as I helped her up onto the chair. I steadied her as she reached her right hand up and into the space beyond the bookshelf's end-board. She pulled her hand back out, sighed, and looked at the ceiling. I could feel her trembling as I held on to her waist.

"I'm not sure I can do it," she said. "I'm so nervous."

"Okay, take a deep breath," I said. "You know what to do."

She pushed her hand back into the secret compartment. I could see her arm moving as she explored the small space. Then she stopped and I heard her sharp intake of breath. She slowly pulled her hand out. Clutched in her fingers was another leather-bound notebook, smaller than her grandmother's diaries.

"I'm buzzing! I'm buzzing!" she said as I helped her down. "I'm bleeding buzzing."

"You're certainly shaking, but I guess you could be buzzing," I said.

She stood in front of the bookshelves and held out the small notebook, almost as if it were radioactive, so we could both see it. She paused, tried to slow her breathing, and rested her left hand on top of the notebook, keeping it closed. We just stood there for a few minutes, gathering ourselves. She then looked at me and nodded once. She opened the front cover. She gasped—so much for slower breathing. Then, when I had a clear view, it was my turn to gasp. We stared and processed what we were seeing.

"Holy shite!" I whispered. "Well, I guess we now know who JB was."

"Don't you think this situation is tailor-made for the term *gobsmacked*?" Callaghan said in a voice taut and tense. "For that is exactly what I am right now."

Pasted inside the front cover of the notebook was a classic publicity photo of the one and only Josephine Baker, topless in her famous banana skirt, strings of beads around her neck, her ebony skin aglow. Yes, the famous, iconic Josephine Baker.

Neither of us spoke for a few moments. Okay, I really don't know how long the silence reigned. I was still wrapping my head around this revelation.

"Jack, I think my grandmother may have had an affair with Josephine Baker. I think I need to sit down."

I helped Callaghan over to the couch and lowered her down into the cushions.

"It's astonishing," I said. "At the time, Josephine Baker was one of the most famous entertainers in the world, not to mention going on to become a decorated wartime spy. What a wonderful twist in what's already an extraordinary story."

"I don't know how you can construct complete sentences right now," Callaghan said.

"Neither do I. Maybe it's the writer's curse," I replied. "Anyway, I'm buzzing and gobsmacked, too, if I understand what you mean by those terms."

Then we sat side by side and read the diary, page by page, until we finished it. I silently thanked Constance Stanley for her beautiful handwriting. It was easy, and a joy, to read. When we'd finished reading, we just sat there for a few moments to let it all settle in our minds. Callaghan turned back towards the beginning of the secret diary, to an entry from October 1925, when it all started:

It was an exhibition utterly bereft of inhibition. She was the most striking blend of raw beauty, pure talent, and a bizarre, almost antic sense of performance. It was like nothing I'd ever seen on the boards. When she was on stage, my gaze never ever wandered from her. Such confidence. Such presence. In an instant, she somehow left my knees weak and my heart full. I have no explanation beyond the visceral.

Those in the audience around me used the word "exotic" to describe her allure and her act, but I confess I barely noticed the colour of her skin. I only saw radiance and brilliance and, yes, a kind of unconventional, singular beauty.

I knew the Théâtre des Champs-Élysées well, having once been taken on a tour by a friend who works there. When the show was over, I slipped down the side staircase behind a curtain to the bowels of the theatre, where the dressing rooms were crammed together along a single corridor. Many of the actors, musicians, and dancers were milling about, flushed and glistening from the fervour of their performance.

I found her in the third room I entered. Alone, her bare back to me, she was seated before a large mirror and vanity. She looked into the mirror and saw me behind her at the door. She smiled and nodded before speaking to my reflection.

"You're too far away. I can't see you in the dim light," she said in an American accent. "Come in, please."

Without thinking, I walked straight into her dressing room and stood just next to her chair, both of us still looking at one another only in the mirror. I had yet to say a word.

Josephine Baker took in my full reflection, and I hers. As is my habit, I was fully clothed. She was not but made no effort to cover herself. Though I tried, I could not tear my eyes from her captivating form in the mirror. This seemed to please her, for she looked at me through slightly hooded eyes, a wry smile warming her countenance.

"Why don't you close that door," she whispered, leaning towards me. "And then we can be formally introduced without risk of interruption."

I was not myself and moved as if in a trance to close the door. When I walked back towards her, she suddenly swivelled in her chair to face me. I stopped in front of her. She narrowed her gaze and looked me up and down. Then she reached out and took both my hands in hers.

"You are a vision," she said, still whispering. "Who are you?"

I have no memory of what I said. But I do remember what happened thereafter.

"I have to stop reading this or I might spontaneously combust," Callaghan said, fanning herself. "Oh, be still my beating heart. That has got to be one of the most erotically charged passages I've ever read."

"Um . . . I second the motion," I replied. "Is it warm in here?"

She smiled.

"I can't believe it, but it's all right here in my grandmother's own hand. It's true. This all happened! The drama, the intensity, the emotion, the heartbreak, the euphoria, the drinking, the sex, the pain, it's all here."

"Okay, so let's just recap," I said. "Your grandmother seems to have had a tumultuous, torrid, brief, high-octane flare of a relationship with Josephine Baker. That all tracks. Baker was known to have had sexual relationships with women, not to mention with plenty of men, often at the same time. But we'll need to verify the timeline and locations to make sure it all holds water."

"And Josephine Baker broke her heart. I'm not sure I can ever forgive her for that. It's so sad." Callaghan was looking off dreamily. "I love that my grandmother called her Jojo in her diaries. She had a pet name for her American, Black, woman, dancer, singer, spy, lover, who, by the way, was Josephine Baker!"

"I'm stunned," was all I could say—though short, it's still a complete sentence.

While the notebook's documentary evidence was clear, it was not yet confirmed. So I reached up for the leather-bound diary for 1926. I found the entry I was looking for, having read it not that long ago.

"Right, so this entry is dated January 14, 1926, and it says, 'Stole a long weekend with WO in Berlin.' We already know WO is actually JB. But we now have a date, too."

I pulled out my iPad, which I now kept at Callaghan's, and Googled Josephine Baker.

"Well?" she said as she looked at me in anticipation.

"Just another few seconds. I want to find at least one more reference so we're on safe ground," I said, my fingers flying over my iPad. "Okay, I just found two more references. Let me read this Facebook post to you from an online history and culture site called DW Culture. Here we go: 'On January 14, 1926, Josephine Baker performed for the first time in Berlin at the Nelson Theatre. She shimmied across the stage in her iconic banana skirt, defying all conventions for a dancer, sealing her place as an icon of the 1920s and the first Black superstar.'"

"Wow, the same date that put my grandmother in Berlin, too. Jack, this really happened, didn't it?"

"It certainly looks that way," I agreed. "This is new information about an icon of the era, as seen through the rich and insightful eyes and voice of your grandmother. This makes the idea of finding a publisher for these diaries—and the Josephine Baker notebook, too—even more compelling."

"Hmmm. Hard to disagree," Callaghan said. "And I have been coming to terms with the idea since you raised it earlier. I think I'm there, at least in principle. But before we show anyone, let's just think through any implications of specific, and perhaps intimate, entries. I know no one is still alive to be offended, but let's make sure we're comfortable before sharing this."

"You alone have to be comfortable, Callaghan. She is your grandmother," I said. "You've had her all to yourself for your entire life, both when she was alive and since she died, through her words in these notebooks. Going public with them is an important decision, and not one to be taken lightly. If they are ever published, you can't put that toothpaste back in the tube, if you know what I mean. This is your show and your call."

She sat on the couch with the Josephine Baker notebook opened on her lap. She was deep in thought, or shock, I'm not sure which.

"Her diaries are so alive and so animated," she said, flipping the pages. "But until you mentioned it, I'd never considered that scholars and fans of that era might want to see them. But you're right. Her diaries are more interesting than half the books I've read about that time."

"I truly believe there would be interest among publishers and academics in this new and eloquent first-hand account of Paris in the twenties."

"But I'm not an editor or a writer," she said, looking at me. "If we do decide to do this, I want us to do it together—that is, if you want to. And I want you to be the editor and to write the introduction and anything else that needs composing. That's what you do."

"Hold on a second, Callaghan. Are you sure?" I asked. "I know I offered to help, and I dearly want to, but we've really only known each other for four months. You might want a professional editor rather than a freelance writer."

"First of all, it feels like we've known each other for four decades, doesn't it?" she asked. I nodded. "When you walked into the Café Paul and ordered a pain au chocolat from me that first day, it was fate and destiny and providence standing in front of me, gift-wrapped. For heaven's sake, you were reading a book by my grandmother's favourite writer, after whom I am named. You have a passion for, and a deep knowledge of, Paris in the twenties. Jack, you can't fight this. If we go forward, we were meant to work on this together. The stars and planets, and all other celestial bodies, have never been so perfectly aligned as they are right now. We were made for this and were brought together for this. I'm already thinking about the painting that will grace the cover of this book."

I stayed quiet, given that she seemed to be on a roll. She took a deep breath before continuing.

"Jack, this was meant to be. When Tab A fits so perfectly into Slot B, you don't fight it. You welcome it. You embrace it. And you're grateful for it."

"I can't argue with any of that. So, if you decide we should proceed, count me in."

Then she kissed me. While it wasn't yet official, it appeared to me that she'd already made her decision.

I was right. Callaghan never clearly stated that she'd decided to proceed with Operation Publishing Constance. She just started conducting herself as if she had. I was fine with that. In fact, I was thrilled and excited. I was very rarely excited about the writing I did for my clients. I mean, how enthused can one get when writing a luncheon speech that somehow—however obliquely—extols the virtues and societal benefits of . . . well, you know what the speech is about. No need to dwell on it any longer. But editing the diaries of Constance Stanley, amateur poet and professional observer of 1920s Paris, was a prospect that left me not just enthused but enthralled. And doing it shoulder to shoulder with Callaghan was a dream assignment.

I worked hard over the next few days to wrap up a few writing projects on which I'd been dawdling so I could focus exclusively on the Paris diaries of Constance Stanley. I started at the most basic level. It was tedious work, but it had to be done as a precursor to more rigorous academic inquiry. Yes, I started with volume one of her diaries, and I carefully typed it word for word, date by date, punctuation mark by punctuation mark, into a Word doc on my laptop. Where she had made a rare spelling error, I'd leave it and add *sic* next to it in parentheses. Or when she'd obviously missed a small connecting word, I'd add it in brackets. Fortunately, Constance Stanley had lovely and legible handwriting and had used ink that had barely faded at all over the last century. It took some time, but over the course of two weeks of steady work, I typed in every word of her diaries, including the showstopping JB cahier.

While I was clacking away on my keyboard, Callaghan was carefully photographing every page of every one of the notebooks, including the leather covers and bindings, so we had a complete digital record of the diaries. Given her artistic eye, she also worked her way through her grandmother's photo album identifying candidate shots that might be included in the finished book.

I also contacted the Toronto office of Oxford University Press. They had published John Glassco's *Memoirs of Montparnasse* back in 1970. Despite the half century that had elapsed since, I hoped they might be interested in publishing Constance Stanley's diaries, since they described the same city and era. I secured a contact there from an old client and fashioned an email briefly telling the story of the diaries, the apartment, the Josephine Baker connection, and Constance's granddaughter, Callaghan Hughes, who was leading the effort to have the diaries published. I suggested in the email that I was a writer helping with the project.

I attached several digital photographs of the diary pages, including the coded message that had led to the discovery of the secret notebook. Finally, I scanned and attached a few of the photos that Callaghan had chosen from Constance's album. I sent off the email and attachments one afternoon and wondered if I'd ever hear anything in response.

We didn't have to wait long. I was still awake at midnight when a reply landed in my inbox. The message was from Thomas Henson, an editor at Oxford, and it was not long. It simply said, *Could we discuss this via Zoom tomorrow at 2 p.m. Paris time?* The Zoom link was included. I confirmed immediately.

Because it was a Zoom call, Callaghan and I dressed up just a bit, to give the impression that we were thoughtful, substantive people for however long we could sustain it. When I say we dressed up, I mean that the upper halves of our bodies—the only part visible on Zoom—looked quite respectable. Thomas Henson and his two colleagues also on the call would never know we were both wearing sweatpants just beyond their view.

The call seemed to go well. We could immediately tell that Thomas Henson and his colleagues were deeply interested in the diaries—even excited—based on what we'd sent.

"I'd like to have my London-based colleague Alistair Gibson go to Paris as soon as humanly possible to have a look at the diaries and start the authentication process. We'll need to confirm that the diaries are exactly what they appear to be before reaching any decision on a publishing offer," Thomas Henson said. "In the meantime, it would be very helpful in our deliberations if you could forward more excerpts so we can gain a clearer sense of the writing, the rich detail, and the range of issues and people reflected therein."

We agreed to send representative excerpts from each notebook rather than sharing the entire set of diaries. It just didn't seem right to send off everything we had before we had signed a publishing contract. They concurred.

They clearly felt some urgency about the project, as they wanted their researcher from London to come the next day. That worked for us, and the arrangements were made.

We had everything set up for Alistair Gibson on Callaghan's large dining table when he arrived the next day around noon. We had the actual diaries, the photograph of Constance Stanley that had helped crack the code, the secret "JB cahier," a list of places, individuals, and issues discussed in the diaries, and of course, the large photo album. He was impressed with what we'd pulled together for him.

Alistair asked for paper and ink samples from three different leather notebooks, which we happily provided. We assumed he was going to confirm scientifically that the notebooks and inks used were in fact from the 1920s. Made sense. There had been plenty of literary hoaxes over the years, perpetrated by fortune-hunters who had simply created phony diaries of famous people. Hitler's diary was likely the most famous fraud in this vein.

Alistair also took lots of pictures—not just of the diaries, but of the apartment, too, and the bookshelves and hidden compartment. He even took a couple of photos of Callaghan and me. By the time he left six hours later, it was easy to tell that he believed our whole story, unreservedly. Everything lined up so well. It was hard to imagine how this could be anything but legitimate and authentic. The real deal, as it were. The results of the paper and ink testing would confirm it all, and I figured a publishing offer would not be far behind.

"I've been putting this off for as long as I can, but it's now March 14, and there's something we really need to talk about," I said to Callaghan as we sat on the couch, an hour or so after Alistair had headed back to London.

"You mean, just how amazing the last few months have been, and how much has changed since we met?" she said. "I mean, you now have a writing credit on a hit song, and we might very soon have a publishing deal for my grandmother's diaries, which you will edit—with input from me, of course. That's what you want to discuss, right?"

"Well, not exactly. While all of that is true, that's not what we need to tackle."

"Okay, so we're going to do this, are we?" she asked with a deep sigh.

"Well, we have to, sometime."

"Do we? I mean, do we really have to?" she said. "Okay, sorry, Jack. Where do you want to start?"

"Well, maybe I can just set the context first," I suggested, feeling my way forward. "If you'd told me a year ago that I'd actually be in a relationship and be laughing every day, and feeling happier than I have since Annie died, I would not have believed it. Yet here

I am, in Paris, with you, on some kind of extraordinary adventure that I don't want to end."

"Excellent! Glad we see eye to eye on it. Good talk. Great talk," she said. "Glass of wine? Dinner? Movie?"

"Callaghan, I have to go back to Toronto," I said quietly. "My son is there. He needs me and I need him. My home is there. I've got a lot of work to do with the guys to get ready for the season that starts in about three weeks. I don't want to go back, but I have to. I have obligations. And did I mention a son? I'm sorry."

She suddenly looked sombre.

"I just thought you might stay," she said. "I know you can't hang around here forever, but I really wish you could."

"How about a visit to Toronto sometime?" I asked, grasping for something to look forward to.

"I have three art shows coming up in the next month or so," she replied. "I don't know."

"Oh," I said, caught a bit off guard. "You'd be welcome anytime, for however long you can stay."

"So you really are leaving?" she asked. "I've been down this road before, and it nearly did in my head and heart."

"I have to, Callaghan. I'm sorry," I said, and mentioned the date of my return flight to Toronto. "But we can FaceTime."

"FaceTime?" she said, giving me a puzzled look. "FaceTime? It's not the same as waking up together."

"No, it surely is not."

Despite my good intentions, we left the topic lying there between us, neither of us wanting to have anything to do with it. Her reaction had left me a little troubled.

—

Two days later, Thomas Henson set up another Zoom call. Callaghan and I sat together on the couch, with my laptop resting atop several art books on the coffee table. We both wore shirts that were semi-presentable, yet we once again wore sweatpants just below the camera's eye. Callaghan had seemed quieter and a bit distant or detached since I'd confirmed my departure date. I hoped it was just a passing phase as she came to terms with what would soon be a long-distance relationship.

"Ms. Hughes and Mr. McMaster, we have the results of our exhaustive and rigorous authentication analysis, and I'm pleased to report that the diaries of Constance Stanley have passed with flying colours. But you already knew that. We now have no doubt that the diaries in your possession were indeed penned by Ms. Stanley between 1920 and 1930 in Paris," Thomas Henson opened. "Yes, it is possible that she fabricated the parties, salons, and anecdotes, but the photographs support the legitimacy of the diaries, as do the detailed entries, which all line up chronologically with what we already know about certain events of the period."

"Well, that's certainly happy news," Callaghan said. "Of course, as you say, we've known all along that my grandmother wrote the diaries, but it's still a relief to hear that the authentication process reached the same conclusion."

"We will need a formal book proposal from you, and I'll pass along a format guide to help with that," he said. "But having now seen, authenticated, and verified the diaries—and I must say, if the rest of the entries are as fascinating and revealing as the excerpts you sent, then this is truly a remarkable find. Now, where was I? Oh yes—knowing that we have the true goods, as it were, we are comfortable proceeding with a publishing contract."

"Yes!" I shouted, and sprang to my feet, revealing the conflict between my pressed oxford cloth button-down up top and the ratty orange sweatpants below.

"Yes, well, we're pleased that you're excited. I can tell you, we certainly are, too," he replied. "Now, as you know, we're an academic, not a commercial, publisher, and despite our august history, we're still a rather small operation. With this in mind, I hope you will consider a three-thousand-euro advance against royalties of ten per cent of cover price to be satisfactory. I'm afraid it is the best we can offer."

I looked at Callaghan beside me and nodded once.

"Mr. Henson, that sounds just fine to us," Callaghan replied. "Could I ask whether you'll permit me to paint the image to serve as the cover?"

"Ah, thank you for reminding me," he started. "We have surveyed your artwork and are mightily impressed. We see no obstacle, and only marketing benefits, to using one of your paintings as the cover. Of course, we'd like some input on the image itself, just to ensure it will actually work as a cover and support the book's overall branding profile, if I may be so crass."

"But of course," Callaghan replied. "My colleague and I look forward to collaborating on this exciting project."

She looked at me in a way that made me feel very much like a colleague, rather than what I'd thought I'd been for the preceding four and a half months.

"Well, on behalf of my colleagues here at Oxford University Press, I can only say that we are thrilled to have reached an agreement with you," he said, bringing his hands together in front of him. "We firmly believe this book will be very popular among a small but committed segment of our readers. And it will also further our mission to support scholarship in art, culture, and literature."

"A noble calling, to be sure," I said, for some unknown reason.

"I'll email you a contract for you both to sign," Thomas said. "I may have forgotten to note this, but we support Ms. Hughes's choice of Mr. McMaster as editor, after having checked out your credentials. But we will also assign an editor from our staff to work with you on the book. I'm afraid there won't be a big book tour, subway ads, celebrity spokespersons, or promotional billboards. We don't really go in for that sort of expensive puffery. Nor could we afford it even if we wanted to try."

"No worries, Mr. Henson," Callaghan replied. "We're not much into expensive puffery ourselves."

"Splendid. We'll publish first in Canada and the U.K., and eventually in the U.S. And we'll endeavour to find a Paris partner to translate and publish the book in France, which seems only fitting."

"That all sounds wonderful, Mr. Henson," said Callaghan.

"Let me just say in closing that from what we've seen, we believe this book will make a significant contribution to our understanding of an important, even revolutionary, period in our cultural history."

When he said this, a subdued Callaghan nodded impassively.

Two days later, with Callaghan's blessing, I emailed our book proposal to Thomas Henson, carefully following the format he had provided. It was brief but complete. The day after that, we signed the publishing contract etching it all in stone. This was really happening, though I was unclear as to whether Callaghan and I were still really happening.

I did everything in my power to stop it, or at least slow it, but time defied my paltry efforts and relentlessly ticked away. On the morning of my last day, I suggested we not part at the airport. I didn't want my last few minutes with Callaghan to be spent jostling with tourists queueing in the security line. She agreed, though she hadn't been the same since our talk about my return to Toronto.

We spent the morning as we normally would. Oddly, she'd worn a flannel nightgown to bed the night before and was still wearing it while making coffee. She'd never done that before.

That last morning, when I hugged and held Callaghan for a long time just inside the door of her apartment, she did not reciprocate. I was the only real participant in the hug. I wondered what the hell I was doing leaving and what was going through her mind.

"Jack, I think we should agree on some ground rules as we move forward with the book," she said, a serious look on her face.

"Who are you and what have you done with Callaghan?" I joked.

"Look, Jack, I was up all night trying to figure out another way to handle this, but I just can't," she said. "Being together has been wonderful, and I'm so thankful we met. But you're going back to Toronto, and I have to stay here. I know myself well. I've been on this ride before, and I can't do it again. I just can't handle trying to manage a long-distance relationship. As I said, it nearly killed me the last time. So let's just consider the last four months or so to be a special gift, but it's not possible to sustain it after today. I'm just not built for it. I'm sorry. I truly am."

She paused for a moment when emotion threatened to derail her. I was speechless and, true to the condition, said nothing.

"Please try to understand," she pleaded. "I can't do it again. I just can't. So please, let's say goodbye now and call it a day. I know this may be a surprise. I kept hoping you'd change your mind and stay. I'm sorry, but if you FaceTime me from Toronto, it'll just make the separation worse and more painful. So . . ."

She paused again to gather herself.

"Let's not contact one another after this. I'm sorry. I don't know any other way to move forward."

I was caught completely off guard. My head was spinning.

"Um, I don't know what to say. I don't know what just happened," I said. "So what about the book? Should I be stepping away from it?"

She sighed and lowered her head.

"No, the book wouldn't have happened without you, and I certainly don't know what's involved in the editing," she said. "I'll come up with the painting for the cover, and you carry on with the editing and other writing requirements. We can be on separate tracks for the most part. If you have questions about what to include or what to cut, let's agree to correspond only through email. It won't be easy, but we have to deliver the manuscript to Thomas in a few months anyway. So we'll have to suck it up and manage somehow through email. I don't think I can do it any other way."

"Are you sure about this?" I asked. "I don't know. After what we've had, this seems like kind of an extreme reaction to my return to Toronto."

"I know it seems so, and I promise you if there were any other way . . ." she said, her voice trailing off. "It's my fault for ignoring what I knew to be true—that you would have to return to Toronto sometime. I understand that you have no real choice. Toronto is home. I know. I get it. I deluded myself and thought I might be able to get you to stay. Silly, but true."

"It's not silly in the least. If I didn't have responsibilities back home . . ." I started.

"And a son," she helpfully added.

"Right. If I had no obligations and no son, I'd never leave here."

"You're not helping, Jack," she said. "Look, talking about it doesn't make it any easier. Let's say goodbye and be thankful we were together for a time."

I didn't know what to say. I've always felt I'm at my most inarticulate in unexpected and high-stress situations. I had nothing.

"If you're sure that's what you want," I said.

"It's not what I want! You must know that. You must see that," she said. "It's just what's necessary for me to get through this."

I took a deep breath, maybe three or four.

"Well, then, um, thank you for appearing at a time when I really needed to be shown that I could live my life in colour again. You did that all on your own, and I'm so grateful. Oh, and thanks for making your café colleagues speak to me in French."

Then she cried. So I cried, too. There were flowing tears, heaving sobs, and a whole lot of serious, but I clearly sensed platonic, hugging before I finally forced myself to leave so I wouldn't miss my flight. After she closed her door, I could still hear her weeping as I struggled to walk away.

I was in shock, but I had no time to sort through my feelings or consider how my world had suddenly changed. I figured that was what long flights were for. I didn't really blame her. Well, maybe a little bit. Transatlantic relationships were challenging at the best of times. She had had a terrible experience once before. But I just hadn't expected her strong reaction or her "ground rules." It hurt.

But it wasn't over. Not yet. I just needed some kind of a reconciliation strategy.

My immediate plan was to return to my apartment to do my final packing and cleaning, lock up and leave the keys in the mailbox, and then grab a taxi to the airport. On my walk back, I saw Clementina sitting in her usual spot just outside the door to Café Paul. I slipped into the café.

"Un café et un croissant, s'il vous plaît," I said in my best French accent, which I knew probably still sounded like an anglophone trying out French for the very first time.

"Bien sûr, monsieur," said Étienne behind the counter. His response in French made me even sadder about Callaghan.

I paid and delivered the coffee and croissant to Clementina. I did my best to convey that I was leaving for several months but that I hoped to be back and would see her again then. (But would I?)

She grabbed my hand with both of hers and kissed it.

"Merci, monsieur. Merci pour tout."

I was leaving with more stuff than I'd had when I'd arrived, including two well-packaged pieces of art, both created by the talented artist Callaghan Hughes. One was the Latin Quarter street scene

I'd bought at her art exhibition, and the other the framed charcoal sketch of me sleeping where my face, striated with the light spilling through the window, revealed contentment, even happiness—but that was then. I was impressed with the stunning details around the folds and rolls of the sheets draped partway down my shoulder. The depression and creases my head made in the pillow were also rendered with great skill. It looked so real. I loved it. Along with the art, I had my big wheelie bag, my guitar, and my backpack and laptop. So I had my hands full. But I somehow managed.

I was of two minds that final morning. I can't deny that part of me was excited about returning home, to Will, to the guys, to the park and the ball hockey to be played there. I'd been gone for five months, longer than I'd ever been separated from my home, family, and friends. I missed it all. But in those five months away, I'd met and fallen for one Elizabeth Callaghan Hughes, a woman as different from Annie as anyone I'd ever met. After landing in Paris, I'd felt the fog in my head and heart lifting day by day, week by week. To me, cause and effect were obvious. In honesty's clear, clean light, I realized I felt much more myself leaving Paris than I had when arriving—at least until Callaghan's breakup bombshell that morning.

I'm not sure I'd have drawn this conclusion at an earlier age. I'm not convinced I'd have possessed the self-awareness to see it. But now, at sixty-two years old—yes, as hard as it was for me to believe, let alone accept, I was indeed sixty-two—I felt like I was recovering, returning, rebuilding, renewing, restoring, resetting. Perhaps the best metaphor might be—Callaghan's curveball aside—that I was rebooting my life after a catastrophic system failure. My heart and head were coming back online after a nearly three-year shutdown. All right, all right, I realize the computer crash comparison is—however accurate—well, inadequate, and obviously short-changes Annie. But it's just an analogy and it's what came to me in that high-stress moment.

What allowed me to see this, though, was the accumulation of life experience, and the incremental wisdom and maturity that had come with it. I see now that this idea of automatic age-related maturity might be the twelfth item on our list of things that actually make me feel my age. But this one is much more welcome and helpful than, say, frequent nocturnal visits to the bathroom, or the stiffness and pain in my legs the morning after a ball hockey game. So that brings us up to an even dozen. Surely this is a fitting item on which to call this list complete and closed. I was never a fan of the baker's dozen concept, or the misfortune that seems to have followed the number thirteen around for centuries. So let's stick with our list of twelve, shall we? An even dozen and we'll call it a day.

But Callaghan had just blown up all my theories on my growth and recovery. It almost felt like I was right back where I had started from the previous November. I still felt sick.

As I loaded my luggage into the trunk of the taxi, I happened to look up and saw Callaghan across the street, watching me with tears streaming down her face. Caught off guard a second time that morning, I started across the street towards her, but she shook her head and held up her hand. I understood—or maybe not—but that didn't make it any easier. I stopped and waved before getting into the taxi. I had to turn around and look out the rear window to see her as we drove away. As melodramatic as it sounds, we looked at one another until the taxi turned onto a side street and we were gone. It played out like the midpoint of a Hollywood rom-com, though the comedy part was lost on me. I truly didn't know if I'd ever see her again. I had no idea how things had gone so badly off the rails.

I was miserable for the entire flight home. I felt like I'd made a huge mistake leaving Paris, but also that I didn't have much choice. I needed to get back to Will and everything I'd left behind. I'd been gone for five months. I couldn't just live in Paris indefinitely when my history, family, friends, and life were in Toronto. Reality was reasserting itself. I was returning home to the warm embrace of my community. That felt good. But I was also leaving a part of me behind in Paris. And that felt—well, sitting on the plane that afternoon, it just felt horrible. And I had no real plan to fix it. Not yet.

PART 3

TORONTO

CHAPTER 14

WILL MET ME AT THE AIRPORT. When he hugged me, I had a little meltdown right there in the Arrivals area. I didn't break our greeting embrace for an uncomfortably long time as I wrestled with my tear ducts and voice control.

"Dad, it's okay, I'm here. You're home now," he said. "And I missed you, too."

"Son, I love you and missed you, and am happy to be home, but that's not what's messing me up at this precise moment."

"Right. I hear you, Dad," he replied. "Callaghan is something else. I really like her, and she's obviously good for you. I'm not surprised leaving was hard."

"Let's go home, Will."

I'd only been home for about twenty minutes when clarity landed a cruel blow. The fear that I may have made a big mistake by leaving

Paris and Callaghan had tipped over into the realm of certainty. I had blown it, big time. My heart had understood from the start, but now I knew it in my head, my gut, and my bones, too. Sure, it was nice to be back home with Will, my hockey tribe, and everything from my old life that made me happy. But of course, there was one thing—or more accurately, one person—who made me very happy, and she was not here in Toronto. She was an ocean and five time zones away and had understandably imposed a moratorium on contacting her. I was at least beginning to understand her feelings on the matter but felt every bit of the distance and silence dividing us.

I arrived a little late at Rivals for the big draft night. The rest of the captains were already seated with their spreadsheets, um, spread out in front of them, ready to go. I received a standing ovation when I appeared, and lots of double-edged comments about my new status as a hit songwriter. I bowed deeply, then went around the table gripping shoulders, high-fiving, and fist-bumping before pulling up next to Harris, my co-captain. Before the draft got underway, I was coerced into providing a quick summary of my five months in Paris. I tried to make it clear that it had been a very good period for me and that I now felt much more myself than I had when I left. And just to avoid a plethora of bilateral conversations about the topic, I did fess up to meeting someone who had helped me get past the last two years after losing Annie.

"Yeah, we heard that from your son," Nathan said. "Will said he really likes her. I figure it's a good sign when your son likes your new girlfriend."

"Well, let's not get ahead of ourselves," I cautioned. "We're currently on a break, and to make it clean and simple, she's asked that we not communicate while we're apart, at least for a while. Besides, we're not even in the same country right now, so who really knows what the future holds? What I do know is, I'm back, and I hope in more ways than one. Thanks for all the support. I couldn't have made it without you guys."

"Well, that sucks, Jack. Sorry, man," said Nathan. "But enough about your star-crossed love life, is your game back up to the standard we expect from you?"

Everybody laughed, including me, though I was just going through the motions. Superficial chuckling at best. It's hard to laugh genuinely when you're gutted. But I put on a brave face for the boys. It wasn't their fault Callaghan and I were no longer together.

"I guess we'll find out when the season opens, but I hope my game is back," I said. "I played once a week in Paris and I don't mind telling you that, well, I was a star week in and week out, slipping checks, passing tape to tape, and picking corners—you know, the usual."

"Yeah, yeah, we'll be the judge of that," said Nathan. "Just come to play next Tuesday."

On the one hand, it did feel good to be back home in the bosom and banter of my community. But on the other, I knew my thoughts would turn to Callaghan the instant I was on my own again. I was not looking forward to that. I felt like the victim of a hit and run, still trying to process what the hell had just torn me apart, torn us apart.

The draft proceeded without incident, other than Teddy spilling his beer all over the table. When we were done, I liked the look of our team, but really, the draft system ensured that unless captains were idiotic in their player selections, the teams ended up evenly matched. The stars, the middling players, and those who weren't very good at all were evenly distributed, one pick at a time, across the six teams. As a league, we aimed for parity among the teams. We never wanted one squad to run away with the season, or to go winless, so we'd designed a draft process that yielded teams of similar quality. Of course, throughout the draft, there were plenty of wisecracks about the teams' names, jerseys, and players.

For something different, we'd decided to name each squad after teams in the KHL (the Kontinental Hockey League, active in Russia, Europe, and Asia). Over the years, we'd already run through the original six NHL teams, then the first expansion teams in 1967, then the teams at the junior AHL level. So the teams of the KHL were next up on our list. Harris and I would helm Jokerit, a Finnish team in the KHL. Our dark blue jerseys featured a comical court jester's head emblazoned on the front, complete with the funky hat and its dangling protuberances adorned with bells. Admittedly, playing while wearing a jersey with a multicoloured jester's head across our chests, it might be hard to muster much dignity. But we'd give it our best shot.

Harris and I walked home together after we'd completed and then celebrated the draft.

"How do you feel, now that you're home?" he asked.

"I think I messed up, Harris, man," I replied.

"You mean leaving Callaghan?"

"Yep," I replied. "I'm really missing her. Being home and surrounded by reminders of Annie, I'm now missing both Annie and

Callaghan, and I can't speak to either of them. It was hard enough losing Annie. It feels like I've now lost Callaghan, too."

"Look, J-Mac, I don't know what happened over there, but I can handle the team for a few weeks," Harris said. "Why don't you go back to Paris for a bit longer? Try to figure out a solution. Maybe she can come here for a while?"

"It might come to that if I can't figure anything else out," I said. "I've wanted to FaceTime her, but I gave her my word, and I don't want to threaten what we might be able to rekindle by breaking that promise."

"Believe me, I get it," Harris said. "I was really taken with her. I don't think I've ever met anyone quite like her, and I only had a couple days' exposure."

And so the weeks passed. Four games into the season, I didn't feel like I was in any better shape, though my perspective may have been a little distorted. My performance in our games was lacklustre at best, and nowhere near my level of play in the school parking lot on Rue Descartes. I was back, but I wasn't back, if you know what I mean. I was starting to accept that my mental and emotional states had an impact on how well I played. An idea not entirely bereft of logic—I'd just never fully considered the connection before.

Each day, missing Callaghan seemed to occupy more of my mental space and deplete more of my physical energy. Even though my whole life was wrapped up in this family, this house, this community, this city, I kept asking myself, *What am I doing here?* I tried not to overthink it, but it did not take a genius to know I wasn't happy. I knew I wanted to be somewhere else, or more precisely, with someone else. I kept my promise to be incommunicado, and as a stopgap measure, I threw myself into my old life to take my mind off the mistake I strongly suspected I'd made. That strategy worked to a certain extent, but only as a temporary balm. Distracting oneself from the central issue is not an effective long-term play. When my self-inflicted busy days were over and I crawled into bed drained and exhausted, the futility of my distraction gambit draped itself over me. I wanted to call Callaghan at least once a day. I even tried once. I called her mobile, but it just rang and rang. She never picked up. I left an apologetic message admitting to breaking our agreement and asked her if we could talk, if only just once. She didn't call. I feared I'd broken her trust and doomed any future reconciliation. I felt sick to my stomach afterwards.

"Dad, what is up with you since you've come home?" Will asked one morning. "It's like you're back to how you were before you went to Paris."

"Will, I'm adjusting to my new reality after five months on a different planet. It's just taking me some time to get resettled."

"Really? If you want my view, you seemed very happy, very content, and very comfortable when I was with you in Paris, which was a radical change from how you seemed to be before you left. Something was responsible for that turnaround, and I don't think it was the flaky pain au chocolat and great wine in Paris."

"Look, Will, I know where you're going with this, and it's just not realistic for me to pack up my life and move to Paris. This is where I belong. But I can't be with Callaghan and be here at the same time."

"Dad, I didn't say you don't belong here. It's just that something is missing."

Three days later I succumbed. I booked a ticket for Paris leaving the following Wednesday evening—so I wouldn't miss my Tuesday-night game. My return ticket had me arriving back in Toronto the following Tuesday afternoon—again, so I wouldn't miss my Tuesday-night game. The obligation I felt to my teammates was real. My plan was to just show up unannounced on Callaghan's doorstep, fall on my sword, bleed for a while as I confessed I'd made a big mistake, and then convince her to come to Toronto, at least for a while. I feared if I told Callaghan about my return to Paris, she might try to talk me out of it. So I was counting on the element of surprise to weigh in my favour. It was also possible my little plan wasn't fully baked and would blow up in my face. But I just needed to see her.

In the days before my flight back to Paris, I pursued the other elements in my little plan to bring us back together. I spent a lot of time cleaning up (and out) the storage room on our third floor at the front of the house, just outside my office. Then I worked hard to turn it into a space that might help me survive in the coming months and years. You're probably thinking I installed a treadmill or rowing machine. I'm not saying that wouldn't help my survival, and at some point, I probably should do exactly that. But that wasn't the role the repurposed storage room was destined to play.

It was late Wednesday afternoon, and I'd wrapped up some work on the book and put my packed suitcase at the front door. Will was working late, and I didn't feel like bugging any of my ball hockey mates for a lift to the airport. That would have meant explaining exactly what I was doing flying back to Paris just a month after returning home. So I booked a taxi for five o'clock. The cab was due to arrive in a matter of minutes when my phone chirped with a FaceTime call. I was upstairs, sitting on my bed deciding what books to take for the flight. I was surprised when I saw the name illuminated on the screen.

"Callaghan?" I opened. "Are you all right? I can only hear you. Your camera's not on."

"No, I'm really not okay. But that's to be expected under the circumstances," she said, sounding like someone else, distant, formal. "I'm sorry to be the one to break our FaceTime embargo, but rather than email you about this, I have an idea for the book cover that I wanted to run by you."

"It's so good to hear your voice," I said, checking my watch. "Oh, and it's late for you."

"Yes, it is late, I know. But I'm almost home," she said.

"Um, sorry, Callaghan, I have a taxi coming soon to take me, um, downtown for the Blue Jays game."

"That's baseball, right?" she asked.

"Right."

"Okay, I'll be quick," she said. "About the cover art, while it is a Paris diary, I really don't want anything as cliché as the Eiffel Tower on the cover. I'd like to create a painting that captures the whole vibe of the Left Bank. So I'm thinking of a kind of classic sidewalk café experience, without it being clear which one. It could be along Saint-Germain or Montparnasse, but the focus would be on people having a good time and enjoying café life in the 1920s. Does that work?"

"I like the idea. The cafés were the spine of expat life," I replied. "Can't wait to see what you come up with."

"Right, so I'll work towards that and keep you posted."

At that moment, my doorbell rang.

"Just a minute, Callaghan, that must be my taxi driver at the door, and he's early," I said, annoyed with his timing. "Let me just get rid of him for a few minutes and we can talk a bit more before I'll need to bail."

"I really should go," she said, sounding exhausted. "I'll send you the cover image when I get it done. Thanks, Jack."

"Wait . . ." I said. But she'd already ended the call.

Shit. While it was great to hear her voice, it didn't sound like the Callaghan I'd spent so much time with in Paris. That certainly didn't bode well for my little surprise.

The doorbell sounded again. I hurried down the stairs and opened the front door.

There, before me, Callaghan stood on my front walk, a suitcase beside her. She looked up at me, her eyes not just glistening but brimming with tears. Meanwhile, my eyes couldn't quite comprehend what, or who, I was seeing standing in front of me. I just stood there with my yap open and my eyes wide.

"You won't get rid of me as easily as a cab driver," she whispered as I stood there in shock. Then her face kind of collapsed as she burst into tears. "Oh, shite on a stick, I'm sorry. I didn't want to cry but I can't help it. It's been a long and emotional day."

Finally accepting the reality of her presence, I leapt down the steps and took her in my arms. I said nothing. I couldn't speak right then anyway, so we just held on to one another like our lives depended on it. And in that moment, it felt like they did. It took me a few minutes before I could speak. I've always been a big believer in the notion that actions speak louder than words, so I picked her right up off the ground and carried her into the house. I lowered her onto the couch and then remembered her suitcase. With all the willpower I could muster, I pulled away from her to fetch her bag, which weighed about as much as one of those tiny Smart cars. Then we were back on the couch, entwined again.

"I can't believe you're here," I said. "It's a miracle."

"I just couldn't stand not being able to talk to you, or see you, or hold you, after we'd been inseparable for the last several months," she said. "Furthermore, I'm weak. I thought breaking it off and sticking only to email for the book, at least for a while, would be easier on my heart. Turns out I was wrong. It wasn't easier at all. It was misery incarnate. So here I am."

"This all sounds very familiar. If it's any consolation, I've felt just as bereft. So often I wanted to FaceTime you, just to see you and hear your voice and laugh, but I promised I wouldn't. And I just couldn't imperil any future we might have by breaking the one promise I'd made to you that last day," I said, conveniently ignoring the unanswered FaceTime call I'd attempted.

"You honoured your promise, at least for the most part, but I just couldn't handle it," she said. "That's all behind us now. I'm here."

Then she saw my packed suitcase in the front hall.

"Do you always pack so much for a baseball game?" she asked.

Just then I saw the taxi pull up in front.

"Just give me one second, and don't you dare move," I said. "I'll be right back."

I sprinted out to the taxi and cancelled my ride. The driver was annoyed, given how lucrative an airport run was, until I handed him a fifty-dollar bill for his trouble. Then I dashed back into the house to reassure myself that Callaghan was no apparition, but flesh and bone.

"But what about the Cardinals game, or is it the Orioles or Great Blue Herons?" she asked. "I just remember it was some kind of bird."

"It's the Blue Jays."

"Right, Blue Jays. Sorry, I'm jet-lagged and heartbroken in a foreign land and have a lot on my mind at the moment," she said.

"Given what your day's been like so far, I think it's impressive that you picked up the bird reference at all," I said. "And to be honest, I wasn't actually going to a Blue Jays game. I'm sorry for misleading you a wee bit," I said.

I called up my Air Canada boarding pass on my phone and showed it to her. "I was just about to leave for the airport to fly back to Paris. To fly back to you. I couldn't take it anymore, either."

It was her turn to be shocked.

"No way!" she shouted.

"Way," I predictably replied.

"But you see it, don't you? This is just another illustration of how we're fated to be together. I'm telling you, this is destiny."

She held both my hands in hers and looked up at me.

"If we weren't meant to be together, I would have arrived five minutes *after* your cab pulled away. But no! I got here just in the nick of time. Just more evidence that we're supposed to be a team, not living in two separate cities with an ocean between us."

She paused when she noticed her painting hanging above our fireplace, in the space that any art lover would call prime and prominent. Just below, resting on the mantle in a silver picture stand, was her painting of Annie and Will. The proximity of the two works meant that both of my Callaghan Hughes masterpieces could be enjoyed at the same time.

"They both look perfect in this room, as if they were made to be here," she said. "Try to tell me there aren't higher forces at work here."

"I still can't believe you're here, in this city, in this house, on this couch," I said. "I've had a lot of surprises in my life, but I don't think I've ever been as shocked or as happy as I am right now. You're here! You're actually here."

She beamed at me.

"Well, that's kind of what I was going for," she replied, then paused for a few beats before continuing in a more serious tone. "Look, I know I imposed the 'no contact' rule to protect my heart from further damage, but I just don't think we can or should mess with the fates that brought us together. If I'd written our story as a novel, no one would believe it. But we know it really happened and what it really means."

She paused again to catch her breath, but not for long.

"You were sitting in my café reading a long-forgotten book by the very writer after whom I'm named. We got together and clicked immediately. And believe me, I don't click with everyone. In fact, for some reason, it's never happened the way it did with you. Then, all of a sudden, you had a hit song on the radio, fulfilling a lifelong dream. That happened right out of the blue. And if that's not enough, then you miraculously cracked my grandmother's code and we somehow landed a book deal to publish the diaries I've kept and read and cherished for my entire life. You just don't question a run like that. You embrace it and hold on tight, even with the Atlantic between us."

"You don't need to convince me," I said, nodding vigorously in agreement. "When I walked into Café Paul, I was just looking for a pain au chocolat and a coffee, that's all. And I ended up with something a little dearer to me than a chocolate croissant."

"Like the true Pollyanna that I am, I've always believed that good things happen to good people," she said. "You, Jack, are 'good people,' and I try frightfully hard to be 'good people,' too. What else have we in this life?"

"I don't know how it all happened or who was pulling the strings, but I'm grateful I walked into Café Paul that day when I could have gone to countless other cafés instead. There are quite a few in Paris, you know."

She laughed.

"Jack, I know I should have warned you I was coming, but I was afraid you might try to talk me out of it. Plus, there's also my flair for the dramatic to consider."

"Talk you out of it? For the last month it's all I've been able to do to keep myself from trying to talk you into it. I'm sorry. I was an idiot to leave. I've been miserable."

"I'm glad you've been miserable, sorry, but I mean that in the nicest of ways," she said. "All I know is that I've been in pain since you left. And not seeing or speaking to you was supposed to make it easier, but it made it worse. I worried you'd be back here living your best life with your son and hockey buddies, slowly losing any memory of our time in Paris."

"That would never happen, not in a million years. I've been depressed and wracked with guilt the whole time we've been apart. That's why I'm booked on that flight to Paris in three hours," I said. "Oops! Just give me a second to deal with that."

"I'm not going anywhere," she said, leaning her head back against the couch. "Not anymore."

It took me about twenty minutes on the phone with not one, not two, but three different Air Canada reps before I was able to cancel my flights. Because I'd booked them just a few days ago, they were full-fare tickets and came with cancellation privileges. Not that I cared about the money at that moment.

"But how did this happen?" I asked as I sat back down beside Callaghan. "How did you do this?"

"Well, it was pretty straightforward. I'm an artist. I can paint anywhere. When my last show finished two days ago, there was nothing holding me in Paris and a whole lot beckoning from Toronto. So I just came and planned to throw myself on your doorstep—and your mercy—and beg for forgiveness and shelter."

"It is I who needs forgiveness," I said. "I should never have left. And as for shelter, I'll do better than that. Let me show you something."

I took her hand and led her up the stairs to the third floor. In that instant, it felt like we'd returned to synchronous orbits. All that had been lost when I'd flown home a month ago had been somehow restored when she rang our doorbell. At the top of the stairs,

I opened the door and turned on the light in the large space that we'd previously used for storage. Now it was a hastily, but thoughtfully, equipped art studio.

I thought I'd done a decent job transforming the attic into an artist's studio in the hopes it might entice Callaghan to stay. I figured helping her get a foothold in the Toronto art market might help. And that meant creating a place for her to work. I'd painted the walls a neutral eggshell and pulled up the dirty, well-worn carpet. A belt sander that Harris had lent me and a few coats of Varathane made the newly revealed hardwood floors gleam.

She gasped as she stepped into the large room with the sloping roofline and the west-facing window overlooking the street and the park beyond. She ran her hand along one of the four easels I'd ordered. They were the same model she used in her Paris studio—thank you, Amazon Prime. There was a large free-standing cupboard filled with art supplies including palettes, paper, brushes, paints, and canvasses of various sizes. In addition to the overhead lights, there were also three large floor lamps that could be positioned depending on the resident artist's needs. And miraculously, there was already a sink on the east wall, which I'd cleaned and polished. Painters need a sink.

A set of low bookshelves ran the full length of the south wall. I'd procured copies of the art books I could remember seeing in Callaghan's apartment, then ordered others that I thought looked good and might appeal to her. They were loaded into the shelves as if they'd always been there. She touched the books while shaking her head and smiling.

"Just a minute," she said, as she dashed out the door and back down the stairs. "I'll be right back."

While she was gone, I lit the candles I'd placed on the deep windowsill and turned on the bookshelf stereo with the instrumental new age music she favoured. I heard her rushing back up the stairs. Carefully balanced in her arms was every one of her grandmother's leather-bound diaries. She placed them on the top shelf of the built-in bookshelves and then stood back to admire them.

"Perfect," was all she said.

Then I led her to the funky couch along the north wall, where she could lie down and rest when her muse fled the scene. We both sat down and just looked around the newly christened art studio. She was still shaking her head and kept repeating "I can't believe you did this" like a mantra.

"Other than my grandmother, no one has ever done anything like this for me," she whispered. "Ever."

"Callaghan, it's a reflection of what you've done for me," I said. "Whenever you're ready, we can make the rounds of art supply stores and pick up whatever furniture, supplies, and other stuff you need to create your masterworks right here."

"Are you trying to tell me something?"

"Very perceptive of you. In case it's not clear, I guess this is my way of saying you're welcome to stay here as long as you wish."

She just leaned against me and held my arm with both her hands.

"Let me show you the second floor," I said, standing up and taking her hand again.

She was quite capable of walking without my guiding hand, but I just felt the need to have physical contact. It helped reaffirm in my own mind that her presence was in fact corporeal and not spectral.

The week before, I'd finally cleared out Annie's clothes from our walk-in closet. I kept a few items like a favourite sweatshirt of hers, and a cool hat she liked to wear in winter. They both still smelled like her, and I had a tough time for a while after burying my face in the sweatshirt and inhaling her scent. But I donated the rest of her wardrobe to a women's shelter. Annie would have agreed and probably would have wondered why it had taken me so long.

I showed Callaghan the master bedroom. I pointed to the dresser on the west side of the room.

"I hope I'm not moving too fast or making faulty assumptions, but this empty dresser is for you," I said.

Then I led her to the ensuite bathroom.

"That empty shelf is for you, as well as that empty top drawer and the cupboard below the sink," I said, pointing.

Finally, I showed her the walk-in closet, where the shelves and hanging space on two of the three walls were empty and waiting.

"That's all mine over there," I said, pointing again. "But all the rest of this space is for you."

She'd remained quiet through the tour, but her smile never once dimmed below full wattage. Finally, she turned and wrapped her arms around me, closed her eyes, and rested her head against my sternum. Apparently, I wasn't moving too fast or making faulty assumptions. My mind was reeling, but my happiness calmed me.

"I'm sorry I was headstrong about you leaving. I've been there before and didn't want to go through it again," she said.

"I shouldn't have left, and I'm sorry I did," I said, still in mid-hug, standing in what I hoped would be our walk-in closet. "How long can you stay?"

"I have no idea," she replied. "I flew on a one-way ticket and sheer hope. Let's just see how it all feels and we can figure it out as we go along."

"Perfect."

For the rest of the afternoon, I walked Callaghan around the neighbourhood. I wanted to save the park across the street for the end, so we first walked up to and then along Danforth Avenue, shortened by insiders to simply "the Danforth."

"This is a lovely commercial stretch with all sorts of boutiques, restaurants, bookstores, and—wait for it—galleries. It's also the heart of Toronto's Greek community, so if you like souvlaki or spanakopita, or have a penchant for smashing plates on the floor, you have a couple dozen choices on this street alone."

"It has a real community feel to it, doesn't it?" she said.

I nodded.

"Let's hit the park," I suggested. "To me, that's the heart of the community."

We walked down Carlaw until we hit Withrow Park. She loved it all. The trees, the flowers, the benches, the open playing fields, the dedicated dog space, and of course, the hockey pad where we played our ball hockey games in the spring, summer, and fall. In winter, there's ice in the rink.

"And you live across the street from this perfect verdant patch of loveliness," she said.

"Well, for a little while at least, so do you."

Will and Ariel were home when we walked in.

"Hi, Dad," Will called from the kitchen, where, judging by the commotion, he and Ariel were cooking up a storm.

"Hey, Will," I replied as we walked towards the kitchen. "Look who I've brought home with me."

Ariel, who was rinsing some green onions at the sink, and Will, who was stirring something on the stove, both looked around.

"Callaghan!" Will shouted, startling Ariel. "You're here!"

He left his stirring station and crossed the floor to hug Callaghan.

"Will, it's so good to see you again," she said. "We missed you when you left after Christmas."

"I can't believe you're here," Will said.

"That's exactly what your father said."

"Hey, I thought there was a no calling, no talking rule in place."

"There was, but that folly has ended," Callaghan declared.

"Excellent! Good call," Will said. "Oh, Callaghan Hughes, meet Ariel Banerjee. We work together and, well, we do other things together, too."

"So pleased to meet you, Callaghan," Ariel said while giving her a hug. "Will and Mr. McMaster have told me so much about you. I feel like I already know you."

I winced.

"And Will told us all about you when he visited at Christmas," Callaghan said. "I'm sorry we took him away from you for a few weeks."

"No worries. It was kind of nice to have him out of my hair for a bit so I could get some Christmas shopping done," she said with a smirk. "Just kidding, Will—not really kidding."

Callaghan and I laughed. Eventually, Will did, too.

"And, Ariel, we're going to have trouble if you call me Mr. McMaster again," I said. "I'm still coming to grips with my advancing years, so it would help if you just called me Jack, or perhaps Young Jack."

"No problem, Mr.—um, Young Jack," Ariel replied. "My dad feels the same way. Maybe I'll start calling him Young Arjun."

"Well, if he's like me, I think he might appreciate that," I said.

We all had dinner together that night. Both Will and Ariel were accomplished cooks, but when they worked together it was clear that the whole was greater than the sum of its parts. The meal was wonderful. Veal saltimbocca, roasted parsnips and carrots, mushroom risotto, and some kind of salad with a few ingredients I had trouble identifying, including what appeared to be wildflowers.

"If we're going to eat like this every night, my decision to stay for a while may not turn strictly on Jack," Callaghan said.

Under the table, she rubbed her foot against my lower leg to reassure me she'd been joking. I already knew that, and she knew I knew. But her calf massage did feel good. The four of us talked for a couple of hours around the dinner table. The time flew. Callaghan and Ariel hit it off almost immediately and were yukking it up together and eyeing Will and me, almost certainly sharing private jokes about the men in their lives. It didn't bother me in the least.

Callaghan and I cleaned up the kitchen afterwards. One thing I'd noticed about Will's culinary exploits was that he seemed an advocate of the "why use only three pots when you can use all five" approach to the culinary arts. I've always been a "clean up as you cook" devotee. Will was not.

The jet lag eventually caught up with Callaghan, so after we'd finished with the kitchen, we called it an early night. Twenty minutes later, as inexplicable as it would have seemed earlier in the day, Callaghan and I were in the same bed, in our home, in downtown Toronto.

"That Ariel is a crackerjack," she said. "I really, really like her."

"I think she and Will are perfect for each other," I replied. "She's smart and witty, and they seem so comfortable together, as if they were good friends long before romance entered the picture."

Callaghan squeezed my hand.

"Exactly! I'm a big believer in the friends-first approach. I know too many couples who don't seem to be friends even though they're together. I have no idea how they became romantically involved without first connecting as friends. I just don't see how it could ever work," she said. "You, Jack, are the best friend I've had in a long time."

I confess it was briefly unsettling to see her lying next to me. For more than thirty years, I'd only ever shared that bed—or any other—with Annie. Ever sensitive, Callaghan knew it might be strange for me.

"Are you okay, Jack?" she asked. "You know, I can sleep on the couch if this feels a little weird."

"You'll not be sleeping on the couch. I'm fine. I'm just getting used to this. And I want to get used to this," I said. "But would you mind if we switched sides?"

"Of course not," she replied, crawling over me as I slid to my left.

She didn't even ask why. Likely because she knew. I thought it might be easier if I claimed Annie's side of the bed and let Callaghan sleep in the space I usually occupied. It was a small change, but it gave me an entirely new perspective on the bedroom I'd slept in since the early nineties. In all the years I'd lived in this house, I'd not once slept on Annie's side of the bed, at least until that night.

"Oh, um, I was just thinking. Living with Will, and often Ariel, too, under the same roof, you may wish to reconsider your penchant for naked perambulation throughout the house," I gently suggested. "I mean, I love it. What's not to love? But it might freak them out a bit."

"I'd already made a mental note to curtail any nude cavorting unless we're alone."

"Sounds like a plan."

I had missed sleeping with Callaghan, not necessarily for the reasons you might think. Just to feel her warmth next to me brought a deep sense of contentment. Okay, those other reasons were not without merit, either. That night, I enjoyed the deepest sleep I'd had since leaving Paris.

CHAPTER 15

CALLAGHAN'S FIRST GAME as a goalie in the women's league came two weeks after she magically materialized on my doorstep. Goalies are often in short supply in the women's league—and in the men's league, for that matter. One of the teams had no regular goalie. So whoever drew the short straw on any given game night strapped on the pads and took her place between the posts. In other words, there was an opening for an experienced goalie, or even for Callaghan—a few games in a Paris parking lot hardly earned her the coveted "experienced goalie" designation. But she was game. I borrowed goalie equipment from a neighbour who had aged out of the league a few years earlier, and Callaghan was set to go.

It took her about two minutes to gel with her teammates, most of whom I knew. Callaghan had many gifts. Connecting with new people was just one of them. And when she stopped the first nine shots in her first game, some of them even on purpose, she secured her place on the team. She still squealed with delight whenever the ball hit her and didn't end up in the net. I cheered her on at every game.

Callaghan also had a natural competitive streak, which I'd discovered when Will, Callaghan, and I played Scrabble over Christmas. She knew her way around the English language and often challenged words that she didn't think were legitimate. She was usually right. Beyond her competitive streak, she also just loved the idea of being on a team, of belonging not just to a team or a league but to a community. Her chosen career as an artist demanded a creative but solitary existence, at least when she was in painting mode. And she really enjoyed engaging with other people. While she was an extrovert, she was gifted in a field that attracted its share of introverts. So she loved being on a team, whether as counter staff at Café Paul or as a rookie goalie in a Toronto ball hockey league.

Her open personality meant she slipped into the team and the broader community quickly and easily. Everyone made a point of telling me how much they liked her. That made me very happy, because they had all loved Annie, too. We started being invited to friends' homes for dinner and barbecues as a couple. That was a good sign and Callaghan took it all in stride. It struck me that she was among the most genuine people I'd ever met. She never put on airs or slipped into a different persona based on the event or the group. She was always Callaghan. It of course helped that being herself meant being kind, funny, articulate, enlightened, progressive, curious, open-minded and free-spirited. Not a bad cocktail of traits and values when connecting with a new family, a new circle of friends, a new community.

If she was nervous about somehow filling Annie's shoes in the eyes of a community that loved and missed Annie, it never showed. She spoke openly, easily, and almost reverentially about Annie and how she wished she'd known her. Annie did not become a topic to be avoided in Callaghan's presence. It never looked as if she were competing in any way with Annie's memory. I loved her for that and so did everyone else. It all just felt natural. Though she was not consciously trying, Callaghan easily won people over, even those who may have had reservations—sometimes subconscious and always well-intended—about her. Perhaps it helped that I truly believed Annie would have liked Callaghan. Had they met in the park, I think they'd have become fast friends. One night, I even had a dream that Annie came home from a run in the park with Callaghan in tow to join the family for dinner. I told Callaghan in the morning, and she was an emotional wreck—in a good way—for much of the day. She considered the dream to be a good sign, a good omen.

A few days later, Callaghan was painting in her new studio. She'd spent the previous day wandering the streets with her camera, shooting interesting scenes that captured life in our neighbourhood. She had then loaded the photos onto her laptop and examined each shot closely, sometimes cropping them or tweaking the colours to get precisely the image she wanted. Then, with the laptop on a table next to her easel for reference, she had started painting the scenes on canvas. She had three paintings in progress. As she put it, "I get bored working on just one canvas at a time."

I'd been working on another annual report in my office, just next door to the studio. I figured the time was right. I knocked on the studio door and entered when she called out.

"Hey," I said. "These pieces look amazing. And I think there are plenty of art lovers in the area who would love your interpretation of our neighbourhood."

"You're on to my secret plan," she said. "There are so many beautiful scenes within a four-block radius of where we're standing. I'm going to be busy."

"So I've been thinking," I said, changing the subject. "I don't want us to be apart again, but you have a home in Paris, and I have a home here. I love Paris, and I get the sense you find Toronto to your liking, beyond the fact that I happen to live here. How would you feel about splitting our time between these two world-class cities?"

"Have you been practising that very smooth pitch in your office?" she asked with a coy smile.

"Maybe once or twice—you know, just to test-drive the lines and tweak them for maximum emotional impact," I replied.

"Nicely done," she said, nodding. "It seems to have worked."

Then she gave me a pretty good indication of her official response when she suddenly clapped her hands together while jumping up and down on the spot.

"We'd never have to be apart," I continued. "We could spend mid-April to October here so we can both play ball hockey. After all, you're now a much sought-after netminder, so you can't just bail on your team. Then we'd spend November to early April in

Paris at Château Hughes. I can carry on freelancing here and in Paris and you can paint in both cities, too. Toronto gives you an entirely new market to exploit for your stunning work. There's so much logic and common sense driving this plan. Isn't it the obvious solution?"

"Where do I sign?" she said, before embracing me. "That sounds just about perfect to me. And I guess it is logical, as you say, but I prefer to think of it as a continuation of the fated good fortune that seems to have followed us around since you landed in Paris."

Then I stepped forward and hugged her.

"One more thing," I said. "I know it might feel weird to live in the home that Annie and I shared. I get that. So I'm ready to sell the house so we can find a new place for us."

She was shaking her head before I even finished my sentence.

"No, no, this house is perfect in every way and reflects who you are and who Will is, and who Annie was," Callaghan said. "That's part of who we are now. I understand why you'd suggest it, but in this city, I wouldn't want to be anywhere else with you than in this home. Oh, and we're definitely keeping my apartment in Paris."

"I wouldn't want to be anywhere else in Paris."

And so it was settled, thus removing any uncertainty about how we'd move forward together. That felt good. It felt great. Will was thrilled, as was Ariel. And as the news seeped into our circle of friends, the universal response could not have been more positive and supportive, provided we were back in Toronto for the opening of the ball hockey season—a condition we were both happy to honour.

—

Within four weeks of her unexpected arrival, Callaghan had about a dozen canvasses ready. She'd done her research on the Toronto art scene and easily landed two gallery partners to show and sell her work. One was in chi-chi Yorkville and the other just up the street on the Danforth. Over time, the number of galleries showing her work would grow. She also painted two pieces that would vie for the cover of the book. I liked them both but preferred the one with a broader perspective on a classic Latin Quarter street scene, with a nameless but typical café in the foreground and the neighbouring buildings on either side completing the picture. The colour, the café, the people, and the energy all captured the Left Bank in the 1920s perfectly in my mind. Callaghan eventually agreed. The painting would hang in our living room after Oxford University Press had finished with it. I loved it.

While she was painting, I spent lots of time on the book, consulting with Callaghan often, of course. With an August manuscript deadline approaching, there was still lots to do. I carefully read through all the diary entries to determine what, if anything, ought to be left out. It wasn't as hard as I had feared it would be. In the end, about eighty per cent of what Constance Stanley had written found its way into quite a thick book. The entries excluded were short, incomplete, unclear, sometimes incoherent passages, in messy, often nearly illegible handwriting, that I can only conclude were written in the wee hours of the morning after a particularly intoxicating party. Those entries added nothing to the context and would only serve to perplex the reader. I also felt an obligation to Constance Stanley to protect her image as a thoughtful, observant, and eloquent chronicler of the city and time.

After careful thought, we did leave in the secret notebook capturing Constance's brief and stormy affair with Josephine Baker. I wrote an introduction to that section of the book describing the simple code and how we came to crack it and find the notebook. I loved working on the book. It felt so much more important than the annual report I had written for a large human resources consulting agency or the news release I'd drafted for the launch of my adult-diaper client's sleeker but more absorbent product line. Callaghan grew increasingly excited as the manuscript came together. By early August, I'd finished all the additional writing required, including ghostwriting a foreword for Callaghan that she tweaked to put her own stamp on it. Thomas Henson and I agreed that readers would want to hear from the granddaughter of Constance Stanley. I also researched and wrote introductions for each time period covered in the diaries, to provide broader historical context for Constance's anecdotes. Finally, I wrote explanatory notes for any references that readers might find unclear. For instance, where a diary entry referred to "dinner at B. Lipp," I wrote a note that explained what and where Brasserie Lipp was and why it enjoyed such popularity back in the day.

We worked with Thomas Henson, Alistair Gibson, and the assigned editor, Clara Downs, to select more than three dozen photographs to include in two different sections of the book. I then wrote all the captions. Clara assembled the index, for which I was grateful. The task elevated tedium to a whole new plane.

We met our deadline with a week to spare, and Oxford University Press slipped into high gear to get the book out in early December. I was told Christmas sales were critical in the life of any new book.

"Come on, McMaster, pick up the pace!"

I knew that voice. Callaghan often heckled me from the hill where spectators—well, mainly friends and family—gathered to watch our weekly ball hockey games. I'd been chasing down Ted Appleton, never getting close enough to check him. Callaghan was laughing when she shouted from the peanut gallery, as were the others sitting with her. I was still chasing Teddy and decided it was time for some good old-fashioned subterfuge. As he entered our zone, still with the ball, he glanced back to see where I was. Anticipating this, I immediately slowed down and appeared to break off the chase, letting him believe I was giving up, or at least no longer prepared to cough up a lung to reach him. When he turned back to the ball and began his slow, methodical wind-up for a slapshot, I shifted into high gear, which I can still do for fleeting intervals. I extended my arm as far as it would go and was just able to steal the ball before his stick came down for the shot. Needless to say, he was surprised to see me.

"Thanks for this," I said to him as I turned back up the floor and fed a long pass to Harris, who'd been streaking through the neutral zone. I watched as Harris wound up and fired a shot towards the goal. Unfortunately, it was fifteen feet wide of the net and about six feet above the crossbar. And it was not exactly a bullet. If

I hadn't known better, I'd have thought he'd used a pitching wedge rather than a hockey stick. I was a little concerned, as he usually only shoots ten feet wide and three feet high. But I did take some measure of satisfaction from the play.

"That's more like it, Jack-Mac," Callaghan shouted. "Nice play!"

Our team did not hoist the Clayburn Cup that year, but we made it to the finals. We lost a close championship game in overtime, but I was fine. I may not have been quite so sanguine had I messed up and given the opposing team the winning goal. But fortunately, I was head-down and hyperventilating on the bench after my shift when Bobby Hazlett broke into our zone and potted the game-winner. I was happy for him.

Cindy and Zoe Clayburn were on hand in the faceoff circle to present the Clayburn Cup to Bobby, who raised it high above his head. Cameras flashed and the crowd on the hill cheered. We banged our sticks on the concrete to celebrate the winning team's victory and to remember Jason. I was thinking of Annie at the same time.

Callaghan was waiting for me when I stepped off the rink and into her arms. I was hot and sweaty and smelly, but that didn't seem to matter. She embraced me anyway.

The fall slipped by in the blink of an eye, as it usually did. We decided to delay our departure for Paris until just after Christmas to accommodate an important event. In early December, Callaghan and I, and all of our closest family and friends, gathered at Hart

House Theatre at the University of Toronto. It was a big day. Next to a lectern and microphone on the stage was the painting Callaghan had made for the book cover, resting on an easel for all to see. A table off to the side of the stage was stacked with copies of the newly published diaries of Callaghan's grandmother, Constance Stanley. A lone chair sat just to the left of the lectern. It was thrilling just to attend, let alone be partially responsible for making the book happen.

When it was time to start, Callaghan stepped onto the stage and sat in the chair, while Thomas Henson from Oxford University Press stood at the lectern. At my request, I stood at the back of the theatre.

"Ladies and gentlemen, welcome to the official Canadian launch of *Wiles and Guile: The Paris Diaries of Constance Stanley*. I am Thomas Henson, proud publisher at Oxford University Press. I confess, when we were first approached by Callaghan Hughes about her grandmother's diaries, we were a tad skeptical that such a fresh, vivid, and vibrant look at the cultural scene in Paris in that electric and eclectic era, the 1920s, was actually legitimate. We were not about to be hoodwinked by unscrupulous fraudsters attempting to peddle a set of phony diaries. It has happened before, I regret to say."

The crowd was quiet, including the three dozen or so ball hockey players attending to support two of their own.

"However, after careful scrutiny and unprecedented testing and corroboration by leading academics, I can assure you that Constance Stanley is, as some of the American expat writers might have put it back then, the real deal. What a joy to bring these amazing stories of an extraordinary city in a revolutionary time to broader public view and academic examination. As you will soon discover, the voice of Constance Stanley is a major new discovery that will advance our understanding of the Lost Generation and the City of Light a century ago. We are all very excited."

The crowd responded with enthusiastic applause. Okay, I may well have started the clapping from my perch at the back.

"Now it is my absolute pleasure to invite Callaghan Hughes to say a few words. She is an accomplished artist, as you can see by the painting she created to grace the cover of the new book. Elizabeth Callaghan Hughes is the granddaughter of Constance Stanley and is named in honour of both Elizabeth Hadley Richardson, Ernest Hemingway's first wife, and Morley Callaghan, both of whom were friends of Constance Stanley. Callaghan?"

She smiled, rose from her chair on stage, and walked to the microphone. She shook hands with Thomas, then pulled him in for a hug, and finally faced the crowd of about seventy-five. I knew she was nervous, but she was also clearly filled with pride, as her grandmother was about to get her due.

"Thank you all for coming, and thank you, Thomas, for your leadership in bringing this book to a much larger audience than I ever believed possible," she started. "I've been reading and rereading my grandmother's diaries since I was a child, sometimes at her knee. They would transport me back to a singular time in the history not just of Paris but of art and literature and culture as well. The Lost Generation has captivated us since Gertrude Stein coined the term. The diaries of Constance Stanley—my grandmother—deepen and enrich our understanding of a period of significant cultural and societal change. They're also funny, personal, thoughtful, sometimes sad, and even heartbreaking at times. There are so many stories in the book about my grandmother rubbing shoulders with leading figures of the day, including Ezra Pound, Picasso, Hemingway and his wife Hadley, Fitzgerald, Gertrude Stein, and many more. You'll read about the secret diary we found that reveals and charts the clandestine relationship my grandmother had with Josephine Baker, providing new insights into the life of one of the most famous entertainers of her time. I truly hope you enjoy this special book and spare a thought for my wonderful grandmother who passed away so many years ago."

Callaghan paused briefly before lifting her eyes back to the audience.

"These published diaries would not have been possible were it not for the tireless efforts and endless support, not to mention primitive code-breaking skills, of our editor, Jack McMaster, who is hiding at the back. He organized and edited these diaries with care, commitment, and a passion for Paris and the period. Whether you're an historian studying the expat writers and artists of 1920s Paris, or a reader interested in a culturally turbulent and historically significant time, there is something for you in my grandmother's Paris diaries. I hope you enjoy them and learn from them."

She again paused to make sure we were all still with her. We were.

"Let me close by reading a very brief, even innocuous, diary entry my grandmother wrote in the early summer of 1922. This was not long after she arrived in Paris, fleeing the rigid expectations that burdened many, even most, young English women at the time—expectations that limited women's ability to realize their full potential."

Callaghan opened the book and read aloud.

Wednesday, July 12, 1922

It was a Wednesday evening, early, and I was in Brasserie Lipp on Saint-Germain. It's a lively establishment that I'd been told served the best chicken I was likely to have in my life. How could I not partake? I arrived and was shown to a table for two, though I was happily alone. My French still is not strong. Not yet. In fact, if I am to be frightfully frank, I have a long way to go, but I'm not giving up and can feel myself making progress. I looked at the menu and discovered the word 'poulet,' which I know means chicken in my native tongue. I could have just pointed to the menu item to indicate my order, but what fun is there in that? So I spoke to the waiter in French, though he seemed uncertain about my words and wishes. I was about to try a second time when a lovely and attractive woman seated across the aisle from me sprang to my assistance.

In an accent that sounded American, she asked me what I desired on the menu. She then passed along my order to the waiter in what sounded to my less-than-learned ear to be excellent French. I was touched by this gesture and expressed my deep thanks for her help. Then we talked. She had moved to Paris from America with her husband the previous December. She was dressed simply and had a fetching round face wreathed in short brown hair. Not long thereafter, her husband arrived. He was tall and broad-shouldered, with short hair parted cleanly on the side, almost the same colour as his wife's. Introductions followed and soon my chicken arrived. I thanked her again and asked her to repeat her name so as not to forget it. She said it a second time: Elizabeth Hadley Richardson. Then she suddenly laughed and corrected her surname, as she was only recently married and not yet accustomed to it. She was Elizabeth Hadley Hemingway. Her husband, Ernest by name, smiled but seemed more interested in securing wine for their table. I daresay, while he was a handsome man, there was something lurking beneath the surface that left me disquieted.

Kindly, Hadley suggested getting together in the near future to compare notes on Paris. I readily agreed and look forward to it.

"And let me stop there," Callaghan said. "Thank you all again for coming, and I hope you enjoy the diaries of my grandmother, the indomitable and irrepressible Constance Stanley."

Her remarks and reading were pitch-perfect, in my completely unbiased and impartial view. I was proud of her and beamed from the back row. After prolonged applause, Thomas returned to the lectern to introduce a Canadian academic from McGill University who'd written a book about the Lost Generation. She spoke, perhaps for too long, about what was so special about 1920s Paris. After that, plates of small sandwiches and cookies and squares were passed around right there in the theatre. At the same time, a lineup formed of those who wanted to buy books and have them signed. Callaghan insisted that I sit next to her at the table on stage and sign my name next to hers in every book sold. The ball hockey players in the room all filed onto the stage to buy copies, even though I doubt many of them knew much about the goings-on in Paris a century ago. But they came anyway. They came for me and for Callaghan.

In the coming days, I watched for reviews of the new book, but only found a few in esoteric history journals. Frankly, I was told finding any reviews for a book of such admittedly niche appeal was highly unlikely. The reviews I did find were positive. One hailed Constance Stanley as "a newly discovered voice who wrote with passion and insight about Paris and the Lost Generation writers and artists who created modernism and changed the cultural landscape not just of the city, but of the world."

Now, that was a review that could be excerpted and used on the front cover of subsequent editions of the book—if sales ever justified a second printing. Callaghan was tickled by the few, but positive, critiques. Perhaps her grandmother would now get the belated recognition she deserved.

Maybe it was because the book was finished, published, out in bookstores, and off my plate. Or maybe it was just time. Over the years I'd learned that at a certain point in a new relationship, I had the urge to write a new song. That reliable urge had spawned "Until the New Year" more than forty years ago. I had several songs—most of them not great—written about earlier girlfriends in my "back catalogue." They were heartfelt at the time, back when I didn't always understand what was working in my relationships and what wasn't. I don't play those early compositions much anymore. Each one reflects the state of my mind and heart at a particular moment. In each of those songs, I sound like I've found my soulmate for life. Then the relationship would fail, usually catching me completely by surprise, and I'd retire the song to live somewhere in my memory, seldom to be played.

Then I met Annie. I've always thought "Until the New Year" was the best of my relationship-driven compositions. Perhaps that's not surprising when you consider that Annie and I were together for forty years and married for more than thirty. Is my creativity, my ability to write songs, dictated by the relationship about which I'm writing? An interesting hypothesis—well, interesting to me. My two favourite songs of mine are "Until the New Year," about Annie, and "More Than the Game," about the ball hockey league and my friends who play in it. Both, important relationships to me.

Anyway, this time, the urge to write a new song arrived without warning. When I say "without warning," I'm lying. After all, it had been months earlier, in Paris, when I'd started fooling around with a chord progression and fingerpicking pattern that I thought might serve as the basis for a new composition. What finally and belatedly hit me with clarity now that we were in Toronto was the song's obvious subject and storyline. I should have seen it much earlier.

I liked the underlying instrumentation but still needed to shape the melody to rest on, and mesh with, the guitar part before I could turn my mind to lyrics. I tended to write the music—chord progression and melody—first.

I found and refined a melody I liked, as well as a catchy chorus that afforded harmony opportunities. Finally, though it took a while, I stumbled upon a bridge that was different enough musically from the verses and chorus to be considered a bridge, but not so different that it felt like part of another song just dropped in out of the blue. It is called a bridge, after all. I've learned that bridges are hard, and I need to experiment a bit with different chords and sometimes key changes to build one that works.

So it felt like I had the makings of a new song, with the music and melody for the verses, chorus, and bridge close to fully baked. That just left the lyrics.

A week after the book launch, Callaghan, Will, Ariel, and I were seated in the front row of the venerable Massey Hall to see Jim Cuddy in concert. He had comped us the tickets, which was very kind of him.

You might argue that I should have known—that what happened that night was predictable. Yet I was utterly unprepared, as I'm sure my face conveyed, when I eventually stood up and made my way up onto the stage. Will was by my side and likely was in on the whole thing. I had wondered why he'd taken such an interest in what I planned to wear to the concert.

It happened late in the show, just a few numbers from the end. Jim introduced his next song, or rather, he introduced *my* song.

"Most of you will have heard this next tune," Jim said. "In fact, at this time of year, it's hard to escape it, at least ever since we released it last December. So here's what you might call the song's origin story."

I was slowly freaking out in my seat but was aware enough to notice that the audience had fallen quiet. Clearly the crowd liked a good story, and Jim was a great storyteller. Callaghan had her hand on my knee and was squeezing it as he spoke from the stage.

"Last fall I was looking for, and trying to write, a Christmas song. It had been a while since I'd had a seasonal release and I was getting some pressure to come up with something. But I seemed to be in the middle of a dreaded songwriting dry spell, one that's thankfully passed now. So there I was, in need of a new Christmas song but coming up empty. That is, until I walked by the open control-room door of the recording studio where we often rehearse and write. Anyway, I heard a song I soon learned was called 'Until the New Year.'"

When the audience heard the song title, they started clapping and hooting.

"So, I stepped inside this control room and listened to what I immediately could hear was a relatable, simple, and moving love song about a couple separated at Christmas. Much to my surprise, it was written by a buddy of mine, Jack McMaster."

I'd had no warning of this. Part of me was thrilled that he was going to play the song. How could he not? It was a hit for him last year and was back on the charts as we headed into the Christmas season. But I had had no idea he was going to talk about the song at such length. I looked at Will. He was smiling with his eyes glued to Jim.

"I didn't even know Jack was a songwriter, but he clearly is. He's sitting up front, I think. Can we bring up the house lights, please?"

The house lights did not come up, but rather an actual

spotlight illuminated me, and Will next to me: It was such a bright light, I thought I might be able to see the bones in my hand. I could feel it heating up my body.

"Great! Thanks, guys. There he is. Wave, Jack, would you?"

I stayed seated but gave a little wave. I think I smiled, too, but I'm not really sure. I could well have looked terrified.

"Anyway, back to the story. It was Jack's son, Will, sitting next to him tonight, who was mixing the song in the control room, adding some new tracks to fill it out. You know, a bass line, some drums, strings, and some new harmonies. The remix was a surprise Christmas present for Jack. Well, we don't have all night, so I'll cut to the big ending. I loved the song, and with Will's help, we recorded it with my band on the sly and sent it to Jack, who was lazing around in Paris at the time. I then called him and he very kindly gave me permission to release the recording. I wasn't surprised when it peaked at number two last year, and we're hoping for great things again this year. I wasn't surprised because it's a fantastic song. In fact, I wish I'd written it."

The audience laughed and broke into applause again.

"Finally, you should know that Jack wrote this song more than forty years ago for a wonderful woman named Annie Barnes, his girlfriend at the time. Well, they were married for more than thirty years, until she tragically passed away three and a half years ago, and I hope Jack doesn't mind me saying that. It's part of the poignance, beauty, and meaning of this song. I knew Annie, too. We all miss her."

The crowd, almost in unison, released what sounded like a low moan in sympathy, and then started clapping again. I looked at

Jim, and he moved his arms to indicate he wanted me to stand up and acknowledge the outpouring from the audience.

"Up, Jack. Stand up," Jim directed. "Take a bow."

I stood very briefly and nodded shyly to the capacity crowd behind me. Then I sat down again. Beside me, Callaghan was wiping her eyes and leaning just out of the spotlight's reach.

"Hang on, Jack. You're not done yet. Bring your son, Will, with you and come on up here. We could use your help on the harmonies."

The crowd cheered again. Will stood up first and nodded to me. When your only child is urging you on, you follow through, though my heart was beating out of my chest. At that moment, I wasn't at all convinced I could make any kind of sound with my voice, let alone sing harmonies on key. And believe me, the audience knows when you sing harmonies off key. Callaghan patted my leg and beamed at me as I stood at my seat. That helped. Will and I then climbed onto the stage and stood side by side in front of a single microphone. I hoped no one was expecting us to bust some backup-singer dance moves. I just focused on staying upright as the crowd finally settled down. The bright theatrical lighting meant that from the stage, it looked as if a thick black curtain had descended, so I could see none of the audience except for the first row. I fixed my gaze on Callaghan, and that helped calm me. I prayed the rest of the audience would still be there when the song had run its course.

Before I knew what was happening, Jim started the acoustic guitar intro, and soon we were into the song. The crowd recognized it immediately and cheered. Even standing behind Jim, I could hear his beautiful voice. And it was easy to see that the audience was really into the song, mouthing the words—my words for Annie—along with him.

My feet tapped out the beat and I tried not to pass out. Will had his hand on my shoulder, perhaps as a sign of filial affection, or else to make sure I didn't faint, or flee the scene. We'd agreed on the way up to the stage which harmonies we'd each take. When we hit the chorus, Will and I dutifully leaned in and sang our parts. Courtesy of the two large monitors placed at our feet, we could hear ourselves to ensure we were at least in the vicinity of the proper notes. It was really quite special to be singing harmonies with my own son, our faces close around our shared mic. By the time we rolled into the last chorus, I was feeling much better. I kept my eyes fastened on Callaghan in the front row, and she gave me an intense and sustained look of such love that I very nearly forgot I was singing my own song on the Massey Hall stage with Jim Cuddy and Will. And I could feel Annie, too, as I sang. How could she not be with me when I was singing the song I wrote for her, four decades before?

After the last chord died away, Jim stepped toward me and gave me a hug. He leaned in and whispered in my ear.

"Annie is looking down and is loving this. I can feel it."

"Me, too, Jim," I said. "That was a dream. Thank you."

He just turned me to face the audience and we both stood there, taking it all in. The crowd was on their feet. I feared I might cry, but I didn't. It was close, but I didn't.

It was an experience I'll never forget but hope never to repeat.

"Did you know anything about that?" I asked Will when we were walking back to the car.

"Not a thing," he replied.

"Would you have told me if you'd known?"

"I'd say the jury is still out on that key question," he replied. Then he put his arm around my shoulder. "You did great, Dad. You deserved that and so did Mom."

A week after Callaghan's memorable first Christmas in Toronto with Will and me, she and I boarded an Air Canada flight for Paris. The book launch and the Jim Cuddy concert had delayed our departure by about a month, but it was for the best of reasons. We were both excited about going back to Paris. We were returning to what I now thought of as *our* second home, in the Latin Quarter where Hemingway, Fitzgerald, Morley Callaghan, and so many other luminaries once roamed, including a young and determined woman named Constance Stanley. Callaghan held my hand for nearly the entire flight as I noodled lyrics for the new song, now that I knew what and who it was about.

We were both sad to be leaving Toronto, but also deliriously happy to be headed back to the City of Light. We'd be there for the next several months, at least until the spring—the start of a new season.

A NOTE ABOUT THE ORIGINAL SONGS

I wrote my first song in 1977 when I was seventeen. You really don't want to hear it. But it started something that I've kept up in the forty-five years since. I figure I've written thirty or forty songs. However heartfelt, many of them—perhaps most—are not great. Some are forgotten—not just by friends who might have heard them, but by me, too. But a few of them have stayed with me and remain in the private set list I play for myself, alone in our library where I write. The two songs in this novel are among them.

I wrote *More Than the Game* many years ago as a kind of love song to the ball hockey league I still play in at Withrow Park, here in Toronto. Love song? Yep, love song. I hope the lyrics convey that my feelings for the league, and the community it created, run much deeper than a weekly Tuesday night ball hockey game might suggest.

I wrote *Until the New Year* back in late 1981 when I was in love with a fellow student at McMaster University who had just flown home to Nova Scotia for the Christmas break. I missed her and wrote this song one night sitting on my bed in my campus apartment, seeing my own reflection in my window, bordered by the coloured Christmas lights I'd strung up. More than forty years later, I'm still in love with her and we're still together.

So, the songs are real, even if the story is not.

ACKNOWLEDGEMENTS

This is the second novel I've written during the pandemic. So, I—we all—owe deep thanks and gratitude to the frontline healthcare workers who ran towards the danger every day while the rest of us sequestered in our homes. Unrivalled bravery and commitment.

Of course, this novel would not be in your hands without the tireless efforts of my McClelland & Stewart family at Penguin Random House Canada. I thank my editor Joe Lee, my publishers Jared Bland and Stephanie Sinclair, editorial assistant par excellence Chimedum Ohaegbu, my stalwart publicists Cameron Waller and Dan French, my eagle-eyed copy-editor Erin Kern, proofreader extraordinaire Melanie Little, designer Matthew Flute, and the rest of the team. After nine novels, there's still no place I'd rather be.

I'm also grateful for the years of support from my former editors, Doug Gibson, whom I'll always consider to be my editor emeritus, and Bhavna Chauhan.

Beverley Slopen is the only literary agent I've ever had, and I remain in her debt for taking me on when no one else would.

Fellow writer Rod Carley and I have talked about our respective novels-in-progress at least monthly for some time now. Our conversations kept me motivated as I wrote the manuscript.

There is some ball hockey in this novel inspired by my brothers in the amazing Withrow Park Ball Hockey League. They have become a second family to me since I started playing in the league back in 2003. I'm still playing at sixty-three. My skills have declined in recent years while my recovery time has lengthened, but I'm not done yet.

Some years ago, one of my teammates was Jim Cuddy, famed singer-songwriter and co-founder of Blue Rodeo. He kindly blurbed my second novel when I leaned over on the bench one Tuesday night under the Withrow Park lights and asked him. I thank him for agreeing to appear in this novel as himself, the only real character in the cast. While the novel is fiction, his kindness in the story is a true and accurate reflection of the real Jim Cuddy.

I must also thank—as I always will—the Stephen Leacock Associates for changing—perhaps giving me—my life as a writer in 2008 when a nobody with a self-published novel about Canadian politics miraculously won the Stephen Leacock Medal for Humour. In my mind, all roads in my writerly life pass through Orillia, Ontario.

My old friend Rob Thériault taught me how to play guitar

when we were both seventeen years old. At twenty-two, we loafed around Europe with backpacks, a Eurail pass, and, yes, a guitar. His original compositions inspired me to write my own songs, too—something I've now been doing for more than forty-five years. The original songs in this story are real and I would likely never have written them without Rob's guidance and friendship.

As is often the case, my identical twin brother, Tim, was a very early reader of the manuscript and, as usual, offered thoughtful and honest advice that has made this book better.

In March of 2022, as I began working on this manuscript, I retired from the communications consulting agency I co-founded back in 1995 to fulfill a long-held dream of writing full-time. That only happened because I married Nancy Naylor more than thirty-five years ago. Now you know the first rule of full-time writers: marry well and, if you can, well above your station. I did both and I'll be forever grateful for Nancy's love and support all these years, with more to come. I also owe thanks to our two sons, Calder and Ben, who have always encouraged, and often inspired, my writing life.

Terry Fallis, Toronto, January 2023